The Mistress's Revenge

Tamar Cohen

BLACK SWAN

TRANSWORLD PUBLISHERS
61–63 Uxbridge Road, London W5 5SA
A Random House Group Company
www.transworldbooks.co.uk

THE MISTRESS'S REVENGE
A BLACK SWAN BOOK: 9780552777544

First published in Great Britain
in 2011 by Doubleday
an imprint of Transworld Publishers
Black Swan edition published 2012

Addresses for Random House Group Ltd companies outside the UK
can be found at: www.randomhouse.co.uk
The Random House Group Ltd Reg. No. 954009

The Random House Group Limited supports The Forest Stewardship
Council (FSC®), the leading international forest-certification organisation.
Our books carrying the FSC label are printed on FSC®-certified paper. FSC
is the only forest-certification scheme endorsed by the leading environmental
organisations, including Greenpeace. Our paper-procurement
policy can be found at www.randomhouse.co.uk/environment

Typeset in 11/14 pt Sabon by Falcon Oast Graphic Art Ltd.
Printed and bound by CPI Group (UK) Ltd, Croydon, CR0 4YY.

2 4 6 8 10 9 7 5 3 1

To Jake, because the middle isn't so bad

Never have an affair with anyone who has less to lose than you.

Let me start by explaining.

I know you might see this as incendiary, malicious, even creepy. Call it what you will. But believe me, nothing is further from the truth. The fact is I've been to see a therapist, just as you advised me. So thoughtful of you to think of it. 'I know you think it's mumbo jumbo, so did I, but believe me you'll see the benefits,' you urged me in your most concerned voice right after York Way Friday when you were still in full guilt mode. And how right you were. I'm seeing the benefits already, I really am. Anyway, she told me – incidentally her name is Helen Bunion, can you believe that? And she tilts her head to the side when I talk like a little sparrow. I think it's supposed to let me know I have her complete undivided attention – she told me that getting it all 'out there' would be a vital part of my recovery process.

That's exactly how she said it: 'a vital part of my recovery process'. So what can I do? I don't want to impede my recovery process, and Helen Bunion really is so very concerned about my welfare, so 'out there' it shall get!

Now, I'm aware you will worry about the risk of other people reading this and it all becoming public, and believe me if I can get this 'out there' without risking exposure and all the problems that will bring, of course I will do it. I have only your best interests at heart. You know that. But I'm sure you understand, having experienced the benefits of 'therapy' yourself, that one has to be totally honest (no, what's that word they use instead these days? Transparent. Totally transparent), no matter how painful. So that's what I shall be. As part of my recovery process. I can feel it working already. Thank you so much for suggesting it.

Helen Bunion – she wants me to call her Helen, and you can understand why, but I find it so difficult. It's like calling a teacher by her first name, quite wrong somehow – has told me I should be journalling my emotions.

Did you know that was a verb now? To journal? It's one of those funny made-up verbs that really ought to remain nouns, like 'to impact'. Helen used that one too, funnily enough. She said you'd 'impacted catastrophically' on my life. Catastrophically is a very strong word, don't you think? Still, you'd imagine a trained therapist would know what they were talking about, wouldn't you, so I'll have to assume she has some basis.

So now I'm to journal my emotions. This too will be a fundamental part of my recovery process, or so I'm led to believe. I'm actually quite looking forward to it. Since you've been gone, I've missed having someone to talk to. Remember how we used to dissect every last detail of our lives in those interminable emails we pinged back and forth all day long? 'Our relationship would never have got off the ground if we'd had "proper" jobs,' you often said, making the phrase 'proper jobs' sound like something black and slimy you'd found in your salad. And you were of course right. Fifty, seventy, a hundred emails a day, only possible because we both spend so much time online, sitting solitarily in front of computer screens for hours at a stretch – you at the swanky Fitzrovia offices of the record company where you are both boss and star producer, or else in your small but perfectly formed home study converted from the top-floor box room of your gorgeous detached pale-pink St John's Wood villa (I know you've always maintained you like the view over the gardens and the rooftops, but that box room always seemed such a perverse choice when you could have had the run of the house. 'Sad fuck in a box' you used to head your emails), me in my partitioned cubbyhole in my shabby south London three-bed terrace, largely staring into space.

'Musings of a sad fuck in a box.' The message would ping into my inbox. That heading would go back and forth as the thread grew longer, or I'd change it to 'Musings of an invisible woman in a cubbyhole.' Longer and longer, more and more messages, cataloguing the minutiae of our lives. Every incident in my day was jealously hoarded to be given to you later in an email as a gift. Locking myself out while putting out the rubbish! Buying a Saturday *Guardian* in Tesco only to find someone had already swiped the Guide section! Only now, when there is no one to give them to, and no one who would want them anyway, do I realize how worthless these mundanities were all along.

Who else would be interested in the disastrous meals I make for the kids (yes, still stuck on fajitas, I'm afraid – how amusing you always found my two-dish culinary repertoire) or the fact that the grumpy old man who came to read the gas meter told me off for having so many boxes and bags cluttering the cupboard under the stairs? 'You're putting me at risk,' he told me. Isn't that hysterical? Putting him at risk.

I suppose I could tell these things to Helen Bunion and she would tilt her birdie head at me and listen intently and nod a bit and go 'mmmm' in an encouraging and eminently empathetic way, but it wouldn't be quite the same. And not a very efficient use of £75 an hour! I must say it was very good of you to make me feel there was value in my nonsense. I wonder what you do with all that free time you must have, now you no longer have to read it.

*   *   *

This journalling is a marvellous thing. Really, I don't know where I'd be without it. It's making me see that honesty – sorry, *transparency* – really is the key. I feel lighter already. Of course, you were always the big advocate of honesty. 'I feel like telling Susan everything,' you'd declare impetuously. 'I don't want this to be a hidden thing. That's not the way I feel about you. I want the whole world to know about "us".' The truth would set us free, you always said. And yet in the end, when I suggested (OK, begged, I'll admit, is probably more strictly accurate) that we come completely clean and let your wife and my 'partner' (was there ever a more mealy-mouthed term?) make up their own minds based on all the facts, the truth was suddenly something else, a destructive force that Susan and Daniel needed protecting from. Such a good job you have a handle on all those subtle nuances. Left to my own devices I'd never really understand the difference.

* * *

Sian called in again today. She does that a lot these days. I think she's trying to catch me out, trying to catch me not coping.

'I feel so responsible,' was her constant refrain after York Way Friday. 'I colluded in your affair. I was an *enabler.*'

She actually used that word as well. Enabler. When did we all become so fluent in therapy-speak, I wonder?

Still, she had a point, I suppose. Where would we have been without Sian acting as an alibi while I swept off into the night to meet you, or joining us for dinner and pretending not to notice as the two of us held hands under the table?

'She's getting a vicarious thrill out of this,' you used to tell me, and undoubtedly there was an element of truth in that.

You never could really see the *point* of Sian, could you? In a sense you're right. She's the one university friend I have who, long after I outgrew the rest, has somehow managed to remain stuck on to my life like a stray Post-it note clinging to the back of a suit jacket. Until the affair started we had precious few points of connection left, she and I. I've often said that Sian wears her long-term single status like an aggressive T-shirt slogan, still insisting that it is a lifestyle choice. Remember your TV producer friend's dinner party that you took the two of us to, where she flirted with all the men and regaled the rest of us with lurid tales of twenty-five-year-olds she has slept with (funny how they are always 'gorgeous', these young lovers, though nobody ever seems to meet any of them), then ended up slumped on a beanbag and had to be deposited home in a taxi? Happy to collude with anything that challenged the prevailing Couple Mafia, as she calls it, she was glad at first to *enable* our affair. That's why, in spite of her oft-declared affection for Daniel ('We get each other completely,' she once told you. Do you remember that? How scathing you were?), she encouraged us along, you and I, swept up in the breathless illusion of romance with its reassuring elevation of passion over partnership.

'If it's any consolation, Sally, he had me fooled as well,' she told me today, shaking her head sadly. 'I was totally deceived by him. I feel let down.'

Does that surprise you, Clive, the knock-on effect of your betrayal? The way even my best friend feels let down by proxy?

To her credit, Sian has been through a lot over the past few months – scraped me off the floor more than once, if that's not too hackneyed an analogy. (Imagine me a bit like congealing fat on the kitchen lino, the kind of thing you'd have to dig at vigorously with a sharp knife.) Sian first reacted to news of the York Way Friday bombshell with stunned disbelief. 'He couldn't have . . .', 'Surely he can't have . . .', 'I can't believe he has . . .' But that soon passed into anger. 'How could he have . . .', 'How dare he have . . .'. She feels her faith in human nature, never terribly robust, has been severely tested. She feels misled.

'You'll get over him soon,' she told me today. 'You'll see him for what he is and then, pffff, the scales will fall from your eyes.'

Pffff. As easy as that.

I told her I couldn't wait. And then, because it would make her happy and because I wanted it to be true, I told her it was starting to happen already. 'I'm really making progress,' I said.

And of course I am making progress. Really, I am. Some days I go for long minutes without thinking about you at all.

Sian looked pleased when I told her about the progress. 'I have to be honest, I've been worried about you,' she told me. 'You haven't been yourself recently.'

I didn't bother telling her that myself was the very last person I'd want to be.

Sian was still here when Tilly and Jamie came home from school.

Do you know, more and more, I find myself surprised each day when they burst in through the door. Does that sound awful? It's like as soon as my children go out in the morning, and I'm left here on my own, they cease to exist, and when they come back in the afternoon, I have to relearn them all over again. Does everyone feel like that? Well, you'd know, I suppose, as you've been through it all before. I miss asking your advice on things like that.

Jamie was very keen to tell me that Mr Henshaw was *still* off with an undisclosed mystery ailment. He seemed to think I should know all about Mr Henshaw, so I nodded fervently and hoped nothing more would be required.

Tilly gave me one of those looks. Do all girls do them, I wonder? Those withering looks that make you feel like you've just done something utterly, hopelessly stupid? I expect your Emily spared you those. She's such a

Daddy's girl, isn't she? She saves them for the rest of us.

'I don't know why you bother talking to Mum about that stuff,' Tilly told Jamie. 'She hasn't got a clue what you're on about.'

'Yes she has!' Jamie's face turned a little red. 'I told her about it yesterday.'

'Go on then.' Tilly was looking straight at me, thirteen-year-old eyes fixed unflinchingly on mine. 'Tell us who Mr Henshaw is.'

Helen Bunion talked to me once about engaging with the children and I tried to remember what she said. I knew it had something to do with distracting them by answering their question with a question. Or maybe that's what you're definitely not supposed to do. I have to admit I must have looked a bit vacant, standing there trying to work out whether to distract or not distract, because Sian, who tends to treat children like none-too-bright delivery men who require precise instructions and firm handling, broke in:

'Your mum's not been feeling too good recently.'

Two young sets of eyes fixed on me with sudden interest.

'What's wrong with her then?' It struck me as a little bit bizarre that Tilly was talking about me as if I wasn't even there. But part of me was also relieved. If I wasn't being directly addressed, I couldn't be expected to answer. 'She looks all right to me.'

Jamie wasn't so sure. 'Her eyes do look sort of smaller, like they've been shrunk.'

'I'm not sleeping well, that's all,' I told them. That's an appropriate motherly response, isn't it? To try to diminish your own problems so as not to worry your children. (So often these days I have to ask myself what's appropriate and what isn't. It's as if I'm understudying the role of mother for the first time, without any real vocation for playing it.)

Jamie came and gave me a hug, one eye on Sian looking for approval. Tilly stayed where she was, twisting a strand of hair slowly around her finger.

'You must have a guilty conscience,' she said.

Sian shot me a meaningful look. That word 'guilty', of course. But it's quite clear to me Tilly was just being provocative. And the truth is I don't feel guilty. Not about any of it. I'm sure I ought to, but I actually don't. 'Guilt is so plebeian,' you used to say dismissively. You always thought of it as a wasted emotion. And of course you were right. So clever of you to classify emotions like that – according to their usefulness. I must start doing the same, I really must. Cutting out the emotional chaff must make your inner life so much more efficient. You must have the Volkswagen of inner lives, Clive. I've got to hand it to you.

* * *

You know, I can forgive the fact I begged you to warn me in advance if you were dumping me and you still let me turn up at that restaurant on York Way Friday with a jaunty impatience, and unwashed hair and only my second-best jeans. I can forgive the way you told me it was over before I'd even taken off my coat and then somehow expected we'd find a way of filling the next three tortuous hours, me with my arm still halfway in my sleeve. I can forgive that awful, excruciating, pain-ridden lunch while the waitress hovered uncertainly around the uneaten food, a smile stretching her face as if it might snap, and I tried not to meet anyone's eye. I can even forgive you asking for a receipt (even goodbyes, it seems, are tax deductible). But what I can't forgive is the way you scurried off so gratefully when we got outside and I told you to go. You were halfway down York Way, your laptop bag bouncing insistently against your back, before I realized you really were going to leave me there crying in the rain.

Silleeeee Salleeeee, you used to write in your emails.

* * *

Now, before you say anything, I know you're cross with me. I got your email last night and I'm doing my absolute best to understand how you feel. This journalling is really improving my understanding skills. I think you'd be pleased. 'Please try to understand just a little,' you pleaded shortly before you left me crying on York Way Friday. 'Just try to see things from my point of view.' I think I might be starting to get the hang of it now, this empathizing thing, this seeing things from other people's points of view. It has a lot to recommend it.

So now I'm asking you to try to see this from my perspective. Show a little empathy. You must have picked up a lot of that from your own therapist. Goodness knows you've had enough sessions. Mind you, you always did like to hear yourself talk. I remember you coming back from that first meeting with the therapist so pleased with yourself. 'I had her completely wrong-footed,' you crowed. 'She had no idea what to make of me. I didn't fit into any of her neat little boxes, you see?' But still, you'd think something would have rubbed off from all those sessions, some sort of self-awareness. So I hope you'll try to understand.

There I was last night and I started thinking about Susan and wondering how she was. I know Susan and I haven't exactly been best friends – that Aussie accent can get in the way rather, don't you think, softened though it undoubtedly is after nearly three decades in the UK. More like close acquaintances. But I always liked her. Sometimes I used to think I liked her more than you did. 'I don't want Susan to end up lonely,' I'd say magnanimously. 'She doesn't deserve it.' Or 'How can we build our happiness on Susan's misery?'

You'd always make a pained face when I talked like that. 'I feel just awful about Susan,' you'd say (those were the words you always used to describe your guilt about her – 'awful', 'dreadful', 'wretched'). 'But when two people are as much in love as we are, surely we have a duty to be together, to be happy?' And anyway, Susan would be OK, you'd always say. She was so very capable, so terribly *resourceful*. You made her sound like a library.

Now I have to admit, that word 'bitch' in last night's email did hurt. Do you know, I had to break off from reading it and actually look up other emails from the past, cheerier ones, like the one in which you'd said you would kill anyone who ever hurt me? 'I know that sounds naff but that's how you make me feel,' you'd written. 'It's something very primeval.'

Primeval. What an interesting choice of words. You know, now I come to think about it, that's kind of how I feel a lot of the time at the moment. Primeval.

You know, the interesting thing is that subconsciously I believe I was actually hoping the you who wrote the first email would protect me from the you who wrote the second. Isn't that ridiculous? I should probably save that up and tell it to Helen at the next session. She's really big on the subconscious. It'd be like taking an apple to the teacher.

Anyway, last night I was thinking about Susan. I do that quite a lot since you painted such a vivid picture of your life together. It's been so useful because now I can visualize what she's doing at any time of the day. It makes me feel closer to her somehow. I know that after dinner, the two of you tend to slope off together to the second floor of your lovely St John's Wood house, where you have a cosy duck-egg-blue sitting room with French windows leading out on to a private roof terrace. There you lounge on the vast designer daybed with Susan's ancient, flatulent dachshund and read the papers and watch the telly and comment on the things you've seen or read.

'Just chitty chat, really,' you'd assured me. 'Nothing like the range and depth of the things you and I talk about.'

So last night, I was just a teeny bit at a loose end. These evenings are so long, don't you find? That yawning gap between dinner and oblivion? And I started imagining Susan and you relaxing on the plump velvet cushions. In my head I'd already followed you through your routine. I knew that you'd eat in your gleaming, double-height glass-roofed kitchen, sitting around the blond-wood square table where Daniel and I enjoyed several dinner parties (so strange to think of it now). You'd probably have eaten in the company of your son, Liam, who I never got to meet, and one of his gorgeous, big-toothed, shiny-haired Sloaney girlfriends with their impossibly long legs; and after you'd done the clearing away – your way of showing appreciation for whatever culinary delights Susan had brought home from her upmarket catering firm (successful businesswoman, one-time model, wife, mother, so very, very capable) – the two of you would have made your way upstairs.

And suddenly this idea came to me to call Susan. Don't laugh, but I've always thought the two of us would be closer if circumstances were different. Sometimes I've allowed myself to imagine calling in for coffee on Susan's days off, and sitting chatting over the kitchen table while you sit working at your state-of-the-art iMac in your top-floor studio. Maybe the three of us could go off and get a bite of lunch a little later on.

So I called Susan's number. 'Hello stranger,' she said, and I imagined her meeting your mildly quizzical gaze and mouthing the word 'Sally' before lying back on the cushions, so she didn't see how your mouth froze into an 'o' shape, or your fingers shook as they gripped the edges of *The Times*.

I didn't even know what I was planning to say to her until I actually heard her voice. That unfortunate Down Under accent gives her a rather no-nonsense type of voice, doesn't it, to match her tall, athletic frame, like I imagine a PE mistress might have. (Not that I have personal experience of such things.) 'Take a deep breath and run a couple of times around the quad and we'll soon have you feeling tip-top,' is the kind of thing a voice like that might say. Susan probably wouldn't have much time for journalling. 'Go out and buy yourself a nice frock, or take yourself off to Marrakesh for the weekend,' she'd probably say. 'Much better than sitting in a darkened room wallowing in your own misery.'

I remember once, very early on when we hadn't known

the two of you long, we were all out somewhere and Susan had been talking about pensions and how she'd be entitled to a big chunk of yours, no matter what happened. 'You have to protect yourself, you know,' she'd said. 'If Clive and I ever divorced I'd take him to the cleaner's.' You'd laughed along with everyone else, even though I sensed you'd heard this speech a hundred times before. I wonder if maybe being taken to the cleaner's was something that flashed quickly through your mind when you heard me on the phone last night, saw Susan's mouth stretch soundlessly into the shapes that make Sal-leeeee. I do hope it didn't cause you too much anxiety. Worry is such a *futile* emotion, Helen always says. I don't bother telling her that futility is one of my specialist subjects.

How did it feel, I wonder, lolling on that designer daybed listening to your wife chat away to your mistress? Oops, I mean ex-mistress of course. I can't imagine it was terribly comfortable, although I'm sure you carried it off with your usual insouciance. I expect you were wondering what it was I was saying every time there was a silence (which, let's face it, isn't that often when having a conversation with Susan, although I did my best to hold my own). I expect your heart was hammering rather painfully, despite those warnings your doctor gave you to keep stress to a minimum. (That was one of the reasons you gave me for ending it, do you remember? That all the stress of your double life was taking its toll on your health. You even rolled up your sleeve to show me the little patch of eczema in the crook of your elbow. 'I must start putting myself first,' you said, without even a flicker of irony.)

I must say, Susan was very friendly on the phone, very voluble, as if I'd caught her at a loose end and she was glad of the interruption. She wanted to know all about how I'd been.

'It's such a long time since we last got together with you and Daniel,' she said warmly. 'You must both come round for dinner one night.'

I could imagine the look on your face. I'd have paid good money to see it, I really would.

'I would love that,' I told her, truthfully. 'But in the meantime, why don't we go out together, just the two of us, for a girlie night out?'

'Good idea. Men are so boring, aren't they? I don't know about Daniel, but Clive's such a grumpy old git.'

I laughed.

'At least we'll be able to have a proper chat,' said Susan.

An hour and a half later, your email popped up. It had that 'sent from my iPhone' tag along the bottom and I imagined you barricaded into your en suite, running the cold tap in the sink to cover the tapping of the keys.

I must say, you sounded terribly out of sorts in that email (which, incidentally, contained more typos than I've ever seen in such a short message – don't iPhones have a spell check function?). I can, of course, see why that phone conversation with Susan might have bothered you. Believe me, I'm not as insensitive as you seem to think. But I still think 'bitch' was a little strong.

* * *

Citalopram. That's the name of the happy pills the doctor gave me. I keep wanting to call them Cilitbang. Waging

War on Stubborn Stains. Helen Bunion would adore that. All that hidden symbolism. Might you become just a stubborn stain in time, Clive? Silleeeee Salleeeee.

When I first went to see that doctor, I sat hunched over in the plastic chair next to her desk, feeling like something shrivelled and leathery and dug up from a peat bog. She was in her twenties, a locum at the surgery I've been registered with for years but hardly ever visit. She has long wavy blonde hair and was wearing a perfectly tailored skirt and suede mushroom-coloured knee-high boots so soft they made you want to lean across and do noughts and crosses on them with your finger. She looked at me brightly with her flawlessly (though discreetly) made-up eyes and said, 'And what can I do for you?' That's when I started crying, of course, at the notion of someone maybe being able to do something for me, or someone even wanting to try.

She did a funny thing with her mouth when I cried, scrunching her lips together very tightly and blinking a bit while looking straight at me, her fingers still poised expectantly over her keyboard ready to fill in the 'presenting problem' box. As she waited for me to stop crying, she did the same thing Helen does, tilting her head to one side while maintaining the lip-scrunching expression. I wonder if that's a gesture all medical practitioners are taught in Sympathy Classes. Does your private shrink do that too? I expect they probably do a higher class of sympathy in Harley Street, don't they? Maybe the head tilting is an exclusively NHS gesture.

'Poor old you,' she said.

As I cried, and the young blonde doctor tilted and scrunched, I suddenly had an image of myself as I must look to her – another middle-aged woman in a brown anorak (well, OK, strictly speaking it's called a parka), sobbing in a GP's surgery on a weekday afternoon, and that just made me cry even harder, great snotty gulps that tore from me like vomit. (I can see you frowning at that simile. 'You don't need to resort to shock value,' you'd chide. 'The story should be enough.' You always fancied yourself as a wordsmith – 'I'll write a novel when I have some time,' you'd say, as if it were like bleeding an inefficient radiator.)

When I'd calmed down a bit and got through five tissues from the square, pastel-coloured box she kept on the shelf above her computer, she asked me what was making me so upset. I was in a quandary then. I wanted to tell her the truth, because really I wanted the help she was offering so sweetly, and yet this was, after all, my family practice. I didn't want to bring my children in at a future date, for a repeat asthma prescription or an unexplained rash, and find the same doctor sitting there, meeting my eyes with a quick conspiratorial lip scrunch. I didn't want to see her look at them with pity as she inspected their tongues or shone a light in their ears, knowing their mother was a slut. Can you see my dilemma now?

So I told her between sniffs that my life was a mess, my relationship a disaster, my finances in ruins, my career a joke. I told her all the truths – except the big one. I didn't tell her about you. I don't know that she was actually that interested in the whole truth and nothing other than the truth anyway, to be honest. She was much more concerned about the form she got me to fill in which listed lots of different scenarios and I had to ring the frequency with which they happened to me. When she asked me the one about feeling like you'd be better off dead, she looked very saddened when I ringed option 3: 'a lot of the time'. I was glad then that I hadn't gone for my first choice, option 4: 'all or almost all of the time', which was far closer to the truth. Who wouldn't feel they'd be better off dead if given the choice?

Between my snivels, I asked the sympathetic doctor for 'something to help me sleep'.

'Oh dear, there's nothing quite so awful as going without sleep, is there?' she said, and her long blonde hair made a little whooshing noise through the air as she shook her head sadly to emphasize how very sincerely she was empathizing. 'But, you know, sleeping pills are a very quick fix. They're not actually addressing the underlying issues.' As she said the word 'underlying' her voice dropped suddenly very low, as if the word were a little distasteful. 'So we don't really tend to prescribe them. We prefer to look at alternatives like cognitive behavioural therapy or, in some cases, antidepressants.'

I stared at her blearily over the tissue that was clamped to my nose and asked, 'Will either of those work in time for me to get some sleep tonight?'

The young doctor laughed as if I'd said something quite funny. 'I'm afraid the antidepressants won't kick in for a good few weeks and therapy is pretty much a long-term proposition,' she said.

'So I have to wait a good few weeks before I can get a decent night's sleep?' I asked her stupidly.

She did the scrunchy-lip thing again.

'Poor old you,' she said a second time, at which point I obviously started blubbing all over again. 'You're having an awful time, aren't you? But I'm afraid you're just going to have to grit your teeth and get through these next few weeks. Just keep telling yourself that it's not for long and in just a few weeks you will feel better.'

Just a few weeks?

Is she totally mad?

* * *

I had such a lovely time with Susan last night. She's such fun. I can quite see why you married her.

I'm trying to decide which was the best part, but you know I rather think it might have been getting ready. Does that sound silly? You see, all the time I was getting showered and dithering over what to wear, I was imagining what might be going on in your house, and what might be going through your mind as you watched Susan getting dressed up to come and meet me. Did you try to issue some subtle warning, I wonder? Did you say, 'You know, Sally's never been terribly stable'? Or your favourite: 'She's one of those sad, *damaged* women.' Yes, I rather think you might have. Susan would, of course, have been brisk but kind. 'Oh you're just an old misogynist,' she might have chided. 'Sally's just a little bit socially awkward. Anyway I feel sorry for her.' Susan is always collecting lost causes. It was one of the things you used to complain about most bitterly. 'Oh, I expect one of Susan's misfits will be hanging around at supper,' you'd sigh. Or 'We had to take one of Susan's *dysfunctionals* on holiday with us.'

We started off in the Coach and Horses on Greek Street. Oh, how silly of me. Of course you know where the Coach and Horses is. It was with you I first went there. Now, for goodness' sake don't read anything into my choice of venue. It just happened to be the first place that popped into my head when I was arranging things with Susan. It's just very convenient for both of us, that's all. I can't pretend that the irony of it completely escaped me, however, and I admit I did have a little chuckle when I steered Susan to that exact same table where we sat that one time when you asked me to marry you. Perhaps you've forgotten that little incident. You'd been having one of your periodic meltdowns where you angsted about where our relationship was going and you emailed me, terribly excited, to say you'd come up with some sort of a plan.

When I squeezed into the pub to meet you – it's always so very crowded, isn't it? – you had a smile on your face as big as Brazil.

'I know you're going to think I'm being silly,' you said. How ridiculous that word 'silly' always sounded coming from you with your ex-boxer's physique, your angry curls, your slightly flattened, much-broken nose. 'But I've come up with an idea that might make both of us feel just a little bit secure.'

I felt relieved then, I remember. Finally, you'd come up with a solution that didn't involve wrecking lives and destroying families. Sliding into the seat opposite you, my cheeks still flushed from my walk through Soho Square, I gazed at you expectantly, waiting for you to provide me with whatever answer had been staring us in the face the whole time.

'I want to ask you to marry me!'

My expression must have been a picture, it really must, because your terribly-pleased-with-yourself smile was already fading when I blurted out the one basic fact that you seemed to have overlooked. 'But you're already married!'

You looked a bit cross then and petulant, as if it was pedantic of me to have become hung up on a technicality at a moment of high romance such as this.

'I know I'm married,' you told me, clearly hurt. 'I just wanted you to know how serious I am about you. I wanted to give you some measure of commitment.'

'How can you commit to me when you're already committed to your wife?' I asked you, quite reasonably I thought.

Again that shadow of irritation passed over your face.

'I thought you'd be pleased,' you said and your voice was small and bruised like an overripe plum.

Ironic now to think that the one marriage proposal of my life (I don't count Daniel's 'Weddings are a waste of money but we should look into whether it's worth doing it for tax reasons') should have come from a married man.

I loved you I loved you I loved you I loved you.

Susan was looking slightly older, I thought (although at forty-six she's not far off my age), but more peaceful. Sorry, does that make her sound like a corpse? What I mean is she'd lost that gaunt look she wore for the last year of our affair. Not that I really got a chance to study her in those days, you understand. My guilt kept my gaze constantly averted, bouncing off the very corners of her so that I only ever took in small pieces – a blue eye sunk like a pebble into damp-sand creases, the corner of a mouth pulled down to the chin by invisible thread, the way sunlight brought the split ends of her straight white-blonde hair into sharp relief.

Last night, though, she was sleeker, shinier, plumper. Her smile had lost the weariness of old. She was wearing her trademark navy blue, but she had a white jacket over her dress with a sequinned trim that sparkled where the lights in the pub hit it. She looked alive.

'You look wonderful,' I told her, truthfully.

'Thank you, love, and so do you.'

It was nice of her to lie, but I could see she was a little bit shocked. You see, I haven't exactly been looking after myself since we last saw one another. (Can it really be three months ago, that hunched figure weeping in the rain on York Way?) Grief has hollowed me out with a blunt spoon, trowelling grooves into flaccid flesh. My hair bears the tell-tale stripes of a bad home-dye, the roots an alarming shade of blood-orange where the chemicals have been absorbed by greedy strands of grey, the rest a rusty brown, like corroded iron. I've lost weight (oh, the wonders of the Misery Diet!) so now I wear my skin like an ill-fitting suit and the bones protrude, lumpen, from my chest. Thank God she couldn't see my legs, where the hairs proliferate like weeds now that no one sees them any more.

'Sorry I'm late,' she bustled, shaking out her hair and trying not to look at the black shadows around my eyes or the slight citalopram tremor of my fingers. 'Clive wanted me to go with him and look at some shoes he wants to buy. He's such a terrible baby about things like that. So that threw my day out completely.'

I imagined the two of you peering into the shop window. It would be that old-fashioned men's shoe shop up near Hampstead – you've told me before that's the only place you'll ever go. I remember how excited you were when you bought that pair of brown suede brogues from there, and how much you fussed about them getting muddy when we went for that walk around the old mental asylum at Shenley in Hertfordshire. All those days out in places expressly chosen because no one else in their right minds would want to go there. All those pub lunches in nameless villages up the A1 with floral cushions tied to the chair seats and mid-week specials, three courses for £9.95.

I remember all that while Susan tells me all about the business of being her, about how hard she's been working and how much she's looking forward to getting away with you next week to the manor house in Scotland owned by your old friend Gareth Powell, the historian.

'It's a wonderful place,' she tells me. 'The full monty – flagstoned floors, big open fireplaces, a housekeeper who brings you cups of tea and homemade cakes.'

Well, it was all I could do not to chime in then, adding to the list. 'How about the faded Persian carpets or the four-poster beds with the extra-fine Egyptian cotton bedlinen?'

Don't be silleeeee, I didn't actually say all that. Nor did I tell her how many times you'd begged me to make up an elaborate excuse so I could have a 'night off' and come to Scotland with you. How you'd already squared it with Gareth, who was excited by the thought of aiding and abetting a love affair. (Funny how right at the end, during that agonizing endless lunch, you told me he'd advised you to give me up. 'You'll always love her, dear boy,' he'd apparently told you, this womanizing, two-faced, hypocritical dandy. 'But you know you have to give Susan another chance. It's the *right* thing to do.') Wafting your open invitation at me, you'd built up a picture of how we'd spend our time in Scotland. ('Make it two nights,' you'd wheedled. 'Please.') We'd get up at six and take the path that threaded down from the gardens through the rocks and on to the beach. 'We'll throw pebbles into the water,' you'd told me, 'and sit on the big rock at the far end and take off our shoes and socks and dangle our feet in the water. And at night we'll lie on the big old squishy tapestry sofa in front of the log fire and make love and then I'll carry you up to bed, and we'll make love some more.' (I didn't like to mention your bad back, not when you were so carried away by the Mills & Boon romance of your little fantasy.)

So this is what was going through my head as Susan was describing how very much she was looking forward to the Scotland mini-break. Of course I never had been able to find a whole night to myself to go with you, let alone two, but I'd pictured it in my head so many times. The house, the housekeeper, the fire, the sofa. Us, us, us. Except now it's not to be us, after all. It's to be you and Susan, walking to the beach in the early morning – you holding her hand to help her over the rocks, the two of you sitting side by side, feet dangling, while you talk about where you can make changes in your marriage, how you can make it stronger.

Oh yes, Susan told me all about how you two have been through a rough patch but are now talking more than you've ever done throughout your marriage. I was very touched that she opened up so much, really I was. I hadn't been expecting such a level of intimacy as, goodness knows, we've never had it before, but as Susan herself said, all the talking and couple-counselling you've been doing recently have obviously made her more 'connected' to her emotions.

Incidentally, don't you think that's a funny term? 'Connected to my emotions.' It's as if there was an option to choose to be unconnected to them, to somehow unbuckle them like a rucksack and shrug them off on to the floor and leave them behind. I wish I could do that. Maybe it's something I could ask Helen Bunion about, whether she can help me disconnect from my emotions. Maybe there's a mental exercise one can do (Helen is very big on mental exercises). Or maybe we could role-play it. I could be me and she could be the rucksack, or the other way around. Or there might be a visualization technique that could work. I could imagine packing those pesky emotions away into the back of a drawer, or a box in the attic.

It felt funny hearing Susan talk about being connected to her emotions, because she's always been such a brisk, practical type of person. Before last night I'd have said she probably thought emotions were a bit like tonsils and could be extracted if they ever got troublesome. But I have to tell you, last night I saw a completely different side of her. It was very enlightening, it really was. For instance, she told me that the two of you have been *hysterical bonding*. That's what she called it. Another bona fide counselling term, it seems. Of course, she said it with a wry smile, drawing some exaggerated quote marks in the air. I didn't have a clue what she was talking about at first – I imagined it to be some kind of frenzied empathizing. But Susan explained – quite coyly for her – how after a marriage has been through a crisis point, a couple will often find them-selves 'going at it like rabbits', even if they've been married, say, twenty-six years. Apparently your marriage counsellor told you it was perfectly normal. 'Enjoy it,' she said.

Straight after York Way Friday, I used to have dreams of being ripped open by a knife. Slashed, slit, flesh-torn. I'd thought at first it was because the ending had seemed like a physical assault, which I was subsequently reliving over and over inside my head. Belatedly though I realized that I was the one wielding the knife. I even knew which one I'd use – the one from the kitchen with the exaggeratedly jagged serrated edge. I'd plunge it into my chest and zig-zag down, cutting myself open as with a rusty tin-opener. It was my heart I was after, of course. I'd rip it out, that hateful pulsating thing, and fling it down on the table in front of me. Then I'd grab a hammer and, still beating, I'd smash it to a pulp.

The hysterical-bonding chat really opened the floodgates. I'd always thought Susan was a bit – and please don't take this the wrong way – two-dimensional. She was always so brusque and practical about everything, it was as if she didn't feel things terribly deeply. But as I say, last night I saw a completely different side of her. It seemed – and I know you'll shoot me down in flames here for this corny image – as if someone had turned on a light inside her somewhere. She exuded this sort of glow of contentment that was really quite warming to see. She told me all about the house-hunting trip you're going on to 'a wonderfully undiscovered part of Croatia' next month. As she talked I couldn't help remembering how you'd ranted and railed against her persistent plans to buy a holiday home abroad. 'We won't know anybody there. What would we talk about, just me and her?' you'd agonized. 'Every minute would be hell because I'd only want to be there with you.'

Susan, with her tremendous pragmatism, has researched the whole idea and found a part of Croatia that has yet to become fashionable and where one can pick up a wonderful old place, full of character, right on the sea for 'virtually nothing'.

'But you've already got a wonderful place right on the sea that you bought for virtually nothing,' I reminded her.

Her face kind of clouded over a bit then and she wrinkled up her nose slightly as if picking up a bad smell.

'The Suffolk house is great, of course,' she said, 'within its limitations. But we don't use it nearly as much as we used to. Remember all those weekend parties? There was a time when Clive was up there all the time working on his new material, but he's much happier to stay home now he's got his studio kitted out.'

Sad fuck in a box.

I remembered how thrilled Daniel and I were in those early years to get one of those treasured weekend invitations. 'Just a few of us, nothing fancy,' you'd say. We'd pile kids and pillows and bottles of mid-range red wine into the Saab on a Friday afternoon and Tilly and Jamie would be almost incoherent with excitement by the time we parked the car two and a half hours later. While your own children, then older teenagers away at boarding school, were always absent from these gatherings, there were always enough others to hold their attention. As we walked along the waterside path from the road, towards the enormous old rambling house with its sloping floors and secret passageways and eccentric warren of bedrooms with windows looking straight out across the estuary, you'd step out on to the quayside to meet us, Jack Daniels in hand.

'I love coming in to mix things up,' you'd say, casting an appraising eye over whichever disparate group of house-guests you'd gathered together that weekend, spilling out on to the gardens to the back and the side, 'and then flying out again and leaving it all behind.'

Of course, that was before anything began, when you were still a mysterious distant figure with a separate life, before the frenzied years when you couldn't even go to the loo without advising me first, the years of texts from service-station toilets and pre-iPhone emails sent from coin-operated public computers. 'I'm delayed', 'I'm on my way', 'Nearly there', 'Got to go. Speak in two and a half hours. I love you.'

Think of me going through Essex,' I used to say if you were stuck up in Suffolk without me. It was our running joke whenever there was any kind of separation. 'Did you think of me in Essex?' I'd ask you when you texted me the minute you arrived home. I wonder now if you ever think of me in Essex on one of your rare trips up? There are probably so many other things to think of.

Susan confided in me (I think this was after her second rum and coke) how she'd felt Suffolk had become a bit 'stale'. She couldn't put her finger on why or when it had started, but it had reached the point where the house parties no longer seemed so much fun, and the weather-clock seemed stuck permanently to 'drizzle'.

'We'll always love that house because there are so many good memories, but it's time for the next challenge. We want to go somewhere new. Start again. Meet a new set of people.'

Will you be mixing things up now, I wondered? Flying in and out with your sunset cocktail hours and your lunch parties bleeding seamlessly into dinner, guests splayed out exhausted across the battered leather sofas ('They're

Danish from the 1970s,' you told me anxiously that first weekend we came. 'I wouldn't want you to think we picked them up in World of Leather.')

Susan was very excited about the Croatia trip, I must say. She said that though you've both been before, you've always seemed a bit half-hearted about it in the past. Recently though, you've apparently become more enthusiastic than she is.

She's thinking in terms of maybe cutting down the amount she works, she told me. Taking on fewer clients. It's not as if you need the money, and 'as Clive can fly in and out for work' if you found the perfect place in Croatia, it would make sense for the two of you to spend more time abroad.

I can see how that would work out quite well. Susan's such a great home-maker and a real people person. She'll soon assemble a new crowd of hangers-on, just as she did in Suffolk all those years ago. And the house no doubt will be stunning. How canny you've both been. But then Susan always was so astute with investments – that's one of the things you both admired and resented about her.

'Oh God, I'm just *useless* about money,' you always professed. 'I've never made a long-term strategy in my life, just stumbled from one immediate decision to another.'

Funny, that.

You used to say we were two halves of the same whole. Now I wonder whether we weren't just two halves of the same hole.

Susan asked me all about Daniel. 'Is it still awful?' she said, with typical bluntness.

Sometimes, you know, I regret being so indiscreet about my disintegrating relationship. I should have taken a leaf out of your book. Even when you and Susan were at your most unravelled, you still gave the impression of being the ideal Sunday supplement couple, with your legendary Sunday lunches, your family picnics at Kenwood, your weekend-long house parties in the country. Me, I turned marital dysfunction into a spectator sport. I practically sold tickets. Available now, a ringside seat to watch two people dissect their relationship piece by microscopic piece.

So strange now to think that for years our friends saw Daniel and me as the poster couple for a healthy relationship. 'It's so rare to see a couple who genuinely like each other,' my friend Jack once said. 'Anyone can love their partner, but not many can manage "like".' In the end I think it was the little things that did for us – the relentless erosion of goodwill that comes with co-managing the demands of children, the secret conviction that the other person isn't quite pulling their weight. It wasn't so much, as women's magazines always claim, that we started to see each other as parents instead of lovers, it was more that we saw each other as *wanting* parents, lacking somehow. We each of us felt unfairly burdened by the other's shortcomings. I always think the downward slide started from there.

'Oh, you know,' I replied evasively. 'It is what it is.'

If ever there was a phrase to sound the death-knell of a romance, that must surely be it. 'It is what it is.' Oh dear.

Susan gave me her sympathetic look, which mercifully didn't entail cocking her head to one side but just fixing me with her very blue eyes.

'Well, dear, if you want my advice, you're better off sticking with the devil you know. All men are basically pretty much the same, so if you've already got one trained you might as well hang on to him.'

Well, there didn't seem much point in arguing with that.

After the Coach and Horses we made our way along Old Compton Street and into Wardour Street, where we found a nondescript French restaurant, part of a formulaic chain, where the waiters did that passive-aggressive Gallic thing of smiling at you as if they actually want to stab you.

On our way in, Susan greeted two people she knew at separate tables. I at first wondered if they might be some of her dysfunctionals, but they looked pretty normal to me.

Over dinner, which Susan insisted on ordering in a loud, cod French accent – she does like to play everything for laughs, doesn't she? You must never stop giggling in your house – she told me the big news about Emily. You ought to have told me, you really should. A grandchild! Just what you've been hoping for. You must be absolutely thrilled. If there's one thing you love it's being needed and now Emily will need you desperately, and Susan too. It'll be a whole new start for the two of you.

I remember Sian saying, not long after it started, 'Clive's the kind of man who can't bear not having any children around to look after any more.' Then she'd looked at me very pointedly and added, 'The big danger is he'll meet a woman who needs looking after instead.' I guess that would be me then.

Halfway through the second bottle of Pouilly Fuissé 2008, Susan's iPhone rang. I must say I find it quite touching the way you both got those iPhones at the same time. I mean, I know there must have been some kind of two-for-one deal going on, but there's still something quite sweet about it, your joint embracing of technology. 'Oh, I haven't got the first clue how the bloody thing works,' you protested when you first got it. (I didn't know back then that it had been a team venture you and Susan had embarked on. Ridiculously, I'd thought that iPhone of yours was all about me, a way for you to check for my emails, even when you were away from your box. Oh, the sheer arrogance of me.)

I could tell it was you straight away from the way she turned slightly away, the low, familiar tone of her voice. I imagined how desperate you must have been to find out what we were talking about, and how subtly you must now be quizzing her, trying to gauge from her voice any newly acquired secrets. For a moment I even thought about texting you, just to put you out of your misery. But that wouldn't have been very sensible, would it?

Susan apologized when she came off the phone. 'Clive has gone so soppy recently,' she said, composing her features into a mock frown. 'It's intensely irritating. He's always on the phone. I can't get rid of him.'

Ah, so that's who you're taking your minutiae to now, is it? Laying the details of your day at Susan's feet like a cat offering up a dead bird to its owner, weaving your trivia together with hers to form a protective shroud around you both. It's touching, it really is.

'He's even talking about renewing our vows.' Susan was speaking through a mouthful of tarte aux pommes, but pleasure wafted up from her like stale perfume. Is there anything quite as painful as someone else's pleasure? I fought a momentary urge to pick up my own plate of crème brûlée and smash it violently into her face, pressing so hard that it filled up her nostrils and she choked on its slimy blandness. Or I could lean across and say, 'Oh, here's a photo you might want to use for the invitations,' and tap the buttons on my mobile phone to bring up the pictures in the hidden folder – perhaps the one of you standing behind me enfolding me in your arms and licking my neck while I giggled and the hand that held the phone shook, or the one you took in the hotel bathroom mirror of us standing entwined, forehead to forehead, with matching white towels around our waists? I wanted to take a wire wool scouring pad to that rosy glow on Susan's cheeks and rub and rub until it was gone.

Now, don't start getting all puffed up and protective. It was just a momentary impulse and of course I didn't do any of those things. Instead I sat and smiled nicely and, once I'd swallowed down the bile with a spoonful of crème brûlée, I told her how delighted I was for her and what a romantic thing it was to do after twenty-six years of marriage. Which, of course, it is.

It wasn't yet eleven when we said our goodbyes at Oxford Circus Tube station. The night was still young and I had no real desire to go home, so instead of getting on the Victoria Line south, I turned and followed the sparkle of Susan's white jacket as she headed north. Gosh, I hope that doesn't make me sound like a nutter! It's just I wasn't in any hurry to get anywhere and I'd had such a lovely evening with Susan, I was strangely reluctant to see her go.

I got into the carriage behind hers. I knew of course which stop she'd be getting off at. I've done that journey before, remember? There was a tricky moment as the doors opened and she suddenly turned her head to the right. But she wasn't looking for anyone, and her gaze slid off me like baby oil. I didn't really have a particular plan in mind. I just had a vague notion of following her home and watching to see if there was a light on upstairs, if you'd waited up for her to come home. Helen Bunion would call that masochistic behaviour, and I suppose she might have a point. But as you know very well, sometimes when pain is just about as savage as it can get, it almost becomes pleasurable. ('Hurt me,' you used to urge me, your face distorted by sex. 'I don't want to,' I'd reply, and your cheek would twitch with disappointment.)

In the event though, I didn't get a chance to follow Susan. I only got as far as the top of the escalator. Just a few yards ahead, Susan was pressing her Oyster card to the machine to open up the barrier. And just a few yards beyond that was you. I hadn't seen you for so long, it took a moment for my brain to register that it really was you standing there. You were wearing that ridiculously expensive coat that I used to call your 'fashion coat' because it looked great but did a terrible job of keeping you warm, and your jeans with the slightly frayed hems and a pair of battered cowboy boots. Your hair was slightly longer than when I'd last seen you and your face wore that delighted smile I remember from so many past meetings, that dent appearing like a thumb imprint in your cheek. I have to admit that for a moment it all rushed over me again, those old feelings that Helen has been helping me file away in my mental filing cabinet. ('Hear the clanging noise as you firmly close it.') An answering smile erupted, quite unbidden, on my face and I took an involuntary step forward until I realized – oh, foolish, foolish woman – that you hadn't even seen me. Your loving look, your dimple, your welcome, which I'd been on the receiving end of so many, many times before, were all for Susan. How touching that you didn't even want her to risk walking the hundred or so yards home on her own down the brightly lit mean streets of genteel St John's Wood. But you always were over-fussy like that. I remember all those texts I used to receive on the bus: 'Are you there yet?', 'Don't let anyone follow you off,' 'Text me the minute you're in your house.' They used to irritate me a bit then, when I accepted them as my due, but now I miss them.

Before you turned to go, your arm wrapped protectively around her shoulders, Susan said something to you and your laugh echoed around the ticket hall. I imagine she was telling you something about our evening together. I wonder what it was that could have been so funny. Your laugh rang in my ears the whole way home, like tinnitus.

* * *

Now, please don't take this the wrong way, but I've never really liked Emily. Is that a terrible thing to say about someone who almost became a step-daughter? Maybe. But then I'm aiming for 100 per cent transparency, let's not forget, and the truth will set me free. So there it is.

The first time I met her was at a launch for one of your artists. You were playing the jovial host, introducing all the disparate guests to one another. When I arrived with Daniel, you leaned in to peck me on the cheek and whispered 'Gorgeous' under your breath. Then you said, in a much louder voice, 'I don't think you've met my daughter Emily, have you?' and called her over. She was one of those painfully thin, over-made-up, over-groomed young women and when she shook my hand, hers was limp as tinned asparagus and her smile looked like it had been painted on over her real mouth. Her eyes, weighed down by several layers of thick mascara, were already flitting beyond me, in search of anyone more interesting. It was like shaking hands with a hologram.

I didn't think much of her at the time, beyond wondering how two intelligent people like you and Susan could have produced someone so vapid and so totally self-obsessed, but after my dinner with Susan, I couldn't get Emily out of my thoughts. I knew just the type of pregnant woman she'd make. One of those who turn pregnancy into a competitive sport, and who have their doctor on speed-dial: 'Are bananas safe for unborn babies?', 'How about paracetamol?' She'd ask people to stand up for her on the Tube, even at four months, and start refusing to eat brie and equating smokers with suicide bombers.

Her bland barrister husband would insist she gave up work (if you can call three days a week at a PR company work) at five months, of course, as she'd be needing plenty of rest. And whenever he was away on business, she'd move back home with Mummy and Daddy, because her 'condition' would make her feel too vulnerable home alone in Notting Hill.

You and Susan will love that, of course, feeling useful and needed again. I know exactly how vindicated you must be feeling. 'Imagine,' you might think to yourself as you look down your dinner table at your smugly pregnant daughter, your glowingly expectant wife, 'I almost gave all this up. What an idiot I've been.'

You might even vow to yourself to spend the rest of your life making it up to them – you always were big on grand, empty promises.

Thinking about Emily, that sacred vessel, and the wonderful future unfolding before you and Susan as doting grandparents, started bringing up all those old sensations I experienced in the first awful weeks after York Way Friday. There was that same pain in my left side, just below my ribcage, that same gasping shortness of breath. I sat up in bed and fumbled in my bedside cupboard.

Since my visit to the young blonde doctor who was only interested in addressing the *underlying* issues of my insomnia, I've been having to collect sleeping pills from other sources. Turns out they're practically a currency of their own in our little part of south London, and I never even knew! All I had to do was mention my problems to a few friends, and the donations have been flooding in. A couple of clonazepam here, a packet of zopiclone there. I even got a delivery of valium all the way from South America, where there are places you can still buy such things over the counter in an enlightened sort of way. Funny to think that three months ago I'd never even taken a sleeping pill, and now I've got so many different varieties of tranquillizers, beta blockers, and anti-anxiety medication, I could practically start up my own pharmacy.

I'll tell you something, it's made me look at my friends

in a completely different way: a noble unsung army of middle-aged invisible women battling in stoical silence against our demons.

* * *

I suppose I should tell you a bit about Daniel now. You might have been wondering where he's been in all this. You always did go to such pains to say how much you liked Daniel. 'Well, you couldn't not like him, could you?' you'd tell me. 'He's so terribly *harmless*.'

Was ever faint praise more damning?

Of course, I'd argue that 'harmless' is relative anyway. Just because someone doesn't set out to do you harm doesn't mean they don't end up harming you anyway, does it? You always claimed to be fascinated by how Daniel and I ever wound up together. But you have to understand that when I first met him sixteen years ago at a party thrown by one of the other minions at the publishing house where I worked, he was relentlessly, *gloriously* eager to please. Three years younger than me, with that thick blond hair he was constantly brushing out of his eyes (how perversely irritated you've always been by Daniel's still-long, foppish hair. 'What's he trying to prove?' you used to ask) and his total lack of guile, he seemed the perfect antidote to my studied jadedness. (In those days I wore my ennui self-consciously and half-heartedly, like an experimental fashion craze – like batwing sleeves or high-waisted flares.)

Where did it go, I wonder, that active wish to see me happy? When did the apathy set in, the dull sense that it was enough simply to refrain from doing me harm? In truth, I think I probably squished it out of him somewhere along the way, along with the guitar-playing and the baggy boxers. I often worry that I have somehow made Daniel less than he was when I first met him. That I have reduced him, like over-simmered stock.

I must say, though, Daniel has been marvellous (well, in that unshowy Daniel sort of way) since York Way Friday, hovering nervously on the edge of my incipient insanity, suggesting useless remedies. 'Perhaps we could take up a class together,' was last week's classic. Get this: 'life drawing'.

In a weird way, though, I think he's quite enjoying the mini drama of it all. After so long being shut out and fenced off from my inner life, there must be a certain satisfaction in witnessing the walls breached, the defences down, the infidels swarming through the gates.

He fields telephone calls with hushed, self-important whispers, when I am too numb to speak. I've heard him hiss the word 'breakdown' in an awed, reverential tone. It's nonsense, of course. A convenient label to help him understand the incomprehensible.

Lately, though, I can tell he's growing impatient and the novelty of my debility is starting to lose its shine. Several times he's asked me rather sharply where I go in the evenings or what has precipitated my 'decline'. After the last few years of leading increasingly separate lives, his curiosity comes as an unwelcome intrusion. Still, I'm tempted to tell him the truth, I really am. Do you remember what I wrote to you, in the agonizing aftermath of York Way Friday? How I assured you so loftily that I would now tell Daniel *everything*, how I owed him that, how I was sick of the lies and the deception? Of course, you saw through that right away, even before I did. You knew it was just a ploy to get a reaction from you, a rather pathetic attempt to exert a power I no longer possessed. You already understood what I had wilfully ignored – that the secret of our affair is the last link that ties me to you, the last intimacy we share, now all other intimacy is gone. You know that for me to give that up means giving you up. All of you. No more emails, no more chats with Susan, no more dinner-party crossovers, no more crumbs of information tossed out by unwitting mutual friends. Telling Daniel the truth would sever irretrievably my connection to you. You knew that and you took a chance on it, never bothering to reply to my scarcely veiled threats, my clumsy implication that if you didn't come back to me I'd trumpet our truth from the rooftops. You knew I didn't have it in me. How right you were.

So Daniel continues to bumble along in his ignorance, and I wonder if that ignorance is a blessing or a curse. 'He doesn't deserve this,' I used to declare periodically in that enjoyably melodramatic way, while we were going through one of our regular *mea culpa*, self-flagellation sessions. 'He's done nothing wrong.'

Of course he hadn't done anything wrong. He hadn't done anything at all, not in years, which was of course somewhere at the heart of all our tangled problems. Can an absence of action be construed as a negative action? It's an interesting conundrum, isn't it?

Shall we go back to the very first time we met, you and I? Why not? Of course, Helen Bunion would find a million reasons why not. 'Don't keep journeying to the past. Put up your mental stop sign!' she would urge me. And I know she's probably right, but tonight, every time I put up my mental stop sign, I find myself wanting to drive a great big articulated lorry straight over it, flattening it to the ground. So humour me a little by letting me pick at that particular, familiar old scab and go back to that first time. It will fill up a few moments while I sit up alone in the semi-darkness, journalling away and waiting for the clonazepam to take effect.

We'd gone for lunch at a pub-restaurant in Hampstead with a huge outside garden. It was the birthday of a woman I'd met through an antenatal class and remained tenuously in touch with, and a group of ten or twelve had gathered around a long table outside, enjoying the watery London sunshine. Cyd, the guest of honour, had saved two empty chairs at the end of the table 'just in case Susan and Clive manage to make it'. She'd met Susan at a yoga class, she explained, and then gone to your house for dinner. 'They're fabulous,' she sighed. 'So friendly and down to earth, you'd never guess they were so successful and so *loaded*.' Yes, can you believe that? That was how she described you – not some sad fuck in a box, after all, but one half of a 'power couple'! I think she might even have used the word 'charismatic'. I expect you rather like that.

Eventually you came strolling in wearing jeans and aviator shades and a bright Hawaiian shirt, apologizing that Susan had been called away to sort out a crisis at a wedding she was catering for. Cyd could hardly contain her excitement at your arrival.

'This is the famous Clive,' she said, scrambling to her feet, as proud as if she'd made you herself in pottery evening class.

Cyd is one of those friends so of the moment that, looking back now, I can't quite believe we ever knew each other. What on earth did we find to talk about, she and I? Still I'm grateful to her now, I suppose, although to be honest, my initial reaction to her introduction was disappointment. I've never been a fan of bulky men, and you are, let's be frank about it, a bulky man, although less so now than you were then ('Being in love is the best slimming aid in the world,' you said later, as the cheekbones began to push through the skin on your face like tumours.) Nor was I sure about the Chinese dragon tattoo on your forearm, or the sheen of product in your tangle of curls.

You walked around the table introducing yourself to the group. Daniel shot up to shake your hand, but I remained seated on the far side of the table determinedly working my way through an artichoke, plucking its leaves like chicken feathers. I didn't want to meet 'the famous Clive', didn't want to get close enough for your secondhand glamour to brush off on me like peeling skin.

'I hear you're a journalist. Who have you written for?' you asked me, and I perceived your interest to be forced, although you later insisted your apparent indifference masked a sudden crippling shyness.

Reluctantly, I picked some names out of the air and you nodded, pretending to be impressed.

'You should email me sometime,' you told me. 'I've got a mate who runs a property newspaper. He'll give you some stuff to write that you might find amusing.'

Amusing.

I'd never before met anyone successful enough to consider work 'amusing'.

'He's a bit pompous, isn't he?' I told Daniel on the way home, negotiating the uninspiring south-east London backstreets with their disconcerting mix of ugly sixties blocks and decayed grandeur.

'Oh, I really liked him.' Daniel always likes everyone. So much less effort than having to form a real opinion.

Then had come the invitation to lunch, at your St John's Wood villa. I'd walked into the enormous square hallway with its sweeping staircase, past the gleaming double-height kitchen and into the 'family room' at the back with its curved wall of floor-to-ceiling French windows. I'd taken in the flamboyant rugs and the out-sized abstract paintings by a sister of Susan's who apparently had once been quite well known, and I'd tried to ignore the sickly feeling that swept over me, the knowledge that our own South London Victorian terrace with its knock-through lounge and under-stairs toilet would never again feel good enough, nice enough, special enough.

A hard, ugly kernel of jealousy lodged like a gallstone in my gut.

I never told you all that, did I? I expect you find it all a bit distasteful. When you come from money, there's an unwritten law that you should pretend to find both the acquiring of it and the spending of it rather a tiresome chore, something you 'frankly' don't really pay much attention to. But when you come from a lacklustre semi on the outskirts of a provincial south-western town, you tend to notice these things.

That lunch was the first time I met Susan. With her rancid dog under one arm and a large tumbler of Scotch in the other hand, she meeted and greeted the disparate group she'd gathered with the ease of someone who genuinely likes people, and has faith that, that being so, there's a good chance they will probably like each other too.

'Aren't they just an amazing couple?' whispered Cyd, gazing at you and Susan as though in the throes of a celestial vision, and taking a long drag on her long joint. 'I just love these guys.'

Of course, it would have been churlish to do anything but love you guys too. There you were with your urbane bonhomie, your table with the theatrical candelabra, groaning with fresh salads and interesting Lebanese mezze, all cooked by the loyal team at Susan's catering firm, your Smeg fridge stocked with wine and beer, your hilarious tales of being rollicking drunk at the Ivy with any number of has-been celebrities.

'They've been married for more than twenty years! And they're still so much in love!' Cyd confided in hushed, awed tones.

The hard pellet of jealousy inside me shifted painfully as I thought about the twelve years of mismatchment Daniel and I had notched up, nearly one hundred and fifty months jammed uncomfortably together like an ill-fitting jigsaw.

Of course, if I'd known then that the sour-faced divorcee neighbour who sat silently at the end of the table and surveyed each forkful of food mistrustfully before popping it into her mouth was sour only because she'd once been your lover, leaving her front door open at night for you to slip out of your house in the first dawn light, and still couldn't understand why you never came any more ('One time I got up to go and she started to cry – that's when I knew it was over'), my jealousy might have been tempered slightly and interfered less with my enjoyment of the gorgeous food and entertaining company.

But then, you always hid all that stuff so well.

The compartmentalizing is something I never could manage to get right. You were, naturally, a black belt in it. How many times did you make the journey straight from Premier Inn to marital bed without even stopping to pass Go? I did admire that, I really did. It probably came from all those years trying to break into the music business, oiling your way into record-company offices, turning yourself into whoever the bosses wanted you to be. What's that they call it nowadays in recruitment terms? A trans-ferable skill. That's what it is, being able to parcel up all the separate bits of your life and keep them from touching one another, like a TV dinner. There's a lot to be said for a talent like that.

And so it began. A loose and meandering friendship. When invited into your and Susan's orbit, we'd get together for lunches on your London lawn, or pile up to your Suffolk bolthole to go crab-fishing from the jetty in front of the house, or, when the weather denied us, adjourn to cosy country pubs, taking over fire-warmed snugs with an arrogant sense of entitlement. And when you weren't around, well, our life went along just as it always did. The children went to school. Daniel decided to start a mountain-bike-hire business and took to cycling off at weekends in a vague spirit of research, returning at the end of the day all red cheeks and sticky lycra. I continued to write patchily and badly for magazines, sitting in the cubbyhole in my dressing gown, pitching ideas to commissioning editors in high-heeled shoes and black, tailored clothes eating dressing-free salads in Tupperware containers at their desks. And yes, eventually I contacted your mate Douggie on the property newspaper, and while the work wasn't amusing, neither was it onerous. We struck up an email relationship, the two of us, which grew into a faltering but real (or so I liked to think) friendship.

'Susan's never allowed me to have a female friend before,' you told me, wonderingly. 'It's quite a big departure for her.'

I scoffed then, do you remember? I couldn't conceive of being 'allowed' to have friends of the opposite sex. 'Daniel knows he'd be out on his ear if he ever tried to tell me who I could and couldn't be friends with. You've got to have trust, haven't you?'

Laughable now, isn't it?

Of course, that was before I knew about the divorcee neighbour and the couple of women you'd picked up in a wine-bar in Brighton, who met up with you for a threesome a few times until you realized they were more interested in each other than in you, or the Brazilian prostitute you were given as a 'reward' for creating a surprise hit for a has-been South American artist, or the crazy 'girlfriend' who liked you to watch while she picked up men in a bar wearing no knickers. Once I knew about all that, I could understand better why Susan might have had certain trust issues – even though she had no idea about any of that stuff – your long, illustrious, blindingly successful career of infidelity.

So, I was the one female friend you were 'allowed' to

have. I was flattered, of course, in my usual shallow way.

'Susan likes you,' you told me. 'And she knows you have been doing some work for Douggie.'

And so the emails crept up, from a couple a month to one a week, until we were writing every day, several times a day – idle gossip and waspish observations. I realized that the more acid-tongued I was about my friends or people I met at your parties, the warmer your response. So together we developed denigrating nicknames for them all. Remember Nurse Ratched, with her thin-lipped smile and her white orthopaedic-looking shoes, and your favourite, the Child Bride, perpetually astonished by her brood of awful children?

And you egged me on, of course. Finding the inevitable snags of thread in the make-up of perfectly nice people and pulling and pulling until great gaping holes appeared, so big you could put a fist through. We excelled, the two of us, in character annihilation and congratulated one another on our own discernment, our membership of a little unspoken club of two. That it was founded on an ability to spot the mundane, the laughable and the weak in everyone apart from ourselves never bothered us, did it? We turned sneering into an intellectual pursuit and called it wit. And boy, how pleased we were with ourselves.

'You're the only person who really gets all this stuff,' you'd say to me. 'You're the only one on my wavelength.'

I'd feel as smug as the kid who got an A plus on her history essay, hugging her 'Well done!' to herself through-out the long school day.

Looking back on it, I was, of course, ripe for the picking. Bored, frustrated, intellectually starved. Your first legit-imate female friend. I wore the label like a medal.

Often in your emails, pinged ten miles from your jumped-up box room in St John's Wood, you'd tell me quite unashamedly how you'd read some mawkish piece in the newspaper and started weeping uncontrollably, or how the tears were plopping on to your keyboard while you listened to opera at full blast and thought about the mother who died when you were just a child, and the largely useless absentee father, a builder turned property tycoon who never quite knew what to do with the son he wanted to make into both street fighter and toff. And about the resentful grandmother who brought you up in that soulless Hertfordshire pile; the long, lonely days spent chasing ghosts through empty, high-ceilinged rooms, and pressing your nose up against the shop window of other people's family lives.

'I don't know how to do love,' you always said proudly, as if it were something that ought to come with an instruction leaflet like an IKEA flat-pack wardrobe. 'I'm an emotional baby.'

But at other times, you'd felt the need to remind me that you could also be very hard. How else, in the days when you were trying to break into the business, could you have kept on knocking at doors that were constantly being closed in your face, taking on men who never gave the benefit of the doubt. Do you remember that time I went with you to visit the father of a young girl you wanted to sign up, an East End wide boy who knew his daughter had talent and wanted a share of it by proclaiming himself her manager? We'd driven out to Essex and taken a stroll hand in hand along the sea-front, then parked up in front of an orange-bricked new-build house with tiny windows and mock Roman columns holding up the porch, and you jabbed your elbow into my side when I started giggling at your sudden cockney accent. 'Orlroight mate?' you said to the gold-chained man in the high-waisted jeans who opened the door – you with your voice dripping with money – and I bit my lip to stop the laughter. Still, there was obviously some kind of recognition there, I thought, some element of grudging mutual respect. 'There's a side to me that you've never seen,' you'd brag. 'A side I won't show you, because I don't want to frighten you off.'

I only saw a glimpse of it once. You'd stopped your ridiculous black Jag at some traffic lights on the North Circular. ('Isn't it awful?' you'd said the first time you got that car. 'It's such a cliché. I *hate* it with a passion.') All of a sudden, a gang of pointy-faced Eastern Europeans jumped up from the side of the road with buckets and squeegee mops. 'Don't fucking think about it,' you muttered, as one of them headed determinedly for your car. 'They're only young,' I murmured feebly, but you weren't listening. Your eyes were locked on the skinny young man approaching the gleaming bonnet. 'Fuck off,' you mouthed, but still he came closer, his expression blank, clearly used to this sort of reaction. As he plunged his squeegee into the mucky bucket and reached towards the windscreen, you suddenly ripped off your seatbelt and leaped from the car in one fluid movement, flinging open your door so wide that it flapped on its hinges. Like I said before, you're one of those power-ful men. Powerful men driving big black cars can be scary, even to hardened, ferret-featured Romanians. Before he turned and ran, water sloshing out of the wildly swinging bucket, I saw a look of genuine fear sweeping over his face.

When you got back into the car, you noticed my alarm, and your face softened with concern.

'Just ignore my stupid outburst. Some things just wind me up, that's all. I'd never do anything to upset you, you know that. I'm such a clumsy idiot.'

But that came later, of course, after the emails had segued into something else. At the beginning, it was just you tapping away in your attic box while Dvořák's 'Rusalka' rang out and the tears splattered on your fingers.

* * *

You should have told me you had been nominated for an award! I'm so pleased for you, really I am. Nobody deserves it more. Well, apart from the record-company minions who do all the boring admin and sound checking and preliminary editing, ready for you to come on and take centre stage. But really, of course, it's your name that brings in the talent. Without it, they'd be out of a job, all those scuttling, muttering minions. So I'm delighted to hear about your nomination. Best Producer. What an honour!

Remember how much you used to enjoy making up different job titles – Sanitation Inspector, Pest Control Impresario – when we were booking into hotels? 'I've never had a problem telling lies,' you once told me, more than a little proud. 'It's something that's always come very naturally to me. I don't even think about it.' Once you think about it, you'd explained, you're done for.

And you were absolutely right – no false modesty there! Do you remember the time we booked into a cheap hotel in a business park just off the A1. It was only 10 a.m., way before normal checking-in time (although terribly convenient for the school drop-off).

'My wife and I have just flown in to Luton from a

Plastics Convention in Panama City,' you informed the pimply clerk. 'We've got a six-hour stopover before we've got to go back to the airport to fly on to Paris, where we live. We're incredibly tired. Can you make sure we're not disturbed?'

The lies flowed out of you as easy as muzak. 'Do flights from Panama City even go to Luton?' I hissed as we crammed into the tiny lift, the sweaty champagne bottles clinking in their M&S carrier bags. 'Who cares?' Your hand inside my coat, your tongue inside my mouth.

So anyway, I'm delighted to hear about your nomination – even if the ceremony will only be shown on satellite telly.

How you'll enjoy adding that little fact to your company website. (Incidentally, I love the new photo you have on there – still five years out of date, of course, but five years is a big improvement on fifteen. Did you get it professionally done? I thought I could detect a hint of airbrush, although to be sure I'm no expert in these things.)

Guess where I read about the award? On Facebook! Isn't that hysterical? I'm now Facebook friends with Susan so I get all the updates about what's going on in your lives. Quite amusing really, considering how much you always loathed the whole social-networking thing. Susan's 'status' (I bet you didn't even know they were called that – those little pithy sentences we use to sell our lives to hundreds of our closest friends) read:

Susan Gooding *Clive nominated for music award. About bloody time!*

About bloody time. So typical of Susan not to gush, but clearly so proud too. And after it, 24 comments from some of her 456 friends. (Yes, I've scrolled through them all, pondering relationships, trying to fit together some of the pieces of the life you kept so well hidden. 'My friends are all so dull,' you'd complain, and I'd think it was some kind of a compliment with its unspoken inference that I was somehow some benchmark of wit. I blush now to think what a high opinion of myself I must have had.)

Lots of the comments were ringing endorsements of Susan herself.

'He couldn't have done it without you, hun.' 'Behind every successful man is an awesomely successful woman,' and so on.

Have you read the comments? You really should take a look. I think you'd find it quite enlightening to see how people view you and Susan from the outside, as it were – presuming to guess at the unknowable dynamic of other people's relationships.

* * *

I watched the awards ceremony. Well, of course I did! Obviously I guessed that you wouldn't feature very prominently in the television coverage. After all, you're not exactly A-list, are you? And at getting on for fifty (oh, how you'd hate me reminding you of that), the camera might not altogether love you. Plus I knew Susan would be wearing something navy and sensible, not split to the navel and held together with safety pins, so it was a fair bet that she wouldn't help you get a starring role on the red carpet.

But funnily enough I did spot you arriving. I know

you'll have watched the footage back already about a million times, so it won't be news to you that you and Susan appeared briefly in the background while that female rapper with the black hair was being interviewed.

'There they are!' shouted Jamie, who, at nine, still believes there's a certain magic attached to appearing on the television, and indeed to knowing anyone who appears on the television. Remember how you always worried so much about my children – 'I'd hate for them to be damaged because of me,' you'd say mournfully. Well, there they both were, sprawled out on the sofa, already texting their friends to tell them someone they know – actually really quite well and has been to their house – is on telly *right now*. You made their night! I know you'll be pleased. ('I only care about the welfare of the children in all of this,' you'd say during our angst-ridden conversations about 'the future'.)

And there indeed you were, making your way self-consciously down the red carpet, trying to look as if you weren't aware of the flashes and the reporters and the crowds of Japanese tourists and mothers-and-daughters in matching rainwear, all wondering if you were anyone important.

I must say, you suit a dinner jacket very well. It lends you a natural authority that the usual jeans and T-shirts sometimes lack. And I liked the way you kept one hand firmly interlinked with Susan's, even when you rather awkwardly waved in the direction of the film crew; reassuring and faintly proprietorial.

'Susan looks lovely, doesn't she?' Daniel remarked, as I think he felt duty-bound to do.

Tilly sniffed, unconvinced. 'Why does she always have to wear blue? It's *sooooo* boring.'

But in truth Susan did look very well. I saw she'd done something different with her hair. It was piled up on her head in big round curls, like a vanilla ice-cream sundae, and her long midnight-blue dress was cleverly cut to disguise her less flattering angles. It was touching to see what a big effort she'd gone to not to let you down. You must have been very proud. It reminded me of how you used to love planning my outfits for me, emailing me in the morning to ask what I was intending to wear that day, or to beg me to put on a particular item of clothing if we were due to meet up. A couple of times you even appeared to weep when I walked into the pub or restaurant or wherever we'd arranged to meet. 'You just look so beautiful,' you'd explain, your eyes travelling over me, sucking me up like a hand-held Hoover. 'I'm jealous of your clothes for touching your skin. I'm jealous of this –' and you'd run a finger down whatever top I was wearing. 'And these –' and you'd stroke the inside leg of my jeans. 'And I'm particularly jealous of these –' Your hand creeping inside the waistband to feel what knickers I had on.

When you and Susan strolled hand in hand out of the camera-shot, I thought that was the last we'd see of you. Daniel, of course, remained constantly on the alert for glimpses as the ceremony got under way. 'Is that them?' he'd ask whenever the television camera panned around the audience. 'I thought I saw Clive up there, top right of the screen.'

But just as I'd resigned myself to the probability that you and Susan wouldn't be making a return appearance, you were announced as a winner! What a fantastic surprise!

I hadn't even expected them to televise the Best Producer award, to be quite honest. I mean, the glamour quota isn't exactly through the roof in that sector, is it? I have to admit I sat up a bit in my seat then, while Daniel positively whooped and hollered. I wasn't too impressed with their choice of presenter for that award, though. I mean, if they're going to choose someone from a reality-TV talent show, they could at least have gone for one of the bigger names, but I suppose they had to take what they could get. Competition for that particular honour couldn't have been that high, I should imagine. And I guess one could say she added a telegenic touch to what might otherwise have been a bit of a drab segment, although it was a little distracting the way her breasts seemed constantly on the verge of popping out of that dress. It would all have to be done with tape, don't you suppose? I imagined her boobs covered with little sticky strips like a child's wrapping-up. Well, you were the one who was closest to her. Maybe you noticed something?

When she started to read the list of nominees, slowly and carefully as if reading were a skill she'd only recently mastered, I sat up a little straighter in my chair, realizing you were about to come on-screen again. Sure enough, there you were, your head filling the television like God. Just before the camera swung round to the next on the list, it panned out a little to show Susan sitting next to you, your hands still adorably intertwined. Such a comfort it must have been during those nail-biting minutes of waiting before the result was announced, to have her sitting next to you, that reassuring squeeze of the fingers.

And then all of a sudden the envelope was being opened, and there was your name, sounding so strange on the puffy, pink-glossed lips of the talent-show star. Thank goodness she didn't throw in a little extra line as they sometimes do: 'Couldn't happen to a nicer guy' or 'Justice has been done.'

Daniel broke into spontaneous applause as the camera focused on your face, for a split second frozen in un-comprehending shock, then creasing into smiles as you turned to Susan and kissed her long and hard on the lips before springing to your feet and making your triumphant way down the aisle, pausing every few rows to shake a hand, or receive a congratulatory pat on the arm. Then up on to the stage, taking the steps two at a time with youthful vigour, quite as if you weren't someone whose back was inclined to go into spasm at the slightest over-exertion.

When you bent to kiss the reality star, her prodigious breasts were momentarily pressed flat against your dinner jacket and her lip gloss left a faint pink sheen on your cheek.

Moving in front of the microphone, you did that thing one often sees award-winners do, where they gaze silently at the award, as though struggling to find the words to express how they feel. Knowing you, I'm sure you had your acceptance speech written and committed to memory the very day the nominations were announced, but I have to admit you did a wonderful job of appearing modestly unprepared.

When the audience was completely quiet, you looked up

again to the camera, and I wasn't surprised to see tears in your eyes. You always did have that capacity to cry on command. It was one of your many enviable skills.

'Wow,' you said, and for a second I was completely nonplussed, wondering when you'd started using expressions like that. 'I really can't believe this is real. What an honour! So much of what I've achieved over the years has been done on a wing and a prayer, and it wouldn't have been possible if I hadn't had the luck to be surrounded by some amazing people. My team at Trip Records, who have smoothed over my rough edges more times than I can count and talked me out of some of my more foolhardy ideas.' (Typical of you to be self-deprecating while simultaneously bigging yourself up. That word 'foolhardy', with its connotations of youthful rashness and cavalier self-disregard.)

'The fantastic John Peterson, whose dedication to detail and professionalism has given the company its reputation for integrity.' (How clever of you to compliment your loathed vice-president in such a way as to make him sound impossibly dull and worthy in comparison to the dazzling, devil-may-care *foolhardiness* of you.)

'My wonderful children, Liam and Emily, who, despite their often-professed wish to have a father who was a lawyer or a banker or something nice and safe like that, have nevertheless loved me anyway.' (A great touch that, the humble gratitude of an errant father.)

'And finally, my wife Susan.' Immediately the camera was close up on Susan's face, as if it had been hovering all the while in anxious anticipation in the wings.

And guess what? Well, of course you don't need to guess because you were there, and as I say you must have watched the footage so many times since then it'll be imprinted into your brain. Susan was crying! Actual real tears, trickling down her cheeks, which she wiped away with an angry hand. It felt weirdly voyeuristic, seeing her like that, moist-eyed and shyly quivering.

'We've been married now for over a quarter of a century.' (Cue a spontaneous smattering of applause from the audience.) 'And not a day goes past when I don't learn something new about her, something that makes me realize afresh just how incredibly fortunate I've been and how little I deserve her. Everything I am, I am because of her. Everything I've achieved, I've achieved because of her. All I can say is I must have done something pretty special in a past life to have been rewarded with all this. I thank you all.'

By the end of your speech, which I must say was very well received, being neither too long nor too dry (unlike the winner who preceded you, who made that classic mistake of going for a note of jaunty comedy, which always makes the audience feel short-changed, as if they'd like to snatch the award back and give it to someone who really appreciates it), the tears were sparkling in your eyes like cheap caster sugar. Meanwhile poor Susan, to whom the camera kept cutting back and forth until I felt quite nauseous with the movement of it, had mascara snaking like spilled oil down her left cheek. You've got to hand it to Susan, she's never been a terribly vain person, which, I reflected, seeing her black-streaked face magnified on our widescreen television, was just as well.

'I really should send Clive a message of congratulation,' Daniel said absently. 'I'll definitely do it tomorrow.'

Sometimes I don't know why Daniel even bothers saying half the things he says. Both of us know he won't really text you a message of congratulation, even though the intention is there and he'll probably end up convincing himself that he actually has done it, so genuinely does he mean to carry it out. Daniel has what Helen Bunion calls Delivery Issues. He can come up with no end of plans and ideas, but it's in the enactment of them where he falls down.

'Daddy, if you won an award, would you thank me and Tilly?' Jamie asked.

I must say I had to bite back a bit of a smirk at that one. The idea of Daniel stepping up to the podium to receive some kind of recognition from his peers. What would it be, I wonder, the award for Best Sunday Cyclist? Or perhaps the Lifetime Non-Achievement Award? Mean, mean, mean Sally. After all, Daniel can't really help being a 'serial careerist' (I read that in a magazine the other day, about people who change career so often they never quite get off the first rung). I have high hopes for the teacher training he's halfway through, though – after all, it's already lasted longer than his last 'career' (if you can call selling 'stuff' on eBay a career) – and he hasn't even got into a classroom yet! Some of the time I'm just as sure as Daniel is that there's something really amazing waiting around the corner for him. It's just I'm not quite sure how he would find it without actually getting up off the sofa and at least looking around that corner to see what's there.

'If Dad won an award he'd thank the neighbours and the woman in Londis and that man who helped him fix his bike, and everyone who knows him, and everyone in the world.' Tilly can be merciless sometimes, but in the case of Daniel's fabled long-windedness I think she probably has a fair point. 'And then he'd probably tell them the story of how he had his first job at the age of eleven helping in his uncle's hardware shop *and didn't even expect to get paid for it*. In *those* days you just did it because you were expected to help out.'

Jamie laughed momentarily before remembering that Tilly had said it, so he was honour-bound to find it unfunny. Daniel, meanwhile, had no such reservations and was smiling good-naturedly. I know I probably shouldn't say it, particularly not to you, but occasionally I do wonder if Daniel is all there, or if some tiny little bit of him, the bit that deals with, say, self-awareness, has somehow become dislodged and sneezed out somewhere along the way.

'What about Mum?' he asked, leaning his head back and running his hands through the overly-long blond hair of which he remains justifiably proud. 'What would Mum say in her acceptance speech?'

Tilly glanced over at me, her green eyes sharp like broken bottles.

'Oh, Mum,' she said. 'Mum wouldn't even remember to mention us at all.'

Later, when all the others had gone to bed (when did Daniel start going to bed at the same time as the children, I wonder? It seems to have happened without me even noticing it. We used to watch late films together long after the children were asleep, lying at opposite ends of the sofa, stroking each other's feet through our socks, but nowadays I look up from the News at Ten and find myself sitting on my own, the rest of the house shallow-breathing in the darkness), I got out my laptop and watched the replay of the award ceremony all over again. Amazing, isn't it, this instant repeat facility we all have now, this ability to endlessly relive our lives again and again on YouTube or Catch Up? I wish it had been around when I was younger, I really do. There's so much I seem to have forgotten.

When it got to the section with your speech, I kept my fingers poised over the 'pause' and 'rewind' buttons. I know it's silly, but I wanted to be in complete control.

I freeze-framed through the minute and a half, watching the way your face evolved seamlessly from jokey to tearfully sincere, and how your oh-so-familiar hands played with the rather garish award, your bitten nails pink against the shiny gold-coloured metal. Zooming in again and again until the picture started to blur at the edges, I gazed at your eyes, dark-lashed and puddle-coloured. It was the closest I'd been to you in fourteen weeks. (Not that I'm counting, you understand. Well, no more than I might count the number of weeks after, say, the death of a second-division friend.) I noticed that your curls looked slightly darker, although still flecked through with the occasional dashing streak of silver. Have you had a little bit of salon work done, Clive? If so I must congratulate you, they've been terribly subtle. I know how secretly vain you are about your hair, even while proclaiming that you'd 'just as soon shave the whole lot off and have done with it'. I remember lying in hotel beds in a tangle of boil-washed sheets, watching through the open bathroom door as you reached into your coat pocket and withdrew a nylon-bristled hairbrush and a travel-sized bottle of 'taming serum'.

'I've never known a man take quite so much trouble over his hair,' I told you, amused.

'It's only because it's so dreadful,' you'd tell me, anxious that I shouldn't believe you vain. 'My hair is totally unmanageable.'

There was a trace of pride when you said that, as if your intransigent hair was somehow an indication of an ungovernable personality, someone who chose to live out-side the rules.

I miss running my fingers through your hair, feeling the two slightly raised scars on your scalp, evidence of child-hood misadventures. I miss the way you'd suddenly turn and, with your back now against the bathroom mirror, pull me towards you so that I was gazing up into your eyes, the same distance from you as I am now from my laptop screen. I miss the sudden change in atmosphere, the imperceptible intake of breath, the sexual charge that made the hairs on my arms stand up. I miss it all. I miss it all. I miss it all.

After a while, when I'd stared at your magnified face on the screen for so long I felt my eyeballs must surely carry a negative imprint of your features, I forwarded on until I came to a close-up of Susan. Then, again, I froze the frame. Leaning back on the sofa, I held the computer on my lap at arm's length just looking at Susan, trying to imagine what it must have felt like to be her during those particular heady minutes. I summoned up the disbelief, the elation, the sheer soaring pride. And, of course, the total vindication. Susan's not stupid, she knows people over the years have questioned whether you were just a little too ambitious, too flirty, too self-obsessed to be a Good Enough Husband. Now here was full justification of the compromises she had made. No wonder she looked as if her happiness might smother her!

As the camera panned out to show her sitting in the crowd, flanked by well-wishers, all sneaking looks of ill-concealed envy, I froze the frame again and, leaning forward, placed my thumb squarely over Susan's face, so that she was only visible from the cleavage down. Then, and I know you'll think this rather – what was that word you always used? – twisted, I imagined my own face super-imposed on to her body, so it was me sitting there in my finery, soaking up the attention, the praise, the adulation. It was me you kept glancing over to as you made your word-perfect off-the-cuff acceptance speech, it was me who was feted, it was me who was the cat who got the cream and who, following the after-show party, would lean into you in the back of the taxi home, with one hand on your prized award and the other on your thigh, and whisper of the other rewards that would be yours once we got home.

I pressed my thumb harder over Susan's face, twisting it roughly against the hard screen of the laptop, not caring what smudges I left behind. Harder and harder, as if through sheer force of my will I could rub Susan com-pletely out. But when I took my hand away, there she was still, the big lacquered curls already drooping like five-day-old lilies, the black line of smudged mascara scarring her cheek.

Good old Susan. She always did dig herself firmly into place, embedding herself like a splinter into the very flesh of your life until your skin grew fresh over the top of her and it would have needed something needle-sharp to pick pick pick her out.

* * *

I met Liam yesterday! Isn't that the most bizarre thing? Remember how you always said you'd love me to meet your son one day because you thought we'd get on so well? You were so, so right.

I'd gone to an exhibition at the Royal Gallery that I'd been meaning to see for ages. Blood and Rage, is how the critics styled it. I couldn't really think of anything more apt. So I thought, 'Why not?' Helen Bunion has told me I need to forge new habits that don't include you, break the patterns and set different ones. So why not an exhibition? Why not a bit of blood and rage? New patterns are a great survival strategy, Helen says.

I don't mind telling you, Clive, I need all the survival strategies I can get!

So I went to the exhibition, and it was remarkable. I can't recommend it highly enough. Swollen globs of purple paint, as if the artist had dissected some once living thing over a canvas and then hung it up to admire. (Remember how, when you told me it was over, I said rather rabidly that I felt like a part of me had been ripped off and my insides were leaking out over the floor? Well, now imagine that, except on a painting. Incidentally, please forgive the overblown Jacobean melodrama of all that. I'm honestly embarrassed about some of the things I said. I was over-wrought. I really was.)

After I'd looked around the exhibition, I remembered you telling me your son worked in a swanky brasserie just a street or two away, so I decided to go there for some tea. Well, there's nothing odd about that, is there? There were lots of middle-aged women there queuing for tea on their own, and they can't all be stalkers, can they? Nope, just women with nothing better to do on a Wednesday after-noon than look around an exhibition of paintings that look like slashed, bleeding livers, before enjoying a nice pot of tea. You can't blame them, can you?

I knew he was your son right away. And it didn't hurt that the bill had his name in the corner. Liam. He had a lovely smile, just as I imagined, and your eyes looking down on me. As tall as you, I think, but not as broad, and no sign of the slight paunch that you wear so self-consciously under your clothes like an extra thermal layer.

The tea that he brought me came in a silky bag and smelt of patchouli. I asked if they didn't have any plain PG Tips and he smiled in a way that made it obvious I wasn't the first person ever to ask him that. When he smiled, a little dent appeared halfway down his cheek, just like yours. I looked at it a lot. I hope he didn't notice. You're right. He's nice. I think in other circumstances we'd have been friends. I gave him a ridiculously big tip, wondering if it might make me more memorable. Perhaps the next time he saw you he might say, 'A woman came in today for a cup of tea. She was really nice. You'd have liked her.'

Silly, hey? Silleeeee Salleeeee.

* * *

I do think you need to calm down a bit.

Have you tried any breathing techniques? Helen Bunion

73

swears by them, she really does. Apparently the idea is that you focus so intently on your breathing that you forget about all the other stuff that's causing you stress. Well, like I say, that's the idea. I have to confess I've struggled a little with the whole concept. Helen says I have to take air in while pushing out my stomach so that there's a maximum amount of internal space to fill with wonderful life-giving oxygen. *Breathe in, stomach out; breathe out, stomach in.* That's the bit I struggle with, coordinating the breathing with the stomach. I'll start off fine, but then realize that I'm either breathing out and pushing my stomach out too, or breathing in and pulling it in. Then I'll panic and try to remember what the right combination should be, and my breathing will be getting shallower and shallower, and my stress levels higher and higher. I don't tell Helen that, though. She's very proud of her breathing techniques and I'd feel a bit like I'd failed her if I admitted I couldn't actually do them.

Anyway, I don't mind telling you that that phone call this morning left me a little bit shaken. After all, it was the first time I'd heard your voice in nearly four months. Of course, you didn't sound remotely like you'd sounded on that awards programme the other night. Your voice had that hard, ugly tone you'd used on the ferret-faced Romanian squeegee man, the same gravelly menace. If I didn't know you so well, I'd almost have been scared.

'What the *fuck* were you thinking of?'

I did know, of course, what you were talking about, but I was so surprised at hearing your voice again that I played rather lamely for time.

'Clive! How lovely. What exactly can I do for you?'

74

Could you hear my heart hammering down the telephone line? That wild thumping rhythm drowning out my stupid, lying voice.

'Don't fucking patronize me, Sally. You know exactly what I'm talking about. That fucking piece of shit you wrote in the *Mail*.'

How to play this, I wondered . . . Of course, when the commissioning editor had replied to say they loved the piece, I'd had a feeling there might be, well, repercussions, although I'd assumed they'd take the form of another email tirade. But then, hey, any reaction is better than no reaction – isn't that what you've always told me?

'Oh, you read it, did you?' Of course you'd read it, especially after I emailed you last week on impulse, telling you to look out for it. Could I really have thought the sheer force of my words might win you back? Sometimes my own self-delusion leaves me breathless, it really does. Still, I tried to keep my voice level. 'So you'll have seen then that it was all totally anonymous, so there can be absolutely no comeback for either of us.'

There came a sort of mini-explosion then from your end of the phone. I really thought there might have been some kind of electrical malfunction, but it was just you getting ready to roar.

'No comeback? Are you fucking insane? You write a basically blow-by-blow diary account of our fucking five-year affair without bothering to disguise any of the fucking details—

'I did change the details. I made you ten years older, for a start.'

Of course, I knew that was one of the things that

would have wounded you most, that cruel extra decade arbitrarily yoked around your neck.

'Thank fuck Susan's out of the country on a business trip. So with any luck she won't get to see it; and I don't know how many of my friends would actually recognize me from the gross misrepresentation you managed to get across.'

'So that's all right then, isn't it?'

'No, it's not fucking all right. You could have fucking ruined me. You still could. You have no right to take liberties with my life, my wife, my family.'

'You're overreacting,' I told you, but my voice was already wavering, going squeaky round the edges. It was that term 'wife', of course. That filthy four-letter word.

'No one knows about us. No one ever knew about us. There's no way anyone could put two and two together.'

But, of course, you weren't taken in, and neither did I really expect you to be. We both knew full well that the threat of exposure was the very thing that had motivated me to chart the diary of my fall from grace in print, the predictable, brutal arc of a failed affair. But after all, Susan was abroad, so it all had been really for nothing. Well, apart from the fee, which of course didn't go amiss.

'Aren't you worried about Daniel reading it? Surely you can't want him to find out his *partner*' (the slight emphasis on the word 'partner', as if it wasn't really a proper word) 'was sleeping with his mate for the past five years.'

Funny to think of you as Daniel's 'mate'. I'm not sure you would always have seen yourself that way. In fact I seem to remember you describing him several times as 'spineless' and more than a few times as 'passive aggressive', a favourite term of yours.

'Daniel doesn't read that sort of thing,' I told you, trying to keep my tone chatty and upbeat, although the black pen I had in my hand was busy tearing violent gashes through the paper on my desk. 'And anyway, I'm not sure I even care any more if Daniel finds out.'

You weren't buying it, and who can blame you?

'Don't be fucking ridiculous. Of course you care. If Daniel ever leaves you he'll take your kids with him, and make no mistake about it.'

Make no mistake about it. Did you always talk like that? Or has success made you more pompous?

'I don't know what kind of game you think you're playing, Sally. But I have to warn you, you're about to get in completely out of your depth.'

Well, once you'd said that, there was a bit of a silence, wasn't there? You see, I was still trying to reconcile the snarling voice on the phone with the man who'd once driven all the way to Dorset with me, when I had to pay a duty visit to my father, only to promptly catch the train straight back to London again as soon as we reached the other end. 'I can't bear to think of you sitting in the car on your own all that way,' you'd told me when I'd protested that it was too much to ask. 'Anyway, it gives me the chance to have four whole hours with you to myself.'

Where did that Clive go, I wonder? Is there a parallel universe somewhere populated entirely by those people we believe we know inside out – until they suddenly turn into other people entirely? A place for the people they were until their personalities were abducted and the aliens took over their bodies?

'Are you threatening me, Clive?' I asked you, smiling at the very ridiculousness of the notion.

But your voice when you replied contained no trace of a smile.

'I'm just warning you to stay out of my life, that's all.'

That's all. Just stay out of your life.

A few short months ago, I *was* your life.

How does that happen then?

The truth is, the End of the Affair diary was Helen's idea. She thought it would be cathartic for me to write my feelings down. 'Look on it as a purging,' she told me. Of course, I don't think she really intended for me to get my purgings published in a national newspaper, but I liked the idea of my feelings being recognized, as if being read by thousands of strangers would somehow add authenticity to them. And obviously I rather liked the fact that you might read them too. (How you loved to scoff at the *Mail*'s policy of, as you put it, picking the bum fluff out of people's relationships and masquerading it as news, yet it didn't stop you devouring it avidly.) With that in mind, I tried not to over-exaggerate your faults. Well, not too much anyway. But then, it was all anonymous, so a little bit of over-egging wasn't out of the question. So maybe, yes, you didn't come out of the piece as well as you might have hoped to.

I wrote about the lead up to York Way Friday. It's become something of a leitmotif with me. Sometimes when I'm lying awake at three or four in the morning, those dead, dread hours when loneliness presses around me like a goose-down pillow, I'll go through it all again, like a litany, as if by repeating it enough times I might be able to alter the ending, take a different path, head you off before you reach that inevitable finale. It never works, of course, but still I revisit it all repeatedly like an unexorcized spirit who can't break away.

So when Helen told me to write about it, it wasn't exactly a difficult task. It practically wrote itself, to be honest. The stuff about how we'd been planning to set up home together, then, over the course of just a week, the sudden perplexing slow withdrawal. Then that agonizing lunch in that restaurant on York Way, my arm in my sleeve as you told me it had to stop, *we* had to stop. 'Susan deserves another chance,' you said, describing how she'd fallen apart when you'd told her over dinner in a Mayfair restaurant that you needed some space, weeping hysterically at the table, to the costernation of the waiters, how awful it had been to witness someone so strong, so *resourceful*, unravelling in front of your eyes. The stress had triggered your first-ever migraine. The doctor had been alarmed. 'I have to think of my health,' you'd said as you perused the Australian reds. I wrote about the artichoke soup that sat untouched in front of me, clammy and coagulating, and how you'd pronounced your pasta 'dreadful' but eaten it anyway, and how, once we got out of the door, I told you to go, never expecting you to, and turned around to see your laptop bag bobbing against your thigh as you scurried away. Then that email that came the next day, saying, '*I realize how horrible this must be for you, but I don't really think all those messages you sent last night are helpful, do you? I understand you must be feeling dreadful, but I know I'm doing the*

right thing for all of us. Susan and I are going to be help-
ing our daughter decorate her house for the next couple of
days, so I won't be online.'

And once I'd written the article, well, it seemed silly not
to try to make some money out of it. I mean, it's not as if
the commissioning editors have been beating a path to my
door recently, is it?

Remember how you so sweetly assured me that just
because you were dumping me, it didn't mean you
couldn't still be a kind of mentor to me professionally.
Well, it was a lovely thought, but of course it hasn't
happened, and gradually the property-paper commissions
have stopped coming in and the editors no longer return
my emails, and there turned out to be a gaping hole at the
centre of my 'career'. So, yes, the money from the affair
diary did come in handy. (I even dropped Helen a line to
tell her what I'd done and thank her – she knows how
hard things have been financially.) I've got the newspaper
here, as it happens. And guess what I used as my
pseudonym? Oh, Silleeeee Salleeeee, you don't need to
guess as you've clearly read it already. I thought it was
quite inspired: Susan Ferndown. The 'Ferndown' came
from the road I lived in as a child, and the Susan. Well, it
was just the first thing that popped into my head.

So you see, Clive, it's completely anonymous – I don't
know why you got so cross about it. I think that when
you've had a chance to digest it, you'll see it's not nearly
as heinous as you might have thought. You know I'd never
deliberately set out to do you harm, don't you?

And you know, I've already had loads of comments on
the online version of the paper. Of course, most of them
calling me a marriage-wrecking trollop and saying I only

got what I deserved, but some have been surprisingly sympathetic. One of them was from a Betrayed Wife. (Did you know that term is part of the official terminology of infidelity? BW for short, while the betrayer is a Wayward Spouse/Husband/Wife – WS, WH, WW – or else MM, married man. And I, of course, would be OW, Other Woman. Interesting, isn't it? How we use these pithy little acronyms to cover up our bottomless wells of tortured emotion?) She said that there was no point on the infidelity triangle that wasn't sharp enough to skewer a person. (Don't you just love that turn of phrase? Sharp enough to skewer.) She said she could tell my suffering was acute and that really she and I had much in common, despite being, as she put it, 'at opposite ends of the infidelity continuum'. I was thinking we might actually bond, Mrs BW and I, until I read her last sentence: 'We are not one another's enemies, you and I. It's the men who have betrayed us both who need to be stabbed.'

Stabbed? Well. Obviously at first I thought the woman was a nutter. I mean it's creepy, isn't it? Stabbed. But you know, as the day has gone on, I've found myself thinking about it more and more. I mean, clearly 'stabbed' is going too far, but put yourself in the position of this poor woman, this poor BW. She trusted someone, some man, some *husband*, with her life. Gave herself to him body and soul, only to discover he had two long-term mistresses, and one of them had had his child! Imagine that!

Of course, that got me thinking about that time I thought I was pregnant. Do you remember? We both knew it was ridiculous. I mean, we'd always been so careful – and me already the wrong side of forty. But then I did feel so very pregnant. It couldn't have been Daniel's, of course.

Well, not unless it was the immaculate conception. Helen Bunion would have a field day if I told her about how you and I fussed and planned, and angsted and declared our mutual undying support 'no matter what', only to discover, after two months of waiting, that it wasn't a baby after all, but the start of the peri-menopause! Silleeeee Salleeeee. Of course, Helen would insist it was my subconscious willing myself to have your baby, but then Helen wasn't the one loitering agonizingly in Boots by the 'home diagnostic' kits, dreading bumping into someone I knew and knowing that every other customer was looking at me and thinking, 'At your age? Disgusting.' 'I'll stand by you no matter what,' you'd said in a rather Victorian fashion, just before I did the test.

Well, of course it was negative. Whatever could we have been thinking of? After I'd emailed you the happy news, then and only then came your outpourings of emotion. Deep down, you'd wanted it to be true, you assured me. Then all these secrets would be out in the open, and we could be together properly. Oh yes, you were very unequivocal. After the event. That baby would have been two years old now. I think of it sometimes. Our non-existent spawn that might have brought us together. Your back wouldn't have stood it, probably. Nor would my children. And as for yours . . . Just think of the Sacred Vessel, how she'd have hated being pipped to the post by her own father! Just as well it turned out to be nothing. My reproductive system's final practical joke, its one last pitiful hurrah.

You were very nice about it, I have to say. You didn't say anything about how ridiculous I'd been. And only once did you use that phrase, the one that turned my still-smarting insides to stone: 'May be for the best . . .'

You never did get any further. I think you realized instantly what you'd said. But that was enough. Just those five words that said it all.

So anyway, I felt a certain amount of empathy with my new pen pal, this hurting vengeful BW. Now that Helen and I have role-played it all to death, empathy has become practically second nature to me. I find myself empathizing willy nilly all over the shop – vacant young men on the bus with cheap suits and lardy complexions, brisk dog-walking women oozing barely repressed frustration who inhabit their space like a punch. I feel for them all. It's actually quite exhausting. In fact, the only one I'm still having problems empathizing with, ironically enough, is Daniel.

Of course, I used to empathize with Daniel automatically, without even thinking. Well, at least I think I did (feelings are a bit like childbirth, aren't they? Once they've passed, they're so hard to re-imagine.) It's so difficult to know when that changed. In the early days, we were naturally more disposed to be kind to each other, and to see each other's differences as enriching rather than irritating. Helen likes to talk about the Relationship Bank, where you start with a healthy account and have to work to keep the deposits and expenditures balanced. I tell her Daniel and I have been operating at the limit of our overdraft for years, the goodwill and willingness to make excuses and compromises draining out drop by drop ('Watch those careless metaphors, Sally,' I hear you say) without us really noticing, leaving behind just debts and recriminations. 'We both seem to have mislaid our emotional paying-in books,' I told Helen once, warming to my theme. But I thought her smile was rather forced.

Of course, before the *Mail* article appeared, I had wondered fleetingly what would happen if Daniel somehow underwent a fundamental personality transplant and turned into the kind of person who might read a feature in the paper with 'Affair' in the title, but even in that unlikely event, I knew he'd never recognize his 'partner' of sixteen years from what appeared in the piece. The truth is that even if I stood right in front of Daniel and opened up my soul like a wheeler-dealer opening his coat to reveal row upon row of gleaming contraband watches, he still wouldn't recognize me. If I took off my face, I doubt Daniel could pick me out from a roomful of people.

After you'd hung up on me, I saw I'd had a missed call while we'd been chatting – Helen Bunion. I'd been rather regretting that thank-you email I sent her, alerting her to the newspaper piece, and I knew it wasn't going to be good news. Intuition, I guess you'd call it. (Incidentally, that's another thing Helen and I have been working on – 'honing' my intuition skills so that I'm more able to anticipate outcomes and know when people are genuine. Intuition and empathy – Helen calls it the 'two-pronged attack' in my ongoing battle to become a better, more rounded, more self-aware person.)

Sure enough, when I finally got to speak to her, Helen was wearing the slightly higher-pitched, staccato voice she sometimes clips on to her normal one when something doesn't please her.

'The affair diary was intended as private exercise, not as a slightly underhand way of outing your former lover. How are you ever going to be able to move on when techniques that I'm teaching you for your own personal self-development, and nothing else, are being turned into weapons in your futile, one-sided war against your ex? A war that, as we've been through a million times, you stand no chance of winning?'

It's truly pathetic how much I hate it when Helen is disappointed in me and how I'll squirm and self-justify to try to win her over again.

'It was so cathartic,' I whined.

'That was the idea. But "cathartic" isn't the same as "public".'

'But I changed all the details, and I really, really needed the money.' I bit back the urge to quip 'therapy isn't cheap'. Helen doesn't really do humour.

'If his wife had read that diary, she could easily have spotted the similarities. Don't kid yourself, Sally, that wasn't your underlying intention. You want her to find out, but in such a way that if it all blows up in your face, you can pretend not to know what anyone is talking about. Even after all the work we've done, you're still refusing to own your actions.'

Does your Harley Street therapist say that to you, I wonder? All that stuff about owning your actions? It's one of Helen's *bêtes noires*, my refusal to 'take ownership' of the things I do and have done. It makes me sound a bit like a squatter, doesn't it? Taking ownership of my life. Mind you, if I was a squatter, I could maybe open the door to my life just a crack, take a quick look round, decide it wasn't quite what I was after, and go and find someone else's to take ownership of. Someone better's.

Before Helen rang off, reminding me coolly that she did have other 'clients' who required her attention, she set me yet another exercise.

'Anything,' I said gratefully, eager to redeem myself.

She told me to get a blank sheet of paper and a black felt-tip pen, 'the thickest, blackest pen you can find', and to write out 'in big capital letters the stark, brutal facts of the situation'. Then to force myself to sit and study them until they actually sink in.

Obediently, once I'd put the phone down, I fetched a sheet of paper. I was sitting at what I laughingly call my desk – a glorified table, wedged into the cubbyhole where I work. The cubbyhole is a partitioned-off corner of the dining room which I share with the washing machine, so that important work phone calls have to be made in between spin-cycles. I cleared a space and laid the paper almost reverentially in front of me. Then I dug around in the top drawer of the filing cabinet where I keep the carcasses of pens that in a previous life were once fit for purpose, until I found a black marker still worthy of the name.

Sliding the lid on to the end of the pen, for a moment my citalopram-wobbling hand hovered over the paper. Then I remembered Helen's tight, pinched voice and I started writing down the 'stark, brutal facts of the situation' as she had told me. When I'd finished, I had a list of four points, all written in harsh, impossible-to-ignore black letters.

CLIVE HAS MOVED ON
CLIVE LOVES HIS WIFE
CLIVE DOES NOT WANT ME IN HIS LIFE
IT IS OVER

The words were hard and ugly. There's no softness to capital letters, is there? No gracefully curling 'g's or 'y's, no skittishly kicking 'k' or 't'. Still, I made myself look at them, taking them in, as Helen had told me to, until they stopped being letters and turned into hieroglyphics clumsily tattooed across the page. But by that stage, the message had definitely gone in and was doing a Mexican wave around my head. *Clive is never coming back.*

From somewhere inside me, that secret place below my ribcage, came that familiar scalding acid-rush. I hadn't experienced anything like it since those dark days just after York Way Friday when I'd lie awake in the early hours and feel my insides corroding inch by inch, as though a flesh-eating bug had got into my body and was stripping away tissue from bone, sending my weakened, panicked flabby heart flapping into overdrive, trying to stave it off.

Breathe in, stomach out; breathe out, stomach in.
Breathe in, stomach out; breathe out, stomach in.

I'm concentrating on my breathing, visualizing the breath coursing through my body just as I've been told, and yet the message is there in the pounding rhythm of the blood pumping around my body, in the wild, unbridled pulsing at my wrist. *Clive is never coming back.*

* * *

Susan is wonderful, isn't she? I know it's the word people always use about her, but it's so apt. (Of course, I discount the people who use other words, like 'bossy' or 'controlling'. What do they know?)

I wasn't at all expecting to hear from her yesterday, and had resigned myself to another day of sitting in front of my computer, waiting for emails that never come and obsessively surfing infidelity forums. Then out of the blue, her name flashed up on my phone. Well, after the usual automatic split-second adrenaline attack (What does she know? Has she discovered anything?) I answered, making sure my 'voice smiled' as Helen has taught me to do, and Susan told me that she and Emily were going to be having lunch just around the corner from me (so nice of her to imply that I live on the doorstep of wealthier Balham, rather than the suburban backwaters of Tooting). Did I want to come along?

Well, I didn't need asking twice.

We met in a Spanish restaurant on the High Street, the one that's always in the Sunday supplements.

'I've always meant to come here,' I gushed to Susan. But what I meant was, I'd always wanted to be the kind of person who'd go there. There's a distinction, don't you think?

Susan was looking marvellous again. It's so refreshing the way, even as an ex-model, she values comfort over style. She had on a pair of comfortable-looking jeans with a loose-fitting tunic (navy, naturally), and her wispy, white-blonde hair (more white than blonde today) was artlessly pulled back into a ponytail. Emily, of course, was wearing an A-line, maternity-type top, even though she can't be much more than five months pregnant and hardly showing at all.

'I must sit near a door,' she told the waiter before we'd even been shown to our seats. 'I need to have access to fresh air. You see, I'm pregnant.'

She said 'pregnant' in hushed, awed tones, as if she were announcing she had fifteen pounds of explosives strapped to her body that could detonate at any time.

Once we were sitting down (how nice of that couple to give up their prized window seat when Emily clutched her hand to her chest and started faintly gagging. People are so kind, don't you find?), Emily started perusing the menu in search of a dish that hadn't been expressly created with a view to harming her unborn child. That meant Susan and I had a chance to catch up.

I asked her all about the award, of course. She was typically self-deprecating, but I could tell she was pleased when I said I'd watched it. She told me that afterwards, at the party, you'd hardly left her side.

'There were lots of little dolly-birds there,' she said. 'I told him, "Make the most of it, while you've still got your own teeth," but he just hung around me like a spare part. I can't understand it. Normally, he'd have been lapping up the attention. Must be getting old.'

'Oh, we're *all* getting old,' I told her.

'Rubbish. You look fantastic,' she lied. 'The weight loss really suits you.'

Of course, that was too much for Emily. 'Being too skinny can be awfully ageing though, don't you think?' she asked, addressing the salt pot in front of her. 'I'm *so* much happier now I'm the size of a whale.' She held out one of her slender, birdy wrists admiringly. 'I'm certainly not going to be one of those irritating women you always read about who goes back to a size zero a week after giving birth. I *love* my babyweight.'

'Darling, you're the size of a twig, so do shut up.' Always the adoring mother, Susan.

Susan tells me she's found the perfect Croatian holiday home. It's on the island of Korcula, apparently, so a fraction of what it would cost in Istria or on the Dubrovnik coast.

'But it's still at least twice what we'd budgeted,' Susan confided. 'I'm not going to tell Clive though. Luckily he always claims to be clueless about money and leaves everything up to me.'

You know, if you hadn't always told me so, I never would have got that impression – about you being clueless with money, I mean. I know Susan was always the financial brains of the operation, but you always struck me as someone who knew exactly how much everything was worth. It just shows you how wrong you can be about someone, I guess.

Susan was talking some more about your renewing your vows. She said it was really just an excuse for a great big party, but I could tell it means a lot more than that.

'Of course, you and Daniel will have to be there,' she said. 'It's just going to be our closest friends.'

That was kind of her, wasn't it, to include us among your 'closest friends'? I know she doesn't really mean it, or, if she does, there are probably well over a hundred other 'closest friends' who all come in front of us. But it was still a nice touch, I thought.

She explained that the party was organized for July, in two and a half months' time.

Emily seemed to get very agitated at this. 'I'll be heavily pregnant by then. I really don't know whether I'll be in the right frame of mind for a big party. And you know, I've got that mums-to-be yoga workshop booked for the week after, so I worry it will be too much for me. Honestly, I do think you and Dad could have timed things a bit better.'

Susan rolled her eyes at me behind her glass of wine, but was very placating when she spoke, reassuring Emily that the party wouldn't be too onerous for her, and that she could always take a rest should it prove a little much.

By this time the waitress was at the table – a pretty girl, Portuguese I think, with a gold ring through her eyebrow.

Emily had a long list of questions about the food. Had that one been cooked with nuts? Did this one have raw egg? Pasteurized cheese? The poor waitress's smile started to slide down her face as if it were melting.

Luckily Susan distracted her by pouring a thimbleful of white wine into her glass.

'What do you think you're doing?' Emily shrieked, horrified.

'Just a tiny dribble can't hurt you.' Susan was unabashed.

'For God's sake, Mum, it's as if you want your grandchild to be born with two heads or something.'

Susan's very calm about things like that, isn't she? She didn't act in the least bit embarrassed, although I have to say I was mortified myself. Considering that most of the time Emily talks as if anything louder than a whisper causes her physical pain, she has a really penetrating voice when she sets her mind to it.

But you know, after Emily calmed down, we started talking properly and I have to say that while I wouldn't go so far as to say we hit it off, we did at least find some common ground. All right, that common ground principally consisted of talking about pregnancy experiences and what middle name sounds best with Cressida, but at least I felt a little progress was made. When Susan was in the loo, we even chatted conspiratorially – about you, as it happens. Don't be alarmed, Clive, it was all nice things, obviously. She said she didn't know what had come over you recently, but you were being so ridiculously attentive to her mother it was quite sweet really. (Before you start, that was Emily's word: 'sweet'. I know how much you'd hate to think that particular adjective was being applied to you.) Emily said she and Liam were always teasing you about not deserving Susan, and how nice it was that you finally seemed to be taking what they said on board.

Then we went back to talking about Emily.

By the end of the lunch, I have to say we were all quite jolly. Emily even ventured that everything in the garden with the bland barrister husband might not be completely rosy. Apparently after the twenty-week scan he had failed to show sufficient enthusiasm for her inspired idea of having the scan photo made into a mouse-mat for his mother's birthday. 'I think she'd prefer a smoothie-maker,' is what he apparently said. Emily decided that was rather insensitive of him, but I think he might have had a point, don't you?

Emily told me she was planning to have a baby shower. (I didn't know such things existed outside of *Friends*, but apparently they're all the rage among the young mummies in west London. Honestly, Clive, it's like a little kingdom all on its own, where your sort live, isn't it? The Vatican of London, with different rules and different people and different customs. No wonder you knew I'd never really fit in there.) And guess what? She even invited me along! Well, I happened to mention I'd never been to a baby shower and how much I'd love to see what went on, and she said I could come to keep Susan company (presumably she'll have an oldies' corner, complete with the bland barrister's mousepadless mother). Now, I know you probably won't want me to go – you're so funny about those sorts of crossovers between our lives now. You used to find them quite exciting, do you remember, the thrill of the close shave? – but it would have been very rude of me to say no, wouldn't it? And Susan seemed so genuinely delighted I was going to be there, I really didn't want to disappoint anyone. You can understand that, can't you, Clive?

'I hate letting anyone down,' you used to tell me all the time, clutching your head and arranging your face into that very sincere expression you do so well. Do you remember, how often you used that phrase as you vacillated to and fro between poor ignorant Susan and me, explaining it was a throwback to your own childhood when you'd been constantly let down by the adults around you?

Well, Clive, I also hate to let anyone down. (How considerate we've both become recently. How reluctant to disappoint.) So I'll go to Emily's baby shower. It'll be a novel experience for me. I'm looking forward to it so much. It's like Helen told me: I need to find new experiences to break the old patterns I associate with you.

I do hope she'll be pleased.

* * *

Please don't be alarmed, but I went to look at your house last night.

I know what you're thinking, that it sounds like something a stalker would do, but I was just passing. No, honestly. I was in the area having a wander around Regent's Park. Remember I once suggested we went there, and you said it was far too close to your home and it would be like going on a date together in your back garden? I'd never fully explored it before so I decided to go, and seeing as you'd used that phrase 'my back garden', I thought it couldn't hurt to pop along to your road, just to remind myself where it was.

Of course, it brought back memories of all those dinner parties where Susan and Daniel would chitty chat over the table and, incredibly, never find it odd that the two of us were avoiding each other's eyes. It's lovely, your house, with its eloquently arched windows and curved gravel drive, and obviously Susan does have exquisite taste. The double-height glass kitchen at the back has appeared in more than one interiors magazine. 'Bricks and mortar,' you always said dismissively. 'It means nothing to me. None of it. She can keep the lot.' Yet in the end, you couldn't bring yourself to leave it. Even bricks and mortar, it seems, exert their own pull.

And I can quite see why you wouldn't want to go. Why would you? It's a beautiful house. I love the ornate wrought ironwork around the porch and the way the windows of the drawing room on the first floor ('Don't call it a drawing room,' I can hear you raging. 'It sounds so *poncy*!') catch the evening light at sunset. Oh, yes, I suppose I did linger a little bit longer than strictly necessary, watching how the glass glinted orange then pink, and then how a floor lamp went on in the corner of the room, sending a muted yellow glow through the fluttering opaque curtains.

I could see shadows moving across the room in the amber light. You've got to understand I wasn't spying or anything. Anyone who happened to be standing on that opposite pavement in that exact spot could have seen the same thing. It's just that it was quite a pleasant evening, just the slightest hint of a drizzle, but nothing at all serious. Back home, Daniel would already have got the kids to bed and most likely be snoring on the sofa in front of a low-budget sci-fi movie on Channel Five. I really had nowhere at all I had to be.

On the journey home (and it is a long journey, let's face it, all those stops at platforms crammed with foreign-language students and tourists clutching Hamleys carrier bags), I sat opposite a woman who was silently crying. She was about ten years older than me, in her early fifties probably, and her short hair was dyed very, very red. She had on a pair of green, high-heeled shoes so new they still had the price label on the soles, and I imagined her putting them carefully on earlier that evening, maybe stopping to admire them in the full-length mirror on her wardrobe door, not yet knowing that the night would end with her travelling home alone, with tears making tramlines through her thick foundation. Damaged people. How you used to love them.

'She's very damaged,' you'd airily pronounce about anyone with a hesitant manner, or a nervous laugh, or a less-than-firm handshake. Anyone, in fact, who annoyed you, or puzzled you, or who wasn't as outgoing as you or as able to meet strangers' eyes. (God, how good you are at that – the whole unflinching eye contact. Must have been what made you such a hit with the younger, stroppier musicians. You could probably run workshops on how to do that, you know. 'Eye Contact Skills – Beginners,' you could call the course. You've always loved a lucrative sideline.)

You know what's funny, though? Lately I've been feeling

like I'm the one who's damaged, like every part of me where you've ever laid a finger (and let's face it, there are very few parts where you haven't) bears an ugly black splaying bruise. Does that seem melodramatic to you? I'm so sorry. I see you now, wrinkling your nose in distaste. 'A bit OTT,' you might sniff. Or, worse, 'a bit *obvious*'.

Damaged in transit. Maybe I'll have a label printed up, or a T-shirt.

A bumper sticker might be fun.

Damaged goods.

Silleeeee Salleeeee.

* * *

Sian called me today. Like I say, she has felt awkward since all this business happened, as if those years of being 'a friend to the affair' (incidentally, that's what they call it on infidelity forums – isn't it wonderful?) – providing alibis, joining us for cosy dinners out – makes her somehow responsible for how it has turned out. She raises her eyebrows meaningfully at me when no one else is looking, silently asking how things are going. Am I over you yet?

She thinks we should go out tonight, the two of us, get dressed up, head to Hoxton, hang out in a bar or pub, trying to blend in with the young things. Flirt with some men like we used to do twenty years ago. Sian has never conceded that we might not be quite the same people as we were when we used to traipse our twenty-something selves around the hotspots of late-night London. 'I don't want to be surrounded by 28-year-olds,' I tell her now. 'It makes me feel old.' 'Speak for yourself,' she retorts, smoothing back her carefully highlighted hair with a gym-toned arm. How you used to enjoy mocking her, with her underage boyfriends and designer wardrobe. You refused to see the exposed heart underneath, looking for love in unsuitable places, just like all of us.

Did I ever tell you about the time I met up with Sian a few years ago, the day she'd finally taken possession of a thousand-pound Birkin handbag she'd been lusting after for years? When she arrived at the restaurant where we were meeting, she was like a proud mother, unable to stop fussing over the new arrival, stroking the soft camel-coloured leather and cooing over its shape, its contours. Over the course of the meal, however, the pleasure in her new purchase drained steadily away along with a couple of bottles of good Chenin Blanc. Yet another romance had just bitten the dust and Sian's usual armour-plated self-belief was slipping. 'I'm fed up of it all,' she said eventually, and I remember how shocked I was, to hear her admitting defeat. 'What's wrong with me?' she asked me. 'When did this become my life?' I tried to cheer her up, by reminding her of all her gorgeous young men, all the money she earned as a store buyer – money that she was free to spend on designer handbags galore. She looked at me then, a smudge of mascara scorched black across her cheek. 'A Birkin bag won't care about me when I'm old,' she said. Do you know, Clive, I don't think I've ever heard anything quite so sad.

But today Sian wasn't in the mood for self-pity. I think Sian believes the mourning period should now be over. I think Sian believes a bit of male attention will cure me of you. Well, I can't pretend it wouldn't be wonderful to be cured, finally, of this embarrassing, debilitating affliction.

What a relief it would be to wake up in the morning without subconsciously flinching in anticipation of the hammer-blow of awareness of loss, or to step lightly through my life free of the tumorous mass of you. So tonight I will take the waters of Hoxton in the hope of a cure.

In deference to my imminent restoration to the ranks of the living, I have dressed with particular care, pulling a floaty top on over my suddenly-too-baggy jeans to hide the worst of the Misery Diet's ravages. Tilly came in just now as I was putting on my make-up.

'You haven't worn make-up in months,' she told me, all suspicion. That girl sees everything, you know. Remember how it was always she who'd want to know who I was emailing late at night, or why you always used to call when Daniel was out?

'I'm combating the seven visible signs of ageing,' I told her. It's always good to connect with my children through advertising slogans, I find. It's like a shortcut to understanding. 'I've reached sign five.'

Tilly didn't crack a smile.

'Why is your neck like that?' she wanted to know.

'Like what?'

'You know, like the top of the curtains.'

Ah, pleated. My daughter wants to know why the skin on my neck is pleated.

I look at myself in the mirror and see what she sees – a too-thin 43-year-old whose skin no longer fits, wearing a top that drapes over me like one of those frilly round cloths on what my grandmother used to call an 'occasional table'.

'Liz Hurley is older than I am,' I told her, defensively.

'Who?'

More and more I find I can't even look at Tilly these days. Girls are so unforgiving, aren't they, so critical. I remember being the same with my own mother. She used to wear the most overpowering perfume, the kind that creeps into your nostrils and solidifies there, blocking out the air. When we'd be going out anywhere, she'd always get into the car last (she was always late, my mother), and the smell would hit me like a breaking wave, so I'd have to roll down the window and stick my whole head outside. One time I wanted to borrow a jumper of hers. It was black cashmere and kitten-soft and I knew, in the way teenage girls always know, that it would look loads better on me. Finally she gave in to my wheedling and lent me the jumper to go out in, but when, after a long luxurious bath, I was finally ready to put it on, I found I couldn't. The smell of that noxious perfume lingered in every fibre, every thread. It was the smell of my mother – cloying and heavy and invasive. Attempting to pull it over my head, I found myself gagging and flung it across the floor into the furthest corner of my bedroom. What do you think Helen would make of that, hey? No doubt she'd be able to find lots of ways in which that incident has shaped the person I am today. As for me, I can only really see one. I never, ever wear perfume.

Right, it's getting late, so I must go. Off into the night to be cured. Who knows, this might even be the last journal entry I write. I shall come floating home, pick up this notebook and it'll be as if someone else has been writing all these words – this autistic testament to obsession. I'll gaze at it, puzzled, wondering how it came to be in my house, and who the rabid, ranting writer might be. I might even feel slightly sorry for her, now that I am whole again; this poor broken creature spilling her sour secrets across the page like yesterday's milk. I will be magnanimous, I think. I will try not to judge.

Stupid. Stupid. Stupid.

I'm sitting here in my stupid floaty top, and the paper is already blotchy with my stupid tears. You would be repulsed, I think, if you could see me. Another damaged, stupid woman crying in the night.

Do you want to know what happened? I'm sure you don't, but I'll tell you anyway because it's a funny story. A funny, stupid, stupid story.

So Sian and I went to Hoxton, to be where the young things are. We started in that pub we went to once with the dark-green leatherette benches, and the one tiny toilet where girls in miniskirts squeeze, three at a time, to snort cocaine from the cracked cistern top.

We were witty and caustic, and each successive vodka only made us more amusing.

'We've still got it!' crowed Sian, as a boy young enough to be her son showed us his new tattoo clinging to the sharp edge of his smooth hip bone. It was some kind of a Maori symbol, if I remember. Or maybe not Maori, maybe Aboriginal. Something indigenous anyway. There was something a little unsavoury about the way Sian looked at it, I thought, as if any minute she might flick out her tongue to taste it.

'It's gorgeous,' I think I said.

But really it was stupid. Stupid. Stupid. Stupid.

Then we fell out of that pub, and trip-trapped across the road in our going-out heels, to that other one –

much bigger and more convinced of its own superiority.

There were a couple of people inside who Sian knew from somewhere. I can't remember where. The citalopram and vodka mix seems to have done funny things with my memory. Funny peculiar, not funny ha-ha. Funny stupid.

The people Sian knew were talking to the manager of the pub, a tall man with a dark-brown, topiary-neat goatee and an incongruous tan.

'I've just come back from Sharm el-Sheikh,' he told me.

For some reason Sian and I found that hysterical. We shook with laughter about Sharm el-Sheikh, and somehow ended up convincing ourselves he'd said something very witty.

'He's funny,' Sian whispered to me – the kind of whisper that carries over the top of all the normal voices, and arrives in your ear coated with spit. 'And I think he really fancies you.'

I looked at him with renewed interest. I hadn't really paid much attention before to whether he was attractive, but now she mentioned it, I could see how he might be. And he fancied me? I felt ridiculously, STUPIDLY grateful.

We started talking together, me and Pete. Oh, didn't I say he was called Pete? Stupid name, isn't it? Really stupid.

I have no idea what we talked about, but I had another vodka. Or maybe more. I didn't pay for them. Perks of chatting to the manager.

It's a weird thing with the citalopram and alcohol. You lose great big chunks of time, swallowed up in a black, bottomless worm-hole.

The next thing I remember it was late, and the crowds of young people had wafted off into the night, and a grumpy French barman was stacking the chairs on the tables.

'We're going now,' Sian was saying, her pointedly arched eyebrows speaking a sign-language of their own. 'But you stay here if you want to. Have you got enough cash for the cab home?'

So solicitous, Sian – despite being back to her old *facilitating* tricks. And so drunk. But not, I fear, as drunk as me.

'Stay for another drink,' the man called Pete said. 'I'll make sure you get home.'

I sat there on a stool at the bar, in my stupid floaty top and my stupid going-out heels, and I nodded obediently. It seemed like everyone was looking out for me and had come up with a very sensible plan of what to do next. I was actually quite grateful. Isn't that ridiculous?

Then Pete and I were on our own. He said he lived above the pub and asked if I wanted to come upstairs for another drink. I nodded again like a stupid nodding dog and followed him up the stairs, my stupid going-out heels clicking loudly on every step.

Pete's living room seemed huge, with big high ceilings and massive windows looking straight out on to the building opposite. There was a leather sofa, some rather naff curtains, a framed print of a 1950s Fellini film. (I only know that because Pete told me. I don't want you to think I've turned into the kind of person that looks at a print and says, 'Oh, that's a Fellini, isn't it?')

I was on the leather sofa, and so was Pete. He was so unfamiliar. Every time I shut my eyes and then opened them I had to remind myself again just who he was. I saw him glance at his phone to check for texts and realized he too was probably wondering just who I was and whether he really wanted me to be in his living room. But by then it was too late, and we were embarked on whatever we were embarked on, and neither of us really knew how to get out of it.

When he kissed me, he tasted of red wine and roll-ups. His beard was scratchy and his tan, up close, alarmingly orange. As soon as I felt his tongue in my mouth, fleshy and slightly rubbery like the inside of an outsized mussel, I knew I didn't want to be there.

He stood up suddenly and held out his hand to lead me into the bedroom. I followed unquestioningly, like an abused dog that knows it is about to be walloped but goes along with it anyway.

The bedroom was small and dominated by that Edward Hopper diner print most people grow out of after they leave university. I tried not to look at the unmade bed, where a half-filled ashtray balanced on top of a book called *Awakening the Buddha Within*. Stupid fucking book. Stupid fucking print. Stupid fucking bed.

Pete sat on the end of the bed and pulled me towards him, undoing my jeans. Too late I remembered my hairy legs. I knew there was little chance that Pete would take them for a political statement. There was a fairly good chance that Pete might not know what a political statement was. Stupid fucking Pete.

As he undressed me, his face gave little away, and I suddenly realized that I might be the oldest woman this man called Pete had ever slept with. Even though he must have been approaching forty himself, the average age of the girls in the bar was about twelve, which probably made Pete's normal quarry not much older. I became agonizingly conscious of the puckered skin around my belly-button (how you used to love to rest your tongue there, do you remember, burrowing your nose into the yielding flesh as if it were cheesecake?), the deflated breasts, the focaccia thighs. I saw myself through Pete's dulled blue gaze and wished to be somewhere, anywhere, away from there.

'You all right?'

But Pete didn't wait for a response. His mollusc tongue was roaming my body, leaving its snail's slick on my skin.

And then, with a grunt, he was inside me, pressing down on me like a Breville sandwich-maker. The edge of the stupid fucking Buddhist book was digging into my side and I knew the ashtray must have tipped over. When I dared to look up, Pete's face was raised towards the wall so he was staring directly at the Edward Hopper as he moved up and down. A depressing thing to look at in the throes of passion, wouldn't you think? I wondered what images were going through his head, who he was thinking of. I knew it wasn't me.

I lay there feeling him go in and out, and trying to distance myself from my own body, as Helen Bunion had once tried to teach me to do, so it wasn't me on the bed but some other stupid woman, with her jeans by her ankles and her stupid going-out heels still strapped to her feet. But his rhythmic thrusting was impossible to ignore. I hoped it would at least be over quickly but he went on and on, scrotum slapping against me like a soggy tea towel. On it went and on and on, and each time he did one of his stupid thrusts I thought about you, and how it was your fault that I was there, in this stranger's unmade bed, with last night's cigarette ash pooling under my back.

I hate you Clive, I hate you Clive, went the rhythm of his movements. On and on and on. Bed jerking, ash billowing.

'It's not really going to happen, is it?' I said, when I couldn't bear it any more, and my voice sounded false and ridiculously loud.

That stupid man called Pete looked down then and seemed a bit taken aback, as if he'd forgotten I was even there.

Then he rolled off, clearly relieved.

'Too much to drink,' he said.

Well, I suppose it was nice of him to try to spare my feelings.

He lit a spliff, and I noticed his fingers were covered in thick black hairs, coarse like the stitching in a wound. For a few seconds I stared at them, transfixed, then just as I was about to sit up to leave, all of a sudden, he put the joint down on the floor beside the bed and disappeared down between my legs.

Well, can you imagine? I went completely rigid. I was dry as the proverbial bone down there and his fat stupid mollusc tongue felt like sandpaper. For a few agonizing minutes, he gamely sawed away, while I stared, clenched and wide eyed, at the nicotine-tinged ceiling, trying to pretend there wasn't someone applying exfoliating scrub to my clitoris.

In the end, I put my hand down to touch his head and gently pushed him away.

'It's OK,' I mumbled.

His head stopped bobbing then, and he looked up at me slowly.

'It's OK,' I repeated, almost inarticulate with embarrassment.

'Oh. Right.'

He moved off back to the other side of the bed and retrieved his still-lit spliff. There was a shadow of dark stubble on his back and it crossed my mind he'd probably had it waxed for his holiday in Sharm el-Sheikh.

I sat up and pulled up my knickers and jeans, remembering too late about the ash in the bed.

'I'd better be going.'

Pete inhaled deeply.

'Do you want me to ring you a minicab? Only there's plenty of black cabs driving past all the time, and it'd probably be a lot quicker.'

The thought of me and him sitting together waiting for the ring on the door, me with my coat on, him half dressed and desperate to be alone, clearly filled us both with horror.

'Oh, I'll flag one down outside,' I told him, flailing around to find the armholes in my stupid floaty top.

'Probably best,' he said.

At the front door (at least he walked me down the stairs. Who said chivalry was dead?), he bent down and pecked me awkwardly on the cheek, his stupid goatee rough and scratchy on my skin. Neither of us even bothered to go through the pantomime of exchanging numbers. I couldn't wait to be out of there. And he couldn't wait to see me go.

There were no black cabs passing. Surprise, surprise. So instead I walked to the next junction and waited on the corner there, out of sight of Pete's prying, probing windows. When a taxi finally pulled up, the driver asked me if I was all right and I was shocked to find I was crying – thick, fat, slimy tears with a gob of shame in each of them.

And now I am back home again. Once more writing to

you in this stupid fucking journal. I don't dare run a shower, in case Daniel wakes up and wonders why I'm feeling the need to ablute in the middle of the night, but I long to wash away every trace of that man with his hairy fingers and gravel tongue. There you lie in your perfect house surrounded by your perfect family, while I'm sitting here with a rash on my clit and his snail-trails criss-crossing my body.

I hate you Clive, I hate you Clive. Can't stop that fucking rhythm pulsing through my bloodstream. *I hate you Clive*.

I've got out my laptop and called up the record company's website. There's the photo of you on the 'about us' page, gazing straight out at me, face concertina'd into a smile. Do you remember you once told me you chose the photo deliberately so that any time I wanted to see you, even if you were abroad or somewhere with Susan, I could summon up your smiling face. 'I want you to know I'll always be there for you,' you'd told me. Always, it seems, can have different definitions. So I'm sitting here in my cubbyhole, with all those vodkas still sloshing around my system, looking into your eyes, and thinking how it's your fault I was in that flat, your fault I was in that bed, your fault I thought I needed a man to make whole again all the broken, shattered pieces rattling around inside me. Your stupid fault. Your stupid fault. Stupid stupid stupid.

* * *

Really, Clive. You need to work on your anger issues, as Helen would say.

I mean, I can understand you being upset. It's a horrible thing to have happened. But I really don't see what it's got to do with me.

As soon as I'd put the phone down to you just now (well, as soon as you slammed the phone down on me might be more accurate), I called up your company website to see what you'd been getting so hot under the collar about, but when I checked the comments section there wasn't anything unusual on there. Just the normal pedants nit-picking about one of your more controversial acts. I assume you've already taken the offending comment out. Well, who could blame you?

Mind you, it sounds like the person who wrote it wasn't exactly the sharpest knife in the dishwasher, doesn't it? What was it you said they accused you of? Plagiarism and serial cheating? I mean, you might be able to understand one or the other, but to throw both in together is a bit, well, *odd*, don't you think?

Still, I'm sure you managed to get rid of it before too many people saw it, so I don't think you need to get quite so worked up. I do so worry about your blood pressure, after everything the doctor told you about avoiding stress. Just because we're not together any more doesn't mean we can't continue caring about each other, does it?

I must say, though, I don't appreciate you coming to me in that accusatory tone. It's quite unnecessary. I *empathize* with your situation, naturally, but I had nothing to do with that nasty comment. I'm actually quite shocked you would think I might. What was that you said about the person using 'the same language' as me? Well, don't you think that's just a little bit paranoid? Lots of people use those words, and they don't all go around writing poison-pen letters, do they? And I don't think I've ever used the 'c' word – well, not in that context anyway, no matter how tempting it has been.

How lucky for you that you have the alert that tells you when a new comment has been added. And yes, I can quite see that you would be kicking yourself for not following it up immediately, but at least Susan didn't see it, and that's what counts, isn't it? All in all, I think you had quite a lucky escape really, Clive. You should be feeling quite sanguine really, instead of ringing people up and accusing them of things.

'Don't think you can get away with this, Sally,' you said, before you hung up on me.

I thought that was quite funny, the idea that I might have got away with anything. You see, I feel as if my life has been systematically stripped of everything that once made it worthwhile, every last vestige of value, like an abandoned house. The light bulbs are gone, the appliances too, even the antique tiles from around the fireplace. I feel I have nothing. So you tell me, Clive, what exactly have I got away with? I'd really, really like to know.

* * *

I was thinking about your 'Don't think you can get away with this' comment when I got your latest email this afternoon. There was just that hint of menace in it, I thought. And I remembered that poor Romanian window wiper, and the fear in his eyes.

At first I couldn't quite work it out, why you were using such tough, uncompromising language (what's all that about 'leave Susan alone', as if I'd done something to harm her instead of enjoyed her company on a couple of very pleasant social occasions?) and yet at the same time offering me money. And quite a lot of money. Twelve thousand pounds, in fact. Knowing as you do the precarious state of our finances, I'm sure you appreciate how welcome a £12,000 'gift' would be. We could clear some credit-card debts, pay a couple of months' instalments on the mortgage. No, it seemed like a very generous offer indeed on first reading, and even when I read it again and realized that it was in fact a bribe, my pay-off for disappearing from your lives, I still couldn't help thinking about what I could do with all that money, all the school trips it could buy. I did think your last sentence was a bit unnecessary though, that bit about sending me the money through some indirect means because 'under no circumstances will a face-to-face meeting be taking place!!'. I don't know why you felt the need for those two exclamation marks, really. One would have quite sufficed. 'It would be a very retrogressive step,' you wrote, 'at a point when we both need to be moving on with our lives. Separately.' That word 'separately' meriting a sentence of its own.

Of course, I knew the £12,000 would come from that undeclared stash you'd been given for making that dire rushed single in Holland ('They're paying me in cash,' you'd explained, embarrassed, when you called from your Amsterdam hotel. 'That's the only reason I'm doing it.') – the stash you'd been so nervous about being stolen that you'd ended up hiding it in a plastic bag in the fridge. I know all about the money because of that time we managed a four-day break together and I booked a ridiculously expensive hotel on my credit card which you insisted on repaying in cash, peeling off £1,200 from a wad stuffed into your back pocket and explaining how you'd grabbed it from the fridge earlier that day. 'Tell me if you need more,' you'd said, pressing the creased notes awkwardly into my hand. 'There's plenty more where that came from.' (Not until afterwards, when I stuffed the money down into an old Ugg boot in the bottom of my wardrobe, did I feel a little compromised by that transaction, that wad of grubby notes pressed into hands still smelling of sex.)

But you know, as I started thinking the whole thing through, I began adding up what this whole thing might be worth now we were thinking in purely financial terms. Funny amount, isn't it, £12,000? Anyone else would have rounded it down to £10,000 or up to £15,000, so I wondered if you'd used some kind of formula to work it out – adding up my different grievances since York Way Friday, giving more weight to some than others. I started to do the same. For instance, those endless, sleepless nights, lying in bed while my heart threatened to explode clear through my chest and the movies of you and Susan played out endlessly through my restless mind – those must be worth a few hundred quid each, surely? And what about the citalopram-induced anxieties, the dry mouth, the shaking hands setting out the kids' tea? The loss of income owing to days spent hunched over the computer obsessively checking and rechecking for emails that never come. The cracked teeth ground down to the exposed nerves during the nights, requiring potentially years of expensive dental work. The loss of self, the children asking why Mummy's so different, and once, pricelessly, 'Has Mummy been turned into an alien?'

I went through it all, quite fairly I have to say, totting it all up, making a tally. But you know, even before I finally gave up counting, I knew I wouldn't be taking your money. You see, I realized something interesting, Clive, as I was doing all that adding – that all the money in all the fridges in all the world can't come close to making up for what I've lost.

I really don't want to get heavy with you, you said in that email (which, by the way, I've rechristened the Blood Money Email – in a post-ironic way, of course).

That's an interesting turn of phrase, don't you think? 'Get heavy.' Because, of course, you are a heavy man. A weighty man. Sometimes when you were lying on top of me in one or other hotel bed with the quilted bedcover bunched up uncomfortably against the back of my legs and a dull ache spreading out from the arm pinioned to my side, a sensation of not being able to breathe would sweep suddenly over me and I'd shove you violently off, gasping for air.

'Did I hurt you?' you'd fret. 'You know I'd never do anything to hurt you.'

The women among our group of friends inclined to the view that you were a 'softie' really, a 'pussycat'.

'It's hysterical that he has this reputation as a tough man,' they'd scoff. 'Susan says he wells up at a Yellow Pages ad.'

The men, though, were far more circumspect. I'd seen the way a group of locals standing at the bar would eye you warily when you walked in, raising themselves up almost imperceptibly, pulling abdominal muscles in, following your progress as you went to sit down, alert to you.

'There's something about him that I just don't trust,' my old friend Jack had said on first meeting you.

Ironically, Daniel had jumped to your defence. 'Oh, he might look like a gangster, but he's got a heart of gold,' he'd said. But I'd seen the way men instinctively straightened themselves up when they saw you and I wasn't so sure.

'I can be very hard when I want to be,' you'd told me again when I'd teased you for crying after we'd had sex, or during *World's Strictest Parents*. I'd smiled, imagining you were trying to protest your macho credentials.

Now, when I re-read that line in your £12,000 email – *I really don't want to get heavy with you* – and I remember the fear on that Romanian squeegee man's face, I wonder if you might actually have been issuing a warning.

* * *

The young blonde doctor was dressed head to toe in blue today. Blue shift dress, blue cardigan, blue tights and blue medium-heeled shoes that clicked loudly as she came out into the waiting room to call my name. Do you think I should have read something into that? All that blue?

I'd gone for more citalopram, of course. At the same time as I loathe them, I'm also obsessed with them, flying into a panic if I'm half an hour late for my daily dose. I was down to my last five and had been aware of a constant low-level tug of anxiety.

I can imagine your disdain if you knew I was taking them. 'Opiate for the masses,' you used to call the happy pills everyone and his dog seems to be on. But you know, in the absence of anything else to believe in, I might as well believe in those, don't you think?

'How have you been feeling?' Her head was already tilted to the side before she'd even sat down.

After my pitiful show the last time I'd been in there, I was determined not to cry again. But there was something about the way she scrunched her lips and the way she made it sound as if she really was interested in how I'd been feeling that loosened something inside me.

'Not so good,' I croaked, and a small tear dribbled, incontinent, out of the corner of my eye.

The young doctor looked genuinely sorrowful.

'Oh, poor you.' She looked at me, head still cocked, lips still scrunched, holding my gaze for an almost uncomfortably long time.

'Is it still lack of work that's making you so anxious?'

I'd forgotten I'd told her that particular half-truth. For a moment I was tempted to throw caution to the wind and tell her the whole story – about you, about me, about us, about this. I could always switch practices afterwards, to save the children from being tarred with the Slutty Mummy brush. But something held me back, some last clinging vestige of self-respect, perhaps.

Instead, I nodded in agreement. Well, it's not entirely untrue, after all. Work has been abysmal since York Way Friday, owing partly to me being unable to concentrate on anything for more than five seconds at a time and partly to the downward slide that began not too far into our relationship and gained momentum as our feelings intensified. You'd be very disapproving about that, I'm sure; you with your puritanical work ethic. I remember how you used to make me send over word targets at the start of each day and how disappointed you'd be if I failed to achieve them. I was intrigued in the beginning about how your work drive fitted in with your fabled appetite for hedonism, or the libertinism of which you were so privately and justly proud. But later I realized it was all part of the same thing, the same need to exert control, even over your own supposedly unbridled passions.

The doctor sat very still and gazed at me some more. She'd swivelled her chair away from the desk so that she was facing squarely towards me, the toes of her blue shoes hooked behind the base of the chair.

'Owww,' she said sympathetically, doing an extra emphatic scrunch of the lips. 'Poor old you . . . Have you thought about finding a little job in a shop, just to tide you over?'

A little job in a shop. I'm not joking. I almost wished you'd been there, Clive. You'd have found it priceless, you really would. I started thinking about what a funny story it would make to tell later, how I'd pop my head to the side and do that whole thing with the mouth as I imitated her, but all of a sudden I realized I was sobbing. Proper big, gulping, snotty old sobs. You'd have been absolutely horrified! So then I was glad you weren't there to witness it.

The doctor was clearly quite taken aback by the violence of my emotional display.

'It can seem very hopeless, can't it?' she empathized wildly. 'But you know, it isn't really. How about we up your dose of citalopram?'

Well, I didn't like to argue. Especially not now I've got such a love/hate thing going on with my drugs. I nodded my head docilely. Up with the dosage. Up and up. There are few things in life that can't be improved by more drugs, it seems to me. Yet somehow I felt I ought to mention some of the problems I'd been having since I started taking the pills. It seemed only proper.

So I told her about the erratic sleep, and the struggles to stay awake in the middle of the day, and the headaches and the lack of appetite, and she nodded a lot and crossed one blue leg over the other and began making circles in the air with the toe of her right blue shoe.

'Yes,' she said, encouragingly. 'Mmmmmm . . .'

She agreed that all the things I'd mentioned could be side effects from the drug, but they could also, she informed me, be the effects of the depression.

'We wouldn't want you to have another *episode*,' she said thoughtfully, making me sound more like a jolly series of *Friends* than a psychological basket case. 'So I think we'll pop on an extra 20mg just to be on the safe side.'

So there you have it. I've been super-sized – in a pharmaceutical context, anyway.

Which is good because the rest of me feels diminished, reduced, downsized. I have less sleep, I eat less food, I inhabit less space in the world. Somehow I have less substance now that you are not in my life, so I'll take any kind of increase I can get. I'm sure you can understand that.

The doctor made me fill in the same form as before, where you have to rate how strongly certain statements relate to you. I remembered how saddened she'd seemed the last time so I tried to temper them a little, interspersing a few more threes in with the fours. For instance, with the statement that says 'I feel like a failure and like I've let my family down,' I ringed 3 (a lot of the time), instead of 4 (all the time), because you know, in the odd hours of the night when I'm asleep, I don't actually feel anything at all. Is that cheating? Well, maybe, but it was worth it for her smile of approbation at the end. 'I think I'm starting to see the first faint signs of recovery,' she beamed.

Maybe there ought to be an extra statement on that form. 'I feel like I've let my health practitioner down.'

* * *

I received our formal invitation to the vow-renewal ceremony in the post this morning. I must say, it's hysterical, it really is, so clever. The contrast between the photo on the front of you and Susan getting married in the 1980s (you look like children, the two of you, it's so sweet!) and the photo inside, where you've superimposed your two heads as they are now on to wrinkly old octogenarian bodies, is just genius. I see the hand of Susan in that. You never did really like being laughed at, despite all your protestations to the contrary.

I've propped it up against my computer screen and keep sneaking glances at that original wedding photograph. Susan is much thinner there, of course, and her face is ludicrously young, with that kind of half-drawn quality of the not-quite-adult. She'd only been in the UK a couple of years then, since coming over from Oz as an eighteen-year-old model, and there's something in the protective way she's holding your arm which suggests that, even then, she liked to mother you.

You're also looking much thinner (there's no getting away from it, I'm afraid!). In fact, if it wasn't for the dent in your cheek I'd hardly recognize you! Your hair is much longer and curls over the lapel of your shiny early-eighties suit. I've never seen you in a tie before. It kind of suits you. You are staring out at the camera, and through the camera at me, through a distance of twenty-six years, but I still see you, and I still know you.

Do you know, I hate the life you had before me. I hate the wedding guests in the background who I've never met. I hate the fact that you chose that suit without me in mind, or that I wasn't there to crack up when I saw you in those dreadful shoes. I hate that I never knew you when you were young and handsome and never got to run a finger down a face that was soft and smooth. I hate that I wasn't there. I hate that you left me out. I hate all the time that was robbed, the history that doesn't include me. I hate that somewhere not too far away from that photograph, a sixteen-year-old me is going about my life and you don't even know it yet. I hate it that I don't feature.

That's better.

I've taken the invitation and folded it vertically in half down the centre, so that Susan no longer appears and it's just you in your dated suit with the white flower in the lapel smiling out at the world like someone who has it all in front of him, someone waiting for his life to start.

Waiting for me.

* * *

The oddest thing happened today.

When I logged on to my email account, it was really slow. Slower even than normal (and you remember how much I used to complain when we were trying to rush through a flurry of emails and they'd suddenly slow to an agonizing snail's pace, for no reason other than to spite me). Then I noticed that there was a message I hadn't read which wasn't marked up in bold. It wasn't very interesting, I have to confess, just the commissioning editor at one of the magazines sending a mass email canvassing for ideas, but it was strange the way it was marked as 'read' even though I'd never seen it.

I stared at it a while. Well, let's face it, work being the way it is, I had very little else to do. Then, as is my wont these days, I Googled 'unread email messages marked as read'. (Increasingly, I find myself unable to make the smallest of decisions or form the slightest opinion without Googling it first. How long before I Google 'Do I need to go to the loo?', I wonder.) There were quite a few jargony explanations of technical things that could have contributed towards the unbolded-unread-message phenomenon, but one question really caught my eye. 'Could anyone else have accessed your account and read your emails?'

At first I dismissed the idea, but then I thought about it. And thought about it some more. Then, when I started to get a trickle of emails from people in my contacts list, telling me they'd received a personal email from me, clearly meant for someone else, I started to wonder . . . Could that be you, Clive, making a little mischief?

I looked in my 'sent' folder. Sure enough, I seemed to have sent a message to every name on my list. I have to admit I was a bit apprehensive about the content, but when I clicked on it, it was fairly innocuous. It was a message I must have originally sent to you, saying how bored I was of the piece I was writing, and how I was thinking of retraining as a teacher, or a vet, or an astronaut, basically any other job but this. It was a bit embarrassing, to be sure (Silleeeee Salleeeee), but not as damaging as it could have been. Even sitting on my own in the windowless cubbyhole, I must have blushed thinking of all the other emails that could have been sent . . . the sex ones (do you remember the era of Master and Kitten and their various adventures in steam rooms and jacuzzis and the overspill car parks at B&Q?), or the vitriolic ones where we'd systematically rubbish someone we knew. Compared to those, the email that got sent out from me was unfortunate, but not catastrophic.

It was almost like a warning.

Do you find that fanciful, Clive? You're probably right, but please indulge me a little. These days I must get my entertainment where I can find it.

My password is, as usual, pathetically easy to guess for anyone with a cursory knowledge of my life. (And let's face it, you had a lot more than that. You had the deluxe membership to my life, with all the perks. And even now you've decided to cancel your subscription, I can't take that insider knowledge back, can I? I can't demand you hand back your memories along with your locker key and your entrance pass?) We always had each other's passwords to our dedicated email account. (No secrets between us, we always told each other. Except it was largely an empty gesture as we were the only ones who ever used that account anyway.) It wouldn't take a terribly advanced technological brain (and let's be honest, that isn't you, is it?) to work out that if one email account has as its password the first line of an old address, another email account might just feature the first line of a different old address. I am nothing if not predictable.

Was it you, Clive? Did you come creeping into my account in the night like a thief, sifting through my virtual underwear drawer, emptying out my virtual cupboards? I know I really ought to be outraged by the idea, but something in my ridiculous head persists in being flattered. Don't laugh. It just seems like you've gone to an awful lot of trouble over this. I like the idea that, no matter how fleetingly, I was once more in the forefront of your thoughts, centre stage as it were.

So, believe it or not, I hesitated about changing my password. I mean, there are all the practical considerations, like worrying whether I'd remember what on earth I'd changed it to and also the real possibility that it hadn't been you after all, just some technological gremlin playing a practical joke. So I dithered for most of the day, spending long stretches of time just staring at my inbox on my screen, hoping to uncover some other hints as to your lurking presence. Wondering if, in your little studio (*sad fuck in a box*) in St John's Wood, you might be staring at exactly the same page on your screen. It made me feel quite connected to you, in a comforting sort of way.

But in the end I did change it, of course. While I seem to have lost touch with most of my regular employers after these last months in the antidepressant haze, I'd be pretty stupid to run the risk of alienating them all, wouldn't I? Not while Daniel is still 'in training' (at forty, surely the oldest apprentice in history?) and the family finances so precarious. (I've stopped opening official letters. Did I tell you? Helen told me to give myself a break and not to engage with people or situations that would upset me. I don't suppose she was exactly talking about ignoring all official correspondence, but I've decided to apply the very loosest of interpretations.)

So I thought up another password which I'm guaranteed to have forgotten by tomorrow. The happy pills make me forget all kinds of things. Sometimes it's a problem (last week's dentist appointment, Tilly's art project), but other times it's actually a bonus (stupid fucking Pete). I wrote the password down on a Post-it and dropped it into the drawer of my filing cabinet, but I'm sure to forget I've done that by tomorrow. In a few weeks or months, I might come across that Post-it and wonder why I've scribbled 'Tilly*Jamie94' in big red writing.

I sighed a little once I'd done that, imagining you trying to access my emails but finding yourself locked out. It felt rather mean-spirited somehow. But then I realized that if you'd indeed been sending me some sort of warning, you'd expect me to change the password, and that made me feel at the same time both reassured (you wouldn't take it as a personal rejection) and disappointed (you wanted me to sever this last secret link to you).

Even after I'd clicked the 'password reset' box, I couldn't get it out of my mind, the thought of you spying on my movements from the comfort of your box room, keeping tabs on me, rifling through the shabby records of my life. Did you feel anything, I wonder, reading the words I'd written to other people, after all those millions of words I used to write just for you? Did you have even the teeniest trace of regret when you realized that my life was (just about) limping along without you, that despite the things you used to say about us being one being, we were, after all, 'separate' (your favourite word). For a second I saw us as Siamese twins who had just been successfully operated on. Usually in such cases there's one stronger one, isn't there, one that greedily claims the shared organs, the shared limbs for its own? And then there's the other one, who gets left with the dregs, with a heart too weak to pump on its own and a skeleton that can't support its own body weight. The runt, incapable of sustaining itself independently. No prizes for guessing which of us would be which!

Daniel and I had another of our rare 'heated debates' earlier.

As you know, we hardly ever argue. That would involve a certain investment of emotion on both our parts that both of us are really past bestowing. But this evening, tensions never far from the surface flared rustily into life.

It started with dinner. Daniel and I ate together, the kids having already been fed. (Does that make them sound like livestock? I don't mean it like that.) For some reason, maybe because neither of us was talking, I started listening to Daniel as he ate. You know how when you tune into someone's eating, it becomes quite impossible to focus on anything else? I became fixated on the fork going into his gaping mouth, the noisy, excessive mastication, the obscene undulating of his throat. The noise seemed to grow louder to fill the silence between us, and I stopped even pretending to eat my own food, feeling suddenly nauseous, but Daniel continued putting fork to mouth as if nothing was wrong. Couldn't he hear how disgusting he sounded? It was difficult to believe he wasn't doing it on purpose.

So I started to speak, just to cover up the noise.

I tried to explain (oh, futile endeavour!) that I felt like something was snapping inside me, brittle as a dried-up reed. Don't worry, I didn't mention you, of course. I've become adept at talking around what Helen calls the Elephant in the Room. In fact I'm so good at avoiding that elephant I could probably dance nimbly around it blindfold. But that doesn't mean I've forgotten that fucking great elephant is there. Anyway, I digress. So I was trying to tell Daniel that I was worried about my state of mind. I didn't want to overstate the case, you understand. I wouldn't want to end up sectioned and straining against a straitjacket in some padded cell. But I had a sudden irrational urge to involve him in my life, if only because we share a bed and two children and a drawerful of unopened mail. Since the early days, when he fussed around me like an old woman, enjoying the drama of my sudden emotional collapse, the novelty has worn off, and Daniel has withdrawn into his default position of silent disapproval.

'Some days I feel as if I'm going mad,' I told him.

Daniel looked up from the kitchen table, where he was reading the *Guardian* sports pages over the top of his dinner plate, his newly acquired specs looking unconvincing, like a theatrical prop.

'I feel like that most days,' he told me.

I tried again.

'I'm so tired all the time, and yet I can't sleep. Whenever I close my eyes, I feel like I'm drowning.' It wasn't the most original analogy I know, but I couldn't really think of another way of describing that rush of anxiety, burning its way up through my chest and into my brain, that kept me awake at night, heart pounding.

'Well, I'm *more* tired,' was Daniel's response. 'This training I'm doing is really hard, you know. At least *you* can go back to bed in the afternoon if you're tired. I mean, it's not as if you've got loads of working piling up at the moment, is it?'

Well, it was uncalled for, don't you think? That underhand dig about the work, when I'm the one who has kept us going all this time, through Daniel's myriad failed schemes and half-hearted ventures.

'Depression is not a competition, you know,' I told him, knowing even as I said it that that's exactly what it is. A competition between me and Daniel to see who has made the other the most miserable, each counting up our past resentments, keeping score with old disappointments and unfulfilled dreams.

After that, the atmosphere got rapidly worse.

Daniel is slow to be riled, but when he is, he takes a vicious pleasure in his own bad humour, savouring his sense of his own self-righteousness.

His argument was that my 'depression' (his quotation marks, not mine. You should have seen his expression as his fingers made the gestures in the air, his eyebrows arched in mocking disbelief) was largely self-inflicted and, having been thus inflicted, entirely self-perpetuated.

He feels, apparently, that the antidepressants and the visits to Helen are all manifestations of my unhealthy need to be at the centre of some inflated and ongoing crisis. In other words, Clive, he thinks I'm a drama queen.

Well, given that he only has a fraction of the facts at his disposal, I suppose he could be forgiven for thinking that I'm the sole author of my own misery. (See how I'm trying to empathize even with Daniel – it's practically second nature to me now.) He thinks I should 'snap out of it' and 'think of the children for a change'. I didn't tell him how I can't really think about anything any more, how my brain seems alternately full of rage or full of sawdust. He'd probably just tell me that his brain was under even greater pressure, and we'd enter another level of our new favourite family game: Competitive Breakdowns.

I told him – and I'm not proud of it – that he was an emotional bully. Which isn't entirely either true or fair. I tried to summon up tears to support my cause, but none were forthcoming. He said I was selfish and self-obsessed.

The problem is, of course, that he's right in a lot of ways. (Not that I'd ever use that word about him in his hearing: 'right'.) I've brought it all on myself, every last bit of it. But no matter how many times I remind myself of that, I still can't quite believe it. Because saying I caused it all makes me sound like someone with power, someone who can make things happen. Yet I know that you're the one with all the power, and that everything that has happened has happened *to* me, not because of me.

Daniel became quite heated, and visibly puffed up with his own indignation as he talked. He developed a deep red flush on his neck that spread like ink on blotting paper. I watched transfixed as it bled outwards, staining the skin around the nugget of his Adam's apple, reaching crimson fingers up towards his chin. Meanwhile he threw phrases at me like 'narcissistic personality' and 'emotionally manipulative'. It struck me that he might have been reading the book I borrowed from Helen Bunion's office. I waited for him to drop in something about owning my own actions, which would prove my suspicions beyond any doubt, but he stopped short.

'We used to be happy,' he told me suddenly, and I was so surprised to hear that word coming from his mouth, it was like he was talking in tongues. 'Then something happened. You vacated our relationship.'

I'm serious, that's exactly what he said. *You vacated our relationship*. It made me sound like a fire warden.

'Now I don't even know who you are any more,' he told me, and then he left the kitchen very suddenly. It was a terrific performance, I have to say. I almost could have believed he'd choreographed it in advance.

After he'd left, I stayed leaning against the fridge where I'd been standing. To tell you the truth, I was a little taken aback. Usually Daniel's idea of talking about our relationship is to wait until absolutely backed into a corner, then say something totally noncommittal like: 'We're OK, aren't we?' which can obviously mean absolutely anything, or nothing, depending on your point of view.

When we first got together sixteen years ago, it used to bother me. I'd try everything to get him to open up, convinced that if I could just find the right approach, the right combination of words, I'd unlock the deep well of feeling he clearly harboured, bringing it all to the surface. It took more than ten years before I finally admitted that the problem wasn't finding a way to unleash his suppressed emotions, the problem was believing that they actually existed in the first place. At least, in any form I'd recognize.

I thought about what he'd said about us being 'happy'. Were we ever happy, Daniel and I? Looking back, I recall some happy moments. I can summon them right now. They play across my mind like a PowerPoint presentation. Playing Scrabble under a palm tree on a white sandy Thai beach, lying in bed on Sunday mornings reading the papers with the kids wedged between us watching cartoons, drunken dinners with friends, barbecues in sunny gardens. Those moments unquestionably existed, but then I can find happy moments in every period of my life, yet I wouldn't say these were all happy periods. In fact, I struggle to find one period I'd really call happy. It's easy to rewrite the past, making it fit in with how it's convenient for us to view it now. Yet I still maintain that while Daniel and I kept each other company through some very happy moments in our lives, by and large that happiness wasn't a result of the two of us. We enjoyed some happiness together, but that happiness was shop-bought, rather than home-made.

And what about us, Clive? Did we make each other happy? I can see your face now if I was to ask you that. I can see you making that expression of distaste, as if you'd bitten into a too-sour plum. You always felt happiness was a bourgeois concern, and that when people said they were searching for happiness what they really meant was blandness. Your idea of how other people defined happiness was a Hallmark card, something a bit tacky, a bit tawdry, a meaningless sugar-rush of emotion. So I never asked you.

Yet in one of your emails after York Way Friday (when you were still sending me messages to explain yourself, before you drew up the drawbridge and retreated into defensive silence), you said you'd realized you'd never make me happy. As if after all, I'd turned out to be just like all the rest, trawling for happiness on the shelves of Homebase or in the pages of the Argos catalogue.

At the time I'd argued with you, pretended outrage at your assumptions. Told you I'd never look to someone else to make me feel complete. I was lying, of course. I wanted to be happy, just like all the rest. And obviously I must have thought that you could make me so.

I never once thought that about Daniel. Isn't that terrible? But still, I didn't correct him when he said that thing about how we used to be happy. It's not something you can readily say to someone, is it? No, you got it wrong. I wonder whether he really believes it, or whether maybe Daniel's definition is so different from what we had, that intermittent parallel-worlds kind of contentment, counts as being genuinely happy.

Whatever the truth, Daniel thinks that what has gone wrong over the last few years, the inexorable slide from that pinnacle of happiness (as he now sees it) to where we are today, is down to me emotionally checking out, vacating our relationship. I wonder what he'd say if he knew about you, Clive. You know, something tells me part of him would feel glad, vindicated. If the problems started because of you, it would absolve him of responsibility. It wouldn't be about happiness any more, or lack of it, it would be about lots of other things – sex, excitement, adrenaline, money.

There have been many times over the last few months when I've been tempted to tell him, not out of any altruistic motive, but out of desperation to share my misery around, to let him know just how much I've been suffering. Ridiculous, isn't it? I've rolled the words around in my mouth like mint imperials, rehearsing how they'd sound, preparing myself for his reaction. And yet, of course, I've stayed silent, protecting my link to you, our last surviving secret.

I suspect you see it rather differently, this tie that binds the two of us together. I imagine it's a burden to you now, a shackle you'd much rather shake free. Does it clink along behind you, as you walk with Susan arm in arm, one leg faintly dragging at the back as you pull it along? Does it lie in between you on that huge daybed, nestling down amongst all those smugly plumped-up cushions, taking up space in that all-important middle ground? Is it elephant-shaped, our secret? Does Susan run a curious hand around its invisible trunk, fumbling along invisible ears, wondering, always wondering about that lingering elephant-shit smell?

Like it or not, Clive (and my guess is not – call me clairvoyant), though we may have been surgically separated, we Siamese twins, we nevertheless remain bound together. I feel you straining against the binds. After all, you're the stronger one, you took the legs, the healthy organs, the lion's share of the pumping heart of us. You are aching to be off. And yet still you cannot be altogether free. I feel for you, I really do. It's awful to be forced to carry on wearing the clothes you grew out of months ago. But try to think of it as a badge of honour, a reminder of something you survived.

What's that Nietzsche quote? What doesn't kill you makes you stronger?

But I suppose if you think about it a different way, what doesn't kill you can also leave you maimed.

I've been thinking a lot about what Daniel said. It's now late and once again I'm awake in the night, waiting for the zopiclone to work its way through my system, listening to the asthmatic wheezing of the house around me. Daniel lies asleep beside me, well used by now to my light being on in the early hours, turning his dreams permanently sun-kissed. He is unconscious yet his back still talks to me. Narrow-shouldered and accusatory, his sharp shoulder-blades are like jabbing fingers, silently listing his many grievances.

Could he be right that I 'vacated' a perfectly well-functioning relationship, and all to be with you?

Well, obviously, it started me thinking about those early days. You know, I never really found you terribly attractive at first. I'm sure I've told you that before, in those days when I was so secure in your feelings for me that I didn't feel the need to dissemble, and could afford to be cruel or hard if the fancy took me. Those were the days when truth wasn't a luxury, but a commodity like any other that could be tossed around with impunity, knowing that however hurtful or disagreeable, you'd still come back for more.

It had been inevitable, of course, that sooner or later I'd progress from being your First Legitimate Female Friend to, well, what exactly? Your First Legitimate Female Friend with Benefits?

It started, naturally, with emails. I say naturally, because ours was a relationship that would have been impossible in the pre-email days.

How else could we have become so intense so quickly, so involved in every beating moment of each other's lives, without ever leaving our respective homes? How else could we have left our partners in every single sense of the word (so already Daniel is proved right – I vacated him, as he said), while physically remaining just where we were – you in one of your offices, me in my windowless cubbyhole?

Ours was a thoroughly modern email affair, each nuance played out against the soundtrack of incoming message alerts, so it was only fitting that it started off that way, the messages between us growing steadily both in volume and in intimacy. You commented on clothes you'd seen me wear, protested when I said I was going to get all my hair cut off. Details of your domestic life started creeping into your messages. 'Don't believe everything it says on the tin,' you wrote in one email. 'People would be shocked if they could see what Susan and I are really like.'

You told me how you'd got married so young that you were always trying to recapture the carefree youth you'd never had. That's why there had been all the other women, you said.

Oh, hadn't you mentioned the other women?

Of course, that was a genius move, telling me about the one-night stands, the frenzied flings, the aspiring singer-songwriters, the publicity girls, the prostitutes – the whole long, ignoble line of 'encounters' threading its way through the fabric of your long, glittering marriage. At one stroke you'd advertised yourself as both desirable and available. You needn't feel guilty about being a home-breaker, was your subtext. How can you break what is already broken?

But you were quick to divorce yourself (sorry about that choice of phrase) from the callow-cheating-bastard stereotype. None of this was a reflection on Susan, you said. (I'm paraphrasing now – your voice is so deeply ingrained in me, it's something I feel well equipped to do. I hope you'll look on it as a sort of tribute.) The women were a 'necessary process' you needed to work through on your own, part of the personal development that had been interrupted by getting married while barely out of your teens. You and Susan were a team, you'd grown up together – 'We brought each other up' is the phrase you used – but a team is made up of individuals with their own strengths and weaknesses. Surely I could understand that?

You were terribly good, I have to say. You played it all so perfectly. 'I get the feeling you know exactly what I'm talking about,' you wrote, appealing to my vanity at the same time as probing for a hole in my marital armour through which you could come sliding in. And of course I gave it to you.

'No one can be all things to one person,' I told you. 'Monogamy is an artificial conceit.'

No, I didn't know exactly what it meant either, but of course I knew the message it would send out.

And so it began.

Funny to think that at the start you were the one doing the chasing and me the holding back. I don't remember an exact tipping point where I knew your intentions had changed, but I do remember a dawning awareness that you were deliberately and overtly flirting with me. I like to think I didn't encourage it, but I'm pretty sure I didn't discourage it either, which maybe amounts to the same thing.

Of course, it would be disingenuous to pretend I don't remember the exact moment when we stepped over the line. I'd given you a lift home after an evening picnicking on the Heath with Cyd and assorted friends, watching a jazz band across the lake and drinking chilled white wine as the sun slowly set. Why wasn't Daniel with us that night? I don't recall. Perhaps he had cycled back on his own. He did a lot of cycling in those days. Susan was away for the weekend with your children. So I drove you home, and the sexual tension crackled between us like a bad phone line. What made me turn in through the gates and turn off the engine instead of just pulling in to the kerb to drop you off? (Afterwards you always pressed me for a reason, determined to make that moment part of the folklore of our love-story. How disappointed you always were that I could never come up with anything beyond 'I just thought, why not?') Your face when I turned the engine off was a picture though, it really was. 'Oh blimey,' I think you said, for once lost for words.

All through that long, clumsy first kiss, I kept up an internal monologue: 'This is weird, how *big* his tongue feels, hope nobody can see us, this is probably wrong, this is *definitely* wrong, but it's only a kiss, a kiss doesn't really count.' I'd already decided that it wouldn't go any further. I just wanted to test out how it felt – I was in the infidelity changing room trying on a dress I knew was way too expensive for me, but wanted to experience wearing, just once.

Later, you always referred to that night as Drive-In Movie Night because you claimed that when I pulled into your driveway and switched off the engine, there was a split second before I turned the headlights off where we both remained facing forwards, staring at the illuminated garage wall, as if waiting for some entertainment to begin.

'Drive-In Movie Night was when it all began,' you always said afterwards, conveniently forgetting that it was followed by that strange limbo period where we regressed to a kind of embarrassed, stilted half-friendship. How adept we are at rewriting our own histories. How willingly fact is sacrificed to flow. Now, when I remember that kiss, and your shocked 'Oh blimey,' I know that just as you were wrong about when it all started, you're wrong about when it will end.

It isn't over, Clive. You just don't know it yet.

Once the immediate post-Drive-In-Movie-Night shock had worn off, we began to talk tentatively about what had happened, as if probing a mouth ulcer with a tongue. Of course we both pretended to be horrified. 'Can you imagine if we'd let it go further?', 'How drunk must we have been!', 'Thank God we stopped ourselves . . .' (such experts we two are at turning our failings to our own credit).

We wouldn't discuss it again, we decided. We'd wipe the slate clean. And so we did . . . until Golf Course Wednesday. Where was it we were going that day? I forget. I know you'd taken me to meet your newspaper mate, Douggie, and then driven on somewhere to check out an upcoming band. I rather think there might have been a river beside which we sat awkwardly on a bench, eating sandwiches bought from Marks and Spencer.

Driving back through the heartlands of Hertfordshire ('I'd rather die than live here,' you said preposterously, as we swept past sprawling red-brick mansions with electronic gates and winking alarms), you went very quiet and then suddenly stopped the car by the side of an unmade road flanking a golf course.

'I am totally in love with you.'

Do you remember how that came out – with no pre-amble, no lead-up, you gazing straight ahead with your hands still gripping the steering wheel, engine still on? I made a noise, a startled, unconvincing attempt to demur, but you cut me off.

'I'd leave Susan for you, you know? I never thought I'd ever say that. But I want you to be in no doubt about how strongly I feel about you. I've never felt like this before.'

Until that moment I hadn't been completely sure of my own feelings, but of course I was done for then. Not by the declaration of love, you understand, but by the being put above all the others, above your wife. What woman could resist that?

The first time we had sex was at the Suffolk house one Sunday afternoon, at the tail end of a weekend house party. Susan had left earlier that morning – something about work. When Tilly and Jamie asked Daniel if some of the other kids could travel in the Saab with them, you offered me a lift home with you instead. 'I'll help with the clearing up,' I said, but we both knew what I was really there for. The master bedroom, with its antique

French artfully peeling white wrought-iron-framed bed and deep window seat overlooking the estuary, bore Susan's fingerprints in every one of its Farrow-and-Ball-painted corners. You carried me in there (I didn't know about your back then, or I'd never have let you) and lowered me gently on to the bed, and all I could see were invisible traces of Susan, smeared like excrement over the walls behind you.

Funny to think how unsure I was, even then, even long after the point of no return. Not unsure because of Daniel, strangely. Although this was the first time in over ten years I'd physically betrayed him, I'd done it so many times in my head by that stage that it felt almost like old news.

No, I was unsure about you, about your extravagant curls, your sludge-coloured eyes. Used to Daniel's skinny insubstantiality, you were too present, too unavoidable. When you took off your shirt, I was half repelled and half fascinated by the unexpected body-builder pecs, stretching the skin like shop-bought haggis. I almost told you to stop, almost couldn't go through with it, and yet something in me was thrilled by the sheer new un-familiarity of you.

It would be good, wouldn't it, to reminisce about how fantastic that first time was, how we reached heights of passion never before scaled? But of course it would also be a big fat lie. That first time was a disaster really, with Susan's marks all over the room and your insistence that you were too fat, too old, too married to appeal to me. (Knowing you better, I can see that show of insecurity was just another way of leading me in, giving me the illusion of being in control.) When you pulled on a condom, your erection sank like an undercooked cake, leaving us both gawping like foolish goldfish, wrong-footed (I can hear you now, 'You're mixing your metaphors again') and unsure what to do next.

'It doesn't matter,' I told you, as of course I was honour-bound to do.

But it did matter. We both, in our individual ways, felt there was something wrong with us, something that had made your cock cower like a small, scared thing.

We chose to blame it on Susan, on her presence in the brightly patterned rug, the arched seventies reading light. We called it guilt, but by the time we had put our clothes back on, we both knew it was something else. It was resentment.

The second time we had sex, you cried for an hour. But that's another story. Now, finally, the zopiclone is crawling through my veins. My body greets it with joyful relief, like a much-missed friend.

I loved you I loved you I loved you.

* * *

As soon as I logged on to my email account this morning, I felt something wasn't right. There was nothing I could put my finger on, nothing out of place, just that nagging sense that everything wasn't quite as I had left it.

This time, I have to admit, I felt a little bit apprehensive. I've changed my password, as I've already said. If you'd got into my emails again, you'd have to have been trying very hard.

I called up a contact who once advised me for an article

I was writing on cyber-spying. I pretended I was writing another piece. 'How hard is it to get into someone else's email account if you don't have the password?' I asked.

'Hard, but by no means impossible. You just have to have money and know the right people.'

When he said that, there flashed through my head a vivid recollection of the first time you told me about your hairdresser, Tony. 'He's part of some huge north London crime family,' you'd said, clearly thrilled, and even I recognized the surname. Apparently you'd been going to Tony since your mid twenties and he'd adopted you as an honorary brother. 'Anything you need fixing,' Tony told you. 'Anything at all.' How you relished that contact, your underworld link. 'They're just like the Sopranos,' you emailed me a couple of years ago, just back from a party at the Grosvenor for Tony's anniversary. 'Surveillance, hacking ... Do you know, one of the cousins even told me how to run someone off the road and make it look like an accident? All the way home, I've been itching to try it.' You've always been uncharacteristically coy about it, but I suspect you've called on Tony's family once or twice over the years when business deals have gone wrong, and after I'd put the phone down to the cyber-stalking expert, I couldn't help wondering if you might once more have found occasion to ask for their help.

Am I being ridiculous? Sorry, my sense of perspective seems to have deserted me.

After that call, I remained staring at the screen for a long time, idly clicking in and out of already-read messages in my inbox, wondering if you were following my movements, monitoring me. I tried to feel happy about the idea, like I had before.

My head was pounding with a citalopram headache and my mouth was dry and furry, as if it had been Velcro'd inside.

Was it you, Clive? Were you there?

In the end I closed down my account and lay down on my bed. As someone who works from home, I've always maintained that taking a nap in the daytime is the start of the slippery slope, but this morning I didn't even think about it, just kicked off the old Ugg boots that I wear round the house, and lay down.

I don't know where I am any more. Everything keeps shifting and I can't work out where I'm supposed to be.

* * *

The baby shower was such an education. Really, Clive, you should have been there. You always used to make such a big deal about what a 'girl' you are. You'd have just loved it.

At first, I didn't even think I was going to get to go. After that lunch with Emily and Susan in which I felt like I'd made real headway with befriending Emily, everything went completely quiet. Luckily I hadn't forgotten. I knew when Emily was having her baby shower (what a lovely expression it is, isn't it, that image of babies raining down from above?), so a couple of weeks after that lunch, I dropped her a line.

Don't be disapproving, Clive. I'd asked her for her business card, and it just seemed like a courteous thing to do, to drop her an email asking how she was and explaining how much I was looking forward to my first baby shower. I have to say, she replied pretty much straight away. I got the feeling she was a teensy bit bored, actually. Perhaps she was regretting giving up her 'job' so early into her pregnancy. (Sorry, I don't know why I put 'job' in inverted commas like that. It just came out that way.) Anyway, she said she'd be 'delighted' if I came, and told me all the details. Well, I'm sure I don't need to tell *you* that it was yesterday, camped out in Emily's lovely Notting Hill garden. (It only rained just a tiny bit, and it didn't spoil things at all. You must tell Emily that she needn't have gone and locked herself in the bathroom all that time. Nobody minded in the least about getting a teeny bit wet.)

I'd agonized about the gift, I don't mind telling you. I kept imagining Emily telling you that I'd given her something wildly inappropriate, or cheap or tasteless or any of the myriad of things I could imagine Emily saying. I Googled baby showers to find out what was expected and discovered it's considered good manners to buy presents for both the baby *and* the mother. Expensive business, this baby-shower thing – especially for someone who hasn't worked in the last six weeks. Still, what's another hundred quid on the overdraft? It's a brand-new life we're talking about here! In the end I went for a sweet little babygro from BabyGap (remember our baby, Clive, the puffed-up baby that wasn't?), and I bought Emily some extortionately expensive bath oil from Space NK. Shame that when I arrived, it all went straight on to a huge groaning anonymous pile of presents. I should have attached a gift tag. Emily does have a lot of friends, doesn't she?

I sat next to Susan, of course. We were in dowagers' corner, the two of us and her rheumy-eyed dog, alongside the mother of the bland barrister (clearly forgiven for her unwitting transgression over the scan photo mousemat). Her name's Frieda. Well, obviously you know that already. How ridiculous of me to drop that in when you and Frieda are probably on the closest of terms, her being family and everything. I do think you were being unkind when you used to refer to her in your emails as the unthinking man's Joan Collins. I'm quite sure that isn't really a wig (although I'll admit her forehead appeared to belong to someone else entirely).

Anyway, Susan and I and Frieda got on like a house on fire, we really did, once I'd got used to the way she kept leaning away from the two of us as we spoke, as if she was worried about catching a calorie or something. And her face having just that one expression takes a bit of getting used to, doesn't it? I thought at first that she was going to be really hard work, but Susan managed to loosen her up. (She's amazing like that, isn't she?) She talked quite a lot about you, actually, did Frieda. She obviously considers you two have rather a special bond, in fact she became quite animated really (which naturally made me worry for her face. One got the definite sense that too much expressiveness might cause some sort of surface cracking).

'I think you quite fancy old Clive,' Susan said cheerfully after Frieda had remarked for the second time how you were so much more 'impressive' in the flesh than you'd appeared on the television. There was something in the way she said 'flesh' that made one think of Anthony Hopkins as Hannibal Lecter. You could almost hear the smacking of the lips.

Frieda gave an anorexic smile.

'You're lucky, Susan, dear,' she said in a way that made

it clear that in the normal run of things Susan would not be the kind of person Frieda would envy. 'Clive has still got enough charisma to compensate for the fact that he's getting on a bit, and not what he was.'

Don't shoot the messenger here, I'm just telling you exactly what she said.

To give Susan her due, while she didn't jump up and down in your defence, neither did she wade right in and rubbish you. She said something sharp about charisma not paying the bills and deftly changed the subject. Neither of them seemed to notice that I was finding something endlessly fascinating in the bottom of my glass of wine. The truth is that for all the good 'work' I've been doing with Helen on taking away your power – or what's the term Helen uses? 'Disinvesting' you of your power – I still can't hear your name spoken out loud without feeling something rip all the way up inside me, like I'm being filleted from within with a rusty knife.

Luckily we talked about something else after that. Babies, probably. There was an awful lot of talk about babies. Well, what did I expect? It was a baby shower! There was just one slightly awkward moment, when Susan fixed her blue eyes on me as if she was sizing me up for a coffin, and asked me if I was 'quite all right'.

I made some sort of joke, I think, but though Susan smiled, she wasn't really laughing. She said I didn't seem quite myself (again that phrase, as if not being myself was a bad thing). She said she was surprised that I could afford to take a day off as she'd have thought I would be working during the week.

'Work isn't exactly that great at the moment,' I told her,

promising myself that I wouldn't go into details, wouldn't talk about the endless hours in front of the blank computer screen, the half-finished features, the phone that never rang.

'Well, you must call Clive,' Susan told me decidedly. 'He'll find you some work to do.'

It was a wonderful moment. Quite filmic, I thought. The wife in the garden in her navy polka-dot summer frock, telling the mistress (sorry, sorry, *ex*-mistress) to get in touch with the husband.

'I'm sure *Clive*' (I couldn't help pronouncing the word with a slight wince, the way Tilly does when the wire on her brace digs into the inside of her cheek) 'is very busy at the moment, especially now he's a famous award-winning producer.'

I was aiming for amused detachment, but it probably came across more as a whine.

'Nonsense,' said Susan. 'All he does is sit around all day trying to figure out how his iPhone works while other people do the work for him. Give him a call.'

I nodded, and tried to remember how to arrange my mouth into a smile. There was a burning sensation deep inside my ribcage on the left-hand side as if my heart was being seared like fresh tuna. Luckily, Frieda broke the moment.

'I think I might give Clive a call in that case,' she announced rather startlingly. 'I've got a few ideas for promotional campaigns that I think he'd be very interested in. I've been meaning to get back into the workplace for ages now.'

She said 'workplace' as if it was a foreign city she'd always meant to visit – Prague, for instance.

Susan caught my eye then, and a look passed between

us. For a split second, there were just the two of us, wordlessly colluding, but then back you came, Clive, barging in between us, the elephant on the lawn.

Anyway, the rest of the shower (quite appropriate term that, considering the weather) passed very pleasantly. Like I said, it was a shame Emily got herself in such a state about the rain. It was only a little splash, after all. Susan was very calm about it, I must say. She must have stood outside that bathroom door for over twenty minutes, persuading Emily that her life wasn't really ruined just because the silk tablecloths had got a little bit damp.

'Don't mind me. I'm just one big wobbling mass of hormones,' Emily sniffed when she eventually returned outside, where the guests, slightly bedraggled now, were doggedly eating lunch from sodden paper plates.

It was quite sporting of her, I thought, to make that comment. She's not very good on humour, is she? Least of all when it involves herself. But you could tell Susan had had a word and smoothed it all over.

Good old Susan. And to think you nearly gave all that up, all that goodness. For me!

I could have stayed there all day, in that lovely walled garden in Notting Hill, with the decked dais and the sculpted water feature in the shape of a large egg. In fact, I very nearly did stay there all day. Don't be so suspicious, Clive, I was just enjoying myself, that's all. But then I realized that it was just me and Susan left, and Emily kept talking about how exhausted she was (she's quite right; all that sitting around can get very tiring in her condition), so I reluctantly said my goodbyes.

'Are you sure you're OK?' Susan asked, seeing me out

through the immaculate hallway, tastefully done out in different shades of taupe and ecru. Emily, I decided, was definitely the kind of woman who knows the difference between the two. Would you say that was fair?

Susan said that while it was lovely to see me, she hadn't really thought that babies were exactly my thing.

How could babies not be someone's thing?

I told her it had been a fascinating anthropological experience. That seemed to mollify her a little, and I felt I wasn't some sad, nutty, pre-menopausal woman with too much time on her hands.

On my journey home, I imagined Susan making her way back to your house in St John's Wood, already full of all the stories she would tell you. Were you waiting there for her when she got home? In that amber-lit drawing room with the squashy sofas and low coffee tables and the gold discs lined up on the wall like pirates' treasure? Did you pour her a drink and stroke her cheek and say, 'Well done, you'? Did you talk about your daughter, the Sacred Vessel, and your as yet unborn grandchild and all the other fragile ties that bind you together like spun sugar? Did she say, 'Oh, Sally was there'? And did your heart roar, just for a moment, and your eyes involuntarily blink to shut out the memories? And did you think of me? Did you think of me? Did you think of me?

Oh God, did you think of me?

*   *   *

A man followed me this morning.

No, I'm not saying that to try to be dramatic. It's actually true!

I had gone to the shops to get that maths stuff Tilly's been nagging me to get for weeks. She made a big scene last night, saying not to bother now because the test was over and she hadn't had a compass or a ruler or that funny plastic semicircular thingy so she'd probably failed. She was trying to make me feel guilty, of course. Good job the citalopram Stops All Known Guilt. Dead! (I must ask Helen why I go into advertising speak whenever I think about it. Maybe it's a recognized psychological syndrome.) But I must have had some nagging concern, because I set off purposefully for the hugely expensive stationery shop, and actually made it there, rather than meandering uselessly through all the other shops, vacantly picking things up off the shelves, unsure what I'd set out to buy, which is what I find myself doing more and more.

Anyway, when I came out, I noticed a man, leaning against the lamppost to the right of the stationery shop, smoking a cigarette. Now, that in itself is unusual around these parts, because the yummy-mummy brigade have effectively brainwashed the populace into believing that smoking within a half-mile radius of their offspring is tantamount to child abuse. But the man was also looking directly at me.

At first, and please don't laugh at my conceit, I thought he might just fancy me. After all, there was a time not so long ago when some men did find me attractive ('Gorgeous,' you whispered under your breath as I came in). Then I reminded myself of my unwashed hair, my too-baggy jeans, the sweatshirt of Daniel's that I've been wearing for the last four days and the tortoiseshell reading glasses I'd put on to read prices in the stationery shop and forgotten to take off. (Don't you hate that? That unignorable sign of encroaching age? The missing specs that turn out to be *on your eyes* the whole time?) And besides, there was nothing in the man's gaze to suggest appreciation. He gazed at me steadily but blankly, like I was some kind of digital billboard.

I hurried off in the direction of home, noticing that one of the laces of my tatty Converses had come undone, but feeling too self-conscious to bend to tie it up. When I passed the M&S food hall, I decided on an impulse to go inside. Normally Daniel does the food-shop, but he's much more of a basics kind of person, whereas as you know I like ready-made salads in little pots, and the kind of bread that goes stale in hours. I thought how nice it would be to get something for Jamie and Tilly that they'd really like. That would be the kind of thing a good mother would do, I thought.

But when I was inside, there was so much choice, I couldn't really get my head around it. I thought I might get them a pizza, but then what kind of pizza? Stone-baked, or thick dough, or a plain one to please Jamie, or one with roast vegetables on it, to contribute to their five a day? Or should I go for a ready-made pie? Lattice-topped? Chicken and leek? (Would Jamie notice the leek?) I took one look at the bread section and felt giddy. Irish brown soda? Sunflower seed? Bagels? Rye? In the end it was too much and I stumbled out empty-handed.

And there he was again! The same man as outside the stationery shop. Leaning against a car bonnet (there was a woman in the passenger seat who looked like she was about to spontaneously combust), staring at me.

I know you'll think I'm making it up, so I'll describe him to you. He was in his thirties, dark and quite thick-set, with that kind of close-cropped hair men choose when they're starting to go thin on top. He was wearing a black leather zip-up jacket with two cream-coloured stripes up the sleeves, and pale, artificially faded blue jeans, stretched too tight over his body-builder legs. On his feet he had a pair of dazzlingly white trainers with gold piping. His eyes looked black from where I was standing and, like I said, they were completely blank.

Is he starting to sound at all familiar, Clive? Might you have met him somewhere before? At an anniversary party for your hairdresser, perhaps?

I admit I started to feel very uncomfortable at that point. I wasn't scared exactly, because there were so many people around, but I was anxious. The thing is that recently there have been a couple of times when I've seen something, or thought I've seen something, that turned out not to be there. One time, when I was out with Sian, I thought I saw my brother across the bar, the one who lives in Edinburgh, but it turned out to be no one, a stranger who didn't even look anything like him. Another time, I went to pick Jamie up from his friend's house and after we'd said goodbye to his mother on the doorstep, I tried to get into this blue estate car parked outside and couldn't understand why my key wasn't working, then realized that not only was it not our car, but I hadn't even driven there in the first place! That was embarrassing, you can probably imagine.

So I didn't completely trust myself about the staring man, not even after I'd seen him for the second time. I began to walk home, concentrating on putting one foot in front of the other, which often helps, I find. Do you remember, it was quite sweaty weather today, clammy and wet like just-removed sports socks? I get very tired these days, and sometimes it's as much as I can do just to keep upright, so it took me ages to get to the corner of our road. When I did, I almost screamed out loud. Does that sound a bit too American B movie? Sorry, I don't know how else to put it. Because there he was again, that same dark, squat figure with his whiter-than-white trainers, standing in front of the gate to our house twenty-five metres away, just watching me come round the corner. I stood, absolutely transfixed just where I was, staring at him, just as he was staring at me. Can you imagine how we must have looked to anyone else? I dread to think.

God knows how long we remained like that before, cool and unhurried, he turned around and sauntered away from me in the opposite direction, up the street.

Still I didn't dare move, not until I'd watched him turn the corner at the far end, pausing briefly before he did so to give one last glance in my direction. Once I was sure he had disappeared, I hurried inside my house, grateful that I'd remembered to bring my keys. (Have I told you about the times I've forgotten them, twice in the last fortnight? The hunky Brazilian next door has had to let me in through his house into his back garden and give me a leg up on to the flat roof over our kitchen.) My heart was like a metronome in my chest, loud and painfully sharp, and I stood in our cluttered entrance hall (no ecru, just loads of shoes) trying to remember how to breathe. The house was empty, and I was longing to tell someone what had just happened. Well, obviously, when I say 'someone' I mean you. I was longing to tell *you*.

I rang your phone, for the first time in weeks. It went

straight to voicemail, just as I knew it would. (Do you remember when you first got that phone? 'Now we have a lifeline linking us night and day,' you'd said. 'I want you to know I will always be here for you. Nothing will ever change that.') Rushing to the cubbyhole, I sent you an email, headed 'URGENT'. After twenty agonizing minutes without a response, I gave in and phoned Susan. I knew that if she didn't have a pressing job ongoing, there was a good chance she'd be at home. It was the closest I could get to speaking to you.

She listened quietly while I explained what had happened, trying to keep my voice from quivering. When I'd finished, she was uncharacteristically silent. 'Have you called the police?' she asked me.

I was shocked when she said that. It had never occurred to me to phone the police. What would I have said? A man looked at me in the street? Then I saw him again outside my house? Again, there was a pause after I'd tried to explain all that. Finally Susan spoke, and she sounded strange, like a slowed-down version of herself.

'Look, dear, I know you've been under a lot of stress recently with Daniel and not working. Don't take this the wrong way, Sally, but don't you think you should be seeing someone?'

You know what's funny? When she said that, at first I thought she meant seeing someone as in dating! I really did! I couldn't see what the connection was between the man who followed me and me having an affair. Then it dawned on me that she meant a shrink, or a therapist. Someone like Helen Bunion.

'I'm not mad, you know, Susan,' I said, conscious of the slight warble in my voice. 'It really happened.'

Susan sighed loudly. 'I'm sure it seemed that way,' she said kindly. 'And I'm sure it must have felt very scary at the time. But you know sometimes when you're under a lot of pressure, quite innocuous things can seem threatening. You really should see someone. You've not been yourself.' (And yet again that expression. But if I wasn't myself, I wanted to ask her, who else was I?)

I didn't tell her I was already 'seeing someone'. Don't ask me why, but I didn't want to share Helen with Susan. Helen is my own private thing. I don't want to hand her around like a bowl of greasy peanuts.

Susan got a bit more animated once she'd decided I needed to see someone. She likes to have a mission, doesn't she? Likes to be able to provide a practical solution.

'Leave it with me, I'll ask around and get you some numbers,' she said.

I told her we couldn't afford therapy (and it's true, Helen is a luxury, like quilted toilet paper) but she pooh-poohed me.

'Don't worry, I'll tell them you're on a budget.'

Value Counselling. It's very apt.

'The thing is, Sally,' she went on, 'you must see that it doesn't really make sense, all of this. Why would a perfect stranger stare you out in the street, and then be waiting for you outside your house as though he knew where you lived? It's not very *likely*, is it?'

I had to admit, when she put it like that, it wasn't very likely.

Not unless someone was trying to scare me.

And who would be trying to scare me?

I wish you'd been there, Clive, on the end of that phone

that was to be our lifeline. Am I going crazy, or was he real, that man with the black dead eyes?

The only one who knows is you.

When I went back to the computer just now, I saw that you had finally replied to my email marked URGENT.

In response to my message saying 'Something has happened. Please call me!' you had written just four words. *Leave my family alone.*

Did I invent it all, those mornings (not many to show for five years together, it's true) when I'd wake up to find you lying propped up on your elbow? 'I love to watch you sleep,' you'd say. 'I love watching over you.' Was it all in my head? Your melting eyes? Your trembling hands?

'People move on,' Helen keeps telling me. 'It doesn't mean they weren't ever sincere.'

People move on. I accept that. But what if they've promised to love you for ever? What if they've told you they'll never leave you? What if they've lied and lied and lied again?

Shouldn't people be held to account for that?

Underneath the email from you was one from Emily. I clicked it open to find a rather limp sort of thank-you message. It didn't even specify what she was thanking me for, just a generic 'thank you for your lovely gift'. It was clearly a round-robin message she was sending to all her baby-shower guests and not one that required any response. Still, I found myself double-clicking on 'reply'.

It was so lovely to see you the other day. I know how

long this last stretch of pregnancy can seem. Why don't you and your mum come round for lunch one day next week? Tuesday?

I put in the bit about Tuesday because I wanted to give the impression that some days of the week might be a little more convenient than other days. I didn't want them to know how the days of the week now blur together into one big long sea of empty hours. Once I'd clicked 'send' I felt lighter than I had in days, stronger.

Do you think that's what Helen means by owning my own actions? I do hope so. I want Helen to be pleased.

* * *

The weekends are the worst.

During the week I know there's a good chance you'll be working on your own in your box room (sad fuck in a box), or holding a meeting in your Fitzrovia office, or impressing a new signing with lunch at Le Gavroche.

But the weekends are a different matter.

It starts on a Friday night. I imagine you and Susan meeting after work at the Coach and Horses, or one of the half-dozen private members' clubs you belong to. Possibly you'd each bring a posse from your respective offices, young things usually, who hold you and Susan up as a shining example of everything they aspire to be when they're that old. (Though in reality, of course, they don't believe they will get old. Age is a hypothetical impossibility, like winning the Lottery – they know it happens, just not to them.)

You and Susan would display your fabled largesse, buying everyone drinks, dispensing advice and sympathy, being loud and funny with just the right amount of affectionate putting each other down.

'Aren't they amazing?' they'll ask each other. 'They've been together over a quarter of a century!'

It will seem like an impossibility to them, these young things who probably weren't even born when you and Susan posed for photos on the registry office steps. It will seem a freak happening, like a tsunami or a snowstorm in May.

And you will lap it up, the two of you reflected back to yourselves through all these young eyes. Then the Susan and Clive Show will get louder and wittier. You'll probably take them to the Met Bar to show off how many celebrity has-beens you know.

You'll end up piling home in a taxi with Susan, drunk on your own vitality.

Saturdays are worse. Then my imagination has you waking Susan up late with the papers and a breakfast tray, balancing it next to her on your huge white bed. Then you'll climb back in beside her and the two of you will flick through the supplements, making each other laugh with crass headlines or funny stories about people you know.

You'll get up and potter off to Borough Market. Probably you'll have people coming round for dinner and Susan, queen of her own kitchen, will already know exactly what she wants to prepare. (How I long to be one of those women who opens kitchen cupboards without a sense of trepidation, one of those who actually claims a proprietorial relationship with her appliances – 'My oven is self-cleaning', 'I couldn't live without my blender.') The two of you will walk hand in hand through the packed stalls, and you'll hold the shopping bag (I imagine it to be one of those worthy hessian things with the long handles) while Susan piles in fillets of fish wrapped in waxy paper and oversized vegetables and runny cheese that smells like old dishwater. It doesn't matter that it all costs five times the amount you'd pay in the supermarket. You like the atmosphere of the place, and the way you always seem to bump into someone you know.

Then later, Susan will start preparing dinner while you tidy up a bit (you love having Liam still living at home, but that boy has never learned to clean up after himself, you used to complain). Then you'll both get ready, and you'll tell her she looks beautiful, even though she's probably just put on a different navy dress to replace the one she was wearing this morning. Your guests will arrive – probably other successful couples like yourselves. You'll eat dinner, gush about Susan's food, and laugh loudly at one another's jokes. Then, when the plates are cleared from the blond-wood square table, someone might put out a few small lines of coke to prove you're all still young at heart, and when all the guests have gone you and Susan will dissect the evening, and work out who was damaged and who wasn't, and fall asleep back to back, but still holding each other's hand.

Sunday, of course, is family day. Emily and her bland barrister husband will come for lunch, and Liam will produce whichever Sloaney girlfriend he has on the go. You'll sit around in the light-filled kitchen or, if the weather's good, around the teak table in the garden. Liam will poke fun at Emily's pregnancy. Emily will pretend to be cross. Susan will placate, placate. You will tell amusing stories about the micro-celebs you have met.

The papers will be read, two or three bottles of good Chablis will be drunk and you'll think to yourself, 'I nearly lost this. What a fool I've been. What an idiot, what a prick.'

Helen says I must stop this endless projecting about your life. She says I must stop eulogizing it and try to remember all the times you complained about how dull weekends were, with your dull friends and your dull, dull routine. She says I must take the energy I'm expending on imagining your life and invest it back into mine. I must stop thinking of your family, she tells me, and start thinking about my own.

But weekends in my house are small, mean things where people sniff blindly around each other like laboratory mice.

'Can we go somewhere today, like *normal* families do?' Tilly asked earlier today, while we sat eating cheese sandwiches for lunch.

To be fair, Daniel's look of dismay was fairly fleeting (as opposed to mine, I fear).

'Of course we can go somewhere, sweetie,' he said, throwing me a loaded glance that could have had any number of meanings. 'Where would you like to go?'

But Tilly couldn't think of where she wanted to go, and Jamie wanted to stay home and play Modern Warfare 2.

'I'll stay with Jamie and you two go out,' I said, trying not to sound too eager. 'What's on at the cinema?'

Tilly looked at me scathingly.

'Don't bother,' she said.

Don't laugh, but sometimes, Clive, I feel I'm not equipped to cope with the teenage years. It's like I've only done the introductory course, got the grade 1 certificate, but now we're getting on to intermediate territory and I'm hopelessly out of my depth. I know you've already successfully negotiated all of this. Do you remember how you used to tell me you were so glad you'd be around to give me advice when I reached this stage? Do you remember that, Clive?

In the end, nobody went out today and Tilly spent the afternoon in her room on Facebook while I shut myself up in the cubbyhole and surfed definitions of 'broken-hearted' on the net.

* * *

Before Susan and Emily arrived for lunch today, I sat down at my computer as always.

Can you imagine my surprise when, in place of the usual '0 messages' in my inbox, there were eleven bold new messages, waiting for me like Christmas presents under the tree?

Finally, I thought, my luck is changing. I believe in luck a lot more these days, incidentally. I always used to dismiss it, do you remember? 'You make your own luck,' I used to declare. But now I'm not so sure. Now I think luck might be one of those things like curly hair that just happen to you, whether you like it or not. It's quite a comforting thought, in a strange way.

So there I was, naively excited at the sudden riches in my inbox. But as I opened them, I began to feel ever so slightly sick.

They were all from clients of mine, magazines and websites I've written for before and cultivated over the years, and one after another they all said the same thing: 'We're sorry you feel that way. Our working relationship is now at an end.'

Thank God for the happy pills! While on one guttural level I absolutely knew something awful had happened and that whatever it was, it spelled disaster for me, it was as if I was absorbing all this information through a filter, so that by the time it arrived in my brain it was already watery and tepid.

Most of the messages were replies to an email I seem to have sent to all the people on my 'work contacts' list. I read it with an almost dispassionate interest, as if it was written by someone else (which, come to think of it, was partly true!).

As before, the message that had been sent out was an old one which I had once sent to a friend, also a freelance writer, to whom I often used to moan about work.

I won't bore you by copying out the whole thing (and I suspect it's probably unnecessary anyway, hey, Clive?), save to say that it started off by me ranting about how bored I was with freelancing, and how idiotic most of the commissioning editors were, and how I couldn't be bothered to even pretend to be interested any more. 'I just do it on autopilot and think of the money.' I went on to list some of the ways in which I'd been cutting corners – sloppily copying out chunks from old newspaper cuttings and telling commissioning editors that certain experts were 'impossible to get' when really I just couldn't be bothered. Then I'd gone on to slag off particular publications and personnel for being 'tight-fisted' or 'moronic' or, in one inspired instance, 'insufferably bland'. That's when the sender of the message had been particularly clever, personalizing each message by substituting the name of the addressee. (That personal touch is so important, wouldn't you say?)

The final paragraph had me recounting a particularly unedifying personal anecdote about how I'd gone out the week before with a (named) contact who was deputy editor on a magazine and we'd had a meal and three bottles of expensive wine on her expense account and she'd been sick into her handbag on the way home.

Needless to say, as I cast my eye down the list of unread messages (which, by the way, seemed to be growing by the minute), there was one from her as well.

Isn't it funny how you can spend twenty years building up a career and pffff, it's over in a heartbeat, vanished into nothingness just like the baby that never was?

I sat wedged into my cubbyhole and tried to summon up a sense of outrage, but to be honest, there was little forthcoming. To tell you the truth, I won't miss it – the phone interviews scribbled down on the backs of envelopes because I've run out of notebooks, the greasy begging phone calls to commissioning editors, the endless quest to find a new angle on the same tired old ideas.

I tried to put a positive spin on the whole sorry situation and not think about the wider economic implications of my sudden enforced unemployment or of the unopened official letters already piling up in the drawer. Only when I thought about you, Clive, did the pharmaceutically generated equanimity begin to falter.

I imagined you sitting down at your own oak desk in your glass-sided Fitzrovia office and, just as I had done, clicking on to your inbox, where I know you routinely find upwards of one hundred emails have accumulated overnight – invitations, interview requests, approaches from managers. 'It's such a bore,' you used to groan theatrically. 'I don't want to deal with any of it, all I want to do is spend the day emailing you.'

I imagined you getting down to the business of the day, the business of making money and being Clive Gooding, and I couldn't help but make a few comparisons.

I bet you don't have a drawer piled high with letters you're too scared to open! ('Oh, I just send all that sort of boring stuff to my accountant. Life's too short!') I bet your career hasn't been put through the shredder, I bet your children aren't blithely going about their business unaware of the axe of homelessness dangling over their heads. I bet you don't lie awake in the night compiling lists of saleable assets (few).

That's when the acid began to rise and the palpitations to flutter. Even now, seven hours later, I still feel that gorge rising and have had to do lots of highly focused breathing to try to sink it down again. *Breathe in, stomach out; breathe out, stomach in.*

Tell me something, Clive. How is it that every time I think I have nothing left to lose, I lose something more?

So, it's fair to say I was not in the best frame of mind to have Susan and Emily round for lunch. They arrived separately, Emily first. The poor girl was quite flushed, despite that cool breeze we had today. It seemed my neighbourhood had made her nervous. Walking past a group of 'hoodies' on the corner of the next street, she'd felt so intimidated she'd had to zip her Balenciaga handbag right up and hug it to her chest.

'A woman in my condition is so vulnerable,' she told me, as if explaining something to a foreigner. I didn't like to remind her that I'd been in her condition twice myself. Perhaps she thinks people like me subscribe to a different condition altogether, with a completely different experience of pregnancy. Are there different classes of pregnancy in Emily World, do you think? What an interesting view of me she must have!

Susan was late and appeared a bit out of sorts.

'I really should be doing some work,' she told me. 'I'm surprised you have the time to have leisurely lunches, Sally.'

That was quite ironic in the circumstances, wouldn't you say?

I went to the expensive deli yesterday (I can't face M&S after the last time), so I'd bought loads of food for lunch – lovely Greek salad, couscous with roasted veg, goat's cheese tart, ciabatta, a whole plate heaped with cold meats, humous, olives. Then, while I'd been queuing to pay, I'd tossed into the trolley a couple of packs of sushi, some ready-made quiche and a raspberry cheesecake. (I'm finding it difficult to estimate quantities at the moment, or assess what goes with what. Perhaps you'd already noticed?)

'Oh, I didn't know there'd be food.' That was Emily, of course. 'I've already eaten. I have to be so careful about my diet at the moment. Little and often.'

Curious to think what Emily's definition of 'lunch' is, if it doesn't involve food.

So Susan and I ate, or tried to eat, the obscenely over-laden spread – the sweaty quiche, and rubbery goat's cheese tart, the ciabatta so sharp-crusted it cut the roof of my mouth, the oily Greek salad and coagulating couscous. I thought about dinners I've had at your house, where Susan has effortlessly served up vast platters of filo parcels and exotic salads with bits of fruit in, and vats of liqueur-soaked fresh cream trifle. It was not my finest hour.

Emily looked a bit horrified by my house. I don't know whether she's ever visited someone who doesn't have a cleaner before. I tried to look at it through her eyes (there I go again, with my automatic empathizing reflex), and I could see why she might be slightly alarmed. I did try to clean up the kitchen this morning, but got sidetracked by the email nightmare, so there were still piles of unwashed plates in the sink (we do have a dishwasher, I hasten to add, it's just that nobody seems capable of emptying it). The floor was OK, I think, as Daniel had vacuumed in there just a few days ago, but there were a couple of sticky patches where Jamie had spilled orange juice and, of course, Emily happened to tread in those, so her dainty little ballet pumps stuck to the floor and made a rather horrible squelching noise when she pulled them unstuck.

I blamed it all on the kids, and swore the place had been spotless a couple of days ago, which isn't entirely a lie. Well, OK, it is a lie, but it had been much better, at least. I was glad she didn't look in the living room, and rather apprehensive about what she'd find in the bathroom. I did mean to clean the toilet, but it just went clean out of my head. The drugs do that, I find. Funny, because when I first started on the happy pills, I had a massive influx of manic energy and started jumping up to mop the floors in the middle of the afternoon, but these days I don't have the energy even to notice the dirt, let alone do anything about it.

I needn't have worried, because after a mercifully toilet-free hour, Emily announced she was going to meet a friend to go shopping.

'I have absolutely nothing that fits me,' she said with a mock wail. 'I'm the size of a house.'

I think that was probably my cue to contradict her, but do you know, I just couldn't be bothered? I think that emailing business must have been weighing on me more heavily than I'd thought.

After Emily had left (don't worry, she got a cab. After her nasty experience with the hoodies, she wasn't taking any more chances), Susan and I fell into a dispirited torpor.

Susan seemed anxious that I shouldn't form the wrong opinion of Emily. 'She can seem like a complete snob, but she's got a big heart,' she assured me. I was quite flattered that she minded what I thought, but then Susan said gently that she felt I'd been a little 'short' with Emily. That was her exact word: 'short'.

I was quite taken aback when she said that, I have to say. I don't think I was 'short' with Emily at all, and though as Susan pointed out I had called her anally retentive, it must have been quite obvious to everyone that I meant it as a joke. Please don't take this the wrong way, but is Susan sometimes just a little slow in getting things?

While we were having a coffee (how embarrassing that I offered her filter coffee before realizing we only had instant. I don't think she noticed, though), Susan told me that she had a few numbers for me, of people I could 'talk to' – my Budget Counselling is what she meant, not the

Samaritans or anything (I hope!). I think she might have been expecting a bit more gratitude, but, do you know what, I just wasn't in the mood. I don't need to fucking talk to anyone, I need to have my fucking life back. And do you know who has my fucking life? Susan, that's who.

Breathe in, stomach out; breathe out, stomach in.

I changed the subject by quite abruptly asking about you and her and about how the hysterical bonding was going. I am nothing if not a masochist. (Sometimes I think I'd like to take the sharp end of Tilly's compass and jab it again and again into the skin of my upper leg. Through the denim of my jeans. Do you ever get that feeling?)

If Susan was surprised by my sudden change of tack, she didn't say so.

'I actually think we've reached a completely new stage in our relationship,' she said. 'We're so honest with each other now. Sometimes I think we had to go through all that shit earlier in the year, just to get to where we are now.'

Then she went on to confide that just a few months ago things had got so bad between you that you'd talked about moving out.

'I even thought at one stage that Clive could be having an affair,' Susan told me.

Can you believe that? She actually said that to me. That she thought you might be having an affair! (Remember how you professed to hate that word 'affair'? 'That's not how I feel about you,' you said. 'I feel *married* to you.')

Of course, I asked her – well, you'd have done the same. I asked whether she still thought there was any possibility of that.

Susan shook her head, white-blonde bob shimmering like cheap tinsel.

'He swore on my life that he hadn't,' she told me. 'And I believe him. Clive is a lot of things, but he's not an out-and-out liar. He knows my feelings about that. If I thought he'd slept with someone else, he'd be out. Simple as that.'

Hear that, Clive? Simple as that.

So then I did the thing that you're probably not going to like. In my defence, I was still quite churned up about the career-sabotaging emails and Emily and the whole thing. So – and please try to understand just a little bit – I told Susan about an article I'd seen in one of the papers recently that she might find interesting. An affair diary. Now, before you start, I didn't tell her where I'd seen it. I'm not that stupid. I just told her she might quite like to read it. What are the chances that she'll actually go to the trouble of Googling it, hey? And even if she did, she wouldn't put two and two together. I'm sure you're perfectly safe.

Still, I did regret it rather, once I'd closed the door to her. I don't know what came over me, I really don't, blurting it out like that. But rest assured, Clive, I'll be bringing it up with Helen. Clearly there's still much work to be done!

Another sleepless night. I'm thinking about Susan's face when she said that thing about you not being a liar. I'm thinking how much I regret that hurting you involves hurting her. I'm thinking about the line between love and hate and how you couldn't fit one of Tilly's baby-fine hairs between the two. I'm thinking about what we've done to each other and to everyone else. I'm thinking about you. Always about you.

* * *

I can't claim it was altogether a surprise to hear from you this morning. I knew you'd be cross. But really I had no idea you'd be *that* cross. How could I have guessed Susan would go home and look that affair diary feature up? I mean, would you? She must have been very bored last night. Couldn't you have kept her more occupied? Wasn't there some hysterical bonding you could have been getting on with? I told you she wouldn't put two and two together, though. She'd definitely have said something if she had. Yes, I know you said she gave you a 'funny look', but you're inclined to be paranoid. I think it's fine, I really do. But of course I can't pretend not to be excited that you've finally suggested meeting up, even if it's only for you to get 'heavy' with me. ('I don't want to get heavy with you,' you said in that blood money email – remember?) I have a feeling there are going to be a few threats made (yours) and maybe a few tears shed (mine). It will be the first time I've seen you in five months (I don't count that glimpse of you in the Tube station ticket hall, your smile for Susan, your arm around her shoulders).

'We have to sort this out once and for all,' you thundered down the phone this morning, and while I was a bit shocked to hear the naked hatred in your voice, I have to confess I was a tiny bit thrilled as well. It was the indifference that had been hurting more than anything, you see. It was the way you said, 'I'm sorry you're feeling so dreadful,' as if my feeling dreadful was a completely separate thing to how you were feeling, as if the one had no bearing on the other, as if your feelings were suddenly your own private concern. So hearing your feelings so clearly in your voice, knowing I'd provoked some feeling – any feeling – in you, felt good. Call me silly, but the hatred that glinted in your voice, like grit catching the sun, felt like progress.

And so we're to meet up on Thursday. I can hardly believe it. I've got nothing to wear. My clothes lie in an unwashed heap behind the door of our bedroom, while I wear the same jeans and sweatshirt day in, day out. Even if I washed them, they'd still smell of failure. I need something new, something untainted. I'm going to go into the West End and hit the shops. I'm only forty-three years old, for goodness' sake – plenty of time for jeans and sweatshirts when I'm sixty, or seventy. I have a new credit card Daniel doesn't know about. Do you remember I got it just before York Way Friday, so that I could book hotels without it showing up on the joint account statement? Not that Daniel ever pays much attention to that sort of thing, but better safe than sorry, hey? Of course, you could never risk anything like that, not with Susan keeping such a close eye on the family finances. ('Money is so boring,' you used to say. '£50 or £500, it makes no difference to me.')

My new credit card has a limit of £2,000. Even better, I know that none of the unopened letters in the drawer have this company's logo emblazoned across the top. It's like a clean slate. I can start over. And it's not as if it's an indulgence. Buying new clothes will make me feel better. I feel better already, to be honest, just thinking about it. New clothes, new me. I'll have more energy, I'll be able to tackle work again. I'll find some new publications to work for, ones I haven't burned my bridges with. I feel like things can change. I feel there's a chance my life can move forward. Thursday beckons me on, alternately teasing and threatening. In forty-eight hours, I'll be heading off to Piccadilly Circus (not Horsham or Borehamwood or any of the other 'safe' but soulless places we used to frequent. I've been upgraded!) to meet you in a pub with a (hopefully) secluded upper level. I know I'll be shaking with nerves. I hope you'll try to be kind. I know you're only meeting up to warn me off, but I need to remind you of why you loved me. I need to know you still want me (even reluctantly). I need to see myself reflected back in your eyes so that I know I am still real.

Helen says my needs are just wants in disguise. Helen doesn't know how it feels to be me.

* * *

I am not in a good state.

I couldn't sleep last night (surprise, surprise), just like the night before, and took a last-minute emergency zaleplon at 3 a.m. which gave me strange vivid dreams where I kept going up and down in lifts and trying to find you. (Sorry. Is there anything duller than other people's dreams?) When I woke up I felt clammy and out of breath, and my heart was still searching.

As my concession to economy, I went to the chemist and brought home waxing strips rather than the expensive trips to the salon I used to make. Don't worry, I'm not presuming anything will happen. I know you won't be seeing my bare legs, but it's impossible to feel like a woman of worth when you know your legs are furry beneath your clothes and your bikini line is creeping steadily southward. The waxing strips hurt, especially under the arms (don't even ask about the bikini line), but it was a good clean pain, the kind that has a beginning and an end.

After I'd finished, I looked at my naked self in the

full-length mirror for the first time in months and saw myself through your eyes – thin and sallow and smudged with shadows. My legs, where I'd waxed them, were pimpled with a red rash and elsewhere my skin hung loose like a crumpled paper bag.

I am filled with excitement about seeing you tonight, but at the same time filled with dread. I need you to love me. I need you to want me. My needs are wants in disguise, said Helen. But I need those wants beyond all other things.

I started getting ready almost as soon as the kids went off to school. Pathetic, isn't it? You don't have to tell me that. Believe me, I know.

After the home waxing, I dyed my roots. Finally! You wouldn't believe how much grey I'd allowed to grow like a badger stripe down my parting. No wonder Stupid Pete hadn't been able to perform. But let's try not to think about him, shall we? I don't like to think about him.

The colour my hair came out didn't look much like the colour on the packet, I have to say. It was supposed to be Iced Chocolate, but it has turned out a rather dull mousy brown and I have managed to dye the tip of my ear as well. I'm grateful for your failing eyesight. Hopefully you won't notice all my imperfections. As long as your vanity keeps your glasses away, I'll look mercifully airbrushed and permanently in soft focus.

Please be kind. Please be kind.

Sian was furious when I told her I was meeting you, even though I explained you'd only suggested it so that you could have a go at me. Now that she has turned against you, she is like a reformed smoker – as vehement in her disapprobation as she once was in her delight. Your deception has upset her beyond mere loyalty to me. I think you and I were proving some sort of point in her mind. She wanted to believe in the supremacy of love affairs, and finds it bitterly disappointing that in the end it should be the mundanity of marriage that triumphs.

'Haven't you put yourself through enough?' she asked me. 'You'll be right back to square one.'

I didn't tell her that square one looked preferable to where I am now. (Square five? Seven? Ten?)

'Don't worry, I have no expectations except the worst,' I told her, blatantly lying.

'He's a cunt,' she said suddenly. I was quite shocked, I really was. Sian has an exaggerated Catholic streak running through her and doesn't normally use words like that. I wonder if you'd be hurt, if you knew what she'd said? You always pretend to love it when people are abusive to you, but I suspect you'd be a little bit wounded. I think you secretly believed Sian had a soft spot for you.

'It's OK,' I lied again. 'I know he's only coming to tell me to stay away from Susan and Emily. You know how paranoid he is. I'm not expecting anything.'

But still I couldn't help adding: 'What do you think I should wear?'

She refused to answer and when she put the phone down shortly afterwards, her righteous anger hung around in the air like a bad smell. But it didn't matter, because I already knew what I was going to wear. I bought a dress yesterday, black and clingy and satin-shiny with a zip all the way up the back. And then I bought the shoes to go with it – four-inch black wedges that give me slight vertigo when I walk. I'll wear an old jean jacket with it so that it doesn't look like I'm trying too hard. Of course you'll see right through it like a shot.

You'll know it is all for you. All of it.

The question is, will you want it?

Half an hour earlier than I need to leave, but I'm going in a minute, just to get out of the house. Bloody Daniel. Bloody fucking Daniel. When was the last time he expressed an interest in where I'm going? Normally he hardly looks up when I say I'm going out these days. In the beginning he used to at least ask me about my plans (not so much because he was bothered about the answers, but just in the same way as you'd make conversation with one of your children – the point being in the conversation rather than in the answers). Actually, when I think about it, in those early days we might well have been going out together. I often forget about that – those early evenings standing side by side at the sink, sharing the mirror – him to shave, me to apply make-up – chatting companionably. Now those two people no longer seem real, characters in a film I once watched (something starring Meg Ryan?). He hasn't appeared interested in my whereabouts for ages. So why does he have to start asking me questions tonight?

I suppose it must be the clothes. After all these weeks of me slouching around the house in ever baggier jeans and sweatshirts, it must be a bit of a shock to the system – the heels, the dress, the absence of badger stripe, the full slap covering up the worst of the dark shadows, the tell-tale eagerness after all these weeks of lethargy.

It didn't help that Tilly trumpeted it in advance.

'Mum looks like she's going to a Goth wedding,' she said, dropping down on the sofa next to Daniel.

Daniel looked up then, and there I was in my finery, dandified and faintly ridiculous.

Daniel's eyes travelled over me, from the new shoes to the new dress and the new hair.

'You've been shopping,' he said. And his voice sounded like a slap.

'I've had this for ages,' I lied, tugging at the new dress as if it was a rag. 'I just haven't ever worn it.'

Daniel gave me a look I've never really seen before. Tight and hard.

'Where are you going?' he asked, in that same stinging voice.

I got angry then, when he said that. It's not his right to ask me, is it? But Tilly was sitting there and I had to say something, so I made up a story about Gill who I used to work with, and how it was her leaving party. Even as the words were leaving my mouth, they converted to hollow things that bounced empty through the air.

'I don't want you to go.'

I think Daniel even surprised himself when he said that, there was a little giveaway widening of the eyes, but he didn't back down.

'I have to go. They're expecting me.'

Bounce, bounce, bounce.

Jamie glanced up from the floor, where he was lying watching the telly.

'You've done something to your hair,' he said. 'It's younger than your face.'

I pretended to find that amusing, but Daniel didn't crack a smile.

'I have to go,' I repeated lamely. 'I can't let them down.'

'What about us?' asked Daniel. 'What about letting us down?'

You know what's funny? As he said that, I felt a stab of

pure panic that I couldn't immediately place. Then I realized it was because he was looking at me – I mean actually looking at me. Into my eyes. It occurs to me now that it must be months, even years, since either of us did that. The whole eye-contact thing. It felt like an invasion. Plus it was so annoying, him putting me on the spot like that in front of the children. It's not as if I'm always going out somewhere. I hardly ever leave the fucking house.

'You're being ridiculous,' I said, and turned on my lofty heel and teetered back up the stairs. So here I am, far too early, but already desperate to leave. What gives him the right to question where I'm going? What gives him the right to make me feel guilty?

Already I feel like a cheap present wrapped in expensive paper, with my young hair and my old face. I'm trying to claw back some of that good feeling I had earlier when I first got dressed and everything felt full of promise, but it's gone now. In its place is this anger. Why does Daniel always spoil everything? Am I not allowed one single thing for myself?

Right. I'm leaving now, before my nerves fail me. I won't even say goodbye. I'll just call out from the door.

I don't want them to see me go. They always have to try to spoil things.

I'm only going to meet you. It's not a big deal.

Why do they have to make such a fuss?

I won't think about it. I'll just think about nice things. In forty-five minutes I will see you. In forty-five minutes you will see me.

You will see me.

* * *

I have been up since 6 a.m. despite my hangover. Only when I'd been up a while did I realize I had slept without sleeping pills for the first time in months. I've cleaned the kitchen, and made Jamie and Tilly packed lunches. I had to think hard to remember whether Jamie prefers chicken or ham. I wonder who has been making their packed lunches recently. I suppose it must be Daniel.

You're going to think me silleeeee, but memories of last night crowd around my head like Smarties, one on top of the other on top of the other, each one brightly coloured and candy-sweet. Even the images from the early part of the evening, when your anger volleyed from you like machine-gun fire, are soft-edged and sepia-toned.

You'll never know how nervous I was loitering in Boots in Piccadilly Circus until I was just respectably late. I hovered around the make-up counters, sneaking glances in the smudgy mirrors under the pretext of testing out a new eyeshadow or wonder-concealer. How many times did I wish I'd worn something different? Or had my hair professionally coloured? Or splashed out on Botox? Or not got old? Every few seconds I glanced at my phone to check the time and tried to plot your movements. You'd be just arriving (you never could bear to be late), you'd be canvassing the bar, getting a drink.

When I was finally standing outside the pub, my courage almost went AWOL. Really it did. The downstairs bar was full of twentysomething media-types, and my teetering wedge heels made me feel like a fraud, like I was trying to be something I wasn't, a man in drag.

At the top of the stairs I hesitated, trying to compose a face to greet you. How did I look coming through that door? I'd gone for cheery casual. Did it work? Were you taken in? Or could you see, from your seat at a little round table near the wall, my heart slamming itself against my chest?

As soon as I sat down, I understood two things: a) you were angrier than I'd even imagined, and b) you still wanted me.

Does that sound big-headed? It isn't meant to. It's just that I was so worried that your eyes would be blank, like they were on York Way Friday, all feeling drained from them like parched soil. But as soon as I came near you, the smile dying on my face as I met your clench-lipped gaze, I knew you still wanted me. That's something one just can't hide.

There are so many things I want to ask you. What you were feeling at that moment. What you thought when I was approaching you. Whether the anger that had been coursing round your system dissipated away so you had to make a conscious effort to regenerate it. I want to relive every moment of last night, every second, every nano-second. I want to brand it on to my memory with a white-hot poker.

I love you I love you I love you.

I don't mind telling you I was apprehensive at first. Antagonism came wafting off you like sweat.

'You have got to stop this.'

Do you remember, that was the very first thing you said to me? We'll laugh about it one day, of course, but still it took me aback. I hadn't even sat down, was still fishing around in my bag so I could go and buy a drink.

'What?' I asked you. Clever, wasn't it? All the opening

lines I'd been rehearsing in the Tube on the way, and that's the one I came out with. 'What?'

Silleeeee Salleeeee.

That's when you started laying into me. About Susan, and Emily, and even Liam (for goodness' sake!). You mentioned that comment on your company website. Well, when you put it all together like that, of course it was going to sound a bit unhinged. The way you said it, it sounded like I was a mad stalker or something!

I sat silently and listened, and didn't say anything. Instead I let your words flow over me like I was submerging my head in a warm, soapy bath, not really taking it in, but looking at your eyes, and wondering what it meant that you were saying all this stuff and yet your eyes were saying something else.

You'd bought a bottle of white wine, which we'd finished before you'd even reached the website bit. You stood up without even breaking your flow, then stopped suddenly.

'Another?' you asked.

I didn't want you to think I was a pushover, wanted to prove I still knew my own mind (foolish, foolish woman – when did I ever know my own mind?) so I asked for a whisky, a double. When you came back you were carrying two.

As we drank, you expanded on your theme, that I was harassing your family, that I'd gone too far. I looked at your mouth as you spoke and traced your lips in my mind. Could you see I was doing that? Did my eyes give me away?

Somewhere around the second double whisky I tried to explain myself. You'd got it wrong, I told you. You were misinterpreting the facts. York Way Friday had knocked me for six. (I think I may even have used that expression – for the first time in my life. You'll have to forgive me. I was over-wrought!) I'd wanted to stay close to you, which is why I'd made that first call to Susan, but the rest had happened organically. (I think I used that word too. God, I'm embarrassed to remember it all.) And the website comment hadn't been me. Had definitely not been me.

'I've also been under stress,' I told you, not meeting your eyes. 'Some weird things have been happening.' Then I told you about the emails, and the man with the stripes on his leather jacket. You didn't say anything, but I knew you were taking it all in.

By the time we were halfway through the third whisky (or was it the fourth?) I could tell you were mellowing. Your sentences still began with a bluster but it blew itself out before reaching the end.

'I should go,' you said. But we both knew you wouldn't.

'You're looking good,' you told me reluctantly, your eyes travelling over me. 'Susan said you were too thin, but I think it quite suits you.'

I looked at your hand, as it lay on the table between us, tearing a cardboard coaster to shreds. Your fingers were so familiar. I imagined reaching over and putting my hand over yours.

Then all of a sudden, my hand *was* on top of yours. I couldn't remember moving it there, it just seemed to have happened.

There was a split second where we both just looked at our joined hands on the table, as if they didn't belong to us at all, but were some kind of pop-up art installation. I think we were both waiting to see if you would move yours away. When you didn't, I knew. But really I'd known from the start.

Who was it who suggested going to a hotel? I know it doesn't matter now, but I hate to think there are parts of last night I can't remember. I want to play it all again and again like a YouTube clip. I want to relive every second.

I remember the taxi was abnormally large, and we giggled a lot about how big it was. Then we were in one hotel, and the cheapest room was £270, and between us we didn't have enough cash (not even the cash from the fridge – you hadn't been prepared!). You didn't dare use your credit card (not with Eagle Eyed Susan doing the household accounts) and I hadn't brought my one credit card that was still working. We tried to get money from a cashpoint in the lobby, I remember, but it kept saying 'error'.

'Eees faulty,' said a man in a corporate blue suit, in a strong Spanish accent.

We found that hysterical, I remember. 'Eees faulty,' we repeated to ourselves until we were almost crying.

Then we were in another taxi, a different one.

'Take us to a hotel,' you told the driver, imperiously. 'But make sure it doesn't cost more than £187.75.'

Do you remember saying that? I don't think I've ever heard anything quite so funny.

The second hotel had a basement floor with windowless rooms at a discounted rate.

'Eighty-nine pounds?' you queried. 'That's a bargain.' So we bought a bottle of champagne from the hotel bar with all the money we'd saved.

And in the room, it was just like we'd never been apart. Your tongue, your mouth, your body (substantially more of it than before, I thought, the fleshy evidence of too much celebrating). I was glad I'd waxed my legs, glad I'd put on my best pants. 'It's you, it's you,' I kept saying. You must have thought I was mad!

Now, you mustn't mind about that first time, Clive. Really, it doesn't make any difference to me. We were both nervous. How could we not be? And we'd had so much to drink. It was lovely just to lie there holding each other, wasn't it? It didn't matter about the bits that went soft when they should have been hard, or stayed dry when they were supposed to be wet. The only thing that counts is that we loved each other, and that we laughed. 'I love you,' I said, and your eyes said everything that your lips couldn't.

'I've missed this,' you told me later, as we lay on the bed, each bit of us entwined together.

'I've missed you too,' I said.

I'd turned my phone off, but yours was set to vibrate. When it seemed as if the whole bed was shaking with the frequency of your vibrations, we peeled ourselves out of the sheets and went to the shower. How many times have we stood that way before in how many different hotel rooms, water dripping into eyes and from hair, hands soaping under arms, between legs?

When we got dressed I couldn't stop smiling. I steered you in front of the mirror and leaned against you. 'Look at us,' I said. 'We're perfect.'

Of course we weren't at all – you just a little too short, me a little too spiky. But for a second, we blended in together with the moment and it was really perfect.

We said goodbye outside on the main road and you flagged a taxi down for me.

'Let's not spoil tonight with heavy goodbyes,' you said.

I think I laughed, didn't I? How could such a night be spoiled? Anyway, goodbyes don't have to be heavy when they just segue straight into anticipation of the next meeting. All the way home, I smiled. The taxi driver must have thought I was bonkers. 'Good night?' he asked, rather pointedly.

When I got your text making sure I was nearly home, the warmth spread through me like Deep Heat rub. I've missed that so much, you know? Having you worry about me.

Right up until the moment I stepped into our cluttered hallway, my mind was wholly and completely occupied by you. Even the piles of shoes and bags and coats on the floor couldn't dent the bubble of 'us' that surrounded me. Does that sound fanciful? For once I don't care.

The house was dark (hardly surprising as it was 1.30 a.m. Where did all that time go? Hours swallowed up by the consuming greed of us), but there was something restless about the darkness, something that was pacing the floors and crouching in corners.

As soon as I silently pushed open the door of our bedroom, I could tell that Daniel was awake. The tension crackled in the air like static – do you know what I mean? I slid into bed pretending not to notice that Daniel's eyes were wide open and shining in the darkness.

'Where have you been?'

His voice was shockingly loud in the stillness of the sleeping house.

'I told you. Gill's leaving party. It went on far longer than I expected.'

There was a silence then, before Daniel said, 'I don't believe you.'

Do you know, when he said that, I had an over-whelming urge just to tell him the truth. To say, 'I've been in a hotel room with Clive. We're in love. We want to be together.' Of course, I didn't. I know it's too soon and we haven't even discussed a proper exit strategy (that was what you used to call it, do you remember, our ever-changing, convoluted plans to leave our significant others?) that we can both implement together. But I'm so sick of the lies. Now that we're back together I want it all to be different. Completely open. Don't you?

Instead of responding to Daniel, I lay and pretended to go to sleep, but inside I was still buzzing with you. Now, don't take this the wrong way, but after the initial euphoria wore off and I got more used to the idea of us being 'reconnected', I even allowed myself the luxury of being a little bit cavalier. I started thinking about the weight you'd put on, and how it made you look a fraction older. Ridiculous how just one evening together can make one secure enough to become critical again. I imagined you lying awake in your huge bed in St John's Wood and thinking of me.

Now it's 11.35 a.m. and I've been up five and a half hours, and I'm starting to flag a little. I've sent you a couple of emails but I'm guessing you've stayed in bed nursing your own hangover. Hurry up and wake up! I'm desperate to talk to you.

There's so much to say, isn't there?

Half past four and still no word from you. The kids are home from school but I haven't even seen them yet, I don't want to leave my computer. You'll think it silly, I know, but disquiet is pricking at me like cactus hairs. Of course you could have had back-to-back meetings. Or you could have been called suddenly away. Or Susan could be glued to your side. There could be any number of reasons why you can't get to your emails, and I've clutched at them all in turn.

I've been on Susan's Facebook page (I wish you weren't quite so dogmatic about not getting a page yourself) about a hundred times today, trying to gauge what's happening in your house, but there are no updates. It has crossed my mind that perhaps you've already come clean to her, and told her you're leaving and have been in emotional lockdown all day. That would account for the silence. So many things are going through my head. I wish you'd just get in touch. Have you been getting my emails? I was tempted to text you earlier, but I didn't want to take the risk.

The muscles at the tops of my legs are aching from being wrapped around your back so long last night. Every time they twinge I remember what we did, and how your face was and how we looked when we stood together in front of the mirror.

I feel you in every part of me.

It's quarter to seven and Jamie and Tilly have just come in to say they're hungry. I don't know what to make them. Daniel is visiting his brother, Darren, and I can't think of anything to cook. All I can do is sit at the computer compulsively checking and re-checking my inbox.

'I'm sorry having children is so *inconvenient* for you,' Tilly said when I told her I was too busy with work to make them dinner.

I Googled local takeaway places and ordered some pizzas. I know it's extravagant, but sometimes it's good to be spontaneous, don't you think? Don't worry, I wouldn't do that if we were together. We'd take it in turns to cook proper meals that we eat with the kids. (I mean mine, of course. I can't imagine the Sacred Vessel sitting down at the table with us. Well, definitely not at first.) Everything would be so different if we were together, wouldn't it? Every day would be like an adventure.

'This is cool,' Jamie said when the pizzas arrived and I told them to eat them in front of the telly in the living room. But Tilly, of course, refused to see the fun in it. She held her cardboard box on her lap in front of her as if it was an unexploded bomb.

'There's grease soaking through the bottom,' she said, disgusted. 'When did we stop using plates in this house?'

When the boxes were opened, the pizza toppings looked like they were made of melted plastic, and Jamie had been given American Hot instead of Pepperoni. Outraged, he thrust his box under my nose. The oil was pooling, obscenely orange, on the glistening discs of sausage and I almost gagged.

Where are you, Clive? Where are you, Clive? Where are you, Clive?

You were supposed to rescue me from all of this. Surely you remember that?

I have forgotten how to breathe.

I open my mouth and gasp for air like a dying fish. There is a hard rock of pain inside me that I cannot shift, and nothing can get past it. It is cutting off oxygen and blood. It is feeding on me and it is growing.

I am trying to make sense of what you have written in your email, so eagerly anticipated, sitting here patiently at my desk with my journal open in front of me and the computer inches from my eyes, but the meaning dances around the screen, thumbing its nose.

I have sat here all day trying to think what to say.

How could you have been there all day? If you'd sat there all day, you'd have watched my emails dribble in one by desperate one. And yet you never replied. It doesn't make sense.

Last night should never have happened. Believe me when I say, Sally, I despise myself for it.

What do you mean, 'never have happened'? How can you wish something so perfect had never happened? It's like saying Tilly or Jamie should never have been born.

Sitting here in the cubbyhole, I pick at an old scab on my arm until it bleeds. You despise yourself because of last night. Being with me makes you despise yourself. I make people think themselves despicable.

I want you to know I hold myself fully to blame for what happened. I feel I have let everyone down – my family, Susan, even you.

The rock of pain becomes a boulder at that '*even you*' tacked on to the end like a reluctant concession.

I have no excuses for my behaviour and I apologize for any mixed messages it may have sent out. No matter what impression I might have given last night, I can only reiterate what I've been saying for months. I love Susan. I intend to spend the rest of my life making up to her for the hurt I've caused her. I am fully committed to my marriage.

No, no, no, no. Am I saying that out loud? The children and Daniel will think I have gone completely crazy, sitting here in my cubbyhole at 1 a.m., shouting in the dark. But I just don't get it, even though I've read it over and over.

Why are you saying that about your marriage? Are you deliberately trying to hurt me? Is it a new game you're playing, a new test?

I wish you the very best of luck, and hope you'll concentrate on repairing your own relationship with Daniel before it's too late.

With Daniel! Can you really be advising me to repair things with Daniel? Didn't you used to spend whole days telling me he was holding me back, that his very 'niceness' (the word came out of your mouth already in fully formed inverted commas) was impeding my creativity?

Once again I'm asking you to leave my family and myself alone. It's the best thing for everyone, especially for you. And believe it or not, I have got your best interests at heart.

And then, once again, the cruellest mantra of them all.

We must move on with our lives. Separately.

I must have re-read your message a hundred times, but still I can't find the meaning I'm looking for. After my experience with the emails being sent from my account, I wonder whether it actually came from you at all. Maybe Susan sent it herself, or maybe she forced you to send it, standing by your desk dictating what you should say, while you sat mute with misery, typing her bidding with reluctant fingers.

I need to speak to you. If I could just speak to you, we could sort this thing out. It's only distance that keeps you from me. Once we are close to each other, all your resistance melts away. I need to see you. I need to make you see me.

I'm going to call you. I know it's 3 a.m., but I have to

make you remember who I am, how my voice sounds. I have to find out who has got to you between last night and tonight, because this isn't you speaking. I know it isn't. I know you like I know myself, and this isn't you.

Your phone is off. I've forgotten how to breathe. *Breathe in, stomach out; breathe out, stomach in.* In all the years I've known you, you've never turned your phone off, only ever to silent. Not even in the days when passion blinded you to everything. What if one of the kids needed you? What if there was a crisis at work? What does it mean? Why are you hiding? Please don't . . . please don't . . . please don't . . .

Daniel has just appeared in the doorway of the cubbyhole, bleary-eyed and blinking in the dark.

'What's *wrong* with you, for Christ's sake?' he asked, and then he crossed the floor and awkwardly held me around the shoulders.

(Luckily the notebook in which I 'journal' was closed, and my computer screensaver was on. I didn't do that on purpose, mind, I don't care what he sees any more. It just does that after it's been idle for a while.)

It was only when Daniel's arm was wrapped weightily around me like a pet python that I realized, from the sudden sharp silence, that I must have been keening to myself here in the darkness. Rocking back and forth and lowing like a sea-lion.

I'm embarrassed. Really I am.

'You have to see someone, Sal, I'm really concerned about you.'

Nobody does concern in such a grudging, pained way as

Daniel. Sometimes I think it must really hurt him. Even so, I had a sudden urge – a young child's comfort-seeking reflex – to turn my head and burrow into his chest and allow myself to be held and rocked like a baby. What stopped me, I wonder? Was it you, Clive, denying me even those paltry scraps of relief? Instead I held myself stiff and unyielding in Daniel's awkward embrace.

'I *am* seeing someone. I'm seeing Helen.' My voice scraped like underwater coral.

Daniel made a disapproving sound then. He thinks that Helen, like vitamin supplements, isn't scientifically proven. He wants me to see someone with letters after their name.

'Come to bed,' he said.

I told him I would, just as soon as I'd turned off my computer.

'I wish you'd throw that fucking computer away,' he said, in a rare show of strong feeling.

'Who'd earn the money to pay the bills then?' I asked him.

'What money, Sal?'

He had a point, didn't he?

So now he's gone back to bed, and I'm left here, sitting in my swivel chair, with my legs tucked under me and the snot already crusting under my nose.

I wonder where you are, at 4.12 on this fine May morning. Are you pacing around in your box-room studio, thinking of me, hating yourself? Sorry, *despising* yourself, for what you've done?

I don't think so somehow.

What I think is this:

- You are fast asleep in your huge bed, next to your 'wonderful' wife.
- You sent me that message last thing before you went to

bed as a way of clearing your conscience so that you could sleep soundly, knowing you had 'tied up all the loose ends'.

- You think you have 'drawn a line' under the whole 'affair'. (Unfortunate term. Sorry.)
- You are so, so wrong.

The sun is creeping on its belly under the door to the cubbyhole. I am slumped over my desk, my hand barely able to hold the pen, but anger keeps jerking my eyelids open, outrage fizzing through me like tear gas.

I can hear the next-door neighbours already getting up for work. (How I hate them for thinking that this is a normal day. How can they be so obtuse?) This time yesterday my heart was limitless. Now it is a dried-up peach stone (how you'd loathe that clumsy metaphor. Layzeeeee Salleeeee, you'd scold).

Soon Daniel will be up and Jamie and Tilly and the whole thing will start all over again, the whole big bloody pulpy mess that is my life. Meanwhile, you will be getting up feeling like you've had a narrow escape, and bursting anew with fresh good intentions to make it up to Susan. You will feel virtuous and reborn and humble (at least in your own mind). You will pledge to yourself that things will be different from now on. You will push me down to the bottom of your mind like you are mulching compost. You will think that you are free of me. You will be wrong.

I know about you, Clive. I've been inside your head and licked every inch of it, probing my tongue into all its fleshy crevices. I know you, Clive.

I know you.

* * *

I am feeling much better.

I really am. I've stopped taking the citalopram. I think it was impeding my progress. Of course, withdrawing so suddenly has given me some strange reactions, but I kind of like the pain. Do you know what I mean? It's clean and it hurts and for a minute I forget all the other things that hurt. That's a good thing, wouldn't you say?

Another great plus is, I can drink again without blacking out! I haven't told the young blonde lip-scrunching doctor about stopping the drugs. I feel I'd be letting her down in some way. Isn't that ridiculous? I worry she might take it as a personal rejection.

But, you know what? Despite the headaches, even after just three days I'm already feeling the benefits. I've stopped feeling like I'm disassociated from my life. I'm owning my own feelings again. Helen will be so thrilled.

Daniel is less delighted, however. He says I have – let me try to remember the exact wording he uses, because it's really quite funny – 'emotional Munchausen's'. (Can you believe he came up with that quite unprompted? I do think Daniel must have been doing some 'work on himself', as Helen would say.) Daniel believes I'm deliberately putting the kybosh on anything that might make me feel better out of some perverse desire to suffer and, by implication, to make everyone around me suffer too. I tell him I've stopped the pills because my body is a temple and laugh to show him it's supposed to be a joke, but he looks at me like I'm mad. He has taken to calling my friends up to ask them to 'talk sense' into me. I know because sometimes they call me afterwards and say 'Daniel's worried about you'. I tell them Daniel approaches worry like a daily workout routine at the gym, something that's slightly painful but ultimately beneficial, so if not to be embraced, at least undertaken without complaint.

Sian came round yesterday looking very cross.

'I can't accept this level of responsibility any more,' she told me, and when she frowned I was able to see for the first time the full effect of the Botox she's been having. (Did you know she'd started that? Or was that something that happened post York Way Friday? That's how I divide my life now by the way, pre or post that Friday. It's gratifyingly biblical, don't you think?) It was a little disconcerting because it was like talking to two different versions of Sian, the middle-aged frowning one below the eyes and the younger, untroubled one above. Anyway, neither of them seemed to like me very much.

'I'm feeling very compromised,' she told me reproachfully, sounding like a union rep at ACAS. 'The secret of your affair has become a burden that I don't think I can keep shouldering.' (I know you'll think I'm making that up and no one talks like that, but she really did. I'm not lying. It was like she was reading from a script – a really bad one.)

'When I first facilitated' (that word again – has Sian been taking more of those motivational workshops, I wonder?) 'your affair, I thought it would be a positive thing for you, Sal. I could see that you hadn't been happy with Daniel for a while, and hoped the thing with Clive would give you a boost.'

A boost? She made you sound like a vaccination!

Sian went on to say that she could shoot herself now, for

not having tried to talk me out of it, or at least made it clear that she didn't want anything to do with it. She told me she felt she'd been greatly misled by you, but that now we both had to put it behind us. She sounded so genuinely sorrowful I wondered if she might have been having an affair with you herself!

According to Sian, I've been 'wallowing' in my misery for too long.

'You need to put your head up above the parapet for a minute and take a good, hard look around you,' she told me.

Well, when she said that, I started laughing. I couldn't help it. It was that 'head above the parapet'. It made me think of that scene in *Alien* when the thing's head bursts out of John Hurt's stomach and peers around. But my laughter just made Sian's bottom-heavy frown even more pronounced.

'Your kids are suffering, Sal. And when was the last time you did any proper work?'

Well, she had a point about the work, but you know, even while I was docilely nodding, inside I was thinking about something completely different. I was thinking about how you looked at me when we were in the hotel room last week and whether you knew even then that you were going to dump me again as soon as you got home. And I was thinking about you and Susan in your tasteful house, and how you'd be making it up to her, the presents you'd be buying her, the trips you'd be planning. I was the alien that bursts bleeding and slimy and screaming out of a ruptured intestine, and meanwhile you were poring over brochures for beach bungalows in Mauritius or villas in Corsica.

It didn't seem right. It isn't right.

It is wrong.

Three a.m. and here I am again. I find myself curiously attached to the cubbyhole these days. I fear I have become institutionalized.

I am staring at my reflection in a magnifying mirror I found in the back of the filing-cabinet drawer. I am fascinated by the changes I see drawn large on my face. There are hairs sprouting from my chin like Jack's giant beanstalk. Were they there before and I just didn't notice? Or have grief and tears fertilized their growth? The shadows under my eyes have become great pools of black big enough for a person to drown in. I let the muscles around my mouth go slack, and notice how the skin droops down like melted wax. I have a spot on the side of my nose, where no spot has stood since adolescence. I pick at it with vicious pleasure, watching the skin break and enjoying the sudden squirt of pain.

I am becoming grotesque.

Don't worry, I'm not about to start going on about *Alien* again. I do apologize for that, incidentally. I blame the lack of sleep. Daniel thinks I might be getting menopausal. Not that I think he has much of a clue what menopausal might be. Sometimes I think he imagines going through the menopause as something akin to passing through Crewe – not very pleasant while it's happening, but a relief once it's over. I have a sneaking suspicion he imagines I could be 'cured' of the menopause by that nice blonde doctor and it's sheer stubbornness that stops me presenting myself in her consulting rooms for 'tests'.

He doesn't have the first notion what's really wrong with me. Nobody knows that but us. It's yet another bond we share.

I haven't told you yet, but I met Liam again today. Isn't that a coincidence?

I was strolling through the West End, I forget exactly why, when suddenly it occurred to me it might be fun to pop into the Royal Gallery. Well, I'd enjoyed it so much the last time, it really seemed silly not to take advantage of being in the area. I wandered around the new exhibition, which seemed to feature lots of big things in primary colours and a room of what looked like concrete excrement. There was a great big cannon there shooting out massive globs of red wax against the white wall. It seemed unnecessarily violent to me, although all the other crowds of visitors seemed terribly pleased every time it happened. To be quite honest, I didn't really like it but the funny thing is I couldn't stop watching it. It only happened every twenty minutes, but each time it was over, I stood and waited for the next one, and the next. There was something in the way that wax splatted hard and red against the wall that made me think of you and me.

After a couple of hours I'd had enough. I looked at another exhibit that was like an enormous vulva and one that was a pregnant stomach looming obscenely out of a blank wall (remember the pregnancy that wasn't real?). Then I decided to go and have some tea.

Of course, I remembered Liam worked nearby, but it wasn't as if I went in just to see him. Why, he could just as easily have had a day off, or been working a different shift, or been recruited to cover in the kitchens. I had no idea if he would be there, nor was it a major concern. I just want you to know that, in case you start thinking things.

But I can't say I wasn't pleased to see him. It was nice to see a familiar face after all that angry red wax. I'm sure you can understand that.

Now, I don't know if I'm being fanciful here, but I could have sworn Liam recognized me. Does that seem far-fetched? I'm sure you're right, and yet there seemed to be a real warmth in his eyes. The eyes that are almost your eyes.

'I came in a few weeks ago,' I told him, when he came up to stand by my table, taking the pen out from behind his ear.

He smiled in a way that could have been acknowledgement that he too had made the connection or, I suppose, could just have been wary politeness.

The smile made me feel bolder.

'I think I might know your parents,' I told him.

Well, that was fair enough, wasn't it? That's the kind of thing anyone would say. Nothing sinister about it. Liam smiled again and for a moment that dent in his cheek that's so exactly like yours made me forget what I was going to say next, but I think I recovered myself without giving anything away. I told him how I'd met you and Susan all those years ago, and how we'd enjoyed our visits to Suffolk. 'Our very own Brideshead,' I said in a wry sort of way. I was aiming for a mix of casual but friendly. I hope I pulled it off.

He seemed very interested when I told him how helpful you'd always been. (Don't worry, I didn't tell him about the cash from the fridge pressed into my hand in a beige hotel room.) He said he thought he'd heard you talking about me, but I think he might have been being kind.

We had a lovely little chat after that. He really has got a sense of humour, hasn't he? Don't know who he takes after in that respect. I told him how much I was looking forward to the renewal-of-the-vows party and he made a kind of face as if it was going to be a bit of a chore, whereas actually you could see he didn't really mean that at all. He's such a sweetie. I can quite see now why you had such major pre-York Way Friday wobbles about what a divorce might do to the children. You were quite right to be worried.

Liam said he thought you'd been having pre-remarriage nerves, which I thought was quite a jolly way of putting it. He said that he'd been staying in more than normal lately, enjoying a bit of 'mum-comfort' (as he called it) after splitting up from his most recent girlfriend, and you'd seemed a bit out of sorts.

'Usually Dad's the life and soul, but he has been very subdued – for him.'

The good news was that he could report signs of a big improvement over the last few days. 'He's seemed a lot happier and more relaxed. I think he's actually starting to enjoy the whole thing now.'

That's wonderful, Clive. It really is. It's so important to enjoy these occasions, I always think, these rites of passage. Come to think of it, my own life has been rather short on them, having spectacularly failed to get either religion or married, two main prerequisites of a good rite of passage. I do envy you and your family all these life-affirming events – the baby shower, the vow renewing. And how much better that you can go through them all free of that nasty cumbersome 'burden of guilt' you revealed you'd been carting around in our York Way Friday meeting. No wonder you're feeling relaxed!

Liam was quite surprised to hear I'd been at Emily's baby shower. He said he had no idea I was such a good friend of the family. That's an interesting description, wouldn't you say?

I ordered a glass of wine. Now I'm not on the citalopram I find wine tastes so much better and I seem to be able to drink vast quantities without even feeling it. Almost makes up for the withdrawal headaches that still take me unaware, pressing down on my skull like a drying bandage, and the queasiness that comes out of nowhere, sending me running, hand over mouth, to the nearest loo.

'I can't face the patchouli tea,' I told him, and he looked at me as if he didn't have a clue what I was talking about. Which of course he didn't. I expect he's never even heard of patchouli.

That first glass of wine went down so well I ordered another. There's something so civilized about sitting in one of the most upmarket addresses in the world drinking Pinot Grigio in the middle of the afternoon (even if it wasn't the best).

'I expect you enjoy working here,' I said to Liam when he brought the second glass. A bit lame, I know. I just couldn't think of what else to say. He's such an open, friendly chap, isn't he, and yet – and please don't take this the wrong way – there's not a lot, really, to engage with, is there, once you scratch the surface?

Even so, I felt he could have made just the teeniest

bit more effort when I was so patently trying to make conversation with him, instead of just smiling sheepishly and trying to look as if he wasn't glancing around.

'It's all right, yeah,' he said, but his smile had turned down just a notch. 'I'm really sorry that I don't have time to chat, I'm just a bit busy.'

It was true that there were quite a few customers there, but I felt ever so slightly (ridiculously, I know) rejected.

I toyed with the idea of having a third glass, but to tell you the truth I was feeling a bit put out. There was a woman at the next table who kept looking at me in a rather pointed way. She was on her own, just like me, but she was dressed up with studied effortlessness, as if she'd spent hours getting ready for a drinks party where the dress-code was 'smart-casual'. Gauzy patterned top, lots of make-up, statement jewellery and, when she stood up, black leather jeans and high black boots. At her pointy-toed feet was a collection of those carrier bags that designer shops give out with bold writing on the side and thick brocade handles. At first I'd thought she was in her early thirties, but when I looked closer it was obvious she was my age, if not more.

She had her iPhone out and was pretending to be engrossed in something. Apps, I believe they're called, or at least that's what Jamie tells me. Bet you still don't really know what those are, despite being one of the iPhone pioneers. You probably make a joke of it at dinner parties. 'Oh I just use it for making calls and telling the time,' is the kind of thing you say, cleverly proving not only that you're someone who can laugh at himself but also that you're the kind of man who thinks life is too short to read an instruction manual, neither of which bears much approximation to the truth.

Anyway, I could tell she wasn't really remotely interested in whatever was on her iPhone screen. She kept glancing over at me the whole time I was talking to Liam, and then it finally occurred to me that she must have thought I was chatting him up. What is it the media call people like us these days? Cougars. She thought I was a cougar! Isn't that priceless?

Once I'd worked it out, I realized she probably fancied him herself. Now don't get all huffy. He might still be a child to you, but Liam is an attractive young man. Please don't be offended if I say he has a definition around his jaw that you lack. It gives him an illusion of strength, despite his youth and blandness (I mean that in the best possible way, I hasten to add – a blank-canvas kind of way). There was definitely something about the way the pointy-booted woman was stirring the teaspoon in her latte (I'm guessing skimmed milk, aren't you?) while her eyes followed him around the room that made me sense a bit of pheremonal activity.

When I asked Liam that question about whether he enjoyed working there, I could sense her listening in, and when he gave me the brush-off about being too busy, she leaned back and I could swear she was smiling slightly. Sipping the dregs of my wine, I felt a sudden flush of shame as I saw myself through her eyes – a dowdy middle-aged woman in yesterday's jeans and home-dyed hair trying to engage the attention of a man young enough to be her son, who clearly had other places he'd rather be. I wanted to lean across and say, 'It's OK. I had an affair with his father.' Actually, that's not all. I wanted to smear the ghost smile all over her over-made-up face. I wanted to make her re-evaluate and re-frame me. I wanted her to know that men thought of me as a sexual thing. I wanted her to see that I wasn't like her. I wasn't the kind of lonely, brittle woman who sits in soulless cafeterias on weekday afternoons with shopping bags at her feet, looking at boys born twenty years too late.

She was wrong about me.

Liam was wrong about me.

I am not that woman.

* * *

I'm back in the cubbyhole where I belong, looking at the computer screen. Sometimes I think I spend so long here that I'm going to organically grow into the furniture. Half woman, half chair. Hey, if all else fails on the financial front (which, let's face it, looks ever more likely), I could make some money in a travelling freak show. Do they have travelling freak shows any more? If not, that could be a new niche market, don't you think?

Up on the screen is the email from you that dropped into my inbox a couple of hours ago. I wouldn't like you to think I spent my entire life checking my inbox, mind. I do take time out to go to the loo! I'm trying to make a joke here, to keep my lips sealed together in a smile so that it stops my stomach coming up through my mouth. It's not really working.

I've been waiting to hear from you for six days. Ever since you sent that touching 'I despise myself' message. Six days of writing to our secret email account (nothing), ringing your phone (voicemail). I even texted

200

you, a cleverly worded message about needing to talk to you about some research I'd done for Douggie, your newspaper mate (zilch).

Six days of staring at the **inbox (0)** message at the top of my email account, willing it to change and trying to stop my throbbing head from exploding like a nail bomb, spraying the walls with rust-sharpened shards of me.

'Why are you always in here?' Tilly asked me yesterday, actively seeking me out, despite missing valuable *Hollyoaks* time, something almost unheard of.

'I'm sorry, darling, I've got so much work on at the moment.'

'Then how come you never have anything up on the screen apart from your emails?'

She had a point, but it didn't stop me feeling a bit *invaded*, do you know what I mean? I told her that I was waiting on an important work email, but then she pointed out (don't you always forget how much better kids' eyesight is than our own?) that the last email in my inbox was dated from 48 hours ago, and even then it was a message from Tesco telling me about their special offer on wines.

'You haven't forgotten it's my parents' evening next week.' Tilly has this amazing knack of making a question sound like a statement of fact.

I had forgotten, of course, but I didn't tell her that.

So anyway, that's how intently I've been waiting for a reply from you, firing off messages into the abyss, listening to the dull silence of a phone switched to off.

So you can imagine my shock when I suddenly noted **inbox (1)** at the top of my emails. It was you, of course, the jumble of random initials and numbers that announced you were sending this from your 'secret' account.

You're going to think me excessive, I know, but my heart really did start battering against my ribcage, a trapped dog hurling itself at the door.

I didn't even dare click the message open. I wanted to savour the unsullied promise of it, those bold letters that could lead to anything.

Finally I did double click. I couldn't keep staring at it for ever, could I? Then I did a really interesting thing. I think Helen would have found it very 'telling' (that's another one of her key words). I leaned back so that, with my computer-ruined eyes, I couldn't actually read what you'd written and the letters blurred across the screen. I was trying to get a sense of the overall shape of the message, you see – round and jolly? Thin and spiky? – as if that might give me some indication of what it contained. Isn't that mad?

When I really couldn't put it off any more, I leaned forward and skimmed the last line to get a sense of the tone of your message.

You MUST put this behind you now, for your own sake.

It didn't sound good. Sure enough, the rest wasn't any better. Of course I'd half expected that part about seeing Liam, although to be quite frank you're reading far too much into it. Your son works in the middle of the West End. You can't be surprised if your friends bump into him from time to time. I must admit, though, I was surprised when you put that bit about me having sent 436 email messages in the past six days. I'm sure you're exaggerating. It can't possibly be that many. Anyway, most of them were just a few lines long. Some were just a few words. So they don't count, do they? And I don't believe that's an accurate tally of how many times I called your phone before you switched it off, either. You probably just rounded it up to make it sound more sinister.

I was hurt about the blocking thing, though. Why would you block my messages, when you used to say they were all that kept you going? And my phone calls? I didn't even know you could do that. Is that a special app available only to iPhone users? The Blocking Your Exes app? Is there a special app for fixing a broken heart, too? Is there an app for knitting back together a life ripped apart? Don't worry, I'm teasing. I'm not completely crayzeeee. But what I don't know, what I'm still curious about, Clive, is how a few months ago you were sneaking out of bed in the middle of the night to see if I'd left you any messages before I went to sleep, and now you don't even want to see my name in your inbox. How does that happen? How does the person who was loved become unloved? How does someone who says they can't live without you willingly block you out of their life with one click of a mouse?

How does it happen, Clive? I really want to know.

And just remember one thing. Blocking isn't something that can be done unilaterally, no matter who you happen to be.

YOU CANNOT BLOCK SOMEONE FROM YOUR LIFE WHO DOESN'T WANT TO BE BLOCKED.

Now, I must thank you for your concern about my 'psychological state'. I appreciate it, I really do. Equally I appreciate your suggestions that I go to see 'someone qualified to help'. I wonder who you might have in mind when you say that. Who could possibly be qualified to help me? Who knows the answers to the very specific problems behind my 'psychological state'? Who is qualified to know what I need? Who can give me what I want?

Why, Clive, I do believe there's only you.

* * *

Last night, when I finally got to sleep, I dreamed I was having sex with you and woke up some time afterwards drenched in shame, and soaked through with longing.

You know what I miss the most about the sex, Clive? The laughter. That sounds strange, doesn't it, but I know you of all people will understand exactly what I mean. 'I've brought a few props,' you'd say, emptying the contents of an Ann Summers carrier bag on to the hotel bed, and we'd giggle ourselves silly trying to work out exactly what they were for. (Who'd have thought that all these months on, the most vivid memories of sex should be of candy-coloured plastic or the chemical smell of freshly unpackaged latex?)

Remember the Banana Incident? I can't believe you would have forgotten. For once you'd arrived at the hotel empty-handed, but when we'd been in bed a couple of hours, you suddenly remembered something.

'Just stay there,' you commanded, rummaging around in your laptop bag before triumphantly flourishing a banana. Not the most original prop, admittedly, but we were in the mood to have fun and you made a typically theatrical performance of both inserting it and eating it, emerging from under the sheets with your smiling mouth still stuffed with ripe fruit.

It was only half an hour or so later, when we had just

started having sex again, that you suddenly stopped abruptly.

'It's still in there,' you told me, the lust draining from your eyes.

'What do you mean? How can it be?'

'I can't have got it all out. I can feel a great big lump of it still there.'

We stared at each other, do you remember? Half laughing, half panicking, my legs still wrapped around your back, our breath still ragged from the labour of passion.

You were very chivalrous, I have to say, dutifully feeling around inside when it was obvious my own fingers weren't long enough for the job.

'You'll have to use something to fish it out,' you said eventually, admitting defeat.

Half furious with you, half helplessly amused by the situation, I grabbed a teaspoon from the tea-tray and teetered off to the en-suite bathroom, still wearing the ludicrous stilettos you loved me to wear in bed (how clichéd, in the end, are the desires of men).

'Any joy?' you kept asking, pacing up and down outside the open bathroom door like an expectant father while I perched on the edge of the toilet seat, digging around with the spoon. 'Is there anything I can do?' And of course my all-time favourite, 'Shall I pop down to the hotel kitchen to fetch a longer-handled spoon?'

Perhaps it was the idea of you presenting yourself to a bemused hotel cook that galvanized me to probe that bit deeper, but with a sudden comedy squelch, out popped the errant lump of banana.

'Thank God . . . I was feeling so dreadful . . . I'm such a clumsy idiot,' you said as we both gazed awestruck at the spoon with its heaped load of glistening yellowish mulch.

But do you remember how much we laughed afterwards – leaning back against the bathroom walls while tears of relief and hilarity coursed down our cheeks?

'Nothing feels off limits with you,' I emailed you later. 'I never feel embarrassed.'

But you know, things have changed a bit since then.

Now when I look back on those five years of hotel beds and bathroom floors, with the memories of what we did and what I let you do no longer softened by the glow of love, they seem garishly strip-lit and web-cam seedy, the flickering images of bad home-shot porn.

And when I try to recapture the laughter, it's as slippery and elusive as a lump of stray banana.

*   *   *

Helen was not happy with me today.

I don't know whether your supa-dupa Harley Street therapist ever gets cross, but when Helen does, she does this thing where she does a sigh *inside her mouth*. Have you ever seen someone do that? She presses her lips tightly together, so the sigh kind of escapes through her nostrils. She tries to disguise it, but I know exactly what she's doing.

Anyway. She did that a lot today.

The first thing that made her cross was the fact that I'd stopped taking the citalopram.

'I didn't need it,' I told her.

'Do you think you're in a state to judge whether or not you need it?' she asked me.

Well, what is one supposed to say to that? If I said 'yes', she'd probably have said my thinking was distorted by not being on the citalopram. If I said 'no', she'd tell me I needed to go back on the citalopram to get into a better state. It's what's known as a lose-lose situation, I believe.

'Could it be that there's a part of you that enjoys being miserable?' she asked me. 'Is there a part of you that wants not to get better, because getting better means letting go of Clive?'

Do you see what she does, that Helen Bunion? Laying question upon question like papier-mâché, in an ever-growing edifice with a big, empty space at its core.

That's when I foolishly told her about meeting up with you ten days ago. And that's when her inward sighing got really pronounced.

'Sometimes I can't help feeling that you enjoy sabotaging your own recovery, Sally.'

She has these narrow green eyes that she fixes on you as she speaks, and her straight mousy hair is cut into a very tidy bob that she tucks repeatedly behind her ear. Helen was definitely a prefect at school, or a monitor. Did you have monitors at your school, I wonder? (Remember how you hated me saying you were posh? 'I only went to a minor public school,' you said petulantly. 'Only a posh person would know the difference,' I told you.) Helen would have been something like Stationery Monitor – a responsible job but one with minimal potential for conflict or for upset.

'Can I ask you something, Sally?' She did another inward sigh, and I knew she wasn't going to ask anything I wanted to answer. 'Do you really *want* to feel better about things?'

At first I thought it was a rhetorical question, but then I realized she was actually waiting for me to reply.

'Of course I do.' What else could I say, in the circumstances?

'Only it seems to me that for someone who claims to want to feel better, you're doing everything in your power to make yourself feel worse.'

Well, looking at it from the outside, you can see how she'd get that idea, I suppose. So I tried – stupid, I know – to explain how it had been during those two days before our 'date'. How I'd felt alive again, how things had started to have a point to them again.

Helen did exaggerated sighing when she heard that, the kind that takes place quite openly, and her foot, in her sensible low-heeled brown shoes, tapped lightly but insistently on the carpet.

I toyed with the idea of omitting the part where we slept together. It felt embarrassing and overly intimate and I knew she'd disapprove. But then again, I'm paying her £75 an hour to make me better, I can't afford to lie to her, can I? And she can't afford to disapprove of me.

Helen gave an involuntary shake of the head, when I said we'd gone to a hotel.

'Whose idea was that?' Her eyebrows arched so far they almost disappeared into her hair, and she seemed decidedly unimpressed when I told her I was too drunk to remember.

'This man encouraged you to fall in love with him and imagine you had a future together, then dropped you from a great height, without any warning or backward glance, leaving you destroyed, and when he decides he wants a quick leg-over, you jump to it? Is that the kind of woman you recognize as yourself, Sally?'

My head was pounding by this stage and I found myself too distracted by her use of the phrase 'leg-over' to reply. Is that what it was, Clive? Did you get your leg over? Over what, I wonder? Over-easy? Overdue? Over the rainbow?

So Helen repeated it again, the bit about me recognizing myself.

I told her I hadn't recognized myself in months. I told her that even when I look in the mirror to brush my teeth I don't recognize the woman who looks back, her mouth full of toothpaste, her eyes sunken into black shadows.

Helen did one massive inward sigh and then shook her head again with what appeared to be genuine sorrow.

'I have to tell you I think you've substantially set back your progress,' she told me, and though it sounds stupid, I felt tears pricking at the back of my eyes when she said that. I hadn't been aware I'd made any progress, and now I'd gone and set it back.

'Sally, you know this isn't about you wanting Clive back, don't you?'

I looked at her in silence, not daring to blink for fear that the tears would flood out so fast I wouldn't know how to stop.

'This is about you wanting to regain the control you think you've lost, by regaining Clive. But you know you have to put that out of your mind. Clive is gone. You have to concentrate now on the areas of your life where you do still have control: your family, your partner, your work.'

She said a few more things, but I wasn't really listening any more. All I could hear was that phrase repeating in my head – those three little words that mean so much. Clive is gone.

Clive is gone.

Clive is gone.

Helen gave me an exercise to do, there and then, which instantly made me feel marginally better. The word 'exercise' sounds so active, doesn't it? It sounds like you're taking charge of your life, instead of passively waiting around to develop the equivalent of life bingo-wings.

Helen had me write out a list of the ten things that annoyed me most about you, the things that gave me most cause for doubt, even when we were together.

I was so desperate to win back her good favour, I determined to make my list as comprehensive as possible and started trying to work out what things Helen would regard as 'appropriate' in a list of unwelcome traits. And, let's face it, there were quite a few to choose from. Do you remember, Clive, how I was constantly beset with doubts and used to send you long emails detailing them all, which you'd return with your own rebuttals in capital letters. *Too old*, I'd write. To which you'd add 'BUT MUCH BETTER GENE POOL THAN YOU SO WILL CANCEL EACH OTHER OUT'. *Too posh*. 'POSHNESS IS RELATIVE. MOST OF MY FRIENDS THINK I'M COMMON'. *Too married*. BLANK.

After five minutes of anxious concentration, my list read:

1. Pompous.
2. Pugnacious.
3. Judgemental.
4. Egocentric.
5. Too short. (I worried about this one, in case Helen thought me shallow, but to be frank, I was already starting to flag by this stage.)
6. Inconsistent (better).
7. Uses intentionally annoying phrases (in what he believes to be an ironic way), like 'not feeling tip-top' and 'I've gotta be honest with you . . .'.
8. Doesn't love me.
9. Has overdeveloped paternal issues. (OK, I have to

admit I threw that in because I thought Helen might like it. Issues are some of her very favourite things. But it also carries a kernel of truth. You take your role as father a little too far, Clive. Liam and the Sacred Vessel are adults. You don't need to be so involved in their lives. You need to become more . . . separate.)

10. Doesn't love me.
10. Lies.

I was a bit nervous while I was reading out my list. I kept sneaking glances at Helen to see how my points were going down, but she was leaning back in her chair, gazing up into the middle distance with a faraway look in her eyes. Very tricky to gauge.

As I continued down the list, I faltered, and started trying to justify the points as I read them out. Then I realized I'd written 'Doesn't love me' twice. I was mortified, but I couldn't think of anything to replace it. Then I realized I had two number tens.

'I'm not really going bonkers, honest,' I laughed, unconvincingly.

Helen just looked at me without speaking, as if she was rehearsing words in her mind before she shared them.

'That's a very brave list, Sally,' she told me.

Was it? I tried to imagine which of the points might be construed as brave. Not the one about being short, or the one about being old. Oh, I suddenly remembered I hadn't put in the one about being old, I'd decided Helen might not understand that one. After all, you're probably not far off her own age, and only a few years off mine. Come to think of it, I couldn't now remember why it had seemed such a big deal to me at the time. I must have been looking for reasons to find fault. I must have been so secure in how you felt that I felt able to goad you. How didn't I know that it was all an illusion? How didn't I know that the power I must have thought I had was as substanceless as the baby that never was?

'What's interesting about your list, Sally,' (incidentally, does your supa-dupa therapist do that? Use your name all the time? Do you suppose it's to create a bond of intimacy, or is it just to remind us who we are, in case we've forgotten? I rather think it's the latter. These days, I often forget who I am. It's good of Helen to keep jogging my memory) 'is that double admission of "he doesn't love me". It's almost as if you're still trying to persuade yourself that it's true.'

'Or maybe it's just because I'm rubbish at counting,' I offered.

It was a mistake. Helen gave a very pained smile, as if contracting those muscles in the corner of her mouth incurred actual physiological discomfort.

'Why do you think you must make a joke of everything, Sally?' Her green eyes were at a funny angle, so cocked was her head to one side, and she made a funny hmmmmming noise at the end of her question. 'It's almost as if you don't dare acknowledge to yourself the depth of your own pain. You don't have to put an amusing spin on everything, you know. You are allowed to feel devastated. You are allowed to feel angry. It's very important that you give yourself permission to feel deeply and to grieve. You must learn to take yourself and your needs more seriously.'

I didn't remind her that my needs are only wants in disguise. I didn't tell her that the reason I don't allow myself my pain is that I'm worried that if I open those floodgates the tsunami will sweep me away, battering me to a pulp against the rocks. I didn't tell her about the anger that, permitted or not, comes tearing through me like vomit, unstoppable, toxic, acid-smelling.

I didn't tell her about Liam, or about the 436 emails.

I didn't tell her about the headaches. I didn't tell her about the middle-of-the-night keening.

I want Helen to like me.

I want Helen to help me.

I want Helen to make it stop.

* * *

I'm worried about Susan. I really am.

Ever since she came round for lunch that day, she hasn't seemed quite 'herself' (now I'm at it too, that arrogant assumption of 'self' as being something positive, something to aspire to).

I've called her a few times and she has seemed slightly out of sorts, as if she was thinking hard about what to say next, although Susan is usually the most straightforward of people. When I've suggested a night out, she has always been too tired, or too busy. 'This renewal of vows is more hassle than the sodding wedding was,' she told me.

I think she's getting overwrought about it all. I honestly do.

Yesterday I finally managed to get her to agree to a coffee. 'It can only be a quick one,' she warned. She arrived at the Starbucks near your house with half an hour to spare before an appointment at the shop which is altering the dress she's wearing to the big event. She's been on a strict diet to get into the smaller size. Did you know that?

I don't think losing weight really becomes her. It has made her slightly edgier, I think. Less comforting somehow.

Of course, I asked all about the dress. Well, it would have been rude not to, and anyway I was genuinely interested. Is it bad luck for me to describe it to you? I'm sure you and Susan are far too sensible for all that superstition.

She says it's fuchsia-coloured raw silk, slightly ruched around the waist 'to disguise the bulgy bits' (her words, not mine). Won't it be a change to see Susan entirely dressed in a colour that isn't navy, for once? It's as if she's reinventing herself as her second wedding present to you.

As she was talking, I couldn't help imagining what I would have chosen in her situation. You know, after your faux marriage proposal in the Coach and Horses, I used to imagine what I'd wear if it ever happened for real. (In those days, it was more like 'when' it happened for real.) Does that shock you? I know you were a bit wounded when I laughed off your big romantic gesture, but I never told you how, for ages afterwards, I'd pass shop windows and think, 'That'd be a great dress to get married in.'

Of course, the Ideal Frock kept changing. One day it'd be a narrow shift in some kind of ivory colour, as a nod to traditionalism, and the next it would be a wildly unconventional ruffled Spanish-flamenco-style number. I'd imagine your face as you watched me approaching, suitably awestruck and misty-eyed, with that 'What a lucky man I am' smile. I'd imagine the oohs and aahs of the assembled guests (although not the children, I could never imagine either set of children there, and certainly not oohing and aahing). Can you believe I used to do that? It seems so unreal now, but that's how secure I felt. Silleeeee Salleeeeee.

And now it's Susan who's buying the frock. ('It cost nearly £500. Don't tell Clive, will you?' Isn't that sweet?) And it'll be Susan walking towards you in fuchsia pink. (I don't want to rain on anyone's parade, but I do hope she's thought that one through. Fuchsia is so unforgiving, don't you think?) And when your eyes mist up, it'll be for Susan, and when you smile the 'lucky man' smile, it will be because of Susan, and your children will sit in the front row and alternately laugh and cry, and everyone will agree that it's incredible that you've been married for over a quarter of a century, and what a fucking inspiration you are to the rest of us.

And I will be nowhere.

Nothing.

Niente.

Void.

Sorry, I'm digressing. As I said, I thought Susan was rather tense when we met up. Do you think it could be the dieting? I worry that she might be overdoing it.

It's funny, but when she walked through the Starbucks door, I actually thought for a mad moment that you might be behind her, strolling out to get a break from your box room. But then I remembered about the email, and the despising-yourself bit, and the middle-of-the-night keening, and the fact that I was blocked from your life.

I remembered that you weren't about to come loping through the Starbucks door, trailing behind Susan, with an apologetic smile on your face. I remembered that you don't love me any more.

As Susan made her way across to me, I had a sudden wild impulse to tell her everything. I could picture it so clearly, her saying, 'What's been happening since I last saw you?' and me replying, 'Well, apart from fucking your husband, not a lot.' Not that I'd have taken any pleasure in hurting her, I can assure you. I just wanted her to feel some of what I was feeling. It might be a bonding thing, I thought, our shared misery might bring us closer together.

Look at it from my point of view. Here was someone whose life is going absolutely to plan. Long healthy marriage, impressive healthy children, grandchild on the way, house, career, money, friends, travel. What could someone like that ever find in common with someone like me? And yet, I badly wanted me and Susan to be friends. I like Susan, I always have. For once, I wanted it to be her weeping into her skinny latte (oh, that miserable diet!) and me commiserating with her, the same way she so often commiserates with me. I wanted us to be able to support each other. I wanted her to know her life wasn't really so perfect and that she and I shared more than she could possibly know. I wanted her to come to me for comfort. I wanted to be part of her life. I wanted to help.

Oh, don't worry, Clive. I can just picture your face. Do you know that when you frown, the bottom half of your face goes slack and you look every one of your forty-nine years? You've got to stop doing that. Lighten up a little.

Of course, I didn't really say anything of the sort. Even I could see how self-destructive that would be. I'd be cast out into the cold, no prospect of ever creeping back into your affections, or even of getting the crumbs from your family table. No chance of being the ghost at your banquet, the gatecrasher at your feasts. No chats with the Sacred Vessel, no banter with Liam. Outcast. Uninvited. Banished.

Blocked.

Instead, we sat and chatted about the big party. (Susan tells me she's making all the canapés herself! She is a marvel, isn't she? So capable. So creative. You must be so proud.) We talked a little bit about Emily, although Susan didn't seem to want to be drawn very much. I do hope everything is all right between those two. A girl needs her mother at a time like this. And of course, we talked a little bit about you.

'Clive has been quite stressed recently,' she told me. 'He's been terribly quiet, for him.'

Then she told me something quite interesting. She said there had been an occasion, the week before last, when you were supposedly working at home and had locked yourself away in the box room all day. She'd had a day off and had spent most of it pottering around the garden, enjoying the watery early-summer sun. (Oh, how I love these snapshots of domestic life. I feel like I'm almost there with both of you, do you know what I mean?) Looking up, she'd been able to see you through the window of your studio, and she'd watched you sitting in your chair, staring through the glass without moving. 'Every time I looked up, he was in the same position,' she told me. She said you'd still been there when she looked in on you to say goodnight, but she'd woken up just after midnight when you finally came to bed. You'd come around to her side of that big old bed, and you'd crouched down so that your face was practically level with hers. 'I don't deserve you,' you'd told her. 'I'm a stupid old fool and I don't deserve you.'

Of course, when Susan was telling the story it was loads funnier than that. I can't remember the exact phrasing she used, but you know Susan, every story has to have a comic element. Does that ever get on your nerves, by the way? Her insistence on always playing for laughs? Not that it bothers me. Not at all. I need all the laughs I can get, to be honest. It's just that I wondered whether it might start to grate, if you had to live with it all the time.

Even so, I could tell that she was quite touched by that bit when you were crouching by the bed. She said she didn't think she'd ever seen you look quite so sincere.

You'll probably think I'm being paranoid, but there was something in the way she told me that story that made me wonder whether she was saying it because it was an interesting story, or for some other, less fathomable reason. I suddenly remembered telling her about the affair diary piece. Not that she'd ever have recognized either of us from that, of course, but might she have felt that I was trying to imply something, I wonder? Might she, by relating this rather intimate moment, be mounting some sort of a defence?

I tried to push her a bit more by making a joke about how the hysterical bonding must be doing a lot to help her diet. I have to admit, it was hard to bring myself to say that. It's not something I like to dwell too much on, particularly since our recent night in the hotel. Do you remember how you'd always insist that you and Susan never had sex any more? I'd say, 'Oh, all married men say that. It's in the Married Man's Affair Handbook, didn't you know?'

'Yes, but in this case it happens to be true,' you'd say, giving your famous wry smile. 'Believe me, I'd far rather be the having-my-cake-and-eating-it variety of cheating husband, but I'm stupidly old-fashioned. I'm so much in love with you, I can't even contemplate making love to Susan. It wouldn't be fair to any of us.'

'Have you and Clive always had an active sex life?' I asked Susan now, pushing an intimacy that, to be honest, hadn't yet been much in evidence as we sat in the leather Starbucks sofa.

'Oh God yes.' She was almost dismissive about it, and for a moment I wanted to lean across and grab one of her stupid white wisps of hair and wrap it around my hand and yank as hard as I could, pulling out clumps and clumps of it, until they lay on the floor like Singapore noodles.

'Even during that really awful patch when I'd convinced myself there was someone else, the one thing that stopped me making a complete twat out of myself by accusing him of all sorts of groundless stuff was the knowledge that the sex part of things was actually the least of our worries.'

You know, just when I think I can't be shocked any more, something comes along and knocks the breath clean out of me.

Why should I have been surprised? You lied about everything else, why shouldn't you lie about that too? And yet I didn't want to believe it, couldn't believe it.

'You're not looking so hot,' Susan told me. 'Are you sure you're OK?'

I told her I'd been getting headaches from the citalopram withdrawal. And nausea, and dizziness.

'You need to look after yourself a little more.' Susan was all concern now, safely into her comfort zone. 'We're all a bit worried about you.'

I didn't ask her about that 'we'. The word hung in the air like a corpulent fly.

'Don't be silly,' I told her. 'I'm absolutely fine. In fact, I was going to see if you and Emily and Clive wanted to come over for dinner.'

Until the words were out of my mouth I'd had no idea I was actually going to say them. But once I had, I cheered right up. I imagined Susan would probably force you to come, so you'd have to do some major wheeling and dealing to get out of it. You might have to fake a working trip abroad. It would seriously put you out. The thought gave me a sudden stab of intense pleasure.

Susan, however, seemed less than enthusiastic.

'The thing is,' she started (you always know, don't you, that when someone starts a reply with 'the thing is', you're not going to like what they say? Jamie has already started doing it – 'the thing is . . . you're wrong' is what he invariably means), 'it's so near to the vows day that I'm flat-out busy. There are all the flowers to sort out and all sorts of great-aunts and distant cousins once removed to deal with. I don't think we're going to really have time. Also . . .'

Susan trailed into a slight pause after she said that word 'also', and she looked at me as though weighing something up, before carrying on, 'Please don't take this the wrong way, Sally, but I can't help feeling you're getting a little bit, well, *involved* in my family.'

She glanced away quickly when she said that, not really as if she was embarrassed, but more like she was giving me a moment's privacy to digest what she'd said. She's very good like that, isn't she? Very diplomatic.

'I can't help feeling,' continued Susan, 'that you're so worried about your own family's stability that you're sort of taking refuge in mine. Do you know what I mean?'

I must have given her the impression that indeed I didn't

know what she meant, because she went on hastily. 'Please don't think I'm bothered about it from my point of view, although I have to say I think Clive was a bit freaked out when Liam mentioned you'd been in to see him. It's just that I feel you ought to be directing your energies at your own family. You have such great children – I'm sure they'd love to have a bit more of your time.'

Do you know, now I've written that down, I can see it's what psychologists call a 'good-news sandwich'. Daniel learned about it on his teacher-training course. When you have any kind of criticism to deliver, you sandwich it in between two positive comments, so that the person hardly has time to register it before getting hit with the sweetener afterwards. It's very clever, isn't it? Has Susan ever had any kind of psychological training, I wonder? She'd make a wonderful counsellor, although perhaps her rather grating Aussie voice might put a few people off. And sometimes that famous bluntness can seem a little bit, well, insensitive. Not to me, of course. I really appreciate Susan's honesty. It's a marvellous quality. It's just that not everyone I've spoken to feels quite the same way.

To be honest, I didn't really know what to say once Susan had said that. You're going to think I'm paranoid, but it almost sounded as if Susan was warning me off. Yes, I know I'm overreacting, but I was just a little bit hurt.

'I just thought we were friends, that's all,' I said.

Susan's blue eyes looked a little stricken when I said that.

'Of course we're friends, dear. We've known you and Daniel for years and the four of us have always got along very well, haven't we? Clive and I can't wait to have you over for the party. It's only because I care that I can't help worrying about you both, and feeling like you should be focusing a little more on your family.'

She didn't actually add 'and less on mine', but she didn't need to. The unspoken phrase hovered tauntingly in the air.

'Anyway,' she went on, 'Clive and I are flying over to Maui for a week immediately after the ceremony, just to get a bit of down time, a sort of second honeymoon. One of our friends is lending us a ridiculously over-the-top villa there as a second wedding present. But when we get back we'll have tons more time, and maybe we could all get together then. We don't see enough of Daniel these days.'

Can ever a speech have been more barbed? At the mention of the second honeymoon, my guts had started doing something very unpleasant – since coming off the citalopram, they've been playing up rather a lot. Something ugly came up into my mouth and I swallowed it back down with a mouthful of tepid coffee.

'I'm really sorry,' I said. 'I'm not feeling too well.'

Susan was immediately concerned, feeling my forehead with a motherly hand. 'I hope it isn't because of anything I said. I've only got your best interests at heart.'

If it hadn't been for the fear that if I opened my mouth I'd vomit all over the Starbucks shabby-chic battered-leather sofa, I'd have smiled at that one. Well, you couldn't not smile, could you? You and Susan, both with my best interests at heart. I'm a lucky woman, I really am. Between the two of you, you've wrecked my life, pulling at it in a tug of war until it ripped right down the middle like a cheap, worn sheet. But you only have my best interests at heart. Forgive me if I don't altogether believe you. Forgive me if I don't fall on my knees in gratitude at your largesse. Forgive me if I say I want to take my best interests and cram them down your throats until you choke on them. You and Susan and Emily and Liam – the elite club I'm not allowed to join, just to watch from the outside with my nose pressed up against the glass.

You promised me something else. You promised me another life. I'm not after anything I'm not entitled to. I just want what was promised to me.

Is there something wrong with that?

So I missed the parents' evening. I know it's not a great thing to have done, but it happens to lots of busy parents. I don't think there's any need for everyone to make quite such a big thing about it.

Tilly is definitely hormonal. Everything is a crisis with her at the moment. I wonder if I should fix up for her to see Helen for some coping strategies. She might really find it useful.

It's not as if I set out to miss the fucking parents' evening. I was just a little bit upset about seeing Susan earlier in the day, and it went clean out of my mind. I'd been wandering around the West End, buying random things in Topshop, even though all the clothes in there were clearly meant for people thirty years younger. To be honest, I presumed Daniel would have gone to the school anyway. I keep forgetting about this 'training' which seems to absolve him of responsibility for any kind of parenting these days.

'We agreed you'd take over that sort of stuff,' he raged at me after he'd arrived home at seven to find a tearful

Tilly, sobbing in her bedroom writing 'I hate my mum' updates on Facebook. 'It's not like you have anything better to do, is it? When was the last time you did any paid work?'

'I'm working all the time,' I lied. 'I never leave my computer.'

Daniel looked unimpressed.

'Then how come we never seem to have any money? How much is left in the joint account after you paid the mortgage this month?'

I have to confess I was a bit vague. Not because I was fudging the issue, but because it's been so long since I actually checked the balance. And of course, Daniel wouldn't have checked it himself, he has always been more than happy to leave that side of things to me.

'If you're so worried about money, why don't you contribute a bit?' I threw at him.

Daniel looked furious, and to be fair, I could see why. We did actually go through all this when he decided to retrain as a teacher, it's just that I hadn't really taken in all the implications then. I'd been so wrapped up in the fantasy of you and me that nothing else had actually seemed real. And in the back of my mind, I'd assumed that by the time the training was under way, I'd be gone, whisked off to my new life where paying the mortgage didn't feature.

'I suggest you go and talk to your daughter.' He had a weird expression on his face when he said that, as if I was someone he didn't completely recognize, but instinctively knew he didn't like.

Tilly was unforgiving, of course, hermetically sealed off in her hormonal airtight bag. She's going through that unfortunate phase kids reach at thirteen or fourteen where their hitherto dainty features broaden out and coarsen, noses becoming bulbous, skin spotty. She wears her slightly greasy hair across her face like a burka.

Her self-righteous fury rendered her momentarily dumb when I walked into her room. Looking around the walls at all the new posters she'd put up, it occurred to me that I hadn't actually been in Tilly's room for quite some time. When did she stop liking boy singers who looked like babies and start liking bands with leather jackets and scowls?

'Who's that?' I asked her, pointing at one of the posters on the wall.

She turned the full force of her withering gaze on to me. 'Like *you* care!' she said at last.

I told her I was sorry about the parents' evening. I told her I had a lot of things on my mind. To be honest, I was hoping that by taking her into my confidence a bit I might get a little bit of sympathy. I'd forgotten that teenagers don't develop the sympathy gene until much later on, if at all.

'Why don't you just admit it. You don't care about me. You don't care what happens to me. Me and Jamie are just an irritation to you.'

'That's not true.' I was quite indignant. 'I love you both.' It sounded weak and unconvincing, so I expanded. 'I adore you both. But you have to understand that sometimes adults have their own problems. You don't have a monopoly on shitty things happening, you know.'

I'd intended it to sound informal and intimate, but Tilly looked startled by the word 'shitty'. I had to quickly reassure her that I'd call the school first thing tomorrow to fix up a special appointment with her main teachers.

'If you're sure you can fit it into your *busy schedule*,' Tilly sneered.

Sometimes, you know, I feel like I just can't do any more than I'm doing. I know it's not perfect, but it's all I can give at the moment. I wish the children were just a little bit more, well, empathetic. It really would be such a relief.

When I went out of Tilly's room, leaving her staring stony-faced ahead with her iPod headphones stuffed into her ears, I noticed Jamie's bedroom door was slightly open, and there was a slightly muffled breathing coming from inside that made me think he'd been listening to me and Tilly arguing. For a moment, I hesitated, wondering if I should go in and chat to him and explain things. But, you know, my head was pounding and I was still upset about what had happened with Susan, and the scene with Tilly hadn't helped, and all the way home I'd been picturing the large glass of wine I was going to pour myself from the fridge. So I carried on down the stairs.

The thing about kids, as I'm sure you know, is they're very resilient.

* * *

I had half expected your email, of course. The moment I'd made that arrangement with Susan to meet at Starbucks, I'd known you wouldn't like it and realized there was a fairly good chance you'd be getting in touch. I didn't know you'd feel quite so strongly about it, though, I confess. I mean, 'campaign of harassment'. What's that all about? I make a perfectly reasonable arrangement to meet an old friend for a coffee and suddenly I'm mounting a campaign of harassment. Really, Clive, you need to work on your perspective issues. You really do.

As for that part about things being about to turn 'nasty', I do sometimes think you must be plundering your hairdresser's stories for dialogue. That isn't you speaking, Clive. I know you, remember? (Suddenly an image of the ferret-faced squeegee man pops into my head, dirty water slopping out of his bucket as he hurried away.)

I do take your point about you giving me every opportunity for withdrawing voluntarily from your life. The problem has always been that I don't really want to withdraw from your life. Nice of you to give me the opportunities, though. Was that what you were doing when you fucked me on that bed in the windowless hotel room? Giving me an opportunity to withdraw?

It's a good job I didn't have time to sit and analyse that message properly, or I might have got quite depressed. Instead, I had to hurry out of the door to a meeting at Tilly's school. I was quite taken aback when I rang first thing this morning (well, OK, maybe not completely first thing, but definitely before my morning nap. Oh, and maybe it was they who called me and not the other way around, now I come to think about it) and was told that the head teacher and Tilly's form teacher would like to see me at my 'earliest convenience'. I didn't tell them that no time was really convenient for me, or that my packed timetable of compulsive email checking left little in the way of free time.

When I arrived at the school, Tilly was slouched in a plastic chair outside the head teacher's office, chewing on a strand of her hair.

'Everything OK, darling?' I asked her brightly,

principally for the benefit of the head teacher's secretary who was sitting at an adjacent desk.

Tilly gave me a scornful look, scrutinizing what I was wearing. Did your kids do that? Vet everything you and Susan wore to their school in case it somehow reflected badly on them? I imagine it's not so pronounced in the kind of public schools they went to. I expect there's more of a prevailing bohemian liberalism there, as opposed to Tilly's school, where the wrong kind of jeans can permanently brand a parent and bring lasting shame on their offspring. I have to say that, under her critical glare, I suddenly wished I'd made a bit more of an effort. There's nothing quite like being judged by a thirteen-year-old to make one feel wanting. Your email this morning unsettled me so much that I just threw on whatever was closest to hand from the pile on the floor by my bed. Looking down I noticed that the black jumper I was wearing had drips of toothpaste all the way down it, which I tried to scrape off with my fingernail.

The head teacher, Mrs Sutherland, and Tilly's form teacher, a boy-man called Mr Meyer, who didn't look old enough to shave, sat side by side on a sofa in Mrs Sutherland's office. Much to Tilly's obvious annoyance, they wanted to see me first on my own.

'We're a little concerned about Tilly,' was Mrs Sutherland's opening gambit. Well, you can imagine I was a little bit nonplussed. I'd gone in there thinking I was going to get a quick appraisal of Tilly's academic progress, not to listen to any concerns (and to be quite frank, after my coffee with Susan yesterday, I've had just about enough of other people's concerns).

She went on to say that Tilly's attitude had changed

markedly over the past few weeks. That was the exact word. *Markedly*. Apparently she's gone from being a conscientious A student to neglecting her homework and looking blatantly bored, and on occasion being rude in lessons.

'Is there anything happening at home that might be able to explain the change in Tilly's behaviour?' asked the quasi-adolescent Mr Meyer.

Naturally, my first reaction was to tell them to mind their own fucking business. As if I'd tell them what was happening at home. If indeed anything were ever to happen at home, which of course it doesn't (ours being the house where nothing ever happens).

I pointed out that Tilly was at that age where hormones start kicking in and kids start acting completely out of character. I was annoyed to find my voice wavering as I spoke and to realize that I was on the verge of tears.

'Usually the hormonal problems tend to manifest them-selves at home rather than at school,' Mrs Sutherland said doubtfully. 'It's unusual for a girl like Tilly to lose her way so noticeably and so suddenly.'

When Tilly was called in to join us, Mrs Sutherland repeated much of what she'd just told me.

'Have you got any explanations, Tilly?' she asked her. 'Is there anything troubling you? You're such a talented girl. We just want to help.'

Tilly sat sullenly, still chewing on her hair, and shook her head. The teachers turned their eyes to me then, but I found I didn't have anything to add. My mind was still caught up in that phrase Mrs Sutherland had used, about Tilly having 'lost her way'.

My daughter had lost her way. And suddenly I

wondered whether that's what has happened to me too. Have I lost my way, and Daniel also? The three of us wandering blindfold around our lives, bumping into walls.

Have I done that to us? Have I made us like that? Or was it you, Clive? Is it your fault my daughter can't find her way back? Have you ripped up the map that we were all reading from?

Is this because of you?

On the way back from school a very odd thing happened.

I was crossing the main road, past the library, when I saw a man in a familiar jacket sitting on a bench further along. Black leather, with stripes down the sleeve. When I got to the other side, I turned the opposite way and hurried along the road, but I knew without looking that he was following me.

Of course, I knew you had sent him. I kept trying to draw comfort from that. I kept trying to make myself see him as a present from you to me, but my stupid, heavy basketball of a heart was bouncing around uncontrollably in my chest, bruising my insides, and waves of dizziness were passing through me.

Then all of a sudden, he wasn't there any more. The insistent padding of his too-white trainers was no longer echoing the sound of my own footsteps. I slowed down, my pulse still painfully hyperactive, my nerves still stretched tight as catgut. I decided to cut back home through the park, but guess who was waiting by the park entrance?

I'm only joking! I know you know exactly who was waiting there, in his black leather-look jacket and his nasty jeans, leaning against a lamppost, smoking a cigarette. Looking at me. Looking at me. Looking at me.

'Nice day, isn't it?' he said to me as I approached him, trying not to look terrified.

When I didn't reply, he slowly straightened up and ground his fag butt under the sole of his trainers.

'You've been upsetting people,' he told me, and his voice was as casual as Sunday brunch. 'You've been upsetting friends of mine. You need to stop doing that. Do you get what I mean?'

He smiled at me and I noticed that the teeth in the front were several shades whiter than those at the back. Do you think that's some sort of money-saving thing? Did he not think it was worth whitening the back ones because nobody really sees them?

I couldn't speak, of course. I actually wanted to laugh, because it was all so preposterous. Who was this man threatening me at the gateway to the park where Tilly and Jamie used to play on the swings on winter mornings so cold their breath came out in puffs of white smoke? Since when did my life turn into a low-budget gangster movie?

The man was still smiling, but my face was frozen with fear. It had to be some sort of a joke, right? And yet it wasn't a joke. He was the thank-you gift you'd sent me after our night together. But he couldn't be real. This couldn't be real.

I walked past him without speaking, half expecting him to reach out to grab hold of me, or at least to follow me, but he remained immobile. In the park, the Mothers' Mafia were out in force, with their three-wheel buggies and their toddlers clutching their organic muesli bars. I have to say, I was bewildered as I looked at them. Hadn't they witnessed what just happened to me? How could they still be living in a world where the worst thing that could happen was little Jack refusing to wear his tricycle helmet, when just yards away a man had quite clearly threatened to do me harm?

Or had he?

By the time I reached the opposite entrance to the park, I was already starting to have doubts about what had happened. It was too surreal. Things like that just didn't happen. Not in places like this. Not to people like me. I thought again about what he'd said. He hadn't actually made any threats, had he? I could have been wrong. I could have misinterpreted his meaning. By the time I was halfway home, I was starting to feel foolish. And do you know what was the weirdest thing? Really, I *knew* that you had sent him, knew he'd been standing outside my house the other day, knew exactly what he was trying to say. And yet my stupid, useless common sense refused to let me fully confront it.

By the time I put my key in the door, my hand had stopped trembling and I had started to rethink my reaction.

You wouldn't have sent the man with the stripes on his sleeves, if indeed you did, unless you still wanted to maintain a connection to me. He is the go-between, the bringer of conflicted love notes and billets-doux. He is the proof, white trainered and puffed-up chested, that you still care.

The man with the two-tone teeth is another link to you. He scares me, and yet now that he has gone, I find myself wanting to see him again. Is that perverse? Through my bedroom window, I scan the empty pavements opposite looking for a flash of over-white trainer and am almost disappointed to see nothing.

I feel things are moving forward. There's a momentum

about life at the moment, isn't there? The man with the leather jacket represents progress of a sort.

I hope Helen will be pleased.

* * *

The whooshing in my head is getting worse. If I look to the side suddenly, it feels like my brain has come loose in my skull and is skidding around, and I feel light-headed all the time.

I Googled the symptoms and while it could just be the withdrawal from antidepressants, it apparently could also be stress. I feel like my life has slipped out of gear somehow and I can't seem to get it back.

I try to talk to Tilly about what's happening with her, but everything I say comes out wrong and she looks at me as though I'm that alien who has switched places with her real mother.

'Your teachers say you've lost your way,' I babble. But when she looks at me, I can't meet her eyes. I spend a lot of time in the cubbyhole. It feels strangely safe.

This morning, there was a phone call on the landline. Usually a call on the landline can only mean my dad or one of Daniel's ageing parents, phoning from afar with voices tremulous with reproach, or else a recorded message advertising itself in advance with a mechanical click. This time, though, there was a real live, non-parent person on the phone. He was very polite, but there was a hard edge to his voice.

'Mrs Islip?' Don't you love the way people who don't know you often think conferring you with a marital status you don't possess is somehow akin to doing you a favour?

As if they're graciously extending you a particular courtesy you ought to be grateful for?

He was phoning from a debt-collection agency. The whooshing in my head reached epic proportions while he spoke. I owe his client 'a substantial amount' of money, apparently. He wanted to know what 'plans' I had in mind with regard to repaying the money.

My tongue swelled up in my mouth, huge and leaden, like a slab of cold, congealed lasagne. He told me the 'substantial amount' I owed and it sounded ludicrous. Impossible.

'Are you quite sure that's correct?' My voice belonged to someone else.

'I'm afraid it often comes as quite a shock to people to hear the figures out loud. Haven't you been reading the letters we've sent you?'

Of course, he knew very well that I hadn't been. I'm a text-book case, I imagine. Just like all the rest.

'Can I take it you'll be making a payment within the next ten days?' He was so unerringly polite. They must go on training courses for that, don't you think?

'We don't expect the full amount, of course, but my client does need to see some evidence of good intentions. Nobody wants to get the bailiffs involved.'

The bailiffs? I have to tell you, Clive, coming hot on the heels of the man in the leather jacket, this phone call only served to convince me further that I've somehow stumbled on to the wrong filmset. This is not my life. This is not who I am.

But then again, as everyone keeps saying, I'm not myself. So perhaps this is indeed who I am now.

I'm so confused and my head won't leave me alone. It

taps out drum tattoos on the inner surface of my brain.

I need you to help me feel right again.

I need you to turn me back into me.

* * *

I wish you'd get a Facebook page, Clive. I really do. How many times did I used to urge you to do that, when we were still 'together' (what a strange phrase for two people who were clearly such poles apart).

'Oh, I would never do that,' you'd say vehemently. 'I find it so *sinister*.'

Thank God I'm Facebook friends with Susan and Emily. It's so reassuring to go to their pages and be able to keep abreast of all the things that are happening in your lives, particularly since it has become so difficult to get hold of Susan. (I worry about how much this vows business is taking out of her. She's clearly overwhelmed with it all.)

I've just been looking at Emily's page. My goodness, she has a lot of friends, doesn't she? They're all young and attractive, just like her, and lots of them have double-barrelled names that take up three lines on her 'friends' list.

I suspect Emily is finding time weighing on her a bit much. She updates her status several times a day, and it's all about her pregnancy. She clearly imagines she's the first woman ever to have reproduced, and every new development is accompanied with a row of exclamation marks, as if we'll all be as amazed as she is.

Emily Gooding-Brown *is finding it impossible to sleep because the baby keeps waking her up!!!!!!*

Emily Gooding-Brown *can't find any clothes to fit her!!!!!*

Underneath each of her status updates are always a clutch of comments, leading me to suppose that most of her friends are as time-rich as she is.

Georgia Hanley-Corrigan *Not long now babes!*

Often I'll add a comment of my own. I always try to be positive and supportive – I see myself as a sort of trusted auntie figure, and I make sure never to be patronizing. Even if sometimes I do want to just write

Sally Islip *says why not get a life, Emily!!!!!!!*

This morning, I was enjoying a particularly lengthy exchange between Emily and her friend Flikka (I think it's lovely the way so many of her friends have these amusing nicknames, don't you?). They were talking about the summer holidays and Flikka, who is clearly also about to drop, was stating her intention of spending a few weeks at Mummy's place in the south of France. Well, I have to say, Emily got quite agitated.

Emily Gooding-Brown *That sort of heat can be very dangerous for newborns. Risk of febrile convulsions.*

Flikka de Souza *Air con darling!!! Anyway, I will need the break. I'll be exhausted, and Mummy has lined up a divine local lady to come in and help so I'll get lots of yummy lie-ins.*

Emily Gooding-Brown *Lucky you being so laid back. I know I won't let anyone else near my baby once he's born. I'll be like a tigress, I know it!!!!!!!*

I was so engrossed in this that I completely forgot about Jamie, who has stayed off school, complaining of a tummy ache. When I heard him calling me, I almost jumped out of my slack old skin!!!!!!

I dragged myself out of the cubbyhole and pushed open the door of his bedroom. Jamie was sitting up in bed, playing on his PSP.

'I'm bored,' he told me.

Can there be anything more irritating than a child who ought to be at school making you break off work to tell you he's bored?

'Well, go to school then.'

At this, Jamie remembered to put on a vaguely pained air. 'I can't, I don't feel well.'

'You look fine to me.'

Then, to my horror, I realized he was about to cry. Jamie hardly ever cries. I put my arms around him, and realized by how awkward it felt that it must be a while since I held him. He felt much more fragile in my arms than I remembered, his shoulder blades sharp as beaks. I don't know whether this ever happened with you, but when I'm away from my children I always imagine them to be far bigger, far more mature than they actually are, and then I'll hear them on the phone or come across them quite by chance and realize they're still young, and it always shocks me. I expect all parents feel that, don't they?

Jamie seemed very tense at first, but then he kind of slumped into me. We sat there for a while just gently swaying. The thing was, though, that after a while I started to get this really anxious feeling. I get it quite a lot at the moment, but this was worse than usual, like something was slowly burning through me. I began to feel very uncomfortable, sitting there with Jamie, and I know this is going to sound odd, but I missed the cubbyhole. I missed the computer and I missed this journal.

'I know, why don't I take you to school?' I said to Jamie, brightly. 'You can still get there for lunchtime.'

He looked slightly crestfallen. 'Can't I stay here with you?'

The kids don't really get this working-from-home thing, do they? They seem to think we've got all the time in the world to sit around doing nothing. When I explained I was busy, Jamie's face kind of closed up, like a serving hatch. I tried not to notice, and stood up, ready to go. Jamie didn't move.

'You can't go out like that. You're in your dressing gown. *As usual*.'

His voice was different than it had been a few minutes before, as if he'd taken a pencil sharpener and sharpened it up.

When I looked down, I realized he was right. I had on the old fleecy beige dressing gown that Sian is always threatening to burn. How come I hadn't noticed that before? I'd just assumed I was dressed. To be quite honest, I then started to wonder whether I'd actually got dressed yesterday either. I tried to picture what clothes I'd put on, but found nothing came into my head. Uh-ohhh.

Feeling wrongfooted, I told Jamie he could stay at home, as long as he kept himself occupied. But now I'm back in the cubbyhole, I feel resentful. Daytimes are my time. They've always been my time. I know it's wrong, but it feels like Jamie is intruding. I feel like I can hear his breathing, even though I know I can't really. My head keeps whooshing, and the anxious feeling just won't go away. My computer screen is still open to Emily's Facebook page, and her face looks out haughtily from under a cowboy hat.

Sally Islip *feels like her brain is exploding.*

Sally Islip *doesn't understand anything.*

Sally Islip *has lost her way.*

* * *

This morning, there were two more calls from debt agencies. I told them they had the wrong number. I said we'd been getting a lot of calls for Sally Islip and maybe she'd had that number before, but she certainly didn't now.

'I'm terribly sorry to have disturbed you, madam,' said the first man. 'Can I have your name, so we can wipe you from the records?'

My head, with its exploding brain, had to think quickly.

'Susan Gooding,' I said. 'Mrs Susan Gooding.'

'My apologies, Mrs Gooding,' came the reply.

I have to say, it quite shocked me just how easy it was to become your wife. In fact, I can't imagine why I haven't become her before. All it takes is a few words into a telephone, and here I am. Mrs Gooding. I try it out tentatively, like a spoonful of extra-spicy curry.

While the phone was in my hand anyway, I decided to phone Susan. The real Susan, of course. Well, it's been nearly ten days since that coffee in Starbucks, and I wanted to know how she's getting on. You really must watch that diet she's on, Clive. I mean, I know Susan thinks she could do with losing a teensy bit of weight, but she doesn't want to overdo it. Even former models can't afford to get too thin once they reach a certain age.

When I rang, she was at her desk in the office. I could hear lots of loud voices in the background. I must say they did sound like they were having fun, all of them. I envy that sometimes, that camaraderie.

Susan sounded distracted, but she wanted to know how I was, how I was feeling. I said I was fine. I didn't tell her about the debt phone calls, or the man in the leather jacket, or the headache that never really goes away. Instead I told her how much I was looking forward to the big party, and asked her whether she wanted me to come round early to help her prepare stuff.

'That's all right,' she said, and she sounded almost tetchy. I think those companies must be very high-pressure places to work. 'I'll have my family there to help.'

There was something in the way she said 'my family' that made my headache worse. I don't know why. Even after I'd put the phone down, I heard the phrase sounding in my head. 'My family.' Why should she have said it like that? Why should she have said it at all? I just don't get any of it.

Back at my computer, I Googled you to see if there was anything new since I last did it yesterday. I noticed there was a little thing in the *Mirror* about a singer who objected to the way she'd been 'packaged' by you and your record label.

'I feel he has cheapened me,' she said.

I read that sentence a few times. There was something there that resonated.

How many more of us are there, I wonder, who feel cheapened by you.

I imagine our numbers swelling like the tide.

I am begging you. Don't come next Saturday. Not for my sake, but for Susan's. Please don't ruin her big day.

It's a very touching message, I must say, Clive. It's only natural that you should be concerned about Susan. I'm sure you only have her best interests at heart too. (Although that wasn't always the case. Remember? How I used to have to remind you that you were married? How I used to have to make you return home at the end of the evening, shoving you back on to the platform when you attempted to board the Tube home with me? 'Susan's very self-sufficient,' you'd say. 'She won't actually notice I'm not there.' I'm so glad to see how protective of her you've become. God knows she deserves a little cherishing after everything that has happened.)

But you see, you don't need to worry. I adore Susan, as you know. I wouldn't dream of doing anything to upset her. If I didn't think Susan wanted me at the party, I certainly wouldn't go. But she has been so very insistent that I must come. And I promised to bring a bag of baby clothes for Emily. They're my favourite ones from when Tilly and Jamie were little, lovingly folded and smoothed down and packed away in a thick plastic bag in the loft. I'd half a mind to save them until Tilly had children, but now I can see that's quite ridiculous. How old-fashioned will they seem in fifteen or twenty years' time? Silleeeee Salleeeeee. Emily seemed quite taken aback when I told her about them. *U shd kp thm 4 ur kids!* That was her first response. (Took me a while to decipher, I must say. Aren't they clever, these young people, doing away with all those excess letters. Who'd have thought vowels would prove so easily expendable?) But after I assured her that I wanted her to have them, she was clearly pleased. *Gr8. Tnx a mlln!* she replied.

Also, and I know this will mean something to you, as you were always so careful to tell me how concerned you were about Daniel's welfare ('I know I probably sound like the worst sort of hypocrite, but I genuinely care about Daniel,' you'd say, magnanimous to the last. 'I'd do anything not to hurt him.' Anything apart from not fuck his girlfriend, obviously), Daniel is really looking forward to the party.

'It'll do us so much good to have a change of scene,' he said the other night. 'When was the last time we did anything fun together? Please promise me you're not going to change your mind about going.'

He has, in fact, got a point. Increasingly often over the past days, I've been avoiding leaving the house, pleading illness and exhaustion. And to be honest, it's not mere show. The headaches and nausea seem to be getting worse rather than better. I must make an appointment to see the blonde-haired doctor, only I can't bear her look of disappointment if I tell her I've taken myself off the pills. I don't think she'll understand how wanting to *feel* again might be worth putting up with all the other stuff.

Several times, I've backed out of things at the last minute – the pub quiz with Sian and the usual crew, dinner at Daniel's brother Darren's house. Poor Daniel, no wonder he's fed up. You can understand, I'm sure, why it's so important for us to come. I'm quite certain you wouldn't want to do anything to disappoint him.

And besides – how ridiculous is it that I almost forgot to

say this! – I'm also greatly looking forward to it myself. I really am. I feel like it'll be a big turning point in what everyone keeps calling my 'recovery'. You know, Helen is very keen on me confronting things that make me un-comfortable (she calls it 'probing my discomfort zone'), and I think this is just the scenario to test that out (although strangely, Helen doesn't seem keen on me going to the party and has actively tried to dissuade me). You and Susan and your lovely house with its elegant curved driveway and your engaging children and your enviable marriage – you're my discomfort zone (please don't take that the wrong way), and I owe it to myself to probe away until my fears lose their capacity to scare (that's another of Helen's sayings).

So what I'm trying to say in this very long-winded way is that you don't need to worry about anything. I just want to be there to see you and Susan celebrate this auspicious day. Is there anything wrong in that? Please be assured that I'm not going to stand in the corner wishing it was me, or follow you around reminding you of all the things you said. I'm not going to bring up the marriage proposal, or the baby that never was. I'm not going to talk about the five years of hotel rooms paid for in cash. (How much do you reckon we spent over the years? How many thousands? How many tens of thousands?) I'm not going to talk about the other vows you made, the ones you made to me. I won't mention the way you ripped my heart out through my throat and squeezed it till the blood ran through your closed fist and pooled on the floor and all that was left in your hand was a fibrous mulch.

I'm not going to say any of that. So please be reassured. And neither, of course, did I put any of that into the email I sent you just now. Instead I just told you about Daniel and the baby clothes, and how very much we are looking forward to the event. I hope that puts your mind at rest, I really do. This is your big day too, don't forget. You owe it to yourself to relax and enjoy it.

* * *

Well, I can't say it wasn't a shock.

It wasn't even me that found it. As I've said, I don't leave the house so much these days. Not if I can help it. So it was Daniel and the kids who went to the car this morning and found the side window smashed and a brick with a note tied to it lying on the passenger seat. Not terribly original, was it? The brick and the note, I mean. Don't be offended, but I do think it detracted from the overall effect of the gesture – the clichéd aspect of it, I mean.

Of course, it didn't stop Tilly from getting hysterical. She was convinced there was someone watching them as they inspected the car for damage. She was sure that whoever had written that 'BACK OFF!! THIS ISN'T A GAME!!' in such huge red letters was still there, lurking just out of sight, watching to see what effect his actions had had.

Does it make you feel big, Clive? Terrifying a young girl? Does it make you feel like a big, hard man?

Jamie's eyes were huge when he came running back inside the house to tell me what had happened.

'Who did that, Mum?' he asked me. 'Who smashed our window?'

That's pretty much what Daniel wanted to know too.

'Can you think of anyone who might have done that?'

He watched me carefully as he waited for an answer, and I felt a bit like a criminal in an identity parade trying not to look guilty. Do you know what I mean?

'Don't be silly, Daniel,' I said. 'It was obviously meant for someone else. Do you remember that time with the guy at the door with the baseball bat?'

I don't think I ever told you that story, did I? We'd only been living in our first flat for a few months when there was a knock on the door and there stood this massive chap with a baseball bat in his back pocket and his almost-as-massive sidekick, demanding recompense for the dodgy cheque we were supposed to have written. Well, after a long time and a lot of explaining on our part, we finally worked out that the people who'd written the cheque lived at 76b Summerfield Place, while we lived at 76b Summerfield Avenue. He was perfectly charming after that, but it was an alarming encounter nonetheless.

So, it wasn't that much of a stretch of the imagination to convince Daniel that someone had thrown the brick and the warning note through our car window by mistake. After all, he doesn't know anything about the guy with the leather jacket, or the malicious emails sent from my account, or the being followed, or your hairdresser and his family. But still, he did give me a very odd look, which I wasn't sure how to interpret.

Of course, he insisted on calling the police, which made Tilly even more hysterical and Jamie rather thrilled. They arrived a few hours later – in fact, they've only just left really. It's amazing how thorough they were, going through the car, checking the brick and the notes and the door handles for fingerprints. They didn't find any, though.

'Whoever did it knew what they were doing, and obviously wanted to give someone a fright,' a young policeman with a shaving rash told me. I couldn't be sure, but it seemed like he too was looking at me strangely, and I wondered for one mad moment if he thought I might have done it myself. Yes, I know that's just silly, but the whole thing is so surreal, you'd be amazed what passes through one's mind.

After the police left and I managed to slip gratefully back into the cubbyhole, I thought a lot about that note, with its twin exclamation marks, so doubly emphatic.

'This isn't a game!' the note said, and I wondered what exactly might not be a game. Life? The world? You? Me? Us?

I wondered whether you'd written the note yourself, but thought it more likely you'd dictated it. I imagined the thickset man in the leather jacket painstakingly copying down what you told him. Did he buy an extra-thick felt pen especially for the job, I wondered? I thought he was probably the type to stick the tip of his tongue out just slightly between his teeth as he concentrated. I pictured him with his wide forehead slightly furrowed.

Now, of course, I know it could turn out to be nothing to do with you at all, in which case please do accept my sincerest apologies. It could indeed turn out to be an innocent mix-up, some local youths mistaking our old blue Saab for another very similar. Happens all the time. But something tells me that it isn't a mistake. Something tells me you're behind this, Clive. I actually find it quite flattering. (He cares!! See, you're not the only one who can work the double exclamation mark.) But I didn't like that fevered look in Jamie's eyes, or the way Tilly peeped through the living-room window to check the coast was clear before venturing outside earlier on.

The car window has been boarded up with part of a cardboard box. Wouldn't it be lovely if everything was so easy to patch up? Wouldn't it be great to tape a sheet of tatty cardboard over the gaping hole you've left through the core of me?

I don't like what you've done to my family, Clive. I don't like the way you've made us all afraid of dark corners, looking nervously through netted windows. I don't like the way you've put a brick through our lives.

Don't threaten me.

Do NOT threaten me.

Back off. This is not a game.

* * *

'What are you hoping to achieve?'

I'm not joking, Helen was like a stuck record today. She really was. In fact, I was left seriously wondering whether it was really worth paying £75 just to listen to her asking me about what I hoped to achieve, again and again and again. I could just have played a recording of it on a loop for an hour and got the same effect. Maybe I should think about ending my sessions with Helen. I've been considering that more and more recently. Don't get me wrong, at the beginning she was tremendously useful. My personal development came on in leaps and bounds. Well, it was off the scale really. Like I said, I'm so grateful to you for recommending therapy and I can quite see why you took to it. But recently Helen has seemed a little lacklustre, and a little negative, which has got to be one of the worst things you can say about a therapist, surely? I wonder if she's going through some sort of crisis in her own private life. It wouldn't surprise me.

Anyway, the upshot is I think the honeymoon period is well and truly over for me and Helen. I'm starting to think I might have absorbed all I can from her, which is probably a compliment in a way.

Like I said, this afternoon she just seemed to be obsessed with me going to your party tomorrow night.

'What are you hoping to achieve by it?' she kept asking.

I tried to explain again and again that it wasn't a question of achieving anything – it's going to be a lovely social occasion that everyone is looking forward to – Daniel, Susan and even Emily. It would be very bad form for me not to go. But Helen just didn't seem able to grasp this. That phrase 'wilful sabotage' came up several times. To be honest, I'm getting just a bit bored of it. My head was hurting – it felt as if someone was shrinking my skull, tightening it up so that it was pressing painfully against my brain. I kept looking down at my denim-clad legs and feeling disoriented and realized it had been days since I last saw them covered in anything but that old dressing gown.

'Don't you think you might be trying to insinuate yourself back into Clive's life?'

That was the very word she used. 'Insinuate.' I have to say, I wasn't too thrilled about it – it has unpleasant overtones, don't you think? It's a snaky, underhand kind of word.

I told her she was wrong. And of course she is. I'm not trying to 'insinuate' myself into your life. I don't need to. I AM in your life, whether you like it or not. I'm not sure Helen or you have quite grasped that.

After the 'insinuate' word, there was an awkwardness between us that hasn't really been evident in past sessions. Do you find that with your supa-dupa Harley Street therapist, I wonder? That you sometimes sulk about the silent judgements he seems to be making. I decided to punish Helen by withholding choice bits of information that I knew would have rather thrilled her. So I didn't tell her about the brick through the car window, or the man in the leather jacket, nor did I tell her about the phone calls that have been coming regularly now: 'Mrs Islip? It's about your bill . . .' Helen didn't deserve them, I felt. 'Insinuate' had been unnecessary.

Helen tried to get me to focus on Daniel. She seems to think I have stopped seeing him properly and need to be retrained to see him with fresh eyes.

'You're not experiencing him as a complete entity,' she told me.

I have to admit that made me think – the idea of 'experiencing' Daniel. I wonder what form that experience might take, whether I'd absorb him with each of my senses individually, or just let him wash over me like a parachute jump or a day out at Euro Disney.

Helen seems to think that because I've got out of the habit of experiencing Daniel as a complete entity, I've blinded myself to all the qualities that made me choose him as a mate in the first place, and instead I'm investing you with all the credit I'm no longer giving him. That's the phrase she uses, 'investing'. I quite like it, actually. I like the idea that I'm depositing my credit with you, as if I'm making an informed, responsible consumer choice rather than letting things happen to me.

Helen asked me when things with Daniel had become so

'disassociated', and I tried to remember when it had all started – whether we'd always been slightly out of sync, like when bands used to mime on *Top of the Pops*, their lips opening a fraction later than the vocal track, or whether there had been a time when we understood each other.

The truth is that just as every time my children enter a new developmental stage I instantly and completely forget the last, so I've erased from memory my and Daniel's joint past. If I force myself to remember, disjointed vignettes jump into my mind that do seem to show we were, if not passionately in love, at least solicitous of one another. I can see Daniel standing in front of the oven of our first flat in his favourite worn Levi's, cooking up a lavish meal for no other reason than that eating it would make me happy. But did it really make me happy? Do you know, I simply don't remember. When I look back, there is only you. You take up the centre-stage of my memory, spreading out your mass territorially like Jabba the Hutt.

'I'm asking you, for your own sake and for your children's sake, to consider carefully your decision to go to this party tomorrow.' If Helen's sincerity had brimmed over any more, she'd have drowned herself in it.

But you know, Helen doesn't really understand. Sometimes I look at her sensible feet in her sensible shoes and her sensible glasses on her sensible nose and her sensible head cocked empathetically to one side and I just want to throw back my head and roar like a fucking animal, just to see what she does. Try empathizing with *that*, I'd scream, shrieking like a banshee.

Helen thinks she knows me, but she doesn't know me. I thought I knew you, but I didn't know you. I thought you wouldn't hurt me, but you hurt me. None of us really knows the truth about each other. We're all just fumbling about in the dark.

*   *   *

The day of the party and I'm *so* excited. I didn't sleep much last night – not even with two zopiclones and a clonazepam. My eyes are sunk in two vats of black tar.

I finally drifted off to sleep when it was already light, but was woken up not much later by the sound of the phone ringing. Daniel reached out from under the duvet and grabbed it and I listened as he grunted into the receiver, his tone growing sharper and more focused with every sound.

'What . . . I don't understand . . . What bill? . . . Check your records . . . There's been a mistake . . . No, you listen. There's been a mistake . . . You do that, mate.' (Daniel is inclined to go into Blue-Collar-Dialect Mode when dealing with anyone he feels lower down the social evolutionary scale.) 'You send the bailiffs round, and see how quickly we're on to our solicitor.'

I closed my eyes. Well, what else could I do?

'Who was that?' I murmured as if half-asleep.

'Some idiot saying we owe the gas company six hundred quid. Six hundred quid! We don't even use six hundred quid's worth of gas in a year, and anyway we're on direct debit, aren't we? I think it's a scam. Who works on Saturdays anyway?'

Debt-collection agencies, apparently.

Suddenly Daniel went very quiet and I could sense him looking at me.

251

'I haven't seen any of our joint-account statements for a while now, Sally. Do you know what's been happening to them?'

Don't you think that's a cop-out? Asking me as if it's my fault!

I pretended to be asleep, but Daniel got up and started huffing about in that way he does when he's trying to make his presence felt. Something had obviously just occurred to him, and it wasn't something good.

So that kind of spoiled the start to your vow-renewal day, really. Which I think was a bit selfish as we had all been so looking forward to it. I do hope *your* day began better. I imagine you and Susan were up early, with all the chores you had to do. But I'm sure you will have managed a few moments after the alarm went where you lay together in bed looking at each other and giggling gently about the day ahead. Or maybe you will have gone down the traditional route and slept separately last night. Perhaps you woke up this morning in the spare room at Emily's Notting Hill pad, blinking for a moment while you tried to remember where you were. I bet Susan called you first thing. 'Hello, husband,' she might have said. 'Hello, wife,' you'd have replied.

You wouldn't have had to say much more to each other. Those twenty-six years of marriage speak more eloquently than any words of endearment, don't they? (Do you remember when you used to say you'd never been able to talk to anyone the way you could to me? Do you remember saying you could never get tired of hearing the sound of my voice, or ever run out of things to say?)

I'm so glad the weather has held out for the two of you. Really I am. That marquee in the garden could have got terribly muddy, I expect, if it had rained. Of course, it would be nice if it was a teensy bit warmer, but you can't have it all, can you? And Susan's so clever about practical stuff, isn't she? I'm sure she'll have organized indoor patio heaters.

I keep wondering what you're doing at any given moment. It's nearly midday now, so I imagine you'll be setting off to the church – so sweet that you're doing it in a church rather than a registry office, despite your well-worn joke about not wanting to be a member of any religion that would accept you as a member. Don't worry, I'm not in the least offended that we weren't invited to the church bit. I know that's just for your nearest and dearest. (Funny to think that just a few months ago I would have been top of that list. How quickly things change, hey?)

I have to say, today is passing so slowly. Us second-class guests aren't expected at your house until five, so there are still hours stretching ahead until we can leave.

I had the most marvellous idea earlier. I don't know why it didn't occur to me before.

My head was doing its usual whooshing – much worse than usual, actually – after my sleepless night. I was actually starting to wonder if I could even face going out at all. Then I remembered the box of citalopram sitting redundant on the bathroom shelf and I suddenly thought, 'Why don't I take a couple?'

I haven't had one for weeks now, so I'm sure it can't do any harm to reward myself with three or four of them, just to give my seratonin levels a quick boost. Then later I'll take a Sinequan or two in case I start to feel anxious once I get to the party – just to be on the safe side. I've covered all bases, you see. Only the best for your big day.

Daniel asked me again at breakfast about that phone call. I didn't tell him that on weekdays when he's on his course I might get five or six phone calls just like that. Daniel wouldn't understand. He'd just get into a state about it. He tends to overreact. Money has always made him anxious. In the part of the West Midlands where he grew up, the acquisition of wealth was approached much in the same spirit that mothers used to take their kids to chicken-pox parties – you courted it, you got it, and once you had it you bore it with fortitude and stoicism. You certainly never expected to enjoy it.

I told him I didn't know what the phone call was about, and promised I'd try to find the missing bank statements. The thing is, even though he was asking about them, I know he really doesn't want to see them. He's just going through the motions out of a sense of duty. He wants to be seen to be taking action without actually doing it. That's Daniel's modus operandi.

I'm going to have to be careful when I get ready for the party, though. I don't think I'll get away this time with telling him I've had the dress for ages, not when it's so distinctive, so I'll just have to say I got it in the sale. It was so cheap, it would have been rude not to, I'll say. To be quite honest, I don't really care any more whether or not he believes me. Once the trust goes in a relationship, what have you got?

Of course, I shouldn't really have bought the dress at all. It was ridiculously expensive. But you know I want to feel I'm looking my best for the party. I wouldn't want to let you down. Doesn't that sound silly? It's a fabulous dress, though, very fitted and plain and strapless. (I know what they say about women over forty showing their necks and shoulders, but really I think that's just another misogynistic myth, don't you?) And guess what colour it is? Fuchsia pink! Yes, I know that's the same colour as Susan's, I'm not that stupid. I thought she might appreciate a bit of support, that's all. I mean, I'm sure there will be those who might say (and I'm not one of them, believe me) that Susan can't really carry off such a strong colour with her pale skin, so I think that having such a close friend there wearing the same shade will be a kind of validation, don't you think?

Plus, to be quite honest, it looks pretty good on me, I think. I'd never have thought of that colour before hearing about Susan's dress (which is really a compliment to her), but once I tried it on, I realized it actually does suit me. I plan to wear a flower in my hair the exact same bright-pink colour. I think that will look rather Spanish, don't you?

I couldn't get away with buying another pair of shoes, so I'm wearing the same ones I wore when we met up last time. I don't suppose you'll even remember them. Your attention was on other things!

I'm so excited, I really am. I can't remember the last proper party I went to. Of course, your life with Susan is full of parties, I know, but Daniel and I don't tend to get invited to many these days. I think we give off depressing, party-killing vibes. Our mutual misery infects the atmosphere like salmonella. So it'll be a real treat to be out in society again. I hope we can remember how to behave!

The 120mg of citalopram (I went for three in the end, just to be sure) is already pounding around my system, together with the hundreds of coffees I've drunk to keep myself going. I've had a couple of brain rushes, where my heart starts hammering away, and a couple of moments when I had to run to the loo, thinking I was about to be sick. But I also feel bursting with energy. I keep jumping up to check the time on the clock in the kitchen in case my laptop is lying to me, or to check the fridge to make sure there's something for Darren to feed the kids with when he comes to keep them company (no cash in our fridge, sadly!). I even vacuumed the living room earlier on. Jamie was so shocked, he asked me who was coming round. I think he was expecting the Queen! I feel jittery, but at the same time buzzing with anticipation.

Tonight I'm going to see you.

Tonight I'm going to be a part of your world.

Tonight you will not be able to pretend I don't exist.

Tonight you will see me.

Tonight you *will* see me.

Tonight you will see *me*.

All ready. My brain is literally crashing around my skull like a Formula One racing car and I haven't been able to sit still for hours. My stomach keeps clenching like a fist. Maybe I shouldn't have had all those citalopram, but it's too late for that now. I've just taken a Sinequan, so hopefully that should take away the worst of the edgy feeling.

Now that I've got the dress on, I'm having major qualms. It looked so sophisticated in the shop, but now I wonder whether it makes me look like a giant gaudy Christmas-tree decoration, all bright and shiny but hollow inside. And whoever said that thing about older women not showing their necks and shoulders clearly had a point – the skin on my chest is creasing like crushed silk. I've got the flower in my hair, but I can't decide whether to leave it in. Tilly came into my room a little while ago and stared at me in open disbelief.

'Please tell me you're not wearing that thing on your head.'

Children can be so hurtful, don't you agree? They seem to feel they have the right to say anything at all, no matter how offensive, just because they're young. I bet you found that with yours as well. I wish they'd be a little more, well, empathetic.

'I like it. It's fun.'

'It looks stupid. And why do you keep pacing around?'

See what I mean? They always have to find something to pick at you about, something you're doing wrong.

The problem is I am finding it very difficult to stay in one place. Even sitting here writing this is taking for ever because I keep jumping up in between sentences and walking around the room. I think it must be the excitement. I'll bet I'm even more excited than you!

Right now, you and Susan will have finished taking your vows. I wonder how you felt when you saw her coming towards you in that church. Did everyone go 'Ahhhh'? Did your face light up? Did you wish just for a moment that she was someone else, someone who looked a bit like me? Were your children's faces wet with tears? Did their friends tell them how lucky they are to have parents who are still so in love? Did you hold each other's hands in front of your *closest* friends and share a quiet, gentle kiss? Did you tell her she looked beautiful? Did you think of me? Did you think of me? Did you think of me?

There's a noise in my head that sounds like a hand-held blender. Do you know the thing I mean? You use it for squishing soup? I don't think that noise should be there. But maybe it's always been there and I just haven't noticed it before.

Daniel just came in to see if I was ready, and he had a very strange look on his face. I wonder if he's still fretting about the bank statements. For some reason he kept asking me if I really wanted to go, but because of the noise in my head it took me a while to understand what he was saying. Why was he asking that? I think he must be having cold feet. 'I can go on my own,' I told him, but my voice sounded like a record played at too slow a speed.

Then he asked me if I was up to it. Don't you think that's an odd thing to ask? 'It's a party, it's not climbing Mount Kilimanjaro,' I said, but I don't think he heard. In fact, now I'm thinking about it, I don't know if I even said it out loud.

So now we're about to go, and all of a sudden I'm feeling so nervous, I think I might be sick. It could almost be *my* party, for how nervous I am. I could almost be the bride. Isn't that silleeeee? Daniel told me to eat something before we went, but I couldn't even contemplate food. I tried a tiny bite of the digestive biscuit he brought me earlier and it tasted like a lump of hard sand in my mouth. I know there'll be plenty of food at your house, though. Susan is so terribly good at all that stuff. You must be so proud of your wife. Do you repeat that word to yourself as you watch her moving easily between guests at the marquee, making sure no one feels left out, handing out drinks and homemade canapés and warm words? Wife, wife, wife. That is my wife. My wonderful wife. My wonderful life.

Daniel is calling for me now. I can faintly hear him

through the blender noise. It's just as well it's time to stop *journalling*. My hands are trembling so much my writing looks more like a lie-detector graph. (All the lies I've told, Clive. All the lies we've both told. I imagine them all lined up like ranks of soldiers in a parade.) I have to go now. I need a drink. I think everything will be fine once I've had a drink.

I will see you soon. Save a dance for me.

* * *

There's a discoloured patch on the ceiling above our bed where there obviously was once a leak. It's funny, but sometimes I think it looks like a map of Africa, but other times, if I really squint, I can see the head of an animal glaring down at me. Strange, isn't it, how one little thing can have so many different interpretations?

I'll be quite honest with you, though, the bed itself is a bit of a mess.

I'm lying propped up on my elbow writing in this notebook, and all around me is a sea of detritus. Empty pill packets, half-filled water bottles, tissues, unread newspapers, my laptop, my phone. I can even see a banana peel, although I can't imagine who would have eaten that. I don't remember the last time I ate. I think it might even have been at your house. How long ago would that be? Two days? Three? Time has become irrelevant. I think that's a gift. Don't you?

Daniel keeps telling me we have to talk about what happened, but I don't really see the point. To be quite honest, I don't even remember all of what happened. There are whole great swathes of time that seem to have been swallowed up along with the pills.

'We cannot just ignore this.' This is unexpected, coming from Daniel, who normally wouldn't acknowledge the house was on fire if there was an option to ignore it.

'What is there to talk about?' I ask. And of course, I'm right. When you come down to it, there really is nothing to say.

A couple of times, Daniel has tried to force me to explain. 'What was it you kept trying to tell Susan? What the fuck was going through your head when you were throwing yourself at Liam?'

He even managed to get really angry with me.

'I want an explanation,' he has said, puffed up and purple with righteousness. 'You owe it to me.'

I think that's a bit strong, don't you? You don't owe people things if you never promised them in the first place, surely? I never made Daniel any promises. Not one.

So instead of explaining to him, I'll try to sort it out in my own head. You know, so often when you do that, you realize things weren't as bad as you'd imagined them to be, don't you? What in my head might have become an excruciatingly embarrassing episode might well turn out not to have even registered with other people, or if it has, to be just a humorous footnote, something and nothing. I'm sure that'll be the case here. Something and nothing.

Not surprisingly, I remember much more about the beginning of the night than the end. I remember arriving at your house, and seeing the swollen wisteria plant that grows around the front porch reaching all the way up to the wrought-iron balcony, sagging with fairy lights, and thinking how beautiful it would be if I hadn't just had a big argument with Daniel (about weekend parking restrictions, if I remember right), and if the lights weren't jumping about in front of my eyes like fireflies.

Then I remember walking through to the back of the house, and how Susan had created a sort of passageway, lined with tea lights and photos from your two and a half decades together, all reprinted the same size in dramatic black and white. There was one in particular I remember looking at for so long that Daniel hissed I was creating a logjam as other arriving guests queued impatiently behind. It was a photo of you and Susan with Liam and Emily when they were tiny. You had Liam on your shoulders and Susan was holding Emily on her hip, and you were both dressed in shorts and flip-flops as if you'd come straight off the beach. Susan was saying something to a very cross-looking Emily, obviously trying to cheer her up, and her mouth was stretched into an enormous smile as she cajoled her pouting daughter. Meanwhile, you were gazing directly at Susan and your own smile was just for her.

You looked like the cat with the cream. It was a jolt to remember that by the time that photo was taken, just a few years into your marriage, you'd already had two affairs, or maybe three. You once told me, with a certain amount of rueful regret, that you'd even taken a girl's phone number while on your honeymoon, and met up with her after you got back.

'I'm not proud of myself,' you'd told me. 'It was never about not loving Susan. There was just something in me that made me behave like that. I'm very damaged in many ways.'

When we arrived at the back of the house, emerging through the glass-roofed kitchen, where the reflections of tea lights danced on the ceiling like stars, I almost cried when I saw what Susan had done with the garden. The coloured lanterns hanging from the trees, the candles reflected in the mirrored mosaic along the back wall – it was so beautiful. It really was. Glancing up at the house, I saw that every window twinkled with fairy lights, even your studio at the top. I gazed at it for a long time, thinking of all the times you'd emailed me from there. 'I feel imprisoned up here,' you'd declared dramatically. 'I don't belong here. I belong with you.'

Of course, there wasn't much of the garden on show because the marquee took up a lot of space. Inside, Susan had gone for a Japanese-style theme, with long tables and low seating and silk-covered cushions. Everywhere I looked were people gasping about how wonderful it was, and what a special couple you were and how refreshing in this day and age to see such a long, solid marriage. The noise in my head kept getting worse and worse as I struggled to hear what they were saying, and my restless fingers ceaselessly tap-tapped against my glass.

I remember Daniel telling me I'd already had two glasses of champagne. And me replying, 'And? Who made you alcohol monitor?' I remember the smile fading on Susan's face when she saw my dress, but how she recovered herself quickly. 'I seem to have started a trend,' she joked, but Emily standing next to her in a clingy sky-blue dress that made her suddenly enormous bump look like a giant iced gem, looked venomous. 'I brought you those baby clothes,' I told her, my voice hesitant as if I was attempting a foreign tongue. But when I looked for the bag I thought I'd brought, it wasn't there, like the baby that never was.

And I remember you, Clive.

I remember you were talking to a couple I didn't know over by the bar in the marquee. Your hands were gesturing expansively as you told one of your witty anecdotes, and they were both listening raptly. All of a sudden you glanced up, probably trying to remember the punchline (isn't it awful what age does to our powers of joke-telling, how it robs us of that moment of effortless revelation?). I've never fully understood before that phrase about the blood draining from someone's face. Well, not until Saturday night. Your expression was a picture, Clive, it really was. And I have a feeling you quite lost your track in the story you were telling, because the smiles on your audience's faces started to look a little bit strained as they turned around to see what you were looking at. You recovered yourself well, though, I must say. Must be all those years of after-dinner speaking at big music events.

All those things I remember perfectly. And I remember spotting Liam across the room and walking straight over to him, the drugs in my system propelling me forward. He was talking to a couple of young women, I recall, both of them wearing dresses that ended just below their bottoms and enormously high shoes with straps that looked like ribcages going up past their ankles. When I smiled at him, he smiled back, but immediately I realized he didn't have the faintest idea who I was. I remember putting my hand out and saying something about meeting him at the brasserie and he said 'Of course' in a very unconvincing way.

Daniel was right behind me and I introduced him to Liam, explaining where we'd met. 'He served me some lovely wine,' I said. How idiotic was that? The wine wasn't even terribly nice!

And all the time I was conscious of your eyes on me, and it seemed impossible that everyone else in the room could be oblivious to the current running between us. I caught your gaze just once and there was a message in the hard shards of your eyes and the twitch at the corner of your mouth that was as clear as if you'd spoken it out loud. It didn't require any interpretation. I knew you wanted to kill me.

Does that sound fanciful? I can just see you making a disapproving face at my allowing myself to indulge in such flights of fantasy. 'Real life isn't like *Midsomer Murders*,' you'd say. Yet I know without any shadow of doubt that right there, right then, in that Japanese-themed marquee flanked by your wonderful family, celebrating your renewed marriage to your wonderful wife, surrounded by your wonderful friends, you wanted to kill me.

In many ways I was flattered.

After that my memories grow more disjointed. I remember my heart racing as if it wanted to gallop clear out of my chest and back through the fairytale garden and the candlelit passage, and out through the front door and into the street, where the air was fresh enough to breathe properly.

I remember Daniel asking me if I was all right so many times I began to feel like I was trapped in a kind of endless Groundhog Day. I drank more champagne because he kept telling me not to and began to notice there were fireworks shooting across my eyes.

'I want you to leave. Now,' you hissed when you intercepted me coming back from the loo. (Such a hilarious idea to have yours and Susan's faces printed on the loo paper. Liam's work, I imagine. How you must all have roared with laughter.) Your face was closed like a trap.

'Are you threatening me?' I said, in my voice that wasn't my voice.

You walked away, but I knew you were still watching as I crossed the floor and found Susan (how convenient the bright pink of her dress turned out to be – a beacon guiding me in).

'Lovely party,' I said, knowing you could see everything.

Susan glanced across at you, that much I remember. It occurred to me then that you two must have had words about me, before the evening started. Perhaps you'd have done your 'Sally isn't terribly stable' routine. That look that passed between you, complicit, exclusive, was what finally tipped me over, I think.

'I need to speak to you privately, Susan,' I said.

As soon as the words were out, I knew that I was going to tell her everything. I knew then, beyond a doubt, that you were never coming back (finally, that exercise Helen made me do was taking hold). What use was there then in holding on to the secret I'd hugged to me for so long like a wrap-around cardie? Susan deserved to know what kind of man she'd just re-married. But of course, that wasn't my real motivation. Really, I wanted to see it all torn down, the coloured lanterns ripped from the trees, the marquee poles wrenched out of position so the whole monstrous edifice collapsed around the heads of the shrieking guests. I wanted to see the quirky jacket with the fuchsia-pink velvet collar (nice touch, that matching his 'n' hers element) torn from your back. I wanted you exposed. I wanted them to see you for what you were – Liam, Susan, Emily. I wanted to leave a mark on your life that you would never be able to erase. I wanted you to know that I could do you harm.

The lights were still dancing around the corners of my vision, but even so I saw how Susan looked at you again and made a slight face.

'Not tonight, dear. I'm terribly busy. Why don't you call me next week?'

Then things get hazier still.

I know I tried again to talk to Susan, and I remember how she made her excuses and whispered in Emily's ear.

I know Daniel tried to get me to leave, and I know I wouldn't.

Then there was dancing and I was dancing with Liam. I had my arm round his neck, and one of the girls in the impossibly short dresses was standing right by us on her own, her glossy-lipped mouth slightly open in surprise as if I'd just snatched him away from her, as come to think of it, I probably had.

There were speeches. Susan's first. It was short and funny, and I remember laughing until my knees gave way.

'Please let's go,' Daniel said. But I wanted to hear your speech, even though each word sliced at my heart with a cheese grater.

'Twenty-six years ago, I thought I'd married the best woman in the world,' you said. 'Today I *know* I've married the best woman in the world. I want you to raise your glasses in a toast to my beautiful wife.'

My beautiful wife.

People were cheering and raising their glasses, urine-yellow champagne sloshing against the sides.

'Liar, Liar, Liar,' I shouted, but the sound was muffled. Perhaps the guests heard 'Hear, hear, hear,' perhaps they heard nothing.

Daniel did, though. He turned to me while the rest of

the guests were cheering and clapping and tapping their glasses with spoons, until my whole head felt as if it was about to spontaneously combust, and he stared at me as if I was someone he'd never met before.

That wasn't the end, but my mind won't let me remember more. I know I kept trying to talk to Susan and I know she kept avoiding me. I know I went back over to Liam (the shame, the shame, the shame) and I have a memory of sitting on his knee and him being stiff and unmoving and of the girl with the ribcage shoes shaking her head in amused disgust, her long glossy hair shimmering like brown velvet.

Then Daniel was pulling me away and I didn't want to go, but he said you had told him to get me home.

'You're ruining their party,' he shouted.

'They've ruined my life,' I shouted back.

Or maybe I didn't. Maybe I just slumped defeated and allowed myself to be dragged off. I don't remember going back through the fairytale garden. I don't remember retracing our steps along the candlelit passageway, past the shorts and flip-flops photo. I don't remember anyone saying goodbye at the wisteria-framed front door. I do remember being sick into a particularly splendid hydrangea, and again by the kerb.

I remember Daniel sitting in the driving seat of the car with his forehead pressing against the steering wheel.

I don't remember anything more.

But that's enough, don't you think?

That's more than enough.

Jamie came into the bedroom to see me a couple of hours ago to talk about his birthday.

To be quite honest, I'd forgotten he had a birthday coming up. I felt a stab of pure panic. Birthdays are when things are expected of you, only I'm having trouble remembering what those things are. There are things I should be doing. If only I could get out of bed.

Daniel wants to call the doctor. I keep trying to imagine the young blonde doctor, with her matching shoes and tights, sitting on the edge of this bed, strewn with the fall-out of the last three days.

'Poor old you,' she might say, eyeing the tissues and the cups and this notebook. 'You are having a rotten time.'

I promised Daniel I'd get up, I told him I'm feeling better.

'We have to talk about what happened,' he repeated. But I sensed a slight wavering, as if it was already losing urgency.

Daniel thinks the doctor will be able to give me a neat pill and make me better. He doesn't know that what's wrong with me is you, and that there is no cure for that.

So I'm about to get up and dressed for the first time since Saturday. I don't want to, but I must.

I've decided that I will turn getting up into a symbolic ritual. I will brush you off like old toast crumbs, I will leave you behind in the crumpled sheets, I will wash you on a boil wash until you are scrubbed raw and disinvested of all power. I will rise like a phoenix from the ashes of the last five years and become the person I was meant to be, the one who inhabits that parallel universe in which I never met you but remained a good mother to my children and a dutiful lover to Daniel. I will make the last five years disappear. Pffff! Like the baby that never was.

I will not think about how you got off scot-free, or what you took from me, or how you lied.

I will be free of you. I will not think of you. I will rebuild everything.

Back in the cubbyhole, while the sickly moonlight trickles under the door and the house winces in its sleep.

I am looking up information on Maui on Google. It looks incredible. Lucky you. You and Susan must be two days into your second honeymoon now, enough time to settle in and become acclimatized. I've worked out if it's 3.20 a.m. here, it must be 4.20 p.m. there. I imagine the two of you will have enjoyed an hour or two's rest after a long lunch somewhere in the shade. I expect you had fresh fish. You always did love that, probably with a simple green salad (you'll both be watching your weight a bit after the blowout of the vows party). Now you might be contemplating a stroll down to the beach. Maybe you'll buy a bottle of chilled white wine to take with you, or else pick up a drink from a beach bar somewhere.

You'll both have your mobiles on you, of course. A busy, successful couple like you two never goes anywhere without being in constant contact with the outside world. And of course there's always Emily to think of. I know she was frantic when she realized you'd be gone for a whole week when she was in her last month of pregnancy.

'You obviously care more about getting a suntan than about your new grandchild,' she'd Facebooked Susan, clearly wounded.

So I know you won't want to risk missing a call from her.

What if I was to send a message to Susan? Now, as you strolled hand in hand following your nap? Would it really hurt? I could apologize for the other night, but tell her I still need to talk to her urgently. 'I think you deserve to know about Clive,' I'd say.

Of course, I won't really do that. It would be cruel to do that to someone on their second honeymoon. I'll wait until she comes back. I won't bother her now.

But do you know what's so silly? Despite what I've just written, I've known all along that I would. As soon as I'd finished that last sentence, I picked up my mobile and started tapping out a text. I want to stop her, you see. I want to stop her before you arrive at the beach and start laying out your towels. I want to halt her mid step, while the sun scalds down on her bent head, and the tie of her halterneck swimming costume digs into the back of her neck. I want her to look up at you in that still-white heat and know finally who you are.

Now it would be 6.15, Maui time. I've sent five texts to Susan and heard nothing.

A few seconds ago my phone finally beeped, but it was a message from your phone. How I hate my treacherous heart for the way it still lurches at the sight of your name in my inbox.

I picked up your message while Susan was sleeping. You are now blocked from both our phones and email accounts. Leave us alone and get some help.

Get some help.

I'm still trying to work out what kind of help I might need. Who do you think, Clive, might be able to help me divest myself of you? I'd really, really like to know. Is there a church body that can exorcize unwanted people from our lives? Is there some sort of salon where I could go to have you stripped off me with hot wax? Is there a doctor who can administer an enema to flush you out? Is there an architect who can rebuild the life you've left in the rubble?

I wish you'd tell me, Clive. I really do. I'll take all the help I can get. I'm not proud. I'll take it all.

Only there isn't any help, when everyone I see is wearing your face, and every moment that passes is a moment further away from you, and when I look ahead all I can see is what isn't there, and the life that's in front of me is a taunting reminder of the life I should have had.

Do you see my problem, Clive?

Do you see?

Just a little empathy and I'm sure you will.

* * *

I was still fast asleep when Daniel woke me up, trying to force a letter into my face. I'd taken a couple of zopiclone – maybe more – and was having trouble surfacing. His face kept swimming in front of me, red and cross.

'You have to wake up. I know you're not really asleep.'

He wasn't right, of course. I was asleep. I love the zopiclone mornings when I can turn sleep off and on at will.

'It's not fair of you, waking me up. You know I have problems getting to sleep.'

Daniel wasn't budging.

'For fuck's sake, it is half past fucking four in the afternoon. The kids are home from school already. How do you think it fucking feels for them to see their mother comatose in her fucking bed?'

I'm probably exaggerating the number of fucks in that sentence for dramatic effect, but I expect you get the general idea.

To be honest, I was a bit shocked to find out it was that late. I could have sworn I hadn't been asleep long. But then I probably needed it, wouldn't you think? Daniel can be so puritanical when he wants to be.

When I finally forced my eyes open, he was still proffering the letter, shaking it impatiently in the direction of my nose.

'This is from the building society. Apparently we owe them six months' mortgage payments. They want £4,590 by the end of next week or they're repossessing the house.'

'They can't do that. They have to send us warning letters first.'

Daniel was ready for that. He's very quick, I must admit. He'd already gone through the drawer in the filing cabinet next to my desk and discovered all the unopened letters, which he fanned out in front of me like a magician's card trick (although thankfully not this journal, which I keep with me in my handbag).

'Here are your warning letters. Months and months of them, along with utilities bills and credit-card bills. All in all, we owe nearly £35,000. What the fuck have you done, Sally?'

Well, put like that it did sound a bit ominous. And when I tried to come up with an explanation, it sounded a bit weak and unconvincing. I mean, I couldn't very well say that for the last five years I'd been having an affair with Clive Gooding and he promised me we would have a future together, so when the work started drying up, I didn't really try too hard to get more. Even Daniel, who is so wilfully blinkered, wouldn't go for that. On the basis that the best form of defence is attack, I decided to remind Daniel of his own dismal past record of financial mismanagement – the fancy kitchen shop that had eaten all our savings, the years working for his brother's company that was always 'about to take off' but never did, and now this sudden decision to retrain as a teacher, with the financial burden that placed on my shoulders.

'You've always been so glad to let me look after all that sort of stuff. Well, maybe you should have taken a bit more of an interest.' I was working myself up into an outrage. 'Maybe I'm sick of having to deal with everything.'

Daniel shook his head in faux incredulity.

'You haven't dealt with anything in months,' he spat.

When I dragged myself downstairs to say hello to the children, like a Good Mummy, I was irritated to find Tilly wasn't there. She'd gone out to one of her friend's houses, according to Jamie. She could at least have let me know, don't you think? I wouldn't have rushed down if I'd known she was gone.

'Will you play Wii with me?' Jamie wanted to know.

I said I would, still in Good Mummy mode, and we played a couple of rounds of Wii tennis, but I was finding it a real strain to swing the controller, and I kept forgetting which player was me. My head was still all over the place. 'Am I the pink one? . . . Am I the one with the glasses?'

'Never mind, Mum,' Jamie told me as I flopped back down on to the sofa and closed my eyes. 'It doesn't matter.'

He's very intuitive when he wants to be.

The longer Tilly was out, the crosser I became. I didn't know why she hadn't just said she was going, and she'd left her mobile behind, so we couldn't call her. I lay on the sofa and tried to ease myself back into the welcome oblivion of sleep, but I could hear Daniel crashing about in the kitchen, slamming down pots. Every now and then he'd come in and stand in the doorway of the living room glaring at me, but I refused to open my eyes, and eventually he'd go away.

By the time Tilly came home, I was ready to have a real go at her, but when she appeared in the living room, my newly reawakened Good Mummy antennae sensed that there was clearly something up.

'A strange man came up to me on the corner of our road,' she said, and while her body language was full of bravado, her voice was that of a small child.

The man had apparently told her he was a friend of mine and asked her to pass on his best wishes, but there was something about him that she hadn't liked, something she described as 'creepy'.

What did he look like? I wanted to know. But of course I knew already. Shortish and thickset with closely cropped hair and a leather jacket with stripes on the sleeves.

'Who was that then?' Daniel glared at me accusingly.

'Just someone I met through work who lives around here,' I replied.

'Nice friends you have nowadays.'

So now it becomes no longer a game. (Was it ever? I'm starting to wonder.) Now my children are involved, and it's beyond a doubt that the man in the leather jacket exists outside of my own head.

You think you can scare me, Clive. You think I'm a Romanian squeegee man who'll run away with his bucket slopping. You think I'm a star-struck singer you can intimidate with your platinum discs and great big faux-gold award. You think you have it all in your favour. But you are wrong.

I only want what's mine.

And if I can't have what's mine, I'll take what's yours.

Thank God Daniel has gone to bed now. I can hear him snoring upstairs. Even his snores sound angry.

'You have ruined us,' was his tiresome refrain after the kids had finally gone to bed. So melodramatic. If he didn't have anything constructive to say, I'd rather he didn't say anything at all. My mum used to say that, I seem to remember. My mum is dead, though. And the dead don't talk.

He seems to think it is my fault we've got into such a financial mess. He's right in a sense, of course, in that I should have opened the letters, and I should have told him when the work started drying up. But I thought it would all be sorted, you see. I thought I would be rescued. I thought you would rescue me. (Interestingly, Helen once accused me of harbouring Rescue Fantasies. Isn't it funny that she should pick up on that? She's quite perceptive, Helen, although of course I strenuously denied it at the time.)

And Daniel shouldn't have left it all to me. He knows that really. He said as much this evening.

'I suppose I must take some of the blame for sticking my head in the sand,' he admitted.

That was big of him, wasn't it? But then in the next breath he was laying into me again. Why hadn't I told him I was having problems? I've always been happy to look after the joint account before. He's not a mind-reader. (Just as well!)

And so it went on and on and on. And when he wasn't talking about money, he was talking about the man who 'accosted' Tilly. He wanted to call the police, if you can believe it. I pointed out he was being ridiculous, that it was just someone I once met.

'I don't know you any more, Sally,' he said. (Don't forget Daniel doesn't work with words, he doesn't recognize clichés as you or I would.)

And then guess what he said? Go on, guess. It's amusing, really it is. He said, 'You need to get some help.'

I'm not making it up! Hand on heart, that's what he said. Word for word, the same as you.

I laughed so hard my face was wet with tears.

Daniel looked at me for a while, convulsing on the sofa, just staring, without saying anything, and then he went to bed.

I'm still laughing now.

I've been checking Facebook again. Well, when I say 'again' that makes it sound like I've made several separate checks, whereas I suppose it's more like one continuous one. I usually have my screen set to Susan's page, although since you've been away there hasn't been so much going on, so I tend to flit between hers and Emily's.

I see Liam has put the photos from the party up on Facebook already. I can't say I was particularly looking forward to seeing them, but there aren't any where I'm doing anything particularly embarrassing. Perhaps he took those ones out. He comes across as quite a sensitive sort. I wonder where he gets that from. Or perhaps I wasn't so embarrassing, after all. Sometimes I do think Daniel might be exaggerating it. I'd know, wouldn't I, if I'd been that bad?

There are lots of pictures of people I don't remember at all, which I suppose isn't that surprising, and a whole series taken at the church earlier, which are just divine.

You do take a good photo, don't you, Clive? And it's lovely the way Susan is so natural in front of the camera. She really doesn't care, does she? It's so refreshing. And really, what is the big deal about an extra chin – it's personality that counts, isn't it?

I simply adore that photo of the four of you – you, Susan, Liam and Emily, standing outside the church, white confetti scattered like dandruff on your shoulders and at your feet. You are standing between Susan and Emily, an arm around both of them, with Liam on the far end, and you're all leaning slightly towards Emily, who as usual has her hand on her bump, obviously saying something about the baby. There's such energy in that photo, four adults so intent on one unborn child. Liam and Susan are laughing, their smiles betraying a strong family resemblance, but you have a slightly different expression, as if you're surveying the scene from one step back, and though you're smiling, it's a much smugger, more contained smile, as if quietly taking credit for all of it – the wonderful wife, the handsome son, the fecund daughter about to produce the beloved grandchild. All of it your doing, your un-merited reward.

With all eyes in the photograph fixed on Emily's neat bump, my attention also keeps returning there, to this unformed being that will be the icing on your cake – the cake that you managed to both have and eat (clever, clever Clive).

I know you, Clive, I know what is going through your head. I know the bargains you will have made with God, that you will turn over a new leaf, make your family proud, be a shining example for this blob of ever-dividing cells that calls itself a baby. Who knows, you might even believe some of them.

The new baby is a new beginning for you, the trapdoor into a future fizzing with promise. I like to imagine the type of modern grandparents you and Susan will make – flying in early from important work assignments in Florida and Thailand and South Africa so as not to miss the baby's birthday, and juggling recording schedules and lucrative catering contracts in order to babysit for the day while the Sacred Vessel goes out. You'll probably turn one of the rooms in your lovely St John's Wood home into a nursery and the baby will quickly get into the habit of staying with you one night a week to give Emily and the bland barrister some time to themselves. You'll hate being called Grandad, I know, so you'll insist on 'Clive', or some cute customized title like Pappy.

You've always told me how much you regret the time you spent building up your career while the children were young, missing out on most of their proudest milestones in pursuit of the next big break. 'You must make the most of this time you have with your kids,' you'd tell me, your eyes, the colour of rotting algae, burning with benevolent conviction. 'It's such a cliché to say it, but you'll never get this chance again.'

The new baby will give you an opportunity to right the wrongs of the past. You'll smother it in attention and baby talc, gasping gratifyingly at every tiny step forward, every new food tasted, every inch grown. You and Susan will set up a savings account for it from birth and add generously at birthdays and Christmases. You'll hold a christening party in your garden and take it on holidays to your new beach house in Croatia. You'll shock yourself with how much you love that child, channelling into it all that redundant passion you used to have for me.

You want to know something silly? I'm jealous of that blob, with its jelly fingers and free-floating toes. I'm jealous of the way it's so protected and shielded from everything that could go wrong. I'm jealous of the way you're all waiting so impatiently for it to arrive. I'm jealous of the unconditional love that awaits it. Is it wrong to be jealous of an unborn child? I don't really think so. I don't see how it's possible *not* to be jealous of the unborn. Especially this unborn. Especially *your* unborn.

Who wouldn't want to be born into a family like yours? Who wouldn't want cool Uncle Liam and straight-talking Grandma Susan (not for her the vanity about titles)? Who wouldn't want a mum who'll pass seamlessly from being the World's First Pregnant Woman to the World's First New Mother, making restaurant owners clear a table in the quietest corner for her sleeping offspring, and affixing one of those ridiculous 'Baby on Board' notices to the back window of her Mini Cooper? (Is it only me who entertains an irrational urge to press down on the accelerator and slam into the backs of cars bearing that arrogant yellow diamond? Do people really imagine the driver behind will think, 'Well, I was considering rear-ending that Mini Cooper, but that sign has given me second thoughts'?)

Once I thought I might be part of your family, your wonderful, high-achieving, post-theatre-drinks-and-a-bite-to-eat-at-Joe-Allen's-style family. Now that blobby, unformed, floating mass that calls itself a baby will be taking my place, sliming its jelly-and-blood-streaked way into your honeyed, moneyed lives. Is that crazy?

I don't think so.

* * *

I'm not feeling so good today.

I've popped a couple of pills, but I'm not getting that surge of energy I've come to rely on. My hands have started shaking again. I'm holding my left hand in front of my face right now and it's as if it's vibrating. I can't stop staring at it.

It's not really surprising I'm in a state, though. After crawling into bed when it was getting light this morning, I was shaken roughly awake by Tilly.

'Mum. Wake UP!'

You know, Tilly has to work on her people skills. She really does.

'Where's the thing for Jamie?'

I'm not my best first thing in the morning these days. I just blinked at Tilly, not having the faintest clue what she was talking about, or why she was using that horrible hissing tone.

'Jamie's birthday present. Where is it?'

Well, you can imagine I was a little bit taken aback, particularly with the xanax still coursing around my system, rendering me partially paralysed.

'You've got the wrong day,' I told her. 'It's tomorrow.'

But even as I was speaking, I was wondering whether tomorrow might not actually be today, if you see what I mean. I have been losing track of the time rather a lot recently. The days seem to be bleeding into each other like wet paint and I'm finding it hard to tell one from the other.

'You *idiot*!' Tilly's face was a tight purple knot, straining against itself.

Then she disappeared and almost instantaneously her face was replaced by Daniel's, also purple, and also not at all pleased.

'What the fuck is going on in your head, Sally?' A big splat of his spit landed on my lip and I had to literally hold my hand down under the duvet to stop myself from wiping it away. I had a feeling he might find that offensive. It might be construed as what Helen calls an *incendiary* gesture.

'There's a ten-year-old boy downstairs quivering with excitement because it's his birthday, waiting for his mum to come downstairs with his birthday present – *the one he told her all about last week*. How am I supposed to tell him she has forgotten all about it? Tell me that!'

Of course I felt really bad, then. I didn't want to think about the way Jamie's bottom lip would wobble when he realized there wasn't any present. He's just at that age where he understands it's not 'manly' to cry, so he suppresses tears until his whole body resonates with them.

'I didn't forget. I just lost track of the days.'

I have to admit it sounded pretty pathetic even as I was saying it. I will make it up to him. I really will.

When I stumbled downstairs (I'm thinking I might start sleeping in the cubbyhole. I find the stairs quite treacherous some mornings. It's a balance thing, I think. Something blocked in my ear, maybe . . . Blocked again. Is there a theme emerging?) I made a big fuss of Jamie and told him his present was too special to open in a rush before school and it would be waiting for him when he came home. He seemed cheered up by that, although he didn't seem to want me to give him a birthday hug.

'It's because your breath smells like yesterday's dinner,' was how Tilly explained it.

Was Emily ever like that with you, I wonder? Any opportunity for a personal slight? I'm trying to empathize. I keep reminding myself about the hormones coursing around her system like migrating salmon, but that vicious streak is something I'm having trouble with.

My daughter has lost her way, that's what the teachers said.

I wish to God she would find it again.

When Jamie had left for school with Daniel, I tried to remember what had been on the list of presents he'd told me he wanted, but nothing came into my mind. I think there might have been a bike of some sort, but I'm not completely sure and that would be a pretty expensive mistake to make, wouldn't it? Particularly for people who are about to lose their house. (I'm saying that, but you know I still don't really believe it. Something will come up. Something always does, doesn't it?) I wish I'd written down what Jamie said, but I thought it would just stick in my memory. I'm going to have to go out to the shops and hope something is jogged. I'm determined to make this a good birthday for him. When he comes home from school, I'll have cake and maybe a bit of bunting, and a present he'll really love. I just have to work out what that is. I'm going to ignore the pain in my head and get dressed. I'm going to make it up to him.

I really am.

Now you're not to panic.

Everything is going to be OK. I'll deal with it all. As

soon as I saw the entries on Emily's Facebook Page a few minutes ago, I knew something had to be done.

Georgia Hanley-Corrigan *Hang on in there, babes. The baby will be fine. I'll be round to the hospital as soon as xx*

Cassandra Wyn-Coleman *Sending you healing thoughts and prayers, Em.*

Flikka de Souza *Piers knows the best obstetrics guy. I'm looking him up right now. Don't let them do anything without getting a second opinion from your own expert first. OK, sweetie?*

How panic-stricken you must be all the way over there in Maui, knowing this drama is going on. Emily in hospital! Some emergency with the baby! Susan must be going out of her mind with worry. Whatever has happened, poor Emily will be needing a mother figure, and with Susan so far away, I'm going to have to step in. I know which hospital she's at, so I'm on my way over now. Hopefully it's some puffed-up drama, but one can't be too careful. I'll just pop in to make sure she's OK, and then I'll get Jamie's present on the way back. Don't worry, I know you'd do the same for me. We must look out for one another, Clive. We are the same.

Fuck Fuck Fuck Fuck Fuck Fuck Fuck Fuck Fuck

How has it all ended up this way?
I only tried to help.

When did I become so out of sync with the rest of the world? It's like I'm speaking a different language entirely from everyone else, and there's no interpreter, no dictionary. When did I start getting it so wrong?

Let me just recap the last six hours to see if I can make sense of it all. What is it that Helen is always trying to get me to do? Oh, that's it . . . bullet points. Let me bullet point the last six hours.

- Went to hospital.
- Found Emily.
- Died a million deaths.

Breathe in, stomach out; breathe out, stomach in.

OK. Let me start again.

When I looked up the hospital Emily's friends had mentioned on Facebook, I found it was in a very chi-chi part of north-west London. I arrived in a bit of a flap, I have to admit. I was so desperate to get there, you see, to be useful. I'd forgotten my Oyster card and got on one of those buses where they don't let you pay with actual money. The driver had some unintelligible accent and he kept saying 'nerkash' at me, and my head was pounding and I just didn't know what he was talking about. 'I don't understand,' I told him again and again, leaning my forehead up against the partition window and pushing the pound coins towards him. 'NERKASH,' he shouted. Eventually an elderly man in one of the front seats leaned forward. 'He's saying "No cash",' he explained apologetically. 'These buses only take Oysters or tickets.'

The hospital itself, when I eventually got there, having had to get off the bus and buy a ticket from the machine, was a bit unprepossessing – low blocks of concrete and glass, surrounded by what seemed to be rather token trees – but inside was a different story. All that blond-wood strip-flooring! Those purple bucket-seats! To be honest, I never realized just how different private hospitals are to NHS ones. No wonder you've always been such a fan of private health care!

The receptionist was very polite and didn't seem fazed by the fact I was still wearing the old Brazil T-shirt I sleep in over a pair of jeans and flip-flops. She showed me the route to the maternity ward on a neat little map of the hospital which she took from a pile on the desk in front of her. Do you know, I had the most insane craving then to admit myself to this hospital. It just seemed like the kind of place where people would take care of you, and not judge you. A well-ordered place, with little maps to get around – maybe we could all come to stay here. *My daughter has lost her way.* You wouldn't lose your way in a place like this. Someone would always be available to find it for you.

When I was on my way up to the maternity ward, the nausea I'd been keeping at bay since the morning surged to the surface. Luckily, with my handy map I could locate the nearest toilet! And how refreshingly clean it was! I knelt in the cubicle by the toilet bowl without any concerns about hygiene whatsoever. In addition to the reassuring smell of disinfectant, there was a pleasant citrussy fragrance. I wish our bathroom at home smelled more like that. It made me realize I hadn't cleaned the toilet in quite a long time. In fact, I couldn't really remember the last time. I made a mental note to buy some lemony-smelling cleaning stuff on my way home.

I don't know how long I knelt by the toilet, but I'm

pretty sure it was quite long because a couple of times people came and tried the outside handle and I could hear the heavy tread of impatient footsteps walking away from the door.

I almost forgot why I was there. Forgot about Emily, the Sacred Vessel, who perhaps wasn't even a Vessel any more, forgot about the thing that called itself a baby, forgot that I was being Susan. Or was I being you?

But eventually I forced myself to my feet (which, I noticed, were a little bit grubby, nails blackened with London grime. I found myself hoping I hadn't inadvertently brought some germs into this pristinely antiseptic environment. I imagined trailing in MRSA on the soles of my flip-flops like old chewing gum). Washing my hands at the sink was a pleasure in itself. I loved the designer hand lotion, and even thought about trying to wash my feet, but didn't feel up to attempting to lift them into the sink.

The obstetrics ward was on the second floor, and had its own stylish reception desk in white and lilac, with soothing down-lighters under the counter. The Scandinavian nurse behind the desk beamed at me as I approached.

'Very popular lady, Emily,' she said, when I announced who I'd come to visit.

I have to admit that as I made my way down the corridor past the slightly ajar doors of the individual rooms, where wan-looking women lay back on jolly purple-printed pillowcases while their well-dressed visitors liberated vast bouquets from their cellophane wrappers, I started to feel quite apprehensive. I'd been in such a rush to come that I hadn't even thought about bringing a gift. I'd thought only of Emily, as any parent would do.

Standing outside room number 7, I hesitated slightly when I heard voices inside. It sounded like there were quite a few people in there. For some reason, I'd been imagining Emily on her own, suffering through whatever had happened to her without the support of her honeymooning parents. I'd forgotten about her bland barrister husband, and her double-barrelled friends with their Notting Hill highlights.

When I pushed open the door, there were at least six people gathered around the bed, and they all fell silent as they looked up at me. Emily, sitting up in bed surrounded by cards and flowers and specialist fruits that might have been guavas, gawped as if witnessing some kind of spiritual visitation.

'I came as soon as I heard,' I gasped. 'I knew you'd be missing your mother.'

Emily's still slender arms crept instinctively around her stomach, which, I now noticed, was still swollen up like a dead thing in the sun.

'Is the baby all right?'

'It's fine. It was just a scare, that's all.'

It was the bland barrister who spoke, the first time he'd ever said anything directly to me. He put his arm protectively around Emily's shoulder and I got a very strange feeling, as if they didn't want me there. I couldn't work it out. We'd almost been friends, Emily and I. She'd even invited me to her baby shower! It could only have been the baby who had turned her against me, that ever-multiplying, ever-dividing blob. It was growing too big, demanding too much space, pushing me out. I thought about my baby. The baby that wasn't, the one who hadn't mattered enough to exist. Do you remember, Clive, how you told me afterwards you wished it had been real? ('Then something would have *had* to happen,' you said. 'We'd have had to be together.') It would have been an uncle or aunt to the thing inside Emily's bloated belly. We would all have been family. But now she didn't even want me near her.

'Thank you for coming, but now I think you should go,' the bland barrister said. (Does he have a name? I can't remember.) 'Emily has been through hell and is completely exhausted.'

Do you know, I had this overwhelming urge then to tell him that I was also exhausted. Suddenly it washed over me, this feeling of being completely and utterly drained, as if someone had sucked every single last drop of energy from me (the thing that calls itself a baby?). I wanted the bland barrister to come and put his arm around me, lead me to one of the comfy-looking padded armchairs (also purple! Some interior designer was having a Prince period, no doubt) and settle me in. I wanted him to crouch down next to me, take my hand and ask me if there was anything I needed. Was that too much to ask, do you think? Just that little gesture?

Instead he remained by the bed, his hand on Emily's fragile shoulder. Emily herself couldn't look at me. Turning her face up to him, she whispered, 'Make her leave.'

Well, I say whisper, but actually it reached all around the room, ricocheting off the walls and eventually pinging back in my face like a stretched elastic band. I think I might actually have sagged against the doorway when I heard it. It felt physical, you see, that 'make her leave'.

'I just wanted to help.'

My own voice was whiny like a child and I tried to disown it, shifting slightly away to put distance between myself and the sound of it.

'We appreciate it.' The bland barrister's voice was stiff and embarrassed. 'But Emily really needs to rest.'

I looked around at the other people in the room – three girls perched on the edge of the prettily patterned bed (yes, shades of purple! How clever of you to guess, Clive!), the two men in the other armchairs. None of them could meet my eyes. Instead they pretended to be studying their hands, or looking out of the window. Two of the girls were flicking through magazines (*Vogue* and *Heat*), but they kept sneaking glances at each other, perfectly shaped eyebrows faintly arched.

I wanted to grab them by their glossy, sleek, pony-tailed hair and smash their heads together, tinted-moisturized forehead crushed against tinted-moisturized forehead, smirk against smirk. I wanted to tie the legs of their skinny jeans around their necks in knots and pull them tight. I wanted to press their leather Mulberry bags over their heads until they suffocated.

Oh Clive, don't be so disapproving. I didn't do any of that. Silleeeee. I even managed a smile (although it might just have been an internal smile, I'm not quite sure).

'Bye then,' I said.

That was quite dignified, don't you think? No hint of reproach or bitterness.

Still, after I'd pulled the door shut behind me and heard the collective squeal of 'OHMYGOD!' from inside, that's when the bitterness came, scouring through me like lemon-scented antiseptic cleaner. Running to the toilet, I leaned over the bowl and vomited up my insides, closing my eyes for fear that what came up would be streaked with blood and clotted with lumps of internal organs. (Does that disgust you? Sorry. Sometimes these days I lose sight of what other people find shocking.)

I don't know what is happening to me. I'm in the dark like that monstrous baby, feeling around blindly with my jelly fingers, kicking against flesh, floating in blood.

And now I suppose I should tell you about what happened next.

The honest truth (though we never were ones for honesty really, were we?) is I'm not quite sure what happened immediately after I left the hospital. I vaguely recall being in a Tube station, but it was incredibly hot and I was standing too close to the edge of the platform and I was scaring myself by how intently I was staring down at the tracks and how easy it was to imagine myself lying down on them.

Then I was outside (thank God) and walking through a crowded shopping area. Did I try on a pair of shoes? I rather think I did. I have a rather shameful recollection of my dirt-ingrained toes peeping out from the end of a gold strappy sandal and the disapproving salesgirl hovering with a redundant pop sock.

I know I did a lot of walking.

I know I cried in Pret A Manger.

I know time was lost. (My daughter is lost. She has lost her way.)

When I finally let myself in through the front door, it was quite a lot later and I knew from the minute I got into the house that things were very wrong indeed. When I walked into the living room, Daniel was sitting on the sofa with an arm around each of the children and they all looked as if they'd been crying.

Daniel didn't speak. Not one word, which I knew was ominous, but Tilly for a change was anxious to break the silence, and her voice when it came was free of its usual cynicism and was once again like a small child's.

'I told you she'd come back. And look, she's got you something. I knew she wouldn't forget. Show Jamie what you've got him, Mum.'

She was looking pointedly at me and I realized I was carrying a plastic shopping bag, but when I opened it, guess what was in there? Lemon-scented bathroom cleaner! And I couldn't for the life of me remember buying it.

'Just what every ten-year-old boy dreams of.'

Daniel had clearly taken over the cynic mantle from Tilly, I remember thinking. Then he spoke again, this time to the children, although he continued staring straight at me.

'Kids, go and get some stuff together for a sleepover. We're going to Uncle Darren's to celebrate Jamie's birthday.'

Tilly, who was half standing, half sitting, looked at Daniel uncertainly, while Jamie burrowed his face in his father's shoulder.

'Is Mum coming?' Tilly wanted to know, and I couldn't tell whether she was hoping for a yes or a no.

'Not tonight. Mum's tired.'

But Daniel was the one who sounded tired.

I knew I'd failed Jamie. How could I not know that? His face was red and puffy, and he wouldn't look at me.

'I'm sorry about the present,' I said. 'Why don't we go out and have a pizza?'

Daniel shut his eyes for a long moment.

'It's eight thirty on a school night. We've already had tea. We've already had cake, that I went out and bought from Londis. You missed it. You missed it all. And now I'm going to take the kids to my brother's.'

While Tilly and Jamie were upstairs putting pyjamas into bags, I remained standing, stupidly holding the fucking bathroom cleaner.

'I don't want you to go,' I said. But even as I said it, I realized I didn't know that it was exactly true. I'm finding the children so draining at the moment, that constant pressure to keep remembering they are there. You know, I remember when I first had Tilly, the health visitor explained that because a baby has no concept of the world outside of itself, it thinks that every time its mother goes out of the room, she has disappeared from the world completely. I remember being so horrified by how terrifying that must be. But now the same thing seems to be happening except in reverse. When the kids step out of my sight, they cease to exist, and every time they reappear I have to re-learn them all over again. It's exhausting.

'Just for a night, yes,' I said, but it was impossible to tell if it was a question or a statement.

As soon as the children came back downstairs, Daniel met them in the hallway.

'You're going to have such fun with Uncle Darren,' I told Jamie, but the smile I'd stuck on to my face kept peeling off at the edges. 'And when you come back home, I'll have everything prepared for a fantastic belated birthday. I just need to get a good night's sleep.'

Jamie's eyelids were so swollen his eyes had virtually

disappeared. They looked out at me like two raisins in a puffed-up scone.

'Your feet are dirty,' he said.

* * *

The children left the night before last, yet already it is hard to believe they were ever here. Whenever I catch sight of a football sock drying on the radiator (in truth, already dried and stiff with excess powder) or a frayed copy of *Twilight* I am jolted twice over – first with the memory of their existence and secondly with the memory of their loss.

You think loss is too strong a word? You think I exaggerate?

They are not coming back.

Daniel arrived yesterday and packed more of their things into a big case. He told me he was through with reasoning with me and now he was trying to shock me into taking control of my life.

'The kids will be back when they have a fully functioning mother,' he said.

What do you suppose a fully functioning mother consists of, Clive? Are mothers perhaps a bit like appliances? Do we need regular servicing to maintain our full and splendid array of functions?

I wish I knew.

Daniel seemed cross to find me in bed. (He's becoming very judgemental these days, I think. I'm sure he used to have more tolerance.) I had the laptop with me, of course, and my mobile, but I'd unplugged the landline. I didn't like the way it kept looking at me. I also had an almost-empty aerosol can of whipped cream which I'd found in the fridge and kept squirting into my mouth whenever I felt light-headed with hunger.

In truth, though, I haven't felt hungry much. My head still hurts, although it's better when I'm lying down, and any sudden movement sets my insides swaying dangerously.

Daniel made a big fuss about pulling up the blinds and flinging open the windows. Anyone would think the room smelled or something, the way he was huffing about. I could tell he was building up to say something. His pursed-lipped silence was wound tightly around him like a kimono. Eventually he couldn't bear it any more.

'Don't you even care?' he burst out.

Well, what does one say to something like that?

'Don't you care that you're in danger of losing everything? The kids? The house? Me?'

I was a bit nonplussed by that last 'me', I have to say. It seemed inconceivable that Daniel might yet see his leaving as a loss, rather than a consolation prize.

Daniel said I was 'insane' to have stopped the anti-depressants. Isn't that ironic? It's insane to stop the drugs that are a sign of being insane? When I told him I'd started taking them again, in fact I'd taken three that very morning, he didn't seem any more mollified.

'You have to get a grip,' he told me.

By that stage he'd come to the side of the bed and was crouching down so that he was at my level. I think they might learn that at teacher training – how important it is not to tower over the child.

For a moment his face, just inches from mine, went soft like wax, and his features moulded themselves into the expression of someone who cared. It was the look I recognized from old photos, the look of someone who wishes you only good things. Suddenly a lump came tumorous into my throat and I thought I was about to scream. I wanted desperately for Daniel to hold me, pull me into him, stroke my hair and soothe me like a baby; the way he did when my mother died, not minding the snot on his jumper or my blotchy puffed-up face. That's what I wanted, so what did I do? I laughed. I couldn't seem to help it. Stupid giggles that I wanted to bat away from me like flies.

'A grip? Where do I get one of those?' I asked him, helpless. 'Can I buy one? Do you have a spare one?'

And all the time, while I was spilling this stuff, I was silently urging him to lean in and put his arms around me and pretend to love me. If I say I was after just a fraction of the protection the thing that calls itself a baby already commands, you'll think I'm crayzeeeee, but it's nevertheless true. But of course Daniel couldn't see beyond the hopeless giggles. He got stiffly to his feet, creaking with disapproval.

'Let me know when you're ready to start putting your children first.'

My children. The words passed through me like gallstones. I had a sudden image of Tilly and Jamie swimming like goldfish in a glass bowl, visible but not attainable. Or perhaps I was the one in the bowl, obscenely gaping mouth pressed up against the glass, and they were on the outside, walking away.

After Daniel had gone, I lay in bed and tried to cry but there were no tears. Instead my phone rang almost constantly. Sian wanted to come over immediately with a bottle of chilled Sauvignon Blanc to offer support. Daniel had rung her, apparently. (Oh, the cosy bonds forged by having a shared loony in your life. I imagined them comparing notes and shaking their heads in a synchronized show of regret.) She sounded hurt when I told her I wouldn't let her in, saying again that she blamed herself for all of it, for buying into the romance of our affair. She had 'enabled' you to gain a foothold in my life, she said again. She had *facilitated* my breakdown. I told her not to worry and that she hadn't actually been all that important. Then she went very quiet and wounded and said I'd changed and how much she missed the old Sally, and mentioned the Sauvignon Blanc again, more for form's sake, I think, than with much expectation of success.

You always had loads of theories about Sian, didn't you? You thought she was passive aggressive, you thought she wanted to punish me for her own childlessness, you thought she fancied me (although, admit it, that was just a little febrile fantasy). You thought she fancied you. You thought I was too good for her, you thought she was too bad for me. You thought, yet again, that she was damaged.

Damaged women. You always were such a sucker for them.

And now I'm the most damaged of them all. And you're nowhere to be seen.

After Sian, there was my dad. Daniel has been busy with his address book, apparently.

My father sounded uncertain, as though not quite sure why he had rung.

'Are you all right?' he asked.

I couldn't be bothered to dissemble. 'The children have gone, Daddy. Daniel took them away.'

There was a pause as he tried to gauge from my tone whether the children going might be construed as a good thing or a bad thing. Eventually, finding no barometer to guide him, he opted for the safety of the platitude.

'Well, we must hope for the best.'

I let him off the hook then. What else could I do?

'How's life with you, Daddy?'

Immediately he sounded stronger. He was on more solid ground now.

'I've been very disturbed by the oil spill. Of course, it's a disaster, but it's galling to see the Americans are on their high horses again, when God knows the wreckage they've left behind them in places like Bhopal.'

You've never met my father, have you? I'm sure you'd pronounce him 'perfectly charming', but I don't suppose you'll ever meet him now. (Remember how you used to declare yourself insanely jealous of the life I had outside of you, the mother you'd never know and the father you'd never met. 'I want your life to start when you met me,' you'd say. 'I can't bear you to have existed before I knew you.')

'I'm worried about the world, Sally,' my father said now, in all seriousness.

That giggle came again then, quite unbidden, tearing from my mouth like a scream.

'I'm worried about it too, Daddy.'

When the phone rang a third time, I thought it would be my father again, perhaps remembering some new affront the Americans had perpetrated, or perhaps having recalled that losing one's children was more serious than he'd first surmised.

'Sally? Helen Bunion here.'

And so I was to have the full treatment, the big guns, no expense spared.

Helen had to inform me that Daniel had been in touch. She had, of course, told him that it wasn't appropriate for her to discuss her clients with an outside party. (What a funny description for Daniel – an outside party. Makes him sound a bit like your wedding-vows bash in the marquee in your garden, doesn't it?) But she had agreed to contact me as he was clearly most concerned.

'It's reached the point where I feel I must urge you most strongly to seek further help,' she told me. 'You are stretching the boundaries of my remit.'

Isn't that classic? Stretching the boundaries of her remit. I even wrote it down, I liked it so much. It's scribbled here in the margin of my journal next to a doodle of a flower. (The flower has petals that droop down as if it's dead.)

You know, I rather think that's what you might have done, Clive – stretched the boundaries of my remit. Maybe all that stretching is what keeps hurting so much.

Helen told me she had 'grave concerns' about my state of mind and urged me, once again most strongly, to contact my GP. She also said I had reserves of strength I didn't even know existed and that I should draw on them, even when I thought I was all done. That bit about drawing on them made me think about the doodle of the dead flower and again I tried not to laugh.

'There is support available to you, Sally,' Helen told me. 'It's vital that you know you are not alone.'

I thought about that once she'd rung off, about the support that is available to me and about the fact that I'm not alone. Except that it's not how it seems right now. Right now I feel like the most alone person that ever was.

'Don't confuse being alone with being lonely,' Helen has always told me, so I tried to work out which one I was and came to the conclusion I was both.

Alone and lonely. The double whammy.

The phone rang again. A withheld number.

And it was you.

'What did you think you were doing?'

Your voice quivered with barely controlled anger. For a minute I thought you were talking about us. What did I think I was doing when I got involved in 'us'? I'd forgotten about Emily.

'Emily had a nasty scare. Naturally Susan and I are getting the first flight back to see her. The baby is going to have to be induced early. The last thing she needed was you turning up and giving her a fright.'

That was harsh, I think. I was trying to help, after all.

'When are you going to accept reality, Sally?'

I stayed silent. Well, there didn't seem much to say.

'We had an affair and now it's over. You have to move on.'

'Where?'

'What do you mean, where?'

'Where would I move on to?'

You sighed then. A theatrically heavy sigh, as if your chest was being slowly compressed by a giant hand, squeezing out every last breath of air.

'I've tried everything to help you, Sally.' (Have you, Clive? Have you tried everything? Have you tried standing by your promises? Have you tried telling the truth?) 'But I have to warn you, one of my contacts has taken great exception to the way you've been harassing my family. He's not the kind of man you mess with and I'm afraid it's now completely out of my hands.'

'Should I be scared, Clive?'

I thought about the man in the leather jacket and the way his teeth at the front were whiter than the others; a man who cares so much about what other people think that he has bleached only the teeth that other people can see. It won't be him, I don't think, this 'contact' who has taken exception to me. Mr Leather Jacket is too familiar now. Perhaps he even quite likes me. It's not beyond the realms of possibility. There has been no enmity in the exchanges that have passed between us. No, there will be someone else, another of Tony's charming relatives perhaps, in a different jacket, who'll tell you to leave everything to him and not ask too many questions, and you will so gratefully acquiesce. 'I don't want anyone to get hurt,' you might say vaguely, self-servingly, just feeling it important to have said it. 'Some people just won't listen to reason,' the man might say, regretfully. 'Some people just need to learn the hard way.'

I think you hoped I would back down then, but I continued:

'Do you remember telling me how you lay awake at nights worrying about what you would do if anything happened to me?'

Your turn to be silent then, after I said that. Then another one of those big, squashed-down exhalations.

'I never said anything I didn't mean. At the time.'

That 'at the time' was such a clever touch – a Get Out of Jail Free card tucked carefully under the edge of the board.

'Life moves on, Sally. People change.'

But that's just where you're wrong, Clive. People don't change. The world carries on spinning inexorably around, but people don't spin with it. They dig their heels into the shifting sand and cling on for dear life.

After you'd put the phone down (wishing things had never got this far), I tried to hold on to the sound of your voice, tried to wrap myself around it like a T-shirt that smelled of you. But it faded far too quickly, and besides it had been hard and unyielding and not at all comforting. I lay for a long time thinking of how it had sounded as it said those three magic words 'at the time'.

The more I thought about that phrase, the more impressed I was. I've got to hand it to you, Clive. That 'I never said anything I didn't mean. At the time' is sheer genius. It gives you carte blanche to say exactly what you want, knowing that you can backtrack at any time in the future with your integrity intact. I really must remember it for next time.

The problem is, of course, that other people might not quite get how it works. Other people might take you seriously. Other people might start to plan their lives around the things you've said. Other people might be left freefalling.

Did you think about that? Did you? Did you?

* * *

So yesterday was the day for phone calls. And today has been the day for knocks at the door. Five separate times people have pushed open the gate with its rusty, grating latch, and walked up the path, the soles of their shoes crunching in the muesli gravel. Five separate times I've heard the leaves of the out-of-control sycamore tree swish and the spindly branches crack as people bent their heads to pass under it. Five separate times that ominous knocking at the door (thank God the electric bell is now finally

301

out of charge. How I hated the funereal drawn-out howl as its batteries slowly ran down.)

Twice I even dragged myself out of bed to stand at the window at the sound of the knock, despite the bolts of pain that pass through me whenever I stand upright. (The stupidity of me, yet again thinking, even now, it might be you at the door, coming to rescue me.) Once I found myself looking down on the completely bald head and protruding belly of a man I'd never seen before; in his fifties, wearing a black nylon jacket zipped all the way to the top, black trousers and black sunglasses. Something told me he wasn't the Milk Tray Man. At first I thought he might have been the contact you were talking about, the one who'd taken such exception to my harassing your family. But then, after peering through the living-room windows and knocking on the front door a few more times, he put something through the letterbox. I couldn't imagine what your contact might have been posting, so after I'd watched him drive away (incidentally, I noticed a child's booster seat in the back of his car! Doesn't that strike you as incongruous?), I forced myself to go downstairs for the first time in two days. There was a letter on the doormat with a handwritten address. When I opened it I discovered it was from a firm of bailiffs. Apparently Daniel and I owe £2544.79 to a credit-card company and they've been sent to collect.

£2544.79. It could have been worse.

I have to admit, the letter did upset me a bit. I'd decided not to take any medication today as I've almost run out, but after the visit from the fat, bald bailiff, I needed something to calm me down. To my delight, nestling under a box of Tampax in the back of my bedside cupboard, I found three Cymbalta that a GP friend had sent me in the first throes of my depression. I washed those down with lukewarm water from the bathroom sink, trying to ignore the persistent whooshing in my brain as I drank.

The second time I looked down to see who was knocking at the door, it was Sian and I withdrew my head quickly in case she looked up. She stood there a long time, I must say, shouting up at the bedroom window, saying she knew I was there. I felt bad then. She does genuinely care about me, you know, whatever you might think – within the restrictions of her own self-absorption. In the end I took two more zopiclones and pulled the duvet up over my head.

When I woke up a couple of hours ago, it was dark. My laptop told me it was 1.24 a.m. and I couldn't work out what day it was. In the end I Googled 'What day is it today?' and found a website that not only told me the day, but also what the temperature was in London, New York and Tokyo.

I immediately clicked on to Facebook to see if I'd missed anything.

I could see from the entries on Susan's page that you were back. There was something from Liam about picking you up from the airport, and something else from one of Susan's workmates commiserating about you having to cut short your Maui trip.

Emily's page had seen a lot of action. Clearly sitting around in a hospital room, even one equipped with its own iPod docking station, left a lot of time for brooding (and I mean that in the existential rather than the 'Iwannacutebaby' way – although that is probably also true).

Emily Gooding-Brown *wants to thank all her lovely friends for being so lovely.*

Emily Gooding-Brown *Amazing how a brush with death helps focus one's priorities.*

Emily Gooding-Brown *can't wait to meet her little one. Hold on, sweetie. Just two more days!*

Emily Gooding-Brown *Bored now.*

There was also message after message from friends and well-wishers, including one from Susan, obviously sent from an airport somewhere.

Susan Gooding *on way back. Will bring grapes. Don't have baby before we arrive.*

Looking at Emily's profile picture, which had been recently updated to show her in full pregnant pose, I remembered how she'd looked at me when I stood in the doorway of her hospital room and how she'd turned her head away and said 'Make her leave.'

Make her leave.

Once I might have been her stepmother, part of her family. 'Emily might be a little hostile at first, but she'll come round to it once she sees how happy you make me,' you'd told me.

At the time I'd believed you. I'd even fantasized about how Emily would be like an older sister to Tilly, taking her on shopping trips and out for lunch. But now I know it to be a lie. All of it. Emily would never have accepted me. I would never have been good enough. Instead she whispers, 'Make her leave,' and her friends smirk and can't meet my eyes.

I keep feeling sick and rushing to the loo, but when I throw myself down on the floor, nothing comes up. The brain zaps are getting worse, and now there's another feeling as well, prickling at the back of my throat. At first I couldn't place it. In fact, it took me ages to work it out. Do you want to know what it is, Clive, that new feeling churning up my insides and rising up my gorge?

It's hatred.

And do you want to know something else?

It's making me feel alive.

The sun is up, but I've drawn all the curtains and pulled down all the blinds. It makes the pain in my head slightly easier.

The knocking on the door started at seven thirty this morning. I didn't look to see who it was, but I heard male voices shouting through the letterbox.

'Mrs Islip? We need to talk to you, Mrs Islip.'

I don't know who she is, this Mrs Islip they're addressing. I think they have the wrong door.

And still the knocking goes on. I haven't looked to see if that contact of yours has come to see me. I'm sure he'll find me if he wants to, bearing gifts from you and love notes tied around bricks.

Earlier Sian came again, shouting up from the doorstep. 'Sally, for *fuck*'s sake let me in.'

I could tell she had her high black work shoes on, they made a satisfying clicking noise on the pavement when she finally walked away.

The mobile has been ringing, of course, but I rarely answer it, only once this morning when it was Tilly.

'Dad won't let me go to the 14–16 club night in Brixton. Everyone's going. It's so unfair.'

Do you ever have that thing where someone's talking to you and the words are making sense, but you just can't work out what they mean?

'You're not fourteen,' I said. Then immediately I had doubts. 'Are you?'

Tilly's voice rose dangerously as she replied. 'You don't even know how old I am. You don't know what is going on in my life. Why did we have to come to Uncle Darren's? Why can't we come home? What kind of a *fucking* mother are you anyway?'

The 'fucking' reverberated shockingly down the telephone line, silencing us both.

Then there was a noise, and she was gone.

Under the duvet, I've been clicking obsessively between Emily and Susan's Facebook pages and your company's website. I see there's another visitor comment, this one commending you as a 'fearless producer'. You'll like that, I know. That word 'fearless' standing out proudly on the screen.

But I know better. I know what you're afraid of. I know the fear that trickles down from your armpits.

You're afraid of me.

I don't believe it.

That's not true. Of course I believe it. Why wouldn't I believe it?

I decided to look at our old email account, just now. Not the secret one we've always used, but the hotmail one you set up last year, that time the original one was out of action for a couple of days. I'd come across a reference to it when I was scrolling through all our old correspondence. (Do you ever do that, I wonder? Go through our old messages. I rather like the idea that we might both unknowingly be on there at the same time, taking a synchronized trip down memory lane.)

It wasn't hard to guess your password. After all, I knew your password to 'our' account. ('I don't want to have any secrets from you,' you told me. Well, you've got to laugh, haven't you?) It was your mother's maiden name, Lyttleton, plus the dates of Liam's birthday. When that didn't work, I tried Lyttleton plus your own birthday. Then, after a quick Facebook consultation (isn't it convenient the way people list their birthdays so prominently?), I tried Lyttleton plus Emily's birthday. Bingo.

The first surprise was that the hotmail address still worked. The second surprise was that it had been active very recently. I scanned down your inbox. The emails were all from the same person. AnnaMillington1977.

1977!

Even before I clicked any open, I had to run to the toilet again. It was that whole list of AnnaMillingtons, and that taunting, damning 1977.

How old would someone born in 1977 be? Shall we work it out? Thirty-three. Ten years older than your daughter. Ten years younger than me. The symmetry is pleasing, I'll give you that.

When I got back into bed, my brain was slamming against the inside of my skull. I tried to ignore it and instead counted the emails in your inbox from Anna

Millington. Eleven. Then I decided to go through them chronologically from the bottom up, starting June 5, five weeks ago.

Your new pen pal is obviously someone who has recently started working for your record company. The first email was a response to one you'd sent which I immediately called up. It read:

You probably think I'm a sad old fuck (sad fuck in a box!) *and if that's the case please tell me to sod off, but I kind of thought there was a spark between us the other night. Am I deluded? (It wouldn't be the first time!)*

Typical Clive, self-deprecating but predatory. A spark between you, hey? That would have been three weeks before your renewal-of-vows party. Was she there, I wonder, Anna Millington? One of the young girls in the short shiny dresses I'd dismissed as Liam and Emily's friends?

To her credit, Anna Millington tried to mount a semblance of a moral defence.

You're not deluded, don't worry. But you are MARRIED and MY BOSS – two pretty good reasons why that spark should probably stay unignited, don't you think?

Smart woman, that Anna Millington. But would you accept that? No, not you, Clive. In the emails that flew between the two of you over the next couple of days, light-hearted banter with a darker undercurrent of flirtation, you were constantly angling for more, stretching the boundaries of your remit, perhaps. But Anna didn't seem to mind.

Two weeks before the party, it seems you went out on a date. Except, charmingly, you refused to call it a date.

Think of it as a work meeting. The kind of work meeting where there's candles and champagne and you arrive in a tight little dress and ridiculously high heels and laugh at all my jokes, read your message that same afternoon. *I've got butterflies in my stomach. Why the fuck do I feel like such a teenager?*

The following day there was a message from you at 6.30 a.m.! Really, Clive, have you never heard of playing hard to get?

I just wanted you to know I had the most magical time. I know you were right to push me out of the door. I know you're right about everything, but I can't stop thinking about you. Even if nothing ever happens between us, I just want you to know that when you walked into that restaurant, I felt like the luckiest man alive.

When I read that last bit, this sound came from me as if it had been ripped right out of my guts – a horrible, tearing animal sound. It was that 'luckiest man alive' that did it. I had a vivid flashback to three years ago, when we'd actually managed to wangle three days together in the South of France, you adding extra time after filming a promo for a new band, and me under the guise of interviewing a horrible British woman living in Nice who'd written a blog about expat living which had become an unexpected internet sensation. You'd picked me up from the airport and when I walked through Arrivals, self-consciously awkward in my unfamiliar heels, you were there waiting for me. After a long kiss, you drew back and, holding me at arm's length, gazed at me in silence.

'I feel like the luckiest man alive,' you'd said at last.

After that early-morning email, there were just two

others in the long chain of messages. Later that day had come Anna Millington's measured response.

I enjoyed last night a lot. Way, way too much. But the fact remains, you are married and, not only that, about to go on holiday to Maui with your wife. (Ah, so you hadn't, after all, mentioned the renewal-of-vows ceremony to your new young correspondent. Or whispered that nastily emotive word 'honeymoon'.) *I want you to take the time from now until the end of your holiday to reflect on what you really want. I won't be a married man's mistress. I'm worth more than that.*

So Anna won't be a mistress. She is worth more. She is worth more than me. Worth is relative. Hers is higher. I am a mistress (an ex-mistress), so mine is lower. The equations go round and round in my head.

That was the last thing in your inbox. But when I went back to the Sent folder, there was one more message, dated just three days ago.

I think about you constantly, you wrote from your iPhone somewhere in Maui.

So now I know.

But really I've always known.

Was I different, Clive? Or was I just the same? Did I just manage to last slightly longer than the others?

It's hot here under the duvet, but I daren't come out. I don't want to hear the doorbell going, or feel my phone vibrating. I don't want to know if it's light outside the blinds. I don't want to see my own body and have to face that I'm real.

I've Googled you again and found a new image of you on a German music website. I don't know what the text says, but I know your face. My God, I know your face.

All the time, my head is pounding, pounding, and my heart rattling in my chest.

I've just flicked back to Emily's Facebook page. Nothing, just more 'good lucks' from people with stupid names. I want to scratch the screen where their photos are, scoring ugly welts through their smug faces. Back to your company website now, that 'fearless' still leaping off the page, then on to Susan's. I keep flicking and flicking until the sites just merge into each other, faces bleeding together, all of it ugly.

It has happened.

While I was clicking on something on Susan's page a short while ago, a new comment flashed up on her wall.

Liam Gooding *Congratulations Grandma!!*

So that's it. You are grandparents now. Yet another bond in your unbreakable defence.

I went back on to Emily's page, and the congratulations were flooding in. Definitely a boy, it seems. You will love that so much, another male to spar with in your fearless way. Do you remember the baby that never was, Clive? I always imagined it as a boy, a tiny thing kicking in your arms, born of love.

Where did this other thing come from? This usurper? Anna Millington would give you babies, make you a family. Perhaps she and Emily could be friends. And Grandma Susan would look after you all.

The photos have already started being posted on Emily's Facebook wall. A purple creature, with a wide greedy mouth, Emily, damply beaming. The bland barrister, proudly smiling . . . And there, there, there, there, there. There is you.

You are holding the thing that calls itself a baby up to your nose, as if you would snort it up like a maggot-fat line of coke. Susan is beside you, looking up, her face freshly tanned and shining in the bright lights of the delivery room.

And then another. You and Susan are on either side of Emily, who holds the thing like it was made of origami. Susan and Emily have their heads bent in supplication, but you, Clive, you are gazing straight at the camera and your expression is one of total triumph.

You think you've won, don't you, Clive?

But you haven't won.

You're not going to win.

You will pay, Clive.

You all will pay.

It came to me earlier on, what I should do. I don't know how long it is since I last wrote, but I know there have been many more vibrating calls, and more feet crunching on the gravel. Emily's Facebook page is full of 'Congratulations' messages. Hundreds of them. (How many friends young people seem to have these days! How on earth do they keep track?) Quite a few of them mention the fact that she can kiss goodbye to sleep. I think it's supposed to be funny.

I tried to get up a while ago, but my head whooshed so badly that I sank straight back down. But I will do it. If not this minute, then next, and if not then, then later.

I will go to the hospital. Well, I know my way now. I will remember to take my Oyster card, and I will wash my feet, and I will make my way past the polite receptionist and up in the lift. Even if it's not visiting hours, I will tell the nurses that my niece has given birth and that I was told it would be all right. They won't object. There are some plus points, after all, to the respectable invisibility of the middle-aged woman.

I will take what is yours. The same way you took what was mine.

And I will not look back.

Fifteen Months Later

Hello. It's been a while.

Sorry, does that sound like a Tim Rice lyric? I rather fear it does.

To be honest, I haven't even been able to pick up this journal in all these months. Strange to think at one stage it was practically surgically welded to my hands. How quickly we ingrates outgrow our support systems, eh, Clive?

I don't need to look at the last entry to remember when it was and what it said. Nearly fifteen months ago, but it remains scratched into my mind with a rusty nail. The bus, the hospital, the baby.

I won't think about the baby.

Of course, there have been a lot of changes since then. I like to think that progress has been made, of a sort.

For starters, I'm no longer the invisible woman in the cubbyhole, half chair, half human. And, for that matter, you're no longer the sad fuck in a box. That's a kind of progress, wouldn't you say, right there?

The cubbyhole is no more, the house is no more. I don't have to hide myself away from Daniel and the children in order to scribble in this notebook. I have all the time in the world now. Funny how I used to dream of having time to myself. Time to do my own thing, free of other people's expectations. Now it often seems as if I have nothing but time. And no one expects anything. Be careful what you wish for. Isn't that right?

I'm lying on my uncomfortable bed now. (How many beds did we share over the years, Clive? I imagine them in a row like a Slumberland showroom, some queen-size, some swollen with pillows, many with those bolted-on headboards-cum-bedside-cabinets you find in cheap chain hotels; all filled with ghosts.) Looking up, I can just about see through the window where October is massing stolid in the grey sky. A room with a view. A room of my own.

Be careful what you wish for.

There's a card from Jamie on the melamine bedside table. It has a picture of flowers on the front, and inside is written, in careful joined-up writing, 'Good luck, Mum.' The letters, so conscientiously rounded, are painful for me to see, it's like someone is sewing them straight on to my heart, so I try not to look at them too often.

Nothing from Tilly, of course.

'She'll forgive in her own time,' Daniel said the last time he brought Jamie to visit. 'It has been very hard on her.'

He didn't have to add 'and on all of us'. It was written in the hollow plains of his face, in the grey hair now threading through the blond.

I remember Tilly's face as she described to me, on one of her rare early visits, how she and Jamie had gone back to the house with Daniel just before it was repossessed, knowing that they had just a few hours to salvage from it whatever they could. Working against the clock, she'd stuffed her things – all the lovingly collected detritus of childhood: cards from friends, photos of girls in pink pyjamas taken at various sleepovers, posters, folded notes written in class and illustrated with smiley faces – into black bin bags and carried them outside. She told me how the neighbours had pretended not to be staring, and as she spoke, hotly remembered shame oozed from every pore. These days I'll grab at any branch to flay myself with and my mental birch filled in all the details her adolescent awkwardness refused to furnish. In my mind I saw the bags lined up on the pavement outside, Jamie's ripped where he had overstuffed them with the broken train sets and remote-control cars he was too big to play with now, but couldn't bear to leave behind. I saw the stained mattresses leaning against the garden wall, and the grubby, misshapen cushions. I saw Tilly's humiliation as she noticed one of her bags was open at the top, a teen bra spilling over the side. Each image was another lash of the birch.

I deserve it, of course. I deserve it all.

My poor, lost girl.

Daniel told me about Sian without meeting my eyes, just a few weeks ago.

'I'm delighted,' I lied.

I'm not, of course. To tell you the truth, the idea of Daniel and Sian together sickens me to a degree I never could have imagined. At night, I torment myself imagining her sleeping on my side of the bed, slotting effortlessly into the life I thought I didn't want. The surprise, I suppose, is that she should have wanted it, although the more I think about it, and about her face when she said that thing – 'A Birkin bag won't care about me when I'm old' – the less of a surprise it turns out to be. To be quite frank, though, I'm horrified at the idea of Sian being the mother to my children that I spectacularly failed to be, the image of her hairbrush in my kids' bathroom, her high-heeled black work shoes next to Jamie's muddy trainers in the hall. Despite all those years of evangelical singledom, my fear is that she will slide into my family like melted butter. And Daniel will allow it, of course, just as he allows most things, convincing himself that the path of least resistance is the very path he would have chosen for himself anyway. Sometimes I force myself to picture it, enjoying the brutal stab of pain that comes from imagining her face next to Daniel's on the pillowcase I bought, or how she might smooth back the damp hair from Jamie's face when he has one of his nightmares. Those things I force myself to confront, yet when I picture her in the early-morning gloom, preparing the sandwiches for Tilly and Jamie's lunch boxes, my mind closes down. Funny, the inconsequential things that prove too painful to be endured.

The night after Daniel told me, I bit a hole clear through my pillowcase. It was quite shocking to see it the next morning, jagged and ugly and soggy with grief. But I said, 'I'm delighted,' because of that need I have to be punished and to suffer.

Sian has yet to make the journey to see me. She wrote me a long letter, though, saying things like, 'If I'd thought for a minute you still had feelings for Daniel, I'd never . . .' and 'You can never know how much I've agonized about this, how much we both have.' So now it's Sian and Daniel who are 'we both'. Now that Daniel is irrevocably lost to me, I can finally, as Helen Bunion had urged for so long, experience him as a separate entity, and I can see how far removed he is from the ineffectual man my warped obsession had made him out to be. Turns out he is stronger than I ever gave him credit for. He has had to be. More importantly, I see now he has something that I never really noticed before, certainly never valued. Integrity. Oh, don't make that face, Clive. I know how you'd scoff. 'I haven't an ounce of integrity,' you used to boast, adding 'thank God,' for comic effect. Now, belatedly, I see how integrity might have its advantages.

There is a folded, unread newspaper next to the bed. Today's. I don't have to open it to know it will carry a picture of your face – perhaps the same one as on your company website. That's the one the papers often seem to choose. How pleased you must be that you selected that so judiciously. Next to it might well be that photograph of me taken at your vow-renewal party. 'The skeleton in pink' is how I think of it. I think that must be the only one the media can get hold of. My friends and family have been very loyal. Much more so than I deserve.

Rarely does a photo of one of us appear without the other. How ironic, after you invested so much in trying to distance yourself from me, that you and I should end up bound so inextricably together, our images forever twinned in the public imagination, like Myra Hindley and Ian Brady.

The other day there was a new photograph of you. I don't mean to offend you, Clive, but I was a little shocked. How old you seem to have got suddenly. And how gaunt. The last time we met I bemoaned that extra layer of fat you wore like a detachable coat lining. And yet now it's gone I find I mourn it. Funny, but that's about the only thing I miss these days. If it wasn't for the associations with what happened, I don't know that I'd feel anything now when I look at your picture. You'd be just another man. Sorry. Another Tim Rice moment. I do apologize. I don't know what has come over me. Really I don't.

My eyelids feel weirdly heavy, probably a result of not sleeping last night. I do believe I saw every shade of night through the uncurtained window, while my thoughts raced chaotically on and my heart hammered away inside me. The walls are so bare in here, there's nothing to look at except the window. For the first time in ages, I longed for a sleeping pill – just one little white lozenge-shaped merciful zopiclone. But I am free of all that now. Whether through accident or design, my body really has become a temple. I've put on weight too, gaining just as quickly as you seem to have lost. Why, it's almost as if I've been sucking you dry, Clive!

To be frank, before last night it had been a long time since I really thought properly about you. I suppose it must be some kind of psychological self-preservation thing. One's mind won't allow one too close to the things one cannot bear to face.

But last night, it all unfurled again, that endless, nightmare carpet that led me here.

I knew I'd have to go through it again today. I knew everyone's eyes would be on me, judging me, my day of reckoning.

To be honest, I've been shocked by the amount of interest there's been in the whole thing. All those letters, all those messages. The few times I've ventured on to the internet I've found forums where people I don't know discuss all aspects of the whole thing – motivation, moral prerogative – as if you and I were characters in a play, rather than real people. So I knew there would be a crowd, but I had no idea until I was driven there and saw the press of bodies outside, some with cameras, even TV cameras, exactly how big it was going to be.

You can't imagine, Clive, how it felt to be in that room. Sitting trying to look as if I was concentrating on what was being said, but all the time aware that everyone was looking at me, crowds of jostling strangers, staring as if I was a character on their favourite soap, not as if I actually existed there in real life just feet away from them.

Oh, silly me. Of course you can imagine it! You're used to all that, you with your public-speaking background.

Mind you, the last time I saw you on the television, on the evening news, a few days ago, you were looking far from at ease, if you don't mind me saying so. They'd filmed you climbing the steps of the courthouse, and you were almost hunched over as if not wanting to show your face. Just the top of your head was visible and I couldn't help thinking how much thinner your hair has become. *She* was holding your hand, of course, and there was no matching shyness from her, as she smiled straight into the camera lenses, almost as if she'd been practising. You must have been very proud of her, although I have to say you didn't look it. You looked, and I almost hesitate to say this as I know how much you'll hate it, but you looked smaller somehow. Diminished. *She*, in contrast, seemed enormous, an Amazon among women, gripping your hand with iron fingers.

Be careful what you wish for.

This room seems so hot, despite the cool October weather outside. I can't get comfortable. I'm lying here propped up on one elbow, and all the muscles in my neck feel like they're straining in the wrong direction. Yet one more consequence of getting older, I suppose.

There's a photograph on the bedside table, propped up against the reading light next to Jamie's 'good luck' card. It's one Daniel brought me of the two of us with Tilly and Jamie on holiday in France seven years ago, so it pre-dates you. I wonder if that's why Daniel chose it. We'd rented a big house in the countryside near Bordeaux with two other families, an eccentric place that had once been a recording studio. There was a swimming pool outside and I remember we had to take turns to act as lifeguards because Jamie was only three or four and treacherously transfixed by the brilliant blue water. Tilly, at eight, was still young enough to be happy most of the time and to believe her parents were basically on her side. We are all sitting on the back steps of the house. Daniel and I on the lower step, Tilly and Jamie above us. I can't remember who took the photograph. Must have been one of the other adults. Funny, I can't even be sure exactly which friends they were. All the holidays from that time blend into one another in a blur of big Greek salads and chilled white wine.

Jamie is leaning over Daniel's shoulder, laughing at

something just out of sight. Possibly the person who took the photo was making one of those faces adults make when they want children to smile for photos. Daniel is looking slightly up at Jamie, and laughing probably just because Jamie is. Tilly's still chubby arms are round my neck and her face is burrowed into my neck, blowing a raspberry most likely. But it is my own face I keep being drawn to. My mouth open in a roar of hilarity, my eyes all but lost to laughter lines. I am indisputably happy. I am unrecognizable.

Of course, I know why Daniel chose this particular photo. To remind me, as if I needed reminding, of what I once had and what I've lost. I don't blame him. I would have done the same.

But you know the odd thing? At the very same time as I mourn that Sunday-supplement family in the photograph, I'm reminded of another memory from that same holiday, or one very much like it. We are driving crossly along the autoroutes of western France. The kids are overheating in the back of the car, uncomfortably trapped by excess pillows and sleeping bags. My feet are wedged into one side of the passenger footwell by a bag of last-minute provisions that wouldn't fit anywhere else. At the wheel, Daniel, oblivious to the clammy irritability pervading the rest of the car, is humming to himself. Every now and again, he breaks off to read out a road sign. He has always fancied himself a linguist and he pronounces the names of the French towns with obscene, though clearly sincere, relish. *Veeeeeeeeeeeeeeeeldeeyer* (Villedieu), *Aavronsh* (Avranches). With every utterance, my stress levels are rising. I will him to stop, but he carries on. *Leeeeeeeeeeeemowj* (Limoges). I have lost the circulation in my feet, the kids are squabbling fretfully in the back as I look down at the map and see that the next turn-off will be for a town called Châteaubriant. As soon as I have seen the name, I hear Daniel's voice in my head saying it out loud, *Shatowbreeeeeonte*, and I know beyond all doubt that if he does, I will throw open the car door and run and run and never stop. My whole body tenses as we get nearer to the turn-off and I await the first signpost to Châteaubriant. My knuckles on the road atlas are white with anticipation. Now, all these years later, I can't remember what happened next, whether Daniel lost interest in pronouncing the French names, or whether he did and I somehow let it wash over me. But I still remember that clenched dread, that conviction that a breaking point had been reached.

Of all the things in life that cannot be relied upon (of which there are, let's face it, many), memory is the most treacherous. ('And mothers', whispers Tilly's voice in my head. She's right, of course. Memory and mothers.)

It seems inconceivable now that there was a time when my children weren't real to me. Now the thought of them, the physicality of them, their smells, their hair, the flush on Tilly's cheek when she's just woken up, crowd my senses every waking moment. Sometimes I can feel Jamie's hot middle-of-the-night breath on my face, or hear Tilly's long-drawn-out 'Mu-uuuuum,' just as if she were right next to me. We always crave what we no longer have. Have you found that, Clive?

I'm not going to lie to you, I've searched in the news footage and the newspaper reports for mentions of Liam. I can understand Emily staying away, but I'd thought Liam might be there to support you. Please don't think it gave me any pleasure that he wasn't. The days when your discomfort was my only solace are long gone, Clive. I hope you can believe that.

Susan came to visit me once. I wonder if she told you.

I could have refused to see her, but of course I didn't. What, turn down an opportunity to flay myself alive, my skin stripped and bleeding? Why would I do that?

I couldn't meet her eyes, yet I didn't want to look anywhere else either. Everywhere I looked there was evidence of what I'd done, the sudden sagging around the mouth, the dullness of her skin.

I'm sure you can imagine the dialogue that passed between us. Well, when I say dialogue, I really mean monologue. And when I say monologue, I really mean just a few lines, repeated over and over, as if sooner or later she must, by perseverance alone, unlock the answer she was looking for.

'Why?' That one came up a lot. 'I thought we were friends.'

And me, hackneyed as ever, with my one-word response. 'Sorry.' Sorry, sorry, sorry and sorry again. A thousand sorries and none of them even scratching the surface.

You know what was funny, though? As she was getting ready to leave, she turned to me with the strangest of looks. 'I could have known,' she said to me, as if I should understand what she was talking about. 'Did it never occur to you that I could have known if I wanted, but I just chose not to?'

I was dreading seeing Susan again today, if truth be told. I knew it was unlikely, of course, that she'd come, all those people gawping, those dreadful memories stirring. But still I couldn't help scanning the crowd for her white-blonde hair (so much whiter now than before) or a flash of navy blue. I knew I couldn't have spoken a word if I'd thought she was there, listening. It was bad enough as it was, sitting there knowing I was going to have to get up and answer all those questions, bring to life all those ghosts. I don't know how you do it, Clive, really I don't, all that public speaking, with every eye, every camera lens fixed on you. I do admire you for that.

I read an internet report earlier this week where the reporter was describing your demeanour in the witness box. He said that you answered the questions put to you with a voice that was 'practised, but lacked conviction'. I thought that was a little harsh. It would be hard to rustle up much conviction in the circumstances.

The same reporter also described the way you arrived at the courthouse with her, yet didn't look at her once during the entire proceedings. What was that about then, Clive? Guilt? Protectiveness? Surely not regret? He described her as 'loyal' in her support. I had to smile then. The idea that you would place a premium on something like loyalty.

I've changed position now. My heart was beginning to race so uncomfortably I could almost see it moving through this formal, dark-grey jacket I still haven't taken off. I was told to dress smartly, but as soon as I'd put it on this morning, I knew it was a mistake. It felt stiff and awkward, like I was wearing armour, which in a sense I suppose I was. Still, I suppose it will come in useful. It's a good funeral jacket.

My mind won't switch itself off. I could murder a drink. You know, some nights I dream I'm in the pub and when I wake up I can still taste the wine in my mouth, even though it's been nearly fifteen months since I last had a drink. Other times, though, I don't really think about it.

Today has been an ordeal, though, as I'm sure you can appreciate. All those long months shut up in that tiny room, all those meetings, all that preparation, knowing that it was all leading up to this one point. Well, it's no wonder the pressure got to me. I know you'll understand.

The first bit was OK, sitting there in my new funeral jacket and safe last-minute black suede court shoes, while other people droned on (amazing how quickly even listening to talk about oneself can become boring). Looking down at my shoes, I thought of the girl I'd glimpsed on the way in, tottering past in towering red patent platforms, and suddenly I felt a stab of regret for all the shoes I'll never wear – the ones with skinny gold ankle straps or purple velvet bows, or pencil-thin heels that wobble as one walks like mini pole vaults clinging to the ground.

You know, every woman harbours hidden shoe aspirations. We may trudge around in our flip-flops or our comfortable Uggs, but in our heads we're convinced that some time in the future we'll be transformed into the kind of woman who wears knee-high mock-snakeskin boots over jeans, or bubble-gum-pink high-heeled sandals. Accepting that I'll never now be that woman felt like a kind of bereavement in a way. The shoes I'll never wear, the paths I'll never take – that kind of thing.

Imagine thinking of shoes at a time like that! You must think I've completely lost my mind!

(Incidentally, I forgot to say how much I like the suit

you were wearing in the news footage. Dark and sober, but with a subtle hint of pin-stripe to give it that slight edge. Not your choice, I'd wager. You never were one for understatement.)

I could tell that it was getting near my time to talk by a gradual heightening of tension in the atmosphere and the way the people in the front started sitting up straighter and feeling around in their bags for tissues, for one last round of surreptitious nose-blowing and coughing before the main event.

I've never been the main attraction before in anything and I have to say I found it quite terrifying. When my name was called, the woman squeezed in next to me put a hand on my arm and I realized it was shaking. As I hauled myself to my feet, she gave me a look of such pure sympathy, my knees almost buckled. 'The only way past it is through it,' she whispered, and it was strange how touching the platitude sounded to me, as if it was the very first time I'd heard it.

Looking out at all those curious faces, I thought for a moment I might not be able to go through with it. I longed to tear off this stupid jacket and bolt for the door. (Can you imagine how that would have gone down? 'Unhinged!' they'd all have said, vindicated. 'We knew it all along!') But I fixed on a point on the back wall and focused all my attention there, just as I'd been advised, and somehow that seemed to do the trick.

Even so, when I started speaking, my voice squeezed from me in rough, dry lumps, like old toothpaste. I tried to pretend it didn't matter and ploughed on, hiding my trembling hands from sight.

At first the questions were gentle, but, as I'd been

warned, no sooner had I begun to relax than they became more probing, more insistent, until finally:

'Why did you do it, Ms Islip? Was it for revenge?'

For a moment I faltered, swaying slightly, trying not to panic. *Obviously it was revenge*, replied the cynical voice in my head. *Why else?* But of course, I said nothing of the sort.

'No,' said my lying, lumpy voice. 'You've got it totally wrong.'

Funny how in the days when you were still desperate for me, you'd tease me for being such a reluctant liar. Yet now I speak fluent falsehood. It's a foreign language I've recently mastered. I wonder if you'd be pleased at how I've progressed, how much more like you I've become.

Scanning the faces in the crowd, I could see no one was buying it. Well, who could blame them? Still, the pantomime continued.

'Can you describe your feelings now, towards Clive Gooding?'

Of course, I'd been waiting for this all along. I thought I was prepared, but even so, your name, spoken aloud like that, hit me like a slap, like a spat expletive. Don't take this the wrong way, Clive, but if the man had yelled out the word 'CUNT' across the hushed room it couldn't have felt more shocking. But you know, even the shock couldn't completely prevent me appreciating the comedy of the question. One time, if I'd been asked to describe my feelings for you, I could have listed every emotion in the dictionary – good, bad, appalling even, and it still wouldn't have come close. But now? Well, when my brain whirrs through all the options, I have to say I struggle to find even one that rings true. Do you know, I rather think the correct answer to the question 'Can you describe your feelings towards Clive Gooding?' might well turn out to be 'None'? But of course, that is not what I actually said.

'I'm sorry . . .' I mumbled, before collecting myself and remembering the lines I'd rehearsed.

'Mr Gooding was a close friend,' I recited in my dried-toothpaste voice. 'I will always wish him well.'

There was a distant murmur then among the crowd after I said that, like tall, malignant trees rustling in the breeze. This, after all, was what they had come for. They were finally scenting blood.

I knew what was coming, of course. I knew what everyone was thinking. Prison is such a *vested* concept, don't you agree? How the blameless thrill at the thought of the clanging of the doors, the stark clicking of locks, the clanking of key-chains – the hard, metallic sound punishment makes. (Of course, you and I know different – the soft sound of boredom and of people crying into pillows.)

I could feel the anticipation building in the room. Would it be over the top to say it felt as if they were closing in for the kill? Of course it would. My apologies. Like I said, I've been so overwrought today.

Still standing, one of my legs started going into spasm, quivering like something battery operated. I wondered if everyone could see it, even those at the back. There was a woman in the third row chewing gum. I watched her jaw move rhythmically and saw myself through her blank stare, the spectacle I had become, the spontaneous happening, the Fourth Plinth, with an out-of-control leg. I tried to make myself breathe properly. What was it Helen Bunion used to say? Something about breathing and stomachs? Instinctively I inhaled a huge lungful of air and tried to let it out as slowly as I could.

Exhale. Exhale. Exhale.

While I was concentrating on exhaling, the next question came, just as I knew it would.

'Ms Islip, do you have any comment to make on Clive Gooding's sentence?'

I want you to know, Clive, that I never wanted you to go to prison. It wasn't I who pressed charges. I know you're well aware of that, but I think it stands repeating. I wouldn't want there to be any doubt. I wouldn't want you thinking any of this was fuelled by spite. Although, having said that, I can't altogether feel sorry for you either. You puffed yourself up so big that it was surely inevitable you must eventually burst.

I did wince when I heard the charge, though. Soliciting Grevious Bodily Harm. It makes you sound like a common thug! How you'll hate that. But like I said before, the legal action wasn't anything to do with me. The CPS was like a dog with a bone, it really was. I have to say, I rather think your high profile might have counted against you in this instance.

Anyway, I think you might get a lot of mileage out of the whole prison experience when you've had a chance to come to terms with it. You're something of a cell-block celebrity in there, so I've heard. Once you settle in, I'm sure you'll find a way of making it work for you, like you always do. Look on it as a kind of career break. That's what I would do. It is possible to rebuild oneself from scratch, you know, even after something like this. That, at least, is something I have learned. And eighteen months really isn't such a long time, when you think about it.

When I think back to that moment in the hospital, that

low-point to end all low-points, I could never have imagined there could be a way back from there. Well, let's be completely honest, by that stage I wasn't imagining anything outside the little bubble of my own head. I don't like to think of the hospital, yet it's constantly with me. Whenever I see that particular purple colour, whenever I smell lemon-scented toilet cleaner, a wave of pure nausea passes over me. I guess, as punishments go, it's not so terrible, but I still try to avoid dwelling on it.

But I want you to understand how it's possible to bounce back, so I'll revisit it once again. Who knows, maybe my experience can be of some comfort to you. Wouldn't that be ironic?

To this day, I don't remember much about getting to that purple place, except that the bus came almost straight away, and I took it as some sort of sign. I was in a state, that much is certain. I don't have to re-read those last journal entries to know that. It's a wonder I managed to get out at all, really. I know I told reception that I was Emily's aunt, and I know I stood outside her room with the memory of her 'Make her leave' echoing through my head.

Through the slightly open door, I could see Emily sleeping. And there, at the bottom of her bed, in its glass incubator, was the baby, or 'the thing that called itself a baby', as I insisted on calling it. (I was bonkers, wasn't I? Truly bonkers. I'm embarrassed to remember it all.) But you know the funny thing was that, even through my madness, something inside me still recognized that as soon as I took one step forward into that room, I would be crossing a line from which there was no coming back. And so I hesitated, and during that split second of hesitation, the baby wriggled in its glass box and threw up a tiny foot, raw and mottled like salami. And do you know what I did? Please don't take this personally, I'm sure you love it dearly, but I *recoiled*. I shrank back and realized I couldn't bear to go near it – that newly boiled *alien* thing.

Well, you can't imagine how strange it felt, after all that time, to find a part of your life that I felt no connection with, no ownership of. And that was it. Twang! The steel cord of my obsession was snapped, as if with bolt-cutters. All those months of angst, the hundreds of pounds' worth of therapy, and all it took in the end was a scrap of purple flesh.

I must have fled the hospital after that, but I have no idea where I went or how. I'm told I was found wandering in Victoria station and spent the next few weeks in some kind of psychiatric facility, before being delivered into my father's care, but I have very little memory of that either. The mind is a marvellous guardian, don't you think? A *minder*, one could almost say, if one was in the mood to make jokes.

I'm sure most people imagine writing the novel was the therapy that helped me out of where I had got to (a dark, horrible place, a Warsaw of the psyche). Those months closeted away in my tiny old bedroom in my father's house in my own private self-imposed prison, turning my journals into the unimaginatively titled *The Mistress's Revenge*, are fast becoming the stuff of book-group legend. No one ever found out about that hospital visit. I never told a soul until now, but I know you understand what it's like to hit rock-bottom, Clive. And I hope you might find this some help.

Hold on a minute, I'm just shifting my weight to the other elbow. It's hard to get comfortable. These hotel beds look so inviting, and yet they so rarely live up to their promise. Don't worry, it's not one of 'our' hotels. They all merge, don't they, when one tries to think about those five years of illicit assignations, into one beige-carpeted, long-headboarded, mirrored blur? The publisher's PR department booked the room for me. I wouldn't have chosen this hotel myself. Too full of German tourists, and with those double-glazed windows that one can't fully open.

God, here I am complaining about my hotel room, when you're spending the night and the next, oh, five hundred and fifty nights (give or take a few) in a prison cell. I do apologize. Sometimes I can be so insensitive. But I'm working on it. Really I am. And I want you to know that though it's true I've never spent a night in an actual prison, I did endure that stint in the loony bin followed by the long months in my father's tiny back bedroom, so I know what it's like to feel incarcerated. My empathizing skills are not entirely forgotten.

Look, I don't want you to think it was intentional on my part – the timing of things. I know it might seem that way, organizing the first book signing for today, the day after you were sentenced. Believe me, I did raise it with the publisher. I didn't want you to think I was capitalizing on your misfortune. But the publicist assured me they couldn't possibly have known when your case would end. It was pure coincidence.

As to whether they could have guessed, well, that's something I couldn't tell you. I don't deal with that side of things. And in the end, what difference does it make? Our lives are separate now. Just as you always wanted.

Whatever I do happens in isolation of whatever you do. That's progress as well, one could say.

And anyway, I had no idea there'd be that sort of a turn-out at today's signing. Obviously the book's done very well over the weeks since publication. And believe me, no one is more surprised about that than me. You'll say the publicity over your court case didn't hurt, but you know, Clive, you have to remember, your court case is real. The novel is fantasy.

'It's fiction,' I explain whenever anyone asks. 'Fiction informed by experience.'

That's better. I've turned to face completely the other way. Now I can see the fat cuttings book the publicist has been keeping that is lying on the desk against the far wall. Do you know, she actually cuts out every print media reference to the book? There are several interviews in there, awkward occasions where journalists have done their best to probe and then pretended to be sporting and said things like, 'Oh well, you knew I had to ask anyway.' But a couple of accounts of your court case have also crept in and I read one last night when I couldn't sleep.

I must say, it seemed to me the reporter was taking a certain relish in the whole thing. She certainly made a big deal of describing – what's her name again? – Anna. That's it. I mean, I wouldn't have thought it had the least relevance to the case that Anna is 'striking', or that she wore a 'figure-hugging Victoria Beckham dress', or that she had once modelled in her underwear for a men's magazine. Neither is it here nor there that you weren't wearing your wedding ring as the two of you arrived at court hand-in-hand, or that your family was 'conspicuous by its absence'. You claimed never to read the stories that periodically appeared about you in the press. ('It's boring enough just *being* me, let alone having to read about me as well,' you used to proclaim.) Of course, like so many things, that wasn't entirely true and you were forever Googling yourself then calling me to rant about some hack who had it in for you. Mind you, after reading that biased report last night, perhaps you had a point.

Apparently, you have lost the 'confident swagger of old'. That's what the reporter said. I've tried to imagine you swaggerless, and admit I'm having trouble with it. Your swagger is so much a part of what makes you, you.

There's a brief description in the piece of the first witness in your case. The reporter doesn't say whether he turned up in the witness stand wearing a black leather jacket with stripes down the arm, but naturally I know who it is anyway. He even has a name: Gary Wilder. Funny, I never would have put him down as a Gary. As I'd thought, he turned out to be a distant relative of Tony's (I don't expect you'll be getting your hair cut by him any more). He admitted to the court that you had asked him to 'deliver a couple of messages' for him, and that yes, it's not inconceivable that these messages could have been 'misinterpreted' as intimidating. When asked why he would have done such a thing, Gary replied that it had been 'a favour, for a friend'.

Well, I couldn't help chuckling a little when I read that, knowing how deeply that would have wounded your pride. This Gary, with his whiter-than-white shoes and his gelled hair and his total lack of self-awareness, claiming friendship with you.

The next witness was the most destructive by far. This was the one I never met (fortunately for me, some might say!), the contact you warned me had taken such exception to the harassment of your family, the one you'd called for help when your good friend Gary Wilder's scare tactics didn't work. His name, it turns out, is Damian, Damian Vaughan. Well, obviously I had a little smile at that, wondering if you'd chosen him deliberately. You always did love to hammer home a bit of symbolism. Damian, it turns out, isn't actually related to Tony, but is an 'affiliate' of the family. That's the very word the paper used. I rather like it. An affiliate. He was apparently drafted in at the last minute when the usual 'affiliate' let them down. Damian came highly recommended for his discretion and professionalism – how unfortunate for you that his wife didn't live up to it. When she realized who you were, well, the pound signs obviously flashed in front of her eyes. I like to imagine that this Damian felt a little pang of remorse when he secretly taped the *award-winning* Clive Gooding offering to pay him £40,000 to have someone driven out of his life for good. (Incidentally, I want you to know I completely believe your account that you only wanted me 'scared off' and not seriously harmed. I'm just sorry that the jury didn't see it that way. But then, they don't know you like I do. They don't know you only had my best interests at heart.) The wife, of course, took the tape straight to the biggest PR person in the country, and four weeks later the story was all over the *News of the World*.

That was the day it all came out. All of it. You, me, the

grubby hotels, the five long years of lies, the phone calls, the threats, my bunny-boiling obsession, your strong-arm intimidation.

I lost a lot of friends that day and, finally, I lost Daniel. Because of losing Daniel, I lost my children. (Although of course I'd lost them anyway. My daughter who'd lost her way.)

You might have been the one who ended up in the dock after the authorities decided to press charges based on that story (not at my behest, I repeat), but you're not the only one who lost things.

I hope you know that.

Judging by the report in the paper, the prosecutor wasn't impressed by your performance in the witness box, which surprised me. I'd have thought you'd have choreographed and rehearsed it to within an inch of its life. There was a picture drawn by a courtroom artist showing the prosecutor wearing those frameless steel-sided glasses beloved of Scandinavians of a certain age. I can almost hear the disdain in his voice as he outlined your credentials to the court – your past achievements, your position of trust as an employer and a father and a husband, explaining that you led such a charmed life that you came to see yourself as beyond the rules of normal society.

'It seems to me that you, Clive Gooding,' the paper reported him saying, 'are a man who considered yourself outside the prevailing moral context of the times.'

Well, let's be frank, he sort of had a point, didn't he?

And what was the example he gave of the 'living proof of your reckless self-delusion'? That'd be me! Sally Islip! The woman who, as the prosecutor put it, refused to fade out quietly after you called time on our five-year affair.

'Like Frankenstein, you found you'd created a monster that you then had no idea how to stop.'

I admit it stung a bit, that word 'monster', although I tried not to take it to heart.

According to the paper, the prosecutor saved most of his vitriol for your ill-thought-out plan to scare me into silence, the so-called 'Damian Solution'. 'In your mind, it was a case of survival of the fittest. And you were in no doubt that the fittest was you. You thought you would get away with it because of your elevated public and private profile.

'But no matter who you are, Mr Gooding,' he apparently told you then, and I imagine him peering at you over the top of his rimless glasses as he spoke, 'there are always consequences.'

Daniel came to see me three days after the *News of the World* story broke. By that time I had already moved in with my father, who knew something momentous had happened, but couldn't quite get a grip on what. ('It's lovely to have you back here, dear. But are you quite sure there isn't anywhere else you ought to be?')

Daniel didn't look at me as he pushed brusquely past into the hall.

'This isn't a social call, Sally. I need some answers.'

I didn't tell him that answers are the very things I was looking for too.

Of course he wanted to know everything . . . except the things he didn't want to know. He wanted to know where and when we'd fucked, but when I started to tell him he screwed up his face as if he was about to be sick and put his hands over his ears and said, 'I just can't listen to this.'

He wanted to know if the two of us had been laughing at him.

'It wasn't like that,' I told him. 'We didn't even think of you and Susan at all.'

Well, you can imagine how that went down.

To be honest, I was taken aback by how very *affected* Daniel was by it all. I had thought him almost indifferent, but now hurt flaked off him like dead skin. I know reading in a national newspaper that your partner has been having an affair for five years with a man you considered a friend, who then paid money to have her, oh, what was the term the paper used, 'physically intimidated', must have come as a shock, but it was the betrayal of 'us' – him and me – that Daniel kept focusing on. In my naivety, I had thought he'd want to talk about you and me, yet that wasn't really what he was interested in at all.

'How could you do that to us?' he said over and over. 'How could you do that to our family?'

'It wasn't about "us", or our family,' I tried to explain. 'It was something separate, something that was just about me.'

He looked at me then as if he was seeing me completely afresh. I'm not going to lie to you, it didn't feel good.

'You really are a selfish bitch.'

But it was said almost completely without rancour, as if it were an objective fact that he had only just learned.

Just like that, I knew he was lost to me. And belatedly I realized what else was lost – the 'we' that, to my surprise, turned out to lie at the very centre of who I was.

And do you know something, Clive? For the very first time, I didn't hurl the blame like shit against your windows.

I'd lost my family, and it was no one else's fault but mine.

That was well over a year ago, and I have to say that since then Daniel has been very decent. Much more so than I deserve. He brings Jamie to Dad's house every month, and Tilly whenever she will agree to come. Or I come to London and stay in a hotel like this one (remember how we used to joke that there couldn't be a hotel left in London we hadn't shagged in? I have to tell you, Clive, we were so wrong, our concept of ourselves wildly over-inflated as usual) and take the kids for dinners or walks in the park. My daughter is fifteen now and out of that gawky in-between age. She is beautiful, in fact. Men look sideways at her in the street. I long to push them aside and hiss, 'Don't you know she's just a child?' But of course, it's too late to play the protective mother now. Not when the very person she most needed protection from was me. I know I damaged my kids, and because of that I'm resigned to the loss of my right to them. (Although never to the loss of them. Never to that.) Daniel says I must earn that right back. (Sometimes now he even talks to *me* in teacher-speak. It's one of the things I focus on if ever I start regretting that we're no longer together, which, I have to say, doesn't happen too often any more.)

Getting the advance money for the book helped. It was enough for a deposit on a flat for Daniel and the kids, and now that Daniel is fully qualified, he can just about cover the mortgage which his parents grudgingly agreed to guarantee. It makes me happy to think of Tilly and Jamie having their own rooms again, after having to share a bed-room at Darren's. I imagine them surrounded by their things – well, the things they managed to salvage anyway. The money keeps coming in bit by bit and hopefully I'll soon have enough to get a little place of my own near my children – somewhere they can come and stay whenever they like – though for the moment I'm quite happy in my little cell at Dad's. *Cell!* There I go again! Such an insensitive idiot! Please forgive me, it wasn't intentional.

I don't know how I shall feel if Sian moves in there with them all. I like to think I will just bite my lip and accept that's how things are, comfort myself with the thought that this is something else to flog myself with, but I'm not completely sure. In the end, it's the pain of being replaceable that turns out to be the hardest to bear. How did that never occur to us, you and me? How did we never take the time to imagine how Susan and Daniel would feel at being so easily usurped? It seems that to all our other crimes we must also add a failure of imagination.

The good news is that Tilly and Jamie are both coming to spend a week with me in a couple of weeks' time to celebrate my dad's eightieth birthday, which is a major milestone. Of course, Tilly will declare herself 'bored to death' the second she steps through the door, but I'll try not to take that personally either. Baby steps, as Helen Bunion used to say.

Daniel hasn't read *The Mistress's Revenge*. I told him not to, and I think he was quite relieved. 'It's pure fiction,' I said. 'But I wouldn't like you to be always wondering.'

Susan read it, though. When she came to see me she told me, in a brittle, most un-Susan-like voice, it had been 'enlightening'. I couldn't meet her eyes when she said that. Instead I focused on her hands, on the obscene band of translucent white flesh where, for twenty-six years, her wedding and engagement rings had been. I couldn't help wondering whether, when you look down at Anna's smooth, perfectly manicured thirtysomething-year-old hands gripping on to yours, you ever feel the loss of Susan's. Do you suppose hands can mould themselves to one another's shape over the course of a long marriage, so that anything else feels ill-fitting and uncomfortable, like new wedding shoes?

Forgive me, I'm rambling, I know.

From my position lying here on my side, I can see a pile of copies of my book on the floor, waiting to be signed – a monument to our own towering hubris, yours and mine.

There's another reading and signing session tomorrow – a different venue, but no doubt the same questions. I find myself wondering if I have the energy to go through it all again.

At today's event, I was surprised when, after the question about your prison sentence ('Mr Gooding's family has asked for privacy at this difficult time and I respect their wishes' was my predictable response), the gum-chewing woman stood up.

'Some people might say you were cashing in on other people's misery,' she said in a flat, disengaged voice. 'Don't you have any regrets about what's happened?'

That's an interesting question, isn't it, Clive? The question of regrets?

For your part, I'm sure you must have many. (By the way, I'm sorry things have been so difficult for you financially. The court case can't have been cheap, and who'd have thought Susan really would follow through on her threat of taking you to the cleaners? It just goes to show, you never really know someone, do you?)

But the question of my regrets is less straightforward.

Do I regret meeting you, for instance?

You'd think that would be an easy one, wouldn't you, after everything that happened, everything that was lost? And yet somehow it isn't.

If I had never met you, I would never have known the feelings I was capable of. It sounds like a cliché, but I believe that to truly know love, even the grotesque parody of love that ours turned into, one has first to know the withdrawal of love. Love, like happiness, is only fully experienced in retrospect.

When I look back on the woman who hovered in the doorway of that hospital room, staring at that baby (although I don't like to think about the baby), she seems like someone else. And yet at the same time, I know that she is still lodged somewhere inside me (as are you, Clive – in a non-sexual way, naturally). She is just – oh, what's the oncological term? – *in remission*.

Did I ever tell you I once worked with a woman who went into hospital suffering from a mysterious abdominal pain only to find she had been carrying within her all her life the remains of her own unborn twin – fragments of bone, teeth, even hair – contained in a cyst and absorbed into her while still inside the womb? Well, in a weird way, that's how I think of that other Sally. Disappeared, but still intrinsically present.

In the end (and please forgive the philosophizing. It's late and I really have nothing better to do – and neither, for that matter, do you, I suspect) we're all just a series of consequent selves. Once I might have found that notion depressing, a grinding cycle of repeated patterns and retold stories. But now I actually find it quite reassuring, because surely along with the baggage, each new self also brings a new possibility of redemption, no matter how remote, just the same as each new day brings a new chance to make amends. I'm sorry, does that sound too Chicken Soup for the Soul for you? I'm hoping maybe your time in prison might soften you and help you reach the same conclusions. You'll find it comforting, I think. And we must take our comfort where we can.

I would write to the prison to tell you all this directly, Clive – I'm aware how much you will come to depend on receiving mail during the long, empty months ahead. (Strange, isn't it, to think of going back to handwritten letters after all those thousands, tens of thousands, of emails?) But in the end, I don't know who it would really be helping for us to be back in contact. That's why I never replied to that note you sent me after you first read my book, although I want you to know it isn't because I hold anything against you. You were under pressure. I know what that's like. You made an error of judgement, that's all.

I'm flattered, of course, about all the nice things you wrote in that note, and I've thought a lot about what you said about us trying again. But really, what good would it do? You have Anna now (be careful what you wish for). I certainly wouldn't want to come between the two of you. Of course, I do see how some of the things I wrote in the book might have given you the wrong idea – all that mawkish sentiment, those outpourings of love. I'm embarrassed about it now. I really am. But I want you to know, Clive, I never said anything I didn't mean. At the time.

In the end, though, if I've learned anything from this at all, it's that life goes on, and we must move on too.

Separately.

Acknowledgements

The publication of this novel is the culmination of a long-held dream and I'd like to thank everyone who made it possible – Bridget Freer, and Viv Schuster, whose generous encouragement kick-started the process; my clever and far-too-glamorous agent Felicity Blunt and my lovely editor Marianne Velmans, who have given invaluable suggestions and much-needed support; also the entire Curtis Brown and Transworld teams, who have been so welcoming (not to mention talented!). For their constructive (if grossly biased) reading, a big thank-you to my wonderful friends Rikki Finegold and Mel Amos, and for putting up with me for the last few preoccupied months, my long-suffering family – Michael, Otis, Jake and Billie. Lastly I'd like to thank my mum, Gaynor, and my late father, Abner, who loved books, and who did me the huge favour of passing that love on to me.

Reading Group Guide: Topics for Discussion

• Sally follows her therapist's advice to chronicle her feelings about the end of her affair with Clive. It makes *The Mistress's Revenge* feel like a private journal or a letter. Who do you think is its intended audience? How effective, do you feel, is its confessional, intimate tone?

• Sally scornfully writes: 'you ... in ... your detached, pale pink St. John's Wood villa ... me ... in my partitioned cubbyhole in my shabby three-bed terrace'. How do differences in wealth, professional reputation, and social status play out in Sally's relationship with Clive?

• What is the effect on Jamie and Tilly of their mother's obsession with her failed affair with Clive? In what ways do they reveal their feelings to Sally? Do you find Sally's seeming disinterest in her own children's lives shocking, or can you understand how a mother could get to that point?

• 'How did it feel, I wonder ... listening to your wife chat away to your mistress? Oops, I mean ex-mistress of course. I can't imagine it was terribly comfortable, although I'm sure you carried it off with your usual insouciance'. Why does Sally feel the need to keep torturing Clive?

• Do you feel that Clive's wife, Susan, suspected Sally of being the other woman all along?

• 'So strange now to think that for years and years our friends saw Daniel and me as the poster couple for a healthy relationship'. Examine Sally's relationship with

Daniel. Why isn't Daniel more assertive about mending their relationship when Sally seems so emotionally disconnected from him? Does the fact that Sally and Daniel aren't legally married allow Sally to feel less guilt about cheating on Daniel? In what other ways does Sally try to justify her actions?

• Sally's publication of her 'End of the Affair Diary' in the newspaper takes her vengeful behaviour to a new level. Does the threat of exposure really not concern her? To what extent does Sally feel she has nothing to lose?

• To what extent is Sally an unreliable narrator? Do you think she's going mad? How did this affect your reading of *The Mistress's Revenge*?

• Sally's cyberstalking of Clive and his family reveals the extent of her obsession. In your opinion, how do sites like Twitter and Facebook change the way we conduct relationships? Do you think this kind of cyberstalking is the inevitable byproduct of social media?

• What was Sally trying to prove when she had a one-night stand with Pete, the pub manager in Hoxton? What role does her use of drugs seem to play in her judgement and her behaviour?

• Clive resorts to blackmail and intimidation. How does he manage to distance himself from these acts? Why doesn't Sally seem to feel more threatened, particularly when her daughter is approached by one of Clive's hired goons? What does Clive's behaviour reveal about his true character?

• How does the domestic financial ruin that Sally ignores, while actively pursuing her own revenge fantasies against Clive, finally bring her own situation with Daniel and the children into crisis?

• *The Mistress's Revenge* ends with a cascade of twists in the plot. How did you feel about this resolution of Sally's affair with Clive? Do you think justice was achieved?

• Share your own worst relationship stories with your book group. Have you ever been in a relationship that ended badly? If there is one moment from a failed relationship that you could take back, what would it be? What's the craziest memento you've ever kept from a love affair or relationship? Can you relate to any of Sally's actions?

• Do you have any revenge secrets or fantasies of your own?